Praise for the Novels of Alec Nevala-Lee

Eternal Empire

"In *Eternal Empire*, lost worlds and mysterious legends collide with modern-day resonance. Alec Nevala-Lee dishes up another sparkling and complex kaleidoscope of Russian lore, from Scythians and saints to serpents and spies, as two resourceful heroines race to decipher the buried secret."

—Katherine Neville, *New York Times* bestselling author of *The Eight* and *The Fire*

City of Exiles

"Alec Nevala-Lee creates a dazzlingly detailed and authentic world of intrigue, weaving a harrowing tale that will enthrall readers with an undercurrent of political ambiguity that evokes le Carré and an intricate, continent-crossing plot reminiscent of *The Day of the Jackal.* Delivering a complex mix of espionage, European politics, Old Testament riddles, and Cold War mysteries, Nevala-Lee is clearly emerging as one of the most elegant new voices in suspense literature."

—David Heinzmann, author of *Throwaway Girl*

"Stylish. . . . Introduces Mormon FBI agent Rachel Wolfe, who's come to London to work with the British police . . . à la Clarice Starling." —*Publishers Weekly*

continued . . .

The Icon Thief

"Alec Nevala-Lee is no debut author; he must have been a thriller writer in some past life. This one has everything: great writing, great characters, great story, great bad guy, and a religious conspiracy to boot. *The Icon Thief* is smart, sophisticated, and has enough fast-paced action to keep anyone up past midnight. I'm jealous."

—*New York Times* bestselling author Paul Christopher

"Twists and turns aplenty lift this thriller above the rest. From the brutal thugs of the Russian mafia to the affected inhabitants of the American art world, this book introduces a cast of believable and intriguing characters. Add a story line where almost nothing is as it first appears, and where the plot turns around on itself to reveal startling contradictions, and the result is a book that grips and holds the reader like a vise. I devoured it in a single sitting."

—national bestselling author James Becker

"Alec Nevala-Lee comes roaring out of the gate with a novel that's as thrilling as it is thought-provoking, as unexpected as it is erudite. *The Icon Thief* is a wild ride through a fascinating and morally complex world, a puzzle Duchamp himself would have applauded. Bravo."

—national bestselling author Jesse Kellerman

"Nevala-Lee's cerebral, exciting debut proves there's plenty of life left in the *Da Vinci Code*–style thriller as long as fresh venues and original characters enhance the familiar plot elements and genre tropes."

—*Publishers Weekly* (starred review)

Also by Alec Nevala-Lee

The Icon Thief
City of Exiles

ETERNAL EMPIRE

✠

ALEC NEVALA-LEE

A SIGNET SELECT BOOK

SIGNET SELECT
Published by the Penguin Group
Penguin Group (USA), 375 Hudson Street,
New York, New York 10014, USA

USA | Canada | UK | Ireland | Australia | New Zealand | India | South Africa | China

Penguin Books Ltd., Registered Offices: 80 Strand, London WC2R 0RL, England
For more information about the Penguin Group visit penguin.com.

First published by Signet Select, an imprint of New American Library,
a division of Penguin Group (USA)

First Printing, September 2013

ISBN 978-0-451-41566-0

Printed in the United States of America
10 9 8 7 6 5 4 3

If the polar sea ice does retreat, the colossal untapped stores of oil, gas and minerals below present the prospect of riches unimaginable for the Kremlin. There were incidental rumours about a more cryptic geopolitics floating among journalists at Moscow dinner parties, claiming that President Putin had asked to have a piece of the polar seabed brought back for him, as one of the entrances to the underground kingdom of Shambhala in the hollow earth is believed to lie beneath the Pole.

—Rachel Polonsky, *Molotov's Magic Lantern*

The empires of the future are the empires of the mind.

—Winston Churchill, September 6, 1943

Prologue

I vaguely reflected that a pistol shot can be heard at a considerable distance.

—Jorge Luis Borges, "The Garden of Forking Paths"

Arkady arrived at the museum at ten. When a guard in white gloves asked him to open his bag, he unslung it from his shoulder and raised the front flap. The guard ran a penlight across the main compartment and thanked him absently. Arkady nodded and took the bag back again, careful to keep it upright. Then he continued into the entrance hall, past the masonry piers and urns of flowers, and headed with the other visitors into the Metropolitan Museum of Art in New York.

On this weekday morning, half an hour after opening, the museum was not especially crowded. Looking around the bright domed space, Arkady took in the flocks of tourists and children, the retirees and art students, and, above all, the guards in their white shirts and black ties. He had known that the search of his bag would be perfunctory, but he was more concerned by another detail. The guards at the doors only rarely carried guns, but today one was wearing a sidearm.

A few minutes later, he was climbing the grand staircase, a visitor's pin secured to his bag. Instead of passing under the arch into the main line of galleries, he turned and went down the hallway of drawings to his left. Later accounts would emphasize his dark complexion and Uzbek features, but in reality, he was simply a slender, rather handsome young man of medium height, with something of the bearing of a former soldier, which was precisely what he was.

He continued into the next wing, a gallery lined with statues by Rodin and Barye, the famous sculptor of hunting scenes. Most of the visitors were filing toward the far end of the hall, where a special exhibition was taking place, but Arkady headed for a door to one side. Security footage would later reveal that he hesitated only briefly before crossing the threshold.

Inside, the gallery was quiet, with a single pair of visitors in sight. It was a large red space with a parquet floor and a bench set beneath the skylight in the ceiling. As Arkady went in, he noticed a guard in a blue polyester suit standing in the doorway of the next room, her back turned.

He had visited this gallery twice before. Without looking, he knew that the walls were covered in canvases by Ingres and Géricault, with one particularly notable portrait, of an elongated nude glancing back over one shoulder, hanging directly across from him. To his left was the work he was here to see, but he did not look at it yet. Instead, he pretended to study the canvas beside it, a painting of a woman being abducted by two men on horses, as he waited for his moment to come.

At last, the other visitors drifted out of the room. Aside from the guard in the doorway, he had the gallery to himself. Keeping her uniform in his peripheral vision, Arkady turned away from the picture before him, his heart quickening, and approached his true object of desire.

It was not a work likely to catch the eye of a casual viewer, a small oil painting, thirteen by twenty inches, depicting a landscape of low mountains. In the distance lay a body of water, perhaps an inland sea. A few groups of herdsmen in pastoral clothes were scattered across the composition. At the center, a woman, naked from the waist up, was milking a mare with a white stripe down its nose.

But the most striking figure was a man lying before a crude hut, clearly out of place among the rest. He was leaning on one elbow against the sloping ground, his body draped in a loose robe, and his head was bowed, as if he was brooding over the remembered geography of some faraway land.

It is not impossible that Arkady Kagan, as he stood before the painting, felt some kinship with this model of exile, so far from home, cut off from those he knew and loved. A second later, however, the feeling passed, and he noticed that the guard in the doorway was gone.

Arkady looked around the gallery. He was alone. It was sooner than he had expected, but he had no choice but to move now.

Opening the side pocket of his shoulder bag, he removed and undid a folded magazine, which was held shut by a pair of rubber bands. Inside was a flat glass bottle the size of a pint flask. Arkady unscrewed the top, allowing a puff of white vapor to escape, and turned back to the picture. He gave it one last look, staring into the face of the exiled poet, and before he could lose his courage, he took a step back and flung the contents of the flask at the painting.

It would later be determined, from the pattern of splashes, that he had swung the bottle three times. The restoration report would note in passing that if the picture had been doused with water at once, it might have been saved, but the guards had been understandably reluctant to act without further instruction. By the time the conservators arrived, the acid had eaten through to the underlying wood, carbonizing the oils and leaving three irreparable holes.

But all that lay in the future. As soon as Arkady had emptied the bottle, he let it fall to his feet. From his jacket pocket, which had not been searched, he drew a hunting knife. Unsheathing it, he went up to the picture and lunged forward, plunging the knife into the top of the painting, above the central mountain. Then he pulled it down, using both hands, in a long vertical slash, slicing through the image of the distant sea and gouging the wood beneath.

He took a step back, breathing hard. His plan, at this point, had been to drop the knife and go to the bench at the center of the room to calmly await arrest. Indeed, he might well have remembered to do this, altering everything that followed, had he not heard a startled gasp from behind him.

Arkady turned. Standing in the doorway was the guard from before. For the first time, he saw that she was surprisingly young, with a sheaf of brown curls pulled back from her forehead. He saw her eyes flick toward the painting, taking in the damage, and then dart back to meet his own.

If the guard had shouted for him to stay where he was,

he would have done so gladly. Instead, as she looked at him in silence, he was suddenly overwhelmed by shame. Before she could say anything, he turned and walked away, the knife still clutched in one hand. Behind him, the stream of melting paint was flowing down the wall, pooling in a black puddle on the parquet floor.

Leaving the room, Arkady found himself back in the main gallery, but he did not return the way he had come. Instead, he headed to the right, ignoring the elevators, and passed into a pair of galleries devoted to Cypriot art. Beyond this was a staircase, which he took, his pulse thudding somewhere up around his ears. As he rounded the landing and continued down the next flight of stairs, a cooler part of his brain reminded him that the alarm would have gone out by now to the museum's communication center, which had a direct hotline to the police.

He descended to ground level and entered the splendidly renovated galleries of Greek and Roman antiquities, his footfalls echoing on the marble. Around him, visitors were staring, but he ignored their looks and pressed on past the headless statues. Only a hundred yards lay between him and the outside world.

Up ahead, where the galleries gave way to the entrance hall, a guard was speaking into a handheld transceiver. When he saw Arkady, his eyes widened, and he lowered his radio with a shout: *"Hey, you—"*

Arkady went past him without pausing. Part of him knew he should halt, but instead, he pushed his way through a knot of startled visitors at the ticket desk. The only way out was through the main doors.

Passing the coat check to his right, he heard more shouts, but he kept going. The exit was forty steps away.

Beyond the row of stanchions, he could make out the light of the summer day outside.

He was nearly there when he heard another shout, the meaning of which became clear only later, and felt a pair of blows strike his chest.

Arkady became aware of two things at once. The first was that he was still holding the knife, which he had intended to leave in the gallery. The second was that he had been shot.

Looking up, he saw a guard standing before him, his face pale and disbelieving, his sidearm drawn. For a second, the two men stood eye to eye. Then Arkady glanced down at his chest. With his free hand, he touched the patch of warmth that was already spreading across his shirt, and then he fell to the floor.

Arkady rolled onto his back, the knife falling from his fingers at last. In the ceiling far above, he saw one of three circular skylights, which reminded him, curiously, of the three holes the acid had left. Feeling nothing but a strange satisfaction, he closed his eyes to that perfectly white sky, the blood pooling across the floor beneath him, and breathed out for the last time.

In the aftermath of his death, there would be rumors of a racial component in the decision to open fire, leading to a number of protests. Ultimately, however, an investigative commission would determine that the guard in question, a museum veteran of ten years, had mistaken the knife in the other man's hand for a gun. Since the situation had given him ample reason to regard Arkady as dangerous, it was concluded that the shooting had simply been a regrettable accident.

Afterward, the press would compare the incident to other famous cases of art vandalism, including one notorious episode three years before in Philadelphia. And while some wondered why the dead man had ignored the more celebrated portrait by Ingres in the same gallery, surprisingly few ventured to guess why he had chosen to attack that particular work, a painting by Eugène Delacroix: *Ovid chez les Scythes*, or *Ovid Among the Scythians.*

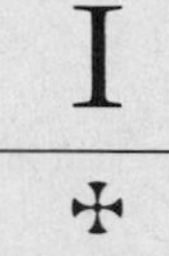

July 27–August 8, 2011

As for the theory of escape—it is very simple. You do it any way you can. If you get away—that shows you know your theory. If you're caught—you haven't yet mastered it. The elementary principles are as follows. . . .

—Aleksandr Solzhenitsyn, *The Gulag Archipelago*

A sense of security, of well-being, of summer warmth pervades my memory. . . . Everything is as it should be, nothing will ever change, nobody will ever die.

—Vladimir Nabokov, *Speak, Memory*

1

Even before the telephone rang, Maddy knew what was coming. As usual, she was the first to arrive at the gallery, and after disarming the security system, turning on the lights, and filling the kettle for tea, she sank down at her desk. The light on the phone was flashing, indicating that she had a message, and although she had tried to prepare for this moment, the sight still filled her with dread.

Before she could listen to her voicemail or check her latest round of email alerts, the phone rang, the display listing a number with a local area code. Maddy regarded it for a second, then snatched up the receiver, answering in her best gallerina's voice: "Beardsley Gallery. How may I help you?"

"Good morning," a woman said smoothly on the other end, giving a name that Maddy forgot at once. "I'm a reporter at the *Guardian* here in London. May I please speak with Maddy Shaw?"

Maddy's rational mind told her to hang up, but part of her wanted to know how bad it was. "Speaking."

"Oh, very good," the reporter said, pausing as if to transfer the phone to the crook of her shoulder. "I'm calling in regard to the incident yesterday at the Metropolitan Museum of Art. I don't know if you've seen the news—"

"I've heard something about it," Maddy said carefully. "A man was shot, wasn't he?"

"Yes, but only after defacing a painting by Eugène Delacroix. Apparently the damage is quite severe. I was wondering if you cared to comment."

Maddy closed her eyes. "And why would I have anything to say about this?"

The reporter pounced on this at once, as if she had been expecting this sort of evasion. "Well, I apologize in advance if my information is incorrect, but I was told that you were the Maddy Blume who broke into an installation three years ago at the Philadelphia Museum of Art."

"And what makes you say that?" As Maddy spoke, feeling as if she were trapped in the kind of conversation that one has in a nightmare, she saw the gallery door open and another employee, the registrar and shipping handler, enter with a look on his face that implied that he already knew everything.

With an effort, she returned her attention to what the reporter was saying. "I'm sure you're aware, of course, that this recent incident has been widely reported, and many stories have referred to the events in Philadelphia. As it happens, your picture appeared in a few places online, and it was recognized."

"It was recognized," Maddy said flatly. "Which means you got a call. Let me guess. Was it someone from another gallery?"

The reporter dodged the question. "I understand that you want to move on. I really do. But people will be asking about this anyway. If you agree to talk to me, we can set the tone for the conversation—"

Maddy was about to reply when she realized that her hand, seemingly of its own volition, had hung up the phone. She also became aware that the registrar was staring at her from his desk. "What have you heard?"

"Everything," the registrar said simply. "It's all over the city. So is it true?"

Before Maddy could respond, the phone rang again. According to the display, it was the same number as before. "It depends on what they're saying. In any case, I don't want to talk about it now."

Something in her tone of voice told him that she meant it. The registrar turned away, switching on his computer, although she could feel the curiosity radiating off him in waves. Her phone rang three more times, then stopped. She waited for the length of a voicemail, then picked up the receiver and deleted all messages without bothering to play them back.

When she was done, she sat there for a moment, weighing the tempting prospect of giving in to despair. Then she saw clearly what she had to do. A glance at the clock told her that there wasn't much time. Ignoring the registrar, who was casting pointed looks in her direction, she opened the topmost drawer of her desk, fished out a flash drive, and inserted it into her computer.

She was copying a set of files when the door opened again and Alvin Beardsley appeared. The gallery owner gave Maddy a nod as he entered, then went without a word to his private office. Maddy remained at her desk for another minute, then put the flash drive in her purse and rose to meet her fate.

The gallery was located in Mayfair, and like most of its

fellows, it was a featureless white cube with track lighting and a concrete floor. In his office, Beardsley was pouring himself a cup of tea. He was a small, round man with a bald head that picked up the colors of the walls around it, mingling them with a peculiar shine of its own. As she entered, his eyes ran lightly across her body, as usual, then settled on her face. "Hello, Madeline. Please, have a seat."

Maddy sat down, seeing herself, as she had on their first meeting, through the gallerist's eyes. Compared to the file photo that had appeared online in recent days, she knew that she looked well, if somewhat too thin, and was no longer able to pretend that she was still in her early thirties.

Beardsley finished pouring the tea and eased into his own chair. Without looking at Maddy, he picked up the phone and instructed the registrar to hold all calls. Hanging up, he turned to regard her in silence. A personnel folder with her name on it was lying on his desk.

Maddy saw no point in trying to postpone the inevitable. "I assume you know."

"Of course I know," Beardsley said. "A reporter from the *Guardian* rang me at home, but I've been hearing about it all morning. I have no choice but to tell you how this looks. When we met, I could tell you were smart, efficient, and willing to work hard, especially for . . ."

He trailed off. Maddy supplied the missing phrase. "For fifteen thousand a year."

"Yes." Turning to the file on his desk, the gallerist flipped it open. "And given your experience with archival work, I was lucky to get you. But it turns out that your résumé neglects to say anything about the most interesting part of your career. Or the fact that you were working under an assumed name."

"It isn't assumed," Maddy said. "It's my mother's. I had it legally changed."

"I imagine that all the attention must have been rather much. Is that why you came to London?"

Maddy already knew where this was going. "The New York art world is a small one. I hoped I could start over here, as an art adviser, but the market wasn't great. My sense of timing has never been good."

"Evidently not. And I'm afraid that the timing here is poor as well." Beardsley closed the file. "If you aren't Gerhard Richter, the market is hurting. Which means that we can't afford this kind of distraction."

The gallerist smiled sadly. "You see, people will talk. And as time goes on, the details of this sort of thing become less clear. They remember that you broke into an installation in Philadelphia and that it had something to do with a scandal at your old firm. Even if you weren't directly involved, it looks especially bad for the archivist at a respectable gallery. You understand?"

Maddy only looked back. Throughout his speech, she had wanted to protest, but she knew that everything he said was true. People didn't remember the details. And saying that she hadn't been in her right mind at the time would only raise more questions. "So you're firing me."

"It isn't as bad as all that," Beardsley said generously. "You're more than welcome to remain until you find another position, which I'm sure will happen soon. There are always opportunities for a girl like you."

His eyes brushed her neckline again. Maddy sat there for another moment, as if she was weighing the reasonableness of his argument, then fixed him with a gaze of her own.

"Actually, that won't be necessary," Maddy said.

"Here's what will happen. I leave today. I get two weeks of severance and a letter of recommendation if I ask for it. And if I require proof of employment to maintain my visa, you'll back me up until I don't need it anymore."

Beardsley laughed uneasily at this. "That's quite a list of demands. And if I decline?"

"I'll return that reporter's call," Maddy replied. "I'll give her the profile she wants. And I'll also explain how this gallery has been helping its clients avoid sales tax on purchases for the last ten years. I'm sure she'll find it interesting, especially the part about the empty crates we send to New Hampshire while the real paintings go to New York. But I'd prefer to part as friends. What do you say?"

They stared at each other in silence. Beardsley opened his mouth, then closed it again.

A quarter of an hour later, Maddy was walking alone up Albemarle Street, carrying a cardboard box. After writing her a check, Beardsley had kept a careful eye on her as she packed up her things and left without looking back.

As she headed for the station at Piccadilly, it occurred to her, with an almost abstract clarity, that her life was a shambles. There was no single moment to blame, only a series of individual choices, all of which had made sense at the time. But it all really came back, she thought, to two decisions. One, in Philadelphia, would always haunt her, while the other—

Maddy was still thinking about this when a voice came from over her shoulder. Although she hadn't heard it in years, and it had spoken only her name, she recognized it at once.

She turned. Across the street, a man was leaning on a

cane. As she watched, he took a step forward, moving gingerly, although his glasses and high forehead were the same as she remembered, and his eyes were still very bright.

Maddy shifted the cardboard box in her hands. “Hello, Alan. Coming to stare?”

Alan Powell smiled. “Not exactly. In fact, I thought we might have a bit of talk. I have a proposal for you. . . .”

2

On the breastplate of the man on horseback, there was the emblem of a flower with four white petals. The rider, whose head was encircled by a halo, was wearing a helmet and a short blue cloak. At the feet of his horse lay something dark and sinuous. Looking more closely, Rachel Wolfe saw a serpent, tongue hissing, transfixed by the spear in the rider's hand.

She had been studying the framed image for a few seconds when a voice came from behind her. "You know what it means?"

Wolfe replied without looking away from the wall. "An icon of St. George, isn't it?"

Vitaly Rogozin chuckled. "That's what most people would say. At least, those who have no sense of history. Some call him a saint, but he's actually far older than my poor broken church."

They were standing outside the study of Rogozin's town house in Bloomsbury. Wolfe turned as the writer fished something from the pocket of his tweed jacket. It was an amulet, the size of a silver dollar, with the image of a horseman and serpent embossed on one side. "You see, here is the rider again, an emblem that goes back to the third century. And on the reverse—"

He turned the medallion over, revealing a woman's hideous face, her head covered in snakes. "The gorgon. No one knows why these two symbols are conjoined, or what the man on the horse really represents. He has gone by many names, of course. But when I look at him, I see the rider of Europe and the serpent of Asia, fighting for the soul of Russia."

Wolfe accepted the amulet from the writer's outstretched hand. "He's also on the Russian coat of arms, below an eagle with two heads, one facing east, the other west." She gave it back. "And under the name of St. George, he's the patron saint of state security."

Rogozin slipped the medallion back into his pocket, the deep lines crinkling around his eyes. "Very true. Although you speak of the history of my country as if you read it in a book. Coffee or tea?"

"No, thank you," Wolfe said, although like many a lapsed Mormon before her, she had begun to drink coffee more regularly. Rogozin motioned her into the study, closing the door behind them. An entire bookshelf near the window was reserved for Rogozin's own work, beginning with his early fictional games and rigorous translations, then evolving into the passionate criticisms of the Putin regime that had made him celebrated around the world.

As they sat down, Wolfe studied Rogozin in silence. He was in his sixties, but he had always seemed older than his years, which had only recently caught up with his famous face. It looked much in life as it did on his dust jackets, creased, cleanly shaven, with piercing hazel eyes and a hairline that had long since disappeared behind the dome of that massive head.

Stationing himself behind his cluttered desk, Rogozin took a sip of cooling coffee and glanced at his computer, which displayed a story about the recent incident of vandalism in New York. "It is always tragic when a great work of art is destroyed," Rogozin said. "As it happens, the rider on that amulet is often linked with the Scythians, who ruled the steppes for a thousand years with their horses and arrows. Does it remind you of your friend?"

Wolfe's answer was one she had given many times before. "A lot of nonsense has been written about that. Ilya Severin isn't my friend. I haven't seen him in a long time, given his upcoming trial. But he was a useful contact."

"He was a thief and murderer." Rogozin closed the window on his computer screen. "A late change of heart doesn't excuse him."

"I've never said it should. But without him, we never would have found out the truth about last year's attack. And I learned long ago to welcome any source of insight, even from those who would otherwise be my enemies."

A smile appeared on Rogozin's face. "I imagine that this is what brings you here today. It's my pleasure, of course. It isn't often that one in my position is asked to give advice to a genuine heroine."

"I'm surprised. Your piece in the *Times* wasn't as flattering to me, or my agency. If I recall correctly, you called me an American cowgirl."

Rogozin gave an indulgent wave of the hand. "I'm a storyteller in search of characters, and you have something of the cowgirl in your face. And while you're far more charming in person, I've made no secret of my disapproval of this country's handling of the Karvonen affair. You dispatch the assassin behind one attack but miss the larger picture—"

"Personally, I have no regrets," Wolfe replied. "Lasse Karvonen was an illegal agent of Russian military intelligence who had been operating undercover for years in London. He murdered five people to obtain a neurological weapon that he used to sabotage the plane of an opposition leader. Eight passengers died in the crash, and one of my own colleagues was severely injured. Karvonen killed two law enforcement officers while making his escape. He would have killed me as well. So don't ask me to apologize for what I did."

"I'm not asking you to apologize," Rogozin said. "Only that you consider the overall situation. In the bad old days, you see, there were two competing sides to the security services, military and civilian, and they kept each other in line. Thanks to you, the military side has been gutted. And one security service, as it happens, is far more dangerous than two."

Wolfe knew that this was perfectly correct. Last year, after Karvonen's death, it had been discovered that his attack was an attempt by the military arm of Russian intelligence to implicate its rivals on the civilian side, as part of a secret war over global energy resources. She would never forget Karvonen's final moments, as he choked on his blood in a tunnel beneath Helsinki, but if she had believed that this would be the end of the story, she had been very wrong. "What makes you say that?"

"I have eyes. I refuse to return to my home country as long as Putin and his kind are in power, but even I can see the signs. If the Serious Organised Crime Agency were good at its job, it would have seen them as well."

"As a matter of fact, we have. After the plot was exposed, military intelligence networks fell apart. They're cleaning house in Moscow, and overseas, illegals have been stranded without resources. Which is very interesting to us. Abandoned agents are notoriously vulnerable to switching sides, if we can find them. And I know you have your connections—"

Rogozin smiled. "If you need my help, things must be even worse than I suspected. Is it true that your agency is being shut down?"

Wolfe sensed him searching for a sore spot. "It isn't clear. The police reform bill has been in the works for a long time. As a liaison officer from the FBI, I'm likely to be reassigned. But that's why I need your insights now."

Rogozin clasped the arms of his chair and rose. "I'll give it the consideration it deserves. Which reminds me that I have a gift for you."

He went around the desk to the nearest shelf, where he pulled down a plain paperbound volume. "Proofs of my latest collection. Uncorrected, of course, but I make few changes these days—"

Rogozin handed her the book. Taking it, Wolfe noticed that he was missing two of the fingers on his left hand. As a reluctant recruit in the Soviet army, about to march into Prague, he had deliberately blown off his own fingers rather than fight against a country whose culture he secretly admired. She handed the book back. "Thank you, but I already have a copy. I'm very interested in your work."

The writer slid the book back on the shelf, then led her to the closed door of his study. "I'm glad to hear it, especially from such an intelligent person as yourself. You must tell me what you think."

"I will," Wolfe said, keeping her eyes on Rogozin's face as he opened the door at last.

Outside, in the hallway, stood two constables. They had been there for the last several minutes, waiting in silence throughout the conversation. Rogozin turned to Wolfe. "What is this?"

Wolfe nodded to the officers, who came forward. "Vitaly Rogozin, I am placing you under arrest. You do not have to say anything, but anything you do say may be given in evidence—"

As the officers took him by the arms, Rogozin reddened, his wrinkled face deepening to the color of a bruise. "And the charge?"

"Conspiring to carry out a terror attack as an agent of Russian military intelligence," Wolfe said. "In particular, providing criminal resources and assistance to the man known as Lasse Karvonen."

Rogozin stared. "You must be joking. You think I was working with Karvonen?"

"Strange, isn't it?" Wolfe replied. "But as you said before, the signs were there."

She stood aside, watching from the corner as the officers took Rogozin into custody, dressing him, with some trouble, in a white forensic suit and placing him in handcuffs. Rogozin had lapsed into a disbelieving silence, but he continued to glower at her. Wolfe looked back, her face without expression, and moved only when the officers led Rogozin downstairs.

Maya Asthana was waiting outside on the sidewalk, standing before a row of Georgian town houses, her dark hair pulled back in a ponytail. Wolfe gave her partner a nod as Rogozin was brought to the hired car idling at the curb. When the officers opened the rear passenger door, she caught a glimpse of the backseat, which was covered in brown paper to avoid contamination of evidence.

As passersby halted to stare, Rogozin was ushered into the rear of the car. The last thing Wolfe saw, just before the door closed, was the writer's face, florid above the fabric of the forensic suit. Throughout all that had taken place, his eyes had never left hers.

A moment later, after instructing the second officer to wait upstairs, Wolfe watched as the car pulled away. Now that the arrest was finally over, she felt a wave of bitter satisfaction, with a grain of fear at the core.

At her side, Asthana had a troubled look on her lovely face. "I hope you know what you're doing."

Wolfe only turned and headed up to Rogozin's office, where the real work was about to begin. "Yes. I hope so, too."

3

"In retrospect, I left at just the right time," Alan Powell said, leaning lightly on his walking stick. "The agency is on the verge of a painful restructuring. Not to mention the mess with Rogozin. I don't know if you've heard about this—"

"It's all over the papers," Maddy said. "I recognized the name of the officer involved. She was your partner, wasn't she?"

Powell smiled. "Yes, although she went her own way a long time ago. She's brilliant, of course, but this time, I fear that she's taken on more than she can handle. Rogozin is a famous writer and dissident. To accuse him of being a spy, especially after he criticized the agency so publicly, invites all kinds of unfortunate interpretations. Which is exactly why I left."

They were walking through Green Park, where she had arrived that morning to find Powell standing next to a spindly young man who introduced himself in an American accent as Adam Hill, an associate at the Cheshire Group. As they headed down the footpath, Maddy noticed that Adam kept one eye on the faces around them, as if to make sure that they weren't being watched.

Powell looked out at the gray ranks of lime trees. "You see, my role at Cheshire allows me to pursue the same sort of work I did when we first met, but more discreetly. It's a small group, just Adam and myself, with a very specific focus. How much do you know about the firm?"

"Just what I've been able to find online," Maddy said. "It's an activist investment and private equity fund. And it's had some trouble in Russia. But you still have stakes in other countries."

Adam nodded. "These days, we're making a serious push into India and other emerging markets. But Russia remains an important region. It's hard for us to invest there directly, given our problems with the current regime, so we've begun to move into advisory work. For a fee, of course."

"And my personal mandate is to investigate illegal activity," Powell said. "Anyone who does business in Russia needs to be concerned about corruption. Our role is to play devil's advocate. And one particular transaction has been taking up most of our time. Have you heard of Vasily Tarkovsky?"

Maddy felt a faint chill, one that was only partially due to the dampness of the day. "He's an oligarch."

Powell seemed to sense her apprehension. "Yes. And I know that you have reason to be wary of such men. But please hear us out. Adam?"

Adam easily took up the thread. "Russia is the world's largest oil producer, and Tarkovsky is the owner of Polyneft, one of the last major oil and gas concerns still in private hands. It holds a valuable portfolio of assets and drilling concessions, including a license to explore offshore in the Black Sea."

"The Tuapse Block," Powell said. "It's worth billions, but because of its considerable depth, it requires advanced technology to exploit, so Tarkovsky needs a Western partner. This will also allow him to avoid working with the Russian state, which would love to funnel the profits into its own pockets. He has been negotiating with several companies, including Argo Petroleum in London. Two American firms are also in contention. And we've been hired to advise the British side."

Maddy saw where this was going. "But you have concerns about the deal."

Powell headed for a bench at the edge of the path, his cane leaving soft pocks on the ground. "We have our reservations. Mind you, all these oligarchs have dirty hands. But I fear that Tarkovsky's involvement goes beyond what he has done in the past. He claims to be in favor of corporate transparency, but there are aspects to his financial dealings that make us wonder—"

He paused. Maddy sensed the reticence there, but she also knew what he was trying to say. "If he's connected to organized crime."

"That's one way of putting it," Adam said. "But to find out, we need information outside the public record. And no matter which offer Tarkovsky accepts, the deal is expected to close in less than two weeks."

Maddy saw that Powell was gazing off at the trees. "So what do you want me to do?"

Powell spoke quietly. He still would not meet her eyes. "We want you to go work for him."

Without a word, Maddy rose and walked away. Behind her, she heard a set of steps. From the sound, she could tell that they were not Powell's, and against her better judgment, she halted. "I can't believe this."

"I understand," Adam said from over her shoulder. "I know how hard this must be."

Maddy turned to face him. He was standing a few feet away, little more than an overgrown boy, with a lot of brains but not much wisdom. "What exactly do you think you know about me?"

"As much as anyone else," Adam said. "You're a gifted art analyst, but you've had a run of bad luck. You worked for a fund manager who conspired with Alexey Lermontov, your former employer, to funnel profits from stolen art to Russian intelligence. Lermontov murdered a colleague of yours who got too close to the truth, then silenced the oligarch Anzor Archvadze before he could expose the plot, using the same poison that led to your breakdown in Philadelphia. And you've been dealing with the consequences ever since."

Adam related this calmly, as if telling a story that had nothing to do with either of them. He struck her as a familiar type, Ivy League, just out of college, who thought little of sacrificing the best years of his life on the altar of finance. "So what did you think I would say?"

"I told Powell that you would probably refuse," Adam said. "But I thought we should try anyway. You may not believe this, but I've wanted to meet you for a long time. If I'd been in your place, I couldn't have made it this far. I also hoped that you'd hear us out. Please don't prove me wrong."

Maddy glanced over at Powell, who was still waiting, apparently unperturbed. At last, she went back. "You have five minutes. What's the deal?"

"It's very simple," Powell said calmly, speaking as if nothing had happened. "In addition to his energy interests, Tarkovsky controls a foundation with offices in London. Its mission is to promote civil society in Russia and cultural exchange with the West, but in practice, we just don't know where the money goes."

Although part of her still wanted to pull away, Maddy sat down again. "So what?"

"In recent years, Tarkovsky has also taken an interest in the repatriation of Russian art from overseas," Adam said, seating himself beside her. "We've recently learned that he's looking to hire a consultant, preferably an American, to advise on one particular transaction."

"And your background makes you an attractive candidate," Powell said. "Tarkovsky is familiar with your case. If nothing else, he'll want to meet you. As I see it, it's the one job in the world—"

"—where my story actually helps," Maddy finished. Turning aside, she laughed, finally understanding why Powell had wanted to see her so badly. "So how is this supposed to work?"

"Nobody at Cheshire will know," Adam said. "We can arrange for the interview, but the rest is up to you. Once you're there, we won't ask for much. We're looking for documentation of cash flows, names of subsidiaries, a sense of how the funds are deployed. A foundation is an ideal vehicle for concealing illegal activity, but there are always records."

"And what if Tarkovsky finds out?" Maddy asked. "I like my head and hands. I don't want to end up without them."

Neither man responded. At last, Powell spoke in a low voice. "Adam, I think we're almost done. I'll see you at the office."

Adam gave a surprised nod. Rising from the bench, he smiled awkwardly and headed alone down the path. Powell watched him go. "Adam's a bright one. He's young, with a sense of history, and he knows what is really at stake. Because this is about more than money."

Maddy studied Adam's retreating back. "I don't see how it's about anything else."

"I can understand why you'd say that. And you wouldn't be the first." Powell glanced down at his hands, on which the scars of old burns were visible. "I've spent my life trying to protect a few basic values. If this deal goes through, Tarkovsky will become one of the largest shareholders in Argo. And I don't want to see a British company in the hands of a possible criminal."

Maddy found herself resisting his tone, with its assumption of their shared concerns. "And why should this matter to me?"

"Tarkovsky has friends in the art world. Once you've obtained the materials we need, you're free to do as you like. If you want to get back in the game, this is the best chance you'll ever have."

Maddy felt a drop of water. As it began to rain, they rose and headed toward the edge of the park. Opening an umbrella, Maddy glanced down at her companion's ruined legs. She knew the story. Powell had been on the plane that Lasse Karvonen had brought down. He had survived, but he had spent months in the hospital, and as she considered this now, she wondered how else it had changed him.

As if reading her thoughts, Powell said, "I hear they've managed to restore the installation in Philadelphia. Of course, it isn't so easy to restore a man's body. Or a reputation. I did you a favor before. Let me do it again. The firm is more than willing to compensate you for your time—"

Maddy walked at his side in silence, slowing her pace to match his steps. She knew that Powell had deliberately chosen to approach her when she was at her most vulnerable, but he was also right. There was nothing left for her in this city, and she was running out of second chances. When they reached the end of the path, she spoke at last. "What does Tarkovsky want to repatriate?"

"It's a Fabergé egg. I'll send you the details. I think you'll find it interesting." Powell paused at the gate, where he turned to face her. "I'll leave you here. Give me a call when you're ready."

With a nod, he headed away. Maddy stood there in the rain, watching as Powell continued down the street. She gradually became aware that her hand had crept into her coat pocket, closing around the object inside, which she had brought from home on an impulse that she didn't fully understand.

A moment later, Powell rounded the corner and was gone. Once she was alone, Maddy withdrew her hand, glancing down at the small conical shape she was holding. It was a chess pawn.

Maddy found herself thinking of Alexey Lermontov, who had fled to London after his intelligence role had been exposed, only to be killed six months later. As she thought back to that day, her memories turned, inevitably, to another man, one she hadn't seen or heard from in years. And as she tightened her fingers around the pawn and slid it into her pocket again, she reflected that there were secrets about her past that even Powell would never know.

4

Owen Dancy, who resembled an oversized baby in a Savile Row suit, lowered his bulk into a plastic chair. Folding his hands on the table, he leaned toward the man he had come to see. "Tell me about Rachel Wolfe."

The prisoner did not reply at once. Studying the plump knot of Dancy's club tie, he found himself wondering why his solicitor was asking this now. "I'm not sure I know what you mean."

Dancy smiled. "In my role as your advocate, it's essential that I understand the nature of your relationship with Wolfe. So far, you've been reluctant to speak of this, however useful you've been in other respects. But recent events have made it imperative that we discuss this now."

Ilya Severin, who had been known long ago as the Scythian, said nothing. They were seated in the interview room at Belmarsh Prison, eight feet square, with windows on all four walls.

As he looked out at the guards, Ilya felt his gaze shift slightly to take in his own reflection. He was dressed in a striped blue shirt that hung loosely on his lean frame. As a remand prisoner, he was entitled to keep his own clothes, but it had seemed easier to go with the standard prison issue. In this regard, as in most other things, his instinct had been to blend in. "What recent events are these?"

Dancy pressed his fingers together. "Your friend is in a bit of a bind. I imagine you know Vitaly Rogozin. A dissident who saw himself as the new Solzhenitsyn, although he lacked the requisite beard. Wolfe believes that he was an agent of military intelligence, and that he was involved with the attack last year that so clumsily tried to implicate the civilian side of the intelligence services."

Ilya took in this information. "So he would have been Karvonen's handler. Was he?"

"I'm curious about this as well. Unfortunately, even my sources have their limits. On the face of things, however, it does seem unlikely."

"Unlikely," Ilya repeated. "But not, at least to your knowledge, incorrect."

Dancy only lifted his hands. "I've told you all I know. The media, not surprisingly, is calling it a politically motivated arrest, which complicates our position. For the upcoming trial, I had intended to use your cooperation with Wolfe as a mitigating factor while minimizing your interest in the intelligence services, which the Crown will use to establish motive. This is why we've made no effort to introduce Lermontov's background into evidence."

Ilya knew that there were other reasons why Dancy's clients had chosen to pass over certain aspects of the career of Alexey Lermontov, the art dealer and paymaster he was accused of killing, but he kept this thought to himself. "And Wolfe's situation has changed things?"

"It presents a delicate problem. We had hoped that your work with Wolfe would be useful, but now it might even be a liability. To evaluate the situation, I need your opinion of her. And I need to know it now."

Ilya waited another moment before responding, aware that all their interactions were built on an unspoken understanding. The year before, Dancy had offered to serve as his advocate, despite the fact that the solicitor's other, unseen clients had good reason to want Ilya dead. Ilya had accepted, perceiving that his enemies were willing to set old grievances aside for the sake of their present advantage. They evidently assumed that the same held true for Ilya himself. Which meant that they would continue to work together only as long as they found each other useful.

With this in mind, Ilya began to speak. "Wolfe is bright, but she lacks imagination. Like most of her kind, she thinks in personalities, not systems. She looks to punish the men who carried out the attack. But she lacks the political will to trace it back to its source. That said, she's not unintelligent. If she arrested Rogozin, she must have had a good reason. But we haven't spoken in a long time."

"So I've gathered," Dancy said. "Is it because she no longer found you useful?"

"No," Ilya replied. "It's because I knew she had nothing left to tell me. Is Rogozin an intelligence agent?"

Dancy pretended not to hear him. "Thank you," the solicitor said, rising ponderously from his chair. "I will take this information into account as I continue to prepare your defense."

Gathering up his briefcase, he left the table. As the solicitor headed for the door, Ilya spoke again. "If the credibility of Wolfe's agency is being questioned, it seems to me that this presents a useful opening for cases on appeal."

Dancy appeared to sense his unspoken point. "Yes. As it happens, Vasylenko's leave to appeal has been granted. We've argued that his sentence was excessive, given his age and lack of proven connection to violent crime in this country. And as you've said, recent events can only work in our favor."

"A good thing you held off for so long," Ilya said. "Vasylenko has been in prison for almost two years. Why wait until now?"

With a smile, Dancy knocked on the door with his heavy fist. "I suppose that the timing seemed right."

A second later, the door was unlocked. Ilya watched as Dancy conferred briefly with one of the guards before disappearing down the hallway. Once he was gone, the guard motioned to Ilya. "Come on, then."

Ilya rose and followed the guard out to the landing. Around him, the prison was quiet, with most of the spur on lockdown.

As Ilya went back to his cell, he reflected that not all of what he had said about Wolfe was true. She had her limitations, but she was not unaware of the larger picture. In the end, however, he had simply said what Dancy wanted to hear, and the solicitor, accidentally or not, had let something slip in response.

Over the last six months, he had felt as if the two of them were engaging in some undefined test, or a delicate, ongoing negotiation. Although its ultimate purpose remained unknown, it was clear that Dancy was acting on behalf of some other party. And it was not Grigory Vasylenko.

As he approached his cell, Ilya pictured the lined face of his former mentor, the aging *vor* who had once commanded the loyalty of the brotherhood of thieves. More than anyone else, Vasylenko had been responsible for transforming him into what he was today, using his anger over the death of his parents to turn him into a thief and killer devoted to undermining the state.

In the end, however, he had learned that Vasylenko had been working for civilian intelligence all along, and that he had taken away Ilya's family to make him a more perfect instrument. After learning of his betrayal, Ilya had devoted himself to tearing down these networks, starting with Lermontov, the civilian side's leading paymaster, and watching with satisfaction as their military rivals were brought down as well, even if his role in exposing the plot had cast him into prison again.

Vasylenko alone still survived. In recent months, while slowly earning Dancy's trust, Ilya had concluded that Vasylenko had grown weak. Even at the best of times, his influence was far less valuable inside than out, and in the absence of a drastic change of situation, the old man would die in prison. The upcoming appeal, in particular, had almost no chance of success.

Yet there were ways in which a *vor* might still be useful, as long as the will was there.

A moment later, they reached his cell, where Ilya waited on the landing as the guard unlocked the door. Ilya went in, and he was about to return to his usual studies when he realized that the door had not closed.

Ilya turned. As he watched, the guard tossed a pair of plastic bags to the floor. "Hurry up, then."

He saw that each of the bags had been stamped with the prison seal. "What's this?"

"You mean the fat man didn't say?" The guard smirked. "You've been transferred. Effective immediately. Get your things."

After a beat, Ilya scooped up the bags. As he gathered up his possessions, he remained outwardly calm, but his mind was racing. On his desk lay an open book, which he slid into the bag, his finger brushing its spine, before quickly packing his clothes and toiletries. "Where are we going?"

The guard motioned for him to come out. "Reception area. You need to be searched before we send you to Block Four."

Ilya's face did not move, but as he carried his belongings out of the cell, he knew what the guard's words meant. The decision that he had been awaiting had already been made. He was being sent to Vasylenko.

5

Maddy sat at a café in Knightsbridge, her newspaper turned to a story about Rogozin's arrest. Next to the paper stood a rapidly cooling cappuccino that she had purchased at an outrageous price before losing all desire to drink it. She knew without looking that Adam Hill was watching from a table in the corner.

She was about to force herself to take a sip when she heard a woman's voice. "Maddy Shaw? Or is it Blume?"

Maddy looked up. Standing before her was a tall blonde in Armani, her bone structure aggressively perfect, carrying a leather folder. Maddy rose. "Either one works these days. And you must be—"

"Elena Usova, Mr. Tarkovsky's personal assistant. Come with me, please."

Without a pause, the woman headed for the door of the café. Maddy scooped up her things and followed, leaving her coffee behind. Out of the corner of one eye, she saw Adam looking after her in surprise.

It was a cool, gray morning. A black sport utility vehicle was parked illegally at the curb, sitting low and heavy on its wide tires. Standing next to the rear passenger door was a chauffeur in a dark suit and tie, with a hard look that made Maddy think that he hadn't been hired based entirely on his driving record. As the women approached, he opened the door. Elena slid inside, and Maddy, after a moment's hesitation, got into the backseat as well.

She found herself in a plush leather interior with a pair of swivel seats facing the rear of the car. Across from them, next to Elena, was a man in shirtsleeves and slacks. It was Vasily Tarkovsky. He was speaking quietly on the phone in Russian, but as Maddy sat down, she could feel his eyes on her face.

As the chauffeur shut the door and went around to the front of the vehicle, Elena opened the folder in her hands and extracted a pen and stapled document. "A standard nondisclosure form."

Maddy looked blankly at the pages as the engine started. "Where are we going?"

"This is the only way we could fit you into Mr. Tarkovsky's schedule," Elena said smoothly. "A car will return you when you're done."

As they pulled away from the curb, Maddy caught a glimpse of Adam on the sidewalk, staring after them as they drove off. She looked down at the nondisclosure agreement without seeing it, studying Tarkovsky as discreetly as she could. He was in his early fifties, more polished than she had expected, with a neat beard and a receding hairline that emphasized his forehead and his intense eyes, which at the moment were directed out the window.

Finally, Maddy signed the document and returned it to the assistant, who slid it back into her folder. In almost the same motion, Elena took out her phone and began checking her email.

Looking outside, Maddy saw that they had crossed the Albert Bridge. They drove in silence for some time, heading south from the city on the trunk road. At last, Tarkovsky finished his call. Without missing a beat, Elena handed him the leather folder, which he opened. Inside, Maddy caught a glimpse of her own résumé, as well as a highly effusive letter of recommendation from Alvin Beardsley.

Tarkovsky spoke without looking up, his English soft but fluent. "You understand what this position entails?"

Maddy sensed that the assistant was watching her closely. "I believe so. You're looking for a consultant to advise your foundation on repatriating works of art from Russia. I've been told that you've taken a particular interest in an object at the Virginia Museum of Fine Arts."

Tarkovsky looked up, his dark eyes lighting on hers. "And the work in question?"

Maddy fell back on her briefing with Powell. "It's one of the fifty imperial eggs made for the Romanovs by the House of Fabergé. Five of them are held in Virginia, which has the largest collection of Fabergé outside Russia. The Peter the Great egg is worth at least twenty million, and inside—"

"Yes, I know what is inside," Tarkovsky said impatiently. "You don't need to tell me that the egg is priceless. What I want to know is if you understand why I have taken an interest in this particular piece."

Maddy switched gears easily. "I think you believe that its legal status is vulnerable to challenge."

"I see," Tarkovsky said. "And how would you rate our chances of success?"

Maddy knew that this was a man who valued honesty in his employees, so she calibrated her answer accordingly. "The case has problems. A number of attempts have been made to contest the ownership of Romanov artifacts, and they've all failed. On the face of it, you have no legal right."

Tarkovsky had listened to this in silence. "Is there any other approach we can take?"

"There's always a way in," Maddy said. "But I'll need to look at the circumstances."

The oligarch closed the folder. "Tell me about the moral aspect. Doesn't my country have a right to its own heritage?"

"Of course," Maddy said, her mind working quickly. "But there are other considerations. Art also deserves to be kept in a place where it can be seen by the greatest number of people."

"But by that standard, art has no place in private collections. Not to mention the art fund where you used to work."

Maddy saw the trap that had been set. "That was a long time ago. And I gained useful experience there. I don't imagine that you see eye to eye with all of your business partners."

This was meant as a light remark, but Tarkovsky didn't smile. "It's about more than business. Your fund traded in art that had been illegally taken from Russia, in collusion with Alexey Lermontov, your former employer. It isn't unreasonable to conclude that you saw the signs but were willing to overlook them, as long as you could advance your career. Am I so wrong?"

Maddy paused. Through the window, she saw that they were passing through a village of gardens and country houses. Over the last two years, she had learned to protect herself and live free from fear, a journey that had finally left her standing alone, a prepaid phone in one hand, at the front porch of a house in Fulham. And as the car turned onto a narrow wooded track, she understood with perfect clarity that she had nothing to prove to Tarkovsky, or to any man.

"Let me tell you something about the art business," Maddy said at last, keeping her eyes on the view outside. "It's based on access and connections. There's a huge incentive to keep transactions secret and to pursue an unfair advantage whenever you can, because the stakes are so high. As a result, it attracts a certain kind of personality. Does that sound familiar?"

She thought she heard the trace of a smile in Tarkovsky's voice. "I suppose so."

"It should. I don't condone illegality, but I suspect that someone in your position knows what it means to make decisions that can come back to haunt you. The real question is what you do next." Maddy paused. "I'm the last person to judge anyone based on what they've done in the past. And I expected that you, of all people, would understand this."

In the long pause that followed, Maddy sensed that she had blown her best chance, but she was also beyond caring. Tarkovsky nodded to his assistant. In response, Elena took a phone from its cradle and spoke into the receiver.

A second later, the car slowed to a stop. As Maddy sat there, her face warm, she heard the chauffeur come around to open the passenger door. She looked across at Tarkovsky. "Are we done?"

Tarkovsky only gave a short nod. After a beat, Maddy gathered up her coat and purse and got up to leave. As she was about to climb out, Elena spoke up. "Can you begin work on Monday?"

Maddy halted halfway out of the car. At first, she wasn't sure she had heard correctly. "Yes."

"Good," Elena said. "I'll give you a call later today to discuss compensation?"

"That would be fine," Maddy said, after realizing that she was being asked a question. She turned to Tarkovsky. "Thank you."

Tarkovsky nodded absently and took out his phone again. Maddy climbed the rest of the way out, finding herself on a flinty private road lined with magnolia trees. Overhead, the sun was breaking through the clouds.

The chauffeur closed the door without looking at her, got back behind the wheel, and drove away. Following the car with her eyes, she saw it approach a guardhouse at an iron gate, with a town car and jeep parked nearby. A moment later, the gate rolled softly back with a low electric whine.

As the car drove through, Maddy saw the house beyond. It was a mansion at the end of a long drive, with five gables and a newer extension surrounded by a lawn and formal gardens. Along the road that led to the house, the grass had been turned into a polo field. On it, she saw a girl of twelve or so, in jodhpurs and a bomber jacket, riding a roan horse near the main house.

Maddy watched as the girl reined in her horse and waited stonily as the car went by. A second later, turning her head, the girl noticed Maddy standing on the other side of the gate. For a moment, their eyes locked.

"Miss?" The voice came from over her shoulder. Turning, Maddy saw that a second driver had appeared by the town car parked next to the guardhouse. He was holding open the rear passenger door.

Maddy walked over to the car, feeling as if she were dreaming. Just before she got inside, reminding herself to call Powell, she glanced back over her shoulder. The girl on the horse was gone.

6

In the underground detention center at Paddington Green, there was a security desk with four monitors. Only one of the sixteen cells was occupied. The camera was set at a high angle, with a white square glued to the monitor to cover up the bathroom area, but otherwise, Wolfe could see the entire room. In it, a man was seated at a desk with a pad of paper. He was sketching something using a felt marker, but from here, she couldn't tell what it was.

The officer headed for the corridor. "You'll want him in the interview room, then?"

Wolfe followed him down the hallway, noticing that Asthana had remained behind. "No. I'll talk to him in his cell. And I want the camera off. It will make it easier for him to open up."

They arrived at a row of featureless blue doors with the round eye of a security camera set above each one. Halting at the cell at the end of the hall, the officer unlocked the door and swung it open.

Wolfe went inside. The cell was twelve feet square, with a Perspex window in the ceiling. Its walls were bright yellow. A vinyl mattress and pillow lay on the bed, next to a bathroom with a toilet and tiny sink.

On the television, a nature video was playing with the sound turned down, showing a mill of army ants marching in an endless circle, each following the scent of the soldiers in front until all had died of exhaustion. Seated beside it was Rogozin. As Wolfe entered the room, he covered the page on his desk with another sheet of paper. Before he did, however, she caught a glimpse of what he had been drawing. It was a sketch of a man on horseback.

Rogozin turned to face her. His thinning hair was uncombed, and he was dressed in slacks and a plain white shirt. Wolfe could still smell the faint odor of the petroleum spirits that had been used to wash the printer's ink from his hands several days before. She had seen the fingerprint card herself, with the prints of the first two fingers on his left hand missing.

The officer closed the door behind him, leaving it unlocked. Once they were alone, Rogozin smiled. "I was wondering if I'd see you again. It seemed unfair of you to leave me without so much as a visit, given how we parted."

"I know. But I thought we could talk." Wolfe pointed to the camera in the ceiling, the red light of which had gone dark. "We aren't being recorded. This is an unofficial conversation. I want to tell you why you're really here."

As Wolfe sat down, she reflected that she had never wanted to be in this position. She had convinced Dana Cornwall, the deputy director of the intelligence directorate, that Rogozin should be held as a terror suspect, allowing them to detain him without charge for fourteen days. So far, however, their searches and interrogations had failed to uncover anything definitive, and with time running out, she had been left with no choice but to confront the prisoner herself.

Wolfe gathered her thoughts. "I'd like to talk to you about Lasse Karvonen. Before he carried out the attack last year, he destroyed his computer, but we've recovered more than a dozen emails from a man who appears to have been his contact in Russian military intelligence."

"So your case should be easy to prove," Rogozin said. "Who was this man?"

"It isn't clear. The emails were routed through intermediate servers to disguise their origins, and all were relatively short. In one of the messages, however, there was a phrase that stuck in my mind. The contact is talking about a woman Karvonen will meet in Helsinki to help carry out his plan, and he writes: *She already fell for you, three times over, before she knew your face or name.*"

As she spoke, she looked to see if Rogozin would react, but he did not. "I didn't know much about Karvonen," Wolfe continued. "But he loved the poetry of John Donne. It's strange, because he was a former soldier, not a literary man. And I wondered if he might have acquired this taste from someone else."

She leaned forward. "So I began looking into Donne. And while I was going through his work, purely by chance, I found a phrase that sounded familiar. *Twice or thrice had I lov'd thee, before I knew thy face or name—*"

Rogozin's expression hardened. "I know the line. But what does it prove?"

"At first glance, not much," Wolfe said. "But when I looked at the original email in Russian, I found that it was a direct quotation from a recent translation of Donne. And the translator was you."

Rogozin gave her a thin smile. "It's always good to

hear that someone has read my work. But I don't see how it gives you a case."

"It doesn't, but it was a start. At first, I thought it just meant that the handler had read your translation, but your books weren't ones I'd expect to see in the hands of an illegal agent. I also knew that you had served in the Russian army, that your position as a prominent dissident allowed you to travel widely, and that you had the confidence of the same opposition movements that were targeted by Karvonen. You also flew out to Helsinki the week after the crash."

"Your men have already asked about this," Rogozin said irritably. "I was attending a symposium. You can check the records."

"I have," Wolfe replied. "But I was also taught, a long time ago, to read behind the meanings of the words themselves. So I had forensic linguists at Hofstra and Georgetown compare your published work with the emails that had been sent to Karvonen. And the analysis concluded, with a high degree of probability, that they were written by the same man."

Rogozin started to laugh. "I can't believe that this is your case against me. I'm not some mindless thug for you to intimidate." He leaned closer, his eyes suddenly bright. "I know it must be hard. Your future seemed so promising, only to be lost in politics, and with a traitor at the desk next to yours, no less. Now you're grasping at straws. And sooner or later, you'll need to let me go."

He sat back in his chair. "Your argument is meaningless. With a small sample of one text and a large sample of another, you can prove anything. On one end, you have a few short messages. On the other, a lifetime's work—"

As Wolfe listened to these words, something occurred to her, but she kept it to herself for now. In any case, Rogozin had touched a nerve. She had killed Karvonen, but the agency had failed to prevent the attack. As time went on, that was the only fact that mattered.

And then there was Arnold Garber. Garber had been an officer at the Serious Organised Crime Agency, working at the desk next to hers, someone she had liked and trusted. Just before the attack, he had disappeared, leaving behind a trail of evidence that indicated he had been working for Russia for years. Intelligence sources had hinted that he was somewhere in Moscow, but no one knew for sure. It was one of the most humiliating law enforcement failures in decades, and ever since, she had been obsessed with finding Garber, if only to ask him why.

Wolfe rose from the edge of the bed. "All right. I was hoping that we might be able to talk, but I'm also willing to do this the hard way. You and I aren't finished. Not by a long shot."

She went to the door of the cell. Before opening it, she looked back at Rogozin, who was still seated at his desk.

"I'm aware that forensic linguistics can be inexact," Wolfe said. "But even after all your objections, I can't help but wonder how you knew that Garber's desk was next to mine."

Rogozin said nothing in response, although Wolfe thought she saw something flicker in his hazel eyes as she left the cell. Closing the door, she went down the hallway, where Asthana was standing with her phone to one ear.

As she approached, Asthana hung up. Before her partner could say anything, Wolfe spoke first, not wanting to lose her insight from a moment before. "Something was missing from Rogozin's house. If he's a writer, where are his manuscripts? His papers have to be somewhere."

"That's a good idea," Asthana said, following her to the end of the hall. "But there's something you need to hear first. That was Cornwall on the phone. The director general wants to hold a hearing into the circumstances of the arrest. It's scheduled to take place in five days."

Wolfe pressed the button for the elevator. "I'm surprised it took him this long."

As she waited for the elevator to descend, she found herself thinking of Powell, who had escaped before the agency degenerated into an endless political nightmare. Five days wasn't nearly enough. But now it was all she had.

The elevator doors opened. Wolfe got in, pressing the button for the first floor.

Caught up in her thoughts, she did not notice, except in passing, that her partner had lingered for a second in the hallway outside. And she did not see Asthana look for a long moment at the closed door of Rogozin's cell, her face unreadable, before entering the elevator as well.

7

The following morning, the gates of Tarkovsky's estate slid back, allowing Maddy to enter for the first time. She was seated in the backseat of the car that had picked her up at home, driven by a silent figure who had resisted all her efforts to engage him in conversation. As they rolled past the guardhouse, she saw two men seated at a bank of monitors. One of them spoke inaudibly into a phone as the town car drove by, passing a sign warning of the electrified fence.

It had been an hour's drive from London. The estate, as Maddy had learned, was located in West Sussex, covering more than three hundred acres outside the city of Chichester. Through her window, she could see a trailed gang mower cutting the grass, with a separate crew filling in the hoof marks on the field with sand. The girl she had seen on horseback the day before, whom she had confirmed was Tarkovsky's daughter, Nina, was nowhere in sight.

At the end of the drive stood the main house, a Tudor mansion fronted with stone and framed by two projecting wings. Next to it ran a modern extension and, to the north, a line of evergreen woods. As Maddy looked ahead, she noted a jeep coming in the other direction, carrying two men in uniform. Powell had instructed her to keep a close eye on Tarkovsky's staff, especially security.

A moment later, the car eased to a stop at the driveway in front of the mansion. As the driver came around to open her door, Maddy saw Elena Usova emerge from the narrow entrance gable. Elena had exchanged yesterday's Armani suit for Versace, but she was carrying the same leather folder as before.

It was a cool morning with a hint of rain, and she could smell damp fir and freshly mown grass as she followed Elena along the footpath. As she walked, she noticed a man in a gray suit watching from the door of the main house, and she increased her tally of security staff to five.

Maddy saw that they were heading for the new building. "We aren't going inside?"

Elena's heels crunched on the gravel of the path. "No. The foundation's employees are housed in the extension. Only Vasily, his family, and his personal staff work in the main house."

Hearing Elena refer to her employer by his first name, Maddy wondered if there was more to their relationship than met the eye. She knew that Tarkovsky and his wife had been separated for years. "It's a beautiful property."

Elena nodded as they passed a walled garden, followed by a pair of clay tennis courts. "The oldest buildings date from the sixteenth century. The main house, which is more recent, was built by Sir Edwin Lutyens. All the stone was quarried here. After Vasily acquired it, he began restoring it to its original state. You'll find that he cares deeply about the past."

When they arrived at the extension, Elena unlocked the door with a keycard. Maddy followed her into a reception area. Inside, a secretary, also tall and blond, was seated at right angles to a security desk, where a guard asked politely to examine her bag. "You'll need to be searched when you leave each day," Elena said. "It's a standard precaution for all employees."

Once the search was complete, Maddy followed Elena up the corridor. The walls were covered in photographs of a yacht under construction, the emblem of a white lotus visible on its hull. This was the *Rigden*, which was being built in Italy by Fincantieri at a cost of nearly two hundred million dollars. When it was launched later this month, it would be one of the largest yachts in the world.

"This building houses the foundation's London staff," Elena said, heading up the hall. "There are eight employees working with our group in Moscow. I'll introduce you to the others in a moment."

The assistant halted at a room two doors down. A flick of the light switch revealed a windowless space lined with file cabinets and shelves packed with books and binders. "These are the archives," Elena said. "It's where the foundation keeps provenance information for art under investigation. You'll want to study our previous projects to get a sense of what we need, then turn to the files on Fabergé to prepare a proposal for repatriation."

Maddy ran her eyes across the files. "Is there a catalog of materials available?"

"Yes. And everything is fully indexed. If you require any translations, you can photocopy the relevant pages and leave them for our service. They'll be ready for you overnight." Elena switched the light off. "If you want to take any materials with you, you'll need to clear it with us beforehand."

"That's fine," Maddy said. She saw a second file room across the hall. "And here?"

"Files relating to the foundation's other activities," Elena said, continuing up the corridor. "You don't need to concern yourself with those."

Maddy nodded, but she did not look away just yet. On one of the shelves, there was a row of black binders, the location of which she quietly noted as she turned to join Elena at the end of the hallway.

Elena opened the last door. Inside, there was a small office with a pedestal desk, two chairs, and a computer and phone. A window looked out on the walled garden beyond. "This is your workstation. Someone in the kitchen will call you about lunch. And a car will come around at six to take you home."

Maddy set her purse down on the desk. "When can I meet with Tarkovsky?"

Elena gave her a glacial look. "Are any aspects of your assignment unclear?"

Maddy, who had worked with women like this for much of her life, returned the stare without blinking. "Not at all."

"In that case, you can begin. If Vasily wants to see you, I'll be sure to let you know." The assistant headed for the door. "I'll check on your paperwork. Someone will be here to see you shortly."

Elena left the office, closing the door behind her. Once she was alone, Maddy exhaled and went to the window with its garden view, thinking back to the binders she had seen in the other room. "We need a sense of how the money goes in and out," Powell had said. "This means travel records, payroll information, but especially the cashbook, a journal of disbursements and receipts—"

Maddy had been doubtful. "But they wouldn't just leave this lying around."

"No," Powell had said. "But even the most secretive enterprise has to maintain this information. Unless they're incredibly careless, you won't have access to the server. But if they're like most businesses, hard copies will be printed and saved. They'll be in Russian, so you'll need to know exactly how they look. Once we know what we have to work with, we'll figure out the rest."

As Maddy stood at the window now, remembering this conversation, she reminded herself to take things one step at a time. Her first task was to find out if the records she needed were really there. And then—

The door of the office opened, breaking into her thoughts. Turning around, instead of the human resources employee she had expected to see, she found herself facing the man in the gray suit who had been watching earlier from the main house. "Please, sit down," the man said. "I am Pavel Orlov, head of internal security. I must ask you a few questions."

For no good reason, her heart began to thump. Maddy awkwardly claimed the chair behind the desk, studying the security chief as he sat down. He had short hair, a worsted tie, and a silver ring with a red stone. "Tarkovsky and I have been over this. He's comfortable with my background."

Orlov smiled. "With all due respect, Tarkovsky will be comfortable when I say so."

Opening the personnel folder in his hands, Orlov began with a question about her most recent employer, then inquired into her time in New York. Maddy had gone over all these matters with Powell, and she responded readily, her uneasiness gradually diminishing.

A moment later, Orlov asked a question she had not been expecting. "Tell me about Ilya Severin."

Maddy sensed a special interest here. "There isn't much to tell. I was only in the same room with him twice."

"Yes, I know," Orlov said. "The first was when you were trespassing in the home of Anzor Archvadze, another powerful man, looking for information to put to your own advantage. The second was at the Philadelphia Museum of Art. You went to break into an installation there, for reasons that remain unclear—"

"It's a long story. I thought I was uncovering evidence of a plot against my life, but it was all in my mind."

"Yet there were men who wanted you dead. Alexey Lermontov knew that you had learned he was trading in stolen art, so he dispatched an assassin to kill you at the museum. Ilya Severin prevented this, then took out Lermontov himself a year later. From what I hear, it's uncertain how he managed to find him. Did you ever wonder if he might come after you?"

Maddy found again that it was easiest to be honest. "No. He has no reason to do so."

Orlov closed the folder, apparently satisfied. "Perhaps not. Indeed, the first time you met Ilya Severin, he spared your life. The second time, he saved it. Do you have any idea why?"

From outside, she could hear the sound of birds in the garden, and she thought once more of the house where Lermontov had died. "I don't know," Maddy said at last. "I imagine he had reasons of his own."

8

Ilya was seated at the table in his cell when the call he had been expecting finally came. He had been reading from his volume of midrash when something made him glance at the door, which was open. There was no one there. All the same, he paused, keeping his eye on the landing. Closing his book, he rested it casually in one hand, the spine facing outward.

A second later, there was the sound of footsteps, and a shadow fell across the threshold. The prisoner standing outside did not attempt to enter. Prison etiquette dictated that you never went into another inmate's cell without permission. "Vasylenko wants to see you."

Ilya rose from his chair. It was association time. For forty minutes every day, prisoners who were not in segregation were allowed to mix freely. Ilya, for his part, had kept to himself. Since his transfer, he had followed his usual routine, reading, walking on his own in the yard, and reporting to his job in the workshop, where inmates filled remanufactured printer cartridges. Until now, he had been left alone. But he had also been waiting for this moment.

Taking his book with him, he left his cell and joined

the other prisoner on the landing. This inmate, whose name was Sasha, was a thickly muscled man with glasses, red hair, and skin so sensitive that, even in this gray climate, he was perpetually pink with sunburn. Six years ago, he had been convicted of torturing and killing his wife and her lover. His arms were covered in tattoos, but to the eyes of a man like Ilya, they were nothing but nonsense.

They descended a flight of metal steps to the association room, a common space with steel mesh running from floor to ceiling and guards stationed at each end. In one corner, a group of West Indians were playing dominoes, shouting with excitement at every move, while other prisoners watched television or stood in a line for the pay phones on the far wall.

Sasha continued through a separate gate, which led to the space reserved for enhanced prisoners. A few cleaners were playing cards, while others were shooting pool. And in the corner was seated a tight circle of inmates, five in all, who turned to look as Ilya approached.

Ilya returned the scrutiny. Most of the men seemed to range from twenty to their early thirties. Some, like Sasha, had the usual meaningless tattoos, while the youngest had no marks at all.

Seated at the center was Grigory Vasylenko. The old man was smaller than Ilya remembered, over seventy by now, his hair and mustache white, along with a fine layer of scruff on his cheeks and chin. He was wearing his jacket indoors, his hands lost in their sleeves, and yet a core of hardness remained, along with a look in his eyes that made Ilya feel as if he were back in Vladimir.

Vasylenko regarded Ilya for a moment, then spoke to his men. "Leave us alone."

At once, the others stood, their eyes fixed on the newcomer, and departed one by one. Vasylenko gestured for Ilya to sit down, then motioned for the book in the younger man's hands, which Ilya handed over. "Still lost in the myths of the Jews, I see. It must have been hard to survive on your own for so long."

"It's what I was taught to do," Ilya said. "I was once told that a man can reach his full potential only when he has been left with nothing."

Vasylenko smiled slightly, evidently recognizing his own words. Looking across at the *vor*, Ilya marveled at how easy it would be. Seated a few feet away from him was the man who, long ago, had ordered the death of Ilya's parents, transforming him into a killer who was unknowingly serving the very forces he hated. More than enough reason, Ilya thought, to end it all now.

But there was another reason to hold back. The death of one man was nothing compared to the survival of the system as a whole. And the possibility still remained, as remote as it might seem, that there was a larger picture elsewhere that he would be allowed to see. "I hear your leave to appeal was granted."

Vasylenko gave an absent wave. "Yes. I do not have much hope of success, but for now, I will go along with the charade. If nothing else, it will be good to have a change of scene."

Looking into the old man's eyes, Ilya saw the true meaning there. "When will it be?"

"One week from now," Vasylenko said calmly. "But I expect that Dancy has told you this already. He claims that you have been quite helpful in giving him insight into the situation on the ground. What have you said?"

"I told him that you're the last of your kind," Ilya replied, knowing that Dancy would have passed along most of this information. “Once, in prison, the thief was king. But I’ve seen the men you control here. Outside, there are those who still honor you and what you represent. But not in this place.”

In response, the *vor* only grunted. “And what do you expect for such insights?”

“Nothing,” Ilya said. “But what I expect and what I need are two different things.”

Vasylenko laughed softly, shaking his head. “I asked you here, Ilyuha, because I wanted to look in your eyes. Dancy thinks you can be trusted. But I know you too well. I’m aware that a man like you, who has so often put revenge above his own best interests, might have other reasons to get close to this lawyer, when in fact you haven’t changed at all.”

“You’re right,” Ilya said. “There are things no man should be willing to forgive. But a man might be willing to forget the past, at least for a time, in exchange for a chance at a future.”

Vasylenko seemed unmoved by this. “These are strong words. But are they true?”

“A year ago, I would have said no. I may say no again tomorrow. But I will be in prison for the rest of my life. I have no fear of this, but I value my freedom and my invisibility. This is not how I want to die, and I have nothing else. But then again, you saw to that yourself.”

As he spoke, Ilya tugged down the collar of his shirt, revealing the pale area of skin where a tattoo had been removed. Vasylenko eyed it dispassionately. “So what are you willing to do?”

“Whatever it takes,” Ilya said, releasing his collar again. “At least for now.”

Vasylenko smiled. "And later? Do you believe you can simply walk away?"

"No. I have no illusions. But I also know that Dancy would not consider taking such a risk without good reason. If you are willing to consider me, you must be out of options. And as I see it, neither of us has a choice."

Vasylenko glanced over at his men, who were watching from their table in the corner. "Perhaps. The world is full of those who think they have what it takes, but there are few with the proper detachment. In your case, I have no doubt that the skills are there, but it will be necessary to prove that you can be trusted."

Ilya had known that this moment was coming. "I understand. Then set me a task."

"Very good," Vasylenko said. "As it happens, the task has already been set. A problem, shall we say, that I need you to resolve."

Lowering his voice, Vasylenko switched to Assyrian, the language used for the most secret communications between thieves. Ilya listened as the old man described what he had in mind, which took only a few words.

When Vasylenko was finished, Ilya sat in silence for a moment, processing what he had just heard. "It can't be done."

"That's a shame," Vasylenko said. His voice was regretful, but in his eyes, Ilya saw a spark of amusement. "Because if you can't do it, Ilyuha, you will never leave this place again."

9

The next day, Wolfe and Asthana went to the library. Arriving at the St. Pancras branch near King's Cross, they met the head of modern literary manuscripts, who turned out to be in his thirties and remarkably attractive. "We were quite lucky to get Rogozin's papers," the librarian said. "Normally, we focus on British authors, but given his longtime residence here, we were glad to make an exception."

After checking their warrant, which they had obtained, for the sake of expediency, by slipping it into a stack of others for the magistrate to sign, he led them down a marble corridor to the manuscripts reading room. Inside, past the rows of carrels, they continued into the stackroom, where Asthana eyed the tall white bookcases. "What's the usual procedure when an archive comes in?"

"We put the papers in the freezer first, to get rid of bugs," the librarian said. "Then we start sorting through the material, which can take some time." He turned into one of the rows. "Here we are."

Following his gaze, Wolfe saw four long shelves, each containing fifteen flat boxes in stacks of five, the spines labeled with a number and Rogozin's name. "Is there a catalog we can use?"

The librarian smiled apologetically. "I'm afraid that what you see is what we have. It generally takes more than a year to fully conserve and catalog any collection. What are you looking for?"

"We aren't sure." Wolfe regarded the rows of boxes, sensing with a sinking heart that it would take weeks to go through it all. "What about nonliterary materials? Rolodexes, pictures—"

"You're in luck. One of the first things we do is cull anything unusual. We've found some odd things over the years." Kneeling, the librarian withdrew a pair of cumbersome cartons from the bottom shelf. He handed them the boxes, which were quite heavy. "Follow me, please."

He led them from the archives to an unoccupied office at the end of the floor, where he smiled politely and left, closing the door behind him. Wolfe counted down three seconds, knowing that this was all the time Asthana needed to make the inevitable remark: "You know, I think he fancies you."

Wolfe smiled as she lifted off the top of her carton. The mess inside was exactly what she had feared, a jumble of knickknacks and junk thrown together without any thought for order. The second box was more of the same, but in the end, they had no choice but to dive in. Donning gloves, they began to sort through the cartons, working slowly and methodically, with Wolfe checking anything in English and Asthana focusing on items in Russian.

An hour later, they emerged with a dishearteningly small stack of items, including an old address book and a stack of floppy disks in a format that would require a considerable amount of trouble to read. Wolfe, her back and eyes aching, was about to pack up the rest of the materials when she noticed something lying under a stack of magazines. "What's this?"

Asthana looked over. "Oh, that? I saw it earlier. It didn't seem very useful."

Wolfe picked it up. On inspection, it turned out to be an ordinary London street atlas. Leafing through it, she observed that it was last year's edition, and at first glance, nothing seemed to have been marked or underlined.

She was on the point of setting it aside when she paused, frowning, and flipped back a page. Looking more closely, she saw that a leaf of the atlas had been torn out of its spiral binding. It was probably nothing, but in the end, she tossed the atlas onto the pile. "Let's go. I'm starving."

On their way out, in the library's reference section, she asked for a copy of the same edition of the atlas, which she brought to a study carrel in the reading room. The absent leaf in Rogozin's copy turned out to contain maps for Acton and Hammersmith, at a scale of three inches to a mile.

Looking over Wolfe's shoulder, Asthana frowned. "That isn't much to go on."

"I know." Wolfe turned to the next page, feeling it between her fingertips. "Thin paper, though. I wonder—"

Switching on the lamp in the carrel, she lifted Rogozin's copy of the atlas and held it at an angle to the light. As she studied the page along one edge, she pulled out her phone and dialed. A second later, it was answered by a man who seemed pleased to hear from her. "Rachel. How are you?"

"I'm good," Wolfe said, still examining the atlas. "Lester, I need a favor—"

A few hours later, they were on Western Avenue, driving through heavy traffic. They had taken the atlas to the police laboratory at Lambeth, where her friend Lester Lewis, a Home Office pathologist, had expedited their request. Electrostatic detection had found indented writing, evidently in Rogozin's hand, on the page beneath the one that was missing. The faint letters left by the pencil's impression had turned out to be an address in East Acton.

Asthana was clearly less than enthused about the errand. As she sat behind the wheel, she turned, as if to cheer herself up, to a favorite subject. "It's obvious Lewis likes you. You should grab that one while you can—"

Wolfe did her best to deflect the topic. "Lewis and I are good friends. If nothing else, we've been through a lot together."

"I'll bet you have," Asthana said, smiling, as they left the main road. "I keep saying you need to bring him to the wedding—"

As she listened, Wolfe realized with a start that Asthana's wedding was less than two weeks away. With so many other things on her mind, she had forgotten all about it, and she didn't want to admit that her bridesmaid's dress was still hanging, unaltered, in the closet of her apartment in Vauxhall.

A moment later, they parked by a strip of vacant land. Opening the glove box, Wolfe took out two flashlights, handing one to Asthana as they emerged from the car into the damp afternoon.

Up the street, a panda car was waiting. As they approached, the door opened and a heavyset constable appeared, his helmet sheathed in a plastic bag. "Afternoon, Officer. It's an honor to meet you."

Wolfe was never quite sure how to respond to such remarks, which reminded her that there were those who still knew her only as the woman who had taken down Karvonen. "You're sure we can get into the house?"

The constable was already heading around to the trunk of his car. "Yes, with the right tools. Won't be a moment."

From the trunk, he took a pair of work gloves, a pry bar, and a flashlight of his own. "Used to be a nice neighborhood. Then the road went to three lanes, which ate up the gardens. They were going to do more, but—"

He gave a shrug, his boots squelching in the grass as they crossed the overgrown lot. Wolfe knew the rest of the story. Most of the houses had been bought up years ago with compulsory purchases. By the time the plan to expand the road was discarded, many of the homes had already been demolished, while those that remained had been boarded up and left to decay.

The house whose address had been found in Rogozin's atlas was a forlorn shell with bay windows, its panes now broken or covered in grime, with ivy carpeting the moldering walls. Moving past the weedy garden, they approached the door, which had been boarded up. As the constable set to work with the pry bar, Wolfe noticed that some of the nails in the plywood looked surprisingly new.

Once the boards were gone, the constable switched on his flashlight, pointing it into the house. "I'd watch your step, if I were you—"

They looked through the open doorway, from which there arose a suffocating smell of dampness. Asthana whistled softly. "Bloody incredible. I can't believe this is still standing."

Wolfe could only agree. Aside from a narrow strip just inside the door, all of the floorboards had been torn up, revealing the thick gray beams underneath. Directing her flashlight toward the gaping hole at her feet, she could see stakes in the basement pointing upward like petrified trees. The ground below was covered in shards of broken porcelain.

"Bailiffs hit this place pretty hard," the constable explained helpfully. "Smashed it all so the squatters wouldn't take over."

"So it seems," Wolfe said. Looking around the ruin of the house, she saw at once that you wouldn't walk along the joists if you could possibly help it. "Give me the gloves. I'm going down."

With some assistance from the others, Wolfe lowered herself into the basement, her shoes landing with a crunch. Beyond the semicircle of light cast by the open door, it was pitch-black, the air heavy with the smell of wet wood. Beneath the dripping water, she heard a soft scurrying sound.

She paused to tuck her pants into her socks. Then she reached up for the flashlight and pry bar, which the constable handed down, saying uncertainly, "Perhaps I should go instead—"

Wolfe eyed the man's ample frame. "No, I'll need both of you to help me back up. Besides, I've had all my shots."

Switching on her flashlight, she went into the shadows. With every step, the smell of dampness grew stronger. Countless scraps of wood and flooring material had fallen down to this level as the bailiffs went to work with their hammers and bolsters. Seasoning everything were the small gray clots of mouse turds.

She let her light play across the walls, which were covered in a network of exposed pipes. In one corner stood a sad Hotpoint refrigerator, its closed door coated thickly with dust. A few feet away, lying on the ground, she saw something else. It was a steamer trunk.

Crossing the floor, Wolfe went up to the trunk, which turned out to be the kind covered in canvas, now old and brittle, secured by a brass clasp. When she tried the lid with one gloved hand, she found it wouldn't budge. She called up to the others. "Can you give me more light?"

Asthana and the constable obliged at once. Wolfe set down her own flashlight, then took the pry bar in both hands. Rearing back, she struck it against the lock of the trunk, the metal ringing under the blow, and felt the clasp give slightly. A second blow knocked the lock off altogether. She set the pry bar aside. Then she reached down and lifted up the lid.

Inside was a mouse's nest. Wolfe saw countless pairs of tiny eyes turn in her direction, paws scampering as the rodents fled from the thicket of grass and leaves that had been woven together inside. At the back of the trunk, there was a hole the size of her fist where the mice had gnawed their way in.

Wolfe tried to laugh but couldn't. A second later, she clearly saw the absurdity of what she was doing. Rising, she picked up the pry bar and flashlight. "This is ridiculous. I'm coming up."

Turning away from the trunk, she began to move gingerly back across the basement floor. As she did, her eye fell on the refrigerator in the corner. It was an ancient model, the kind with a metal door pull, and before she could quite understand what she was doing, she reached for the handle.

The door opened with surprising ease. Looking at what lay within, Wolfe knew at once what had been left here for her to find. But for a long moment, she could only stare silently at the man's body, its withered legs tucked under its chin, that had been awaiting her arrival for so long.

10

Maddy put her plan into effect the following morning. For two hours, she had been studying the files on her desk, a stack of financial records from the Virginia Museum of Fine Arts. As the clock on her computer crept toward twelve, however, she found it increasingly hard to concentrate, and her eyes kept straying to the open door of her office and its view of the hallway beyond.

Over the course of many surreptitious observations, she had determined that each of the binders in the file room had a date on its spine. Most binders seemed to cover a single year, while a few years were divided across two or more. Above each date, there was a printed word in Russian. Yesterday, while glancing at these labels on one of her trips along the corridor, she had finally seen the word that Powell had taught her to recognize: *Журнал*, or *journal*.

The file room itself was frequented primarily by the head of financial operations and his assistant, who shared an office down the hall. The two men ate lunch at their desks and were rarely more than a few feet from the files. To be safe, Maddy knew that she had to wait until both of them were gone.

At shortly before twelve, the moment came. Through her office door, Maddy heard footsteps, followed by voices in Russian. Rising quietly from her desk, she went over to the window, which looked out on the walled garden next to the extension. A minute later, she saw the two men appear outside in their coats, sharing a smoke where the view was most pleasant.

Maddy turned and went back to her desk, on which she had set a black plastic binder identical to the ones in which the financial records were kept. Earlier that morning, she had taken this binder from the archives room where she did most of her authorized work, having already determined that it was the same kind as the ones in the file room next door.

The binder she had selected happened to contain provenance information for works by the artist Nicholas Roerich, a number of whose paintings the foundation had recently acquired. On the spine, in a transparent plastic sleeve, was a descriptive label printed on a square of white cardboard. Keeping an eye on the door, Maddy slipped this label out and set it aside.

From her pocket, she took a second label of the same size, a close copy of the ones used for the cash journals, which she had prepared after discussing her plan with Powell. She slid this label into the sleeve on the binder's spine. Then she picked up the binder and headed for the door.

Outside, the corridor was deserted. Maddy went up the hallway, binder in hand, until she was a few steps away from the file room. Up ahead was a pair of offices occupied by other foundation employees, and beyond that, the reception and security desks, both out of sight from where she stood.

Maddy paused. If she turned left, she would be in the file room; right, and she would enter the archives. It was her last chance to do nothing. She already had the job. If she liked, she could simply stick to the work she had been contracted to perform, and Powell couldn't do anything about it.

For a moment, it seemed like a tempting idea. In the end, however, she turned left instead of right, moving invisibly past the point of no return. Because part of her, she realized, did care after all.

As she had expected, the file room was empty. Without turning on the lights, Maddy went to the shelves, already knowing which binder she needed. Reaching up, she slid it out with her left hand, then, in the same motion, replaced it with the duplicate binder in her right. Then she turned and left the room.

Walking up the hallway at a casual pace, the binder tucked under one arm, she did not think that she had been seen, although her heart was pounding. Back in her office, she shut the door, regretting that there was no lock on the inside. Through the window, she could see the two accountants finishing their smoke.

Maddy opened the binder on her desk. She had been careful to pick a journal from an earlier year, one she didn't think the back office would need that day. Inside was a thick stack of papers organized into sections with dividers and tabs. She began to flip through it, scanning the numbers and unrecognizable words.

At first, not finding what she had been expecting to see, she feared that she had taken the wrong binder. Finally, she saw a page with the layout she had memorized. Ten columns. A date on the far left, followed by a check number, a name, a description in Russian, and a final amount. It was the record of cash disbursements for the entire foundation.

Leaving the binder open, she took out her cell phone. The guard who searched her purse each day wouldn't have allowed her to bring a camera into the building, but fortunately, the camera in her phone worked just fine.

Maddy switched on the camera and held it above the binder. A blurred grid of numbers appeared on the preview screen. She pulled back until it snapped into focus, holding the camera a foot above the desk, and snapped a picture covering slightly more than half the page.

She studied the result. The numbers were small but readable. Going back to camera mode, she took a shot of the second half, then repeated the process on the next page, continuing until she had images of cash disbursements for a total of six months. She had just taken the final picture, and was about to close the journal and slide it into her desk, when there was a knock on her office door.

There was no time to think. Maddy pocketed her phone, then took the stack of files that had been on her desk all morning and dropped it on top of the open binder. Sitting in her chair, she pretended to be looking at something on her computer and called out in a voice that was almost totally calm: "Come in."

The door opened. It was Elena Usova. "We need to talk. Do you have a minute?"

"Of course," Maddy said, clicking her mouse as if to shut a nonexistent window. As she turned to face Tarkovsky's assistant, it took all of her willpower to keep from looking down at the files.

Elena took a seat, her eyes straying down idly to the pile of papers on the desk, on which only the documents from Virginia were visible. "Are you finding everything you need?"

"Yes, for the most part," Maddy said, her voice excessively bright in her ears. "The archives have been very useful."

Elena picked up the file on top of the stack, a copy of the museum's most recent quarterly statement, and began leafing through it. "What about the overall project? Are you close to making a proposal?"

Maddy nodded, aware that the back of her blouse was sticky with sweat. "I've found what looks like a possible approach for repatriation. I just need a little more time to finalize it."

"I see. As it happens, this is what I wanted to talk to you about." Elena tossed the file back on the desk, then turned her cool eyes on Maddy. "We've been forced to move up the timeline. Vasily and I are flying to Washington this week for a series of meetings. He'd like to visit the museum as well. Before he goes, he'll need you to present your recommendation."

Maddy saw the other woman watching for her reaction. "That's ahead of schedule."

"I'm aware of that. But it seemed best for Vasily to combine the two visits. I hope it won't be a problem. Of course, if you aren't prepared, I might be able to convince him to postpone—"

Hearing a hint of satisfaction in the assistant's voice, Maddy wondered if conducting both visits on the same trip had been Elena's idea. In the end, she had no choice but to meet the challenge. "You'll have the report tonight."

Elena rose from the chair. "Very good. In that case, we'll expect you to be packed and ready tomorrow morning. The car will arrive at the usual time to take you to the airport."

Maddy, who was relieved to see that the assistant was leaving, didn't understand what she meant. "The airport?"

Elena smiled. "Oh, didn't you realize? You'll be coming with us to Virginia."

The assistant went to the office door, then paused, turning back to Maddy, who was still staring at her from behind the desk. "I'm sorry," Elena said, one hand on the knob. "Door open or closed?"

11

Once a week, the inmates at Belmarsh were given a form for the prison canteen, brought around to each cell by a smiling woman in uniform. Each prisoner was allowed to spend up to twenty pounds, with the funds deducted from his personal account and the requested items left in his room later that day.

The order form, which consisted of four columns of sixty lines each, had been carefully screened for items of possible harm to others. Its first column was taken up largely by tobacco products. Other items available for purchase included batteries for personal electronics, stationery, postage stamps, and an assortment of toiletries, beverages, and salted snacks.

Ilya had filled out his own form a few days earlier, asking for a jar of coffee and a package of tea, and, in a departure from his usual order, two packs of cigarettes and a few lighters. Although he did not smoke, he did not think that the request would seem unusual, since cigarettes were the closest thing to a universal medium of exchange within the prison walls.

Separately, he had arranged for an additional item that was slightly more difficult to obtain. Several days before, he had spoken quietly with another inmate, a listener who served as a prison counselor and was granted special privileges. The next day, at association, the listener had passed him a flask, the kind that enhanced prisoners were allowed to carry.

Ilya had waited until returning to his cell to open it. When he unscrewed the top of the flask, a single whiff of the colorless liquid inside had been enough to make his eyes sting. Fortunately, he was not planning to drink it.

Now Ilya lay on his mattress, hands folded behind his head, looking up at the ceiling. All of the preliminary steps were complete, but even now, he found himself mulling over two sets of questions.

The first consisted of practical considerations, which was a realm in which he could comfortably operate. Within seconds of hearing what Vasylenko wanted, he had already come up with a list of reasons why it was impossible.

In itself, the task was not especially difficult. There were many ways to kill a man in prison. An inmate's throat could be cut with a sharpened phone card, or, as Ilya had learned from personal experience, a blade could be extracted from one of the safety razors that each prisoner was allowed. The real sticking point was how not to be caught. Ilya had looked at the problem from every angle, and although his solution wasn't perfect, it would have to do.

Yet this left him with a second set of concerns that were not so easily dismissed. He had a name but not a reason. This was an audition for a particular role, one that was rarely afforded the luxury of explanations. To prove that he was still useful, he would need to perform his task without question.

After another moment, he rose. It was early in the morning, and the light coming through the bars of his window was cold and gray. Only a short time remained before he would need to begin.

Going over to his small table, Ilya looked at the book he had left there the night before. On the open page, he had underlined a passage that he had contemplated more than once in recent months. *Russia is a sphinx,* it said. *Rejoicing, grieving, and drenched in black blood—*

If Russia was a sphinx, Ilya thought, with its head in one continent and its body in another, this could only be explained by the soil from which its two halves arose. European Russia ended where the steppes began, in the unforgiving lands, outside of history, that had once been ruled by the Scythians.

But then another nation had emerged in the Dark Ages, as if out of nothing, in the wilderness between empires. Later sources would call them drinkers of blood with hideous faces, but they were more likely a pale, handsome race with blue eyes and red hair that went by the name of Khazars.

Judging from the earliest sources, the Khazars had lived much like their predecessors, a tribe of fierce horsemen and dwellers in tents. But beyond the steppes, the world was changing. Caught between Byzantium and the Arabs, this unallied nation of warriors began to contemplate a grand experiment, centered on the realization that there was a shape to history beyond the cycle of the seasons.

And yet it was never a simple matter to change one's true nature. Reflecting on what the Khazars had ultimately done, Ilya, who knew something about living with a divided soul, reminded himself that one could never entirely escape the darkness at one's heart, and that there were times when it was necessary to embrace it. Nothing of what he had endured so far would have any meaning unless he could pursue it to its conclusion. Because something was coming.

Moreover, he could not avert it from his cell. The only way to see it clearly, and to prevent it from reaching its full culmination, was to follow it as far as he could. Only then could he hope to end it entirely.

And for the sake of that possibility, he was willing to become the Scythian again.

A quarter of an hour later, at just past eight, his cell door was unlocked. Ilya emerged, his towel draped over one arm, and headed with a line of other inmates toward the end of the landing.

He arrived after most of the others, entering a room with wooden benches, a stone floor, and a row of showers. Each stall had a button that, when pressed, would release a trickle of water for thirty seconds. All were already occupied, with a noisy line of the remaining prisoners clutching towels and toiletry bags.

As usual, Ilya went past the others into an unoccupied corner of the room, as if he preferred to wait alone. From here, he could see Sasha, the prisoner who had come to his cell a few days before, standing naked in a stall at the end of the row, his red hair soapy with suds.

Ilya remained where he was, perfectly calm, waiting for the right moment. At last, seeing the flow of water over Sasha's head start to die down, he began to move along the showers, just one figure among many. When he was a few steps away from the last stall, he pulled back the towel that was draped over his arm. In his right hand, he held a measuring syringe that he had taken from the prison workroom, where it was used to inject ink into printer cartridges.

Before Sasha could reach for the shower button again, Ilya walked casually past him and pressed the syringe's plunger. A thin stream of dark liquid arced through the air and struck the other man between his sunburned shoulders. As Sasha began to turn, Ilya kept moving, pulling the towel back over his hand.

Out of the corner of his eye, Ilya saw Sasha standing in the shower, reaching back to feel where the liquid had struck his skin. Ilya continued walking out of the shower room, as if he had decided that it was too much trouble to wait, and headed along the landing to the rows of cells, moving past a pair of guards.

Back in his own cell, he went to the sink. Tossing his towel aside, he carefully rinsed out the syringe, handling it through the plastic bags that he had been given to hold his belongings during his recent transfer. Once every trace of the black fluid had been washed away, he put the syringe on the floor and stepped on it hard, reducing it to shards of plastic.

Going to the window, he tossed the remains of the syringe through the bars, a few bits at a time, so that they were lost on the ground outside, which was strewn with trash that had accumulated between the prison blocks. Then he went back to his bed, lay down, and closed his eyes.

The rest of the story Ilya heard, in fragments, from the other inmates over the course of the day. He heard how Sasha, soon after emerging from the shower, had doubled over, retching, on the bathroom floor; how he had been taken, sweating and convulsing, to the infirmary; and how, since then, there had been no news at all, although the prison was alive with rumors about what had happened.

Ilya listened attentively to the speculation, but he said nothing. Earlier that week, he had carefully emptied the bags of tea from his canteen order and stuffed them with tobacco from the packs of cigarettes. Placing them in the empty plastic coffee jar, he had performed two sets of extractions, the first with butane from the lighters to remove oils and tar, the second with alcohol.

When the solvents had evaporated, he had been left with a solution of almost pure nicotine, which would be readily absorbed through the skin. A single drop on the back of the hand would put a man in the hospital with symptoms of acute respiratory arrest, while sixty milligrams were enough to kill. With the excess solution washed down the drain, it would take days to determine the true cause of death. And by then, he hoped, it would no longer matter.

Final word came that afternoon. As Ilya sat in the association room with Vasylenko's men, another inmate came up with the latest news, which had spread through the prison like wildfire. Sasha was dead.

As the others traded tense whispers, Ilya realized that Vasylenko was looking at him. The ensuing exchange of glances lasted for only a second, but in that interval, a great deal was silently expressed.

A few minutes later, as association time ended, Ilya found himself walking alongside Vasylenko as they headed back to the spur. Ilya spoke quietly in Assyrian. "I still don't understand why."

Vasylenko responded in a low voice. "You will find out in time. For now, let it go."

As the *vor* said this, he slid something into Ilya's

pocket, then went to rejoin the others. Ilya knew what the object was at once, but he did not try to examine it until he had returned to his cell.

Later, with the door safely closed, Ilya studied what Vasylenko had given him. It was a cell phone. And as he shut his eyes, the phone in one hand, he feared that he had never truly changed at all.

12

The Fabergé collection at the Virginia Museum of Fine Arts was housed in the museum's lowest level, where a special exhibition had opened earlier that month. Jewelry, timepieces, and other objets d'art were displayed in niches along the walls, while at the center of the gallery, lit softly in five separate cases, stood the imperial eggs bequeathed by the estate of Lillian Thomas Pratt of Fredericksburg.

Maddy looked at the Peter the Great egg. It was just over four inches high, made of different shades of gold in rococo cage work, with diamonds and other precious stones set above scrolls and bulrushes. Four miniature watercolors on ivory completed the design, with the one facing her now depicting a hut on the banks of the Neva River, beneath the date of the founding of St. Petersburg.

Next to it was a smaller object that had originally been inside the egg itself. Each egg made for the Romanovs had been required to contain a surprise, which, in this case, consisted of a tiny sculpture raised when the top of the egg was opened. It was the bronze figure of a man on horseback, mounted on a bed of sapphire, with a snake being crushed under the horse's hooves.

The director of the museum was a small bearded man in a blue suit. "It's a replica of the equestrian statue of Peter the Great. I don't know if you know the legend behind the statue, Miss Shaw—"

Maddy smiled. "It says St. Petersburg will never fall as long as the statue remains."

Tarkovsky, who was standing a few steps behind her, spoke quietly. "Yes. But I prefer to think of it another way. The statue, like this egg, is a reminder of what Russia was once capable of doing, and what it might do again. But only if it holds fast to its own heritage."

"Spoken like a man who wants to get to business," the director said. "Shall we?"

The director headed upstairs, with Maddy and Tarkovsky following him through the museum. They had arrived earlier that morning, coming by car after flying out from Washington on the oligarch's private Tupolev. For the first time since their departure, she was alone with Tarkovsky himself.

Her nervousness was only increased by the fact that she had not informed Powell of this trip. Maddy knew that Powell would not approve of her spending so much time with the oligarch, preferring that she do her work more discreetly. So far, however, Tarkovsky had kept his distance, and she still wasn't entirely sure what he thought of the argument she was about to make.

Moving through the administrative wing, they entered the director's office. Once the pleasantries were out of the way, Maddy dove in. "As you know, our mission is to preserve Russia's cultural heritage, which includes the repatriation of selected works of art. The price we're offering here is more than fair, and we're committed to restoring this egg to the position it deserves. It won't be locked away, like the Vekselberg collection, but on display at the Kremlin Armory, where it belongs."

"Yes, I've reviewed your proposal," the director said, leaning back comfortably in his chair. "But you understand, of course, that this collection has been here for six decades. Losing any part of it would damage the museum's stature. You can hardly expect the board to give it up without good reason."

Maddy glanced at Tarkovsky, who remained silent. "And we respect this. But we also believe that it's in the museum's best interests to allow this egg to be returned, given the questions that have been raised about the original transaction. It was sold by the Soviet government to an unknown American buyer for four thousand rubles. After the buyer left it unclaimed at customs, it was bought by another dealer, Alexander Schaffer, who sold it to Lillian Pratt for less than seventeen thousand dollars. Today, it's worth at least twenty million."

"None of this is under dispute," the director said. Much of the friendliness was gone from his voice. "And your point is what, exactly?"

"This was not a legitimate sale. A priceless artifact was seized and sold at a discount, with an unexplained gap in the provenance. It's easy to see the museum as only the most recent link in a questionable chain of ownership."

The director smiled tightly. "As it happens, I disagree. The Bolshevik government, whatever its faults, had the legal right to sell its own treasures, and even if the provenance were in question, the statute of limitations ran out decades ago. I sympathize, but you just don't have a case."

Tarkovsky spoke for the first time. His voice was very quiet. "A determined opponent doesn't need a case. All he needs is a lawyer."

The director turned to face the oligarch. "Excuse me. Is that some kind of threat?"

Maddy jumped in quickly. "No. It's a warning. A lawsuit over provenance would be long and damaging. If we've seen this vulnerability, so will others. But there's a second possibility that we'd like you to consider."

As Maddy spoke, she opened the folder she had been holding throughout the conversation. "You recently completed an expansion at a cost of over one hundred million dollars, which means several million in additional operating expenses every year. In retrospect, it was the worst possible time. The state is facing a shortfall. You've already had millions slashed from your budget. And without an additional source of revenue, the situation will only get worse."

She handed the director a copy of the document inside the folder, which was a projection of the museum's financial situation over the coming decade. He took it, frowning. "If you're suggesting that we sell our holdings to pay our operating costs, you're barking up the wrong tree. We're prohibited from selling artworks to cover anything but new acquisitions."

"I'm aware of that," Maddy said. "But there's one exception. A sale to cover operating costs is permissible, under standard museum guidelines, if a work is being repatriated or returned to its rightful owner."

The director glanced up from the document. She thought she saw a hint of interest in his expression. "I'm listening."

"It's quite simple. This is a work of art that belongs in Russia, with a provenance that renders it vulnerable to an extended legal challenge. Under the circumstances, the board of directors, as well as the public, will surely see that a sale is the only possible solution. And if the revenue happens to cover the museum's operating shortfall for the next ten years, that's simply a fortunate side effect."

The director seemed to weigh this. Maddy could hear the ticking of the clock on the office wall as she waited for him to speak again. "If it came to that, it means that we never had this conversation."

"Of course," Maddy said. "We understand the need for discretion in a case like this."

The director was silent for another moment. At last, he said, "We'll take it under due consideration. If I present your proposal to the board, I'll need to abide by their decision. It's not my choice to make."

Maddy felt a rush of something like relief. "That's all we ask. The rest is up to you."

Tarkovsky, for his part, said nothing. A moment later, they wrapped up the meeting, with the oligarch confining himself to a few words of thanks. Maddy thought the presentation had gone well, but when she looked over at Tarkovsky, she couldn't tell what he was thinking.

Outside, it was blindingly hot. Two town cars were waiting at the curb. In one were Elena and Orlov, the security chief; the other, which they entered now, was empty except for the driver, who would return Maddy to her hotel before taking Tarkovsky to his next round of meetings.

As the car started, Tarkovsky glanced out the window. "You did well. I've found that it's often wise to appeal to your rival's best interests."

"I'm glad to hear that," Maddy said. "But I still wouldn't overstate our chances."

"I know. But this was more of a test. I've heard good things about you, and I wanted to see them for myself."

He looked at her directly for the first time. "Lermontov, in particular, always spoke of you highly—"

Maddy froze. For a moment, she was aware of nothing but the throaty murmur of the engine, and she felt for a paralyzing second how close the two of them were. "What are you talking about?"

Tarkovsky glanced away again. "I wasn't sure if you knew. In any event, I thought it best that you hear it from me. I knew Alexey Lermontov. I worked with him years ago, as part of my efforts to recover Russian art from overseas, and often visited his gallery in New York."

Maddy found that her hands had gone cold. "I don't remember seeing you there."

"It would have been shortly after you left. Lermontov often mentioned you. He seemed to think that you were making a mistake by trying to start your own gallery. That your true talents lay elsewhere—"

Listening, she felt something rise in her throat, and she realized that she was dangerously close to being sick. "And you never knew—"

"That he was working for state intelligence?" Tarkovsky said this nonchalantly, as if discussing something of limited interest. "I had my suspicions, of course. Especially given the friends we had in common. As you pointed out, the art world makes strange bedfellows. Your former employer and I found each other useful. Until it was no longer possible."

Maddy fought back her growing sense of queasiness. "And when did that happen?"

Tarkovsky continued to look out the window. "If nothing else, as soon as he was no longer alive."

A silence fell over the car. When Tarkovsky turned to her again, his voice was oddly gentle. "I know this is hard, which is why I wanted to tell you myself. I still want you to work for me. In the end, however, the choice is yours."

He glanced away as the car slowed to a stop. Following his gaze, Maddy saw that they had pulled up at the Jefferson. When the driver came around to open her door, she gathered up her belongings and slid out, looking back once at Tarkovsky, who had remained in the car.

"Think it over," Tarkovsky said. Then the door closed again, hiding him from sight.

13

"The body is that of an adult white male, the carotid arteries cut, a second stab wound above the left kidney," Wolfe said to the board. "Adipocere, or grave wax, has formed over much of the corpse, preserving it, but before it was dumped, the face was systematically disfigured and the teeth and fingertips removed. In the left femur, there's a metal intramedullary rod from an old fracture. We're working to identify it from medical records."

The chairman spoke up, as slim and sleek as a mink. "And you believe that Rogozin was involved with this murder?"

"That's a reasonable conclusion," Wolfe replied. "But I need time to build a case."

"I see," the chairman said. "Unfortunately, time is a rare commodity these days."

Wolfe wanted to say that was common sense, but she held her tongue. The hearing was being held in a conference room in Victoria, not far from New Scotland Yard. She was seated alone at one of four folding tables that had been set up in a square. At the other three sat the nine members of the board, along with Dana Cornwall, the deputy director of the intelligence directorate. Asthana was somewhere behind her, her presence comforting but unseen.

The director general, a bespectacled civil servant with long white hands, was the next to speak. "We've reviewed your decision logs. At the moment, we have no physical evidence and a very tenuous link to Rogozin, who can be held for only five more days without charges."

"Five days is a long time," Wolfe said. "We're going through his files and contacts now. I'm confident that we'll emerge with a case for the Crown that Rogozin was Karvonen's handler."

The chairman nodded sourly. "Except that Karvonen was shot twice before he could be questioned."

Dana Cornwall broke in. The deputy director had aged visibly in the past six months, but she was still an attractive older woman with a manner that commanded attention. "That's bloody unfair. Wolfe had no alternative."

"I'm well aware of that," the chairman said sharply. "No one here is questioning the present officer's bravery. But in my report, I have no choice but to consider the larger picture."

As she listened, Wolfe reflected that the chairman was a lifetime bureaucrat with no law enforcement experience who had been in his current position for less than two years. "I'm still not sure what you mean by this."

The chairman leaned forward. "This case has been a disaster for this agency. Karvonen was allowed to commit several murders practically under our noses, and we were unable to prevent him from carrying out a major act of terrorism. Not to mention the issue of Arnold Garber, an officer who appears to have passed information freely to Russia and may still be doing so as we speak—"

"And it happened at the worst possible time," the director general put in. "This agency is already under scrutiny. In my capacity as head of operations, I'm obliged to evaluate your ongoing involvement with this investigation, considering your public connection to Rogozin—"

Wolfe focused on a point on the wall above the director general's head. "What does that have to do with the merits of the case?"

The director general was eyeing her coolly. "Are you denying that you have a personal stake in the outcome?"

"Not at all," Wolfe said. "But this has nothing to do with my actions, which I carried out in the mutual interest of both our countries."

Even as Wolfe spoke, she heard how naïve this sounded. With the agency on the verge of being reorganized, officers and directors alike were scrambling to position themselves. In any merger, there would always be reductions, and she had no illusions about her own invulnerability.

She chose her next few words with care. "I'm aware that the review process is necessary. But I stand by my decision. All I ask is a chance to see the rest of this through, within the legal period of detention."

The chairman glanced around at the other board members. "Your request has been duly noted. The secretary will testify before the Home Affairs Select Committee next week as to whether this detention is an appropriate use of resources. I only wish we had better news to share."

With that, the hearing adjourned. As Wolfe got up to leave, the members of the board remained seated, talking quietly among themselves, their eyes looking everywhere but in her direction. Her partner was standing behind her. "Come on," Asthana said. "I'll buy you a drink."

As they headed for the door, Cornwall approached. She looked tired, as she often did these days. "Wolfe, they had no right to be so hard on you. Everyone at the agency respects what you've done."

"I appreciate that," Wolfe said, meaning it, although much was also being left unspoken. Cornwall, she knew, had hoped to be promoted to director general, only to find herself tainted by association with the Garber scandal. Wolfe wanted to say something more, but she contented herself with a nod goodbye as Asthana took her arm and led her gently away.

An hour later, Wolfe found herself at a crowded pub in Vauxhall, staring at the few amber inches remaining in her pint glass. In recent months, she had begun to drink more than before, which reminded her of the old joke about why you should always take two Mormons on a fishing trip. Bring only one, the punch line said, and he'll drink all your beer.

Next to her, Asthana was halfway through another monologue about her wedding table cards when she trailed off, sensing that Wolfe wasn't listening. "Cheer up. They were bound to knock you down a little. It doesn't look great for the agency when its star officer isn't even British."

Wolfe managed to smile. "Sometimes I wish Powell were still here. He knew how to ignore the political side."

Finishing her beer, Wolfe ordered another. Asthana was watching her with a mixture of amusement and friendly concern. "I haven't talked to Powell in a long time. You still see him?"

"Occasionally," Wolfe said. "He knows more about

the ties between intelligence and organized crime than I ever will, and we sometimes trade ideas over the phone, but we've fallen out of touch since he joined Cheshire."

Asthana shook her head. "I still think he was a fool to leave, especially given the timing. It looked like they were buying him off."

"I know." Wolfe accepted her fresh pint with a nod. "I understand why he did it, but he refused to see what people would think. He's always been like this, but it got worse after the crash. You wouldn't believe some of the things I've heard." She looked glumly into her glass. "Maybe it's better that he's gone."

Asthana lifted her daiquiri. "That's doesn't seem fair. What's he really done, then?"

Wolfe was about to avoid the question, then heard herself speak before she could help it. "You know Vasily Tarkovsky?"

Her partner frowned. "The oligarch. He's negotiating for some kind of oil venture?"

Wolfe nodded. "Cheshire is advising on the deal. Powell has been looking into Tarkovsky's activities. Most of it is the standard background check. But he's also planted a source on Tarkovsky's staff."

Asthana set down her glass. "What kind of source are we talking about?"

"Someone passing him files under the table. Powell told me yesterday. He wanted my advice about how far to trust her. His source, I mean." Wolfe took another big sip. After the farce of the hearing, which had left her feeling more isolated than ever, she was suddenly eager to share the misgivings she had been bottling up inside. "You see, it's someone we both know. Someone with no business being involved. I told him this, but I don't think he agrees."

Asthana had absorbed this information with what looked like mounting dismay. "Rachel, listen to me. If this comes out, forget the business angle. We're talking about a major diplomatic scandal. Who's his source, anyway?"

Wolfe belatedly realized that she'd had too much to drink, but it was too late to backpedal now. "It's the girl from the Archvadze case. I've told you about her before. Maddy Blume—"

She was about to say more when her cell phone rang. Fishing it with some difficulty out of her purse, she checked the display, then fumbled the phone open. "Lester, how are you?"

"I'm fine," the pathologist said, although his voice was tense. "I just got off the phone with the orthopedic center at the Royal London. They've identified your body. You need to hear the name now."

Wolfe saw that Asthana was watching her intently. Even through her alcoholic fog, she had a premonition of what was coming, and, much later, she would wonder if she had known all along. "What is it?"

Lewis hesitated. "I don't quite know how to say this. It's Garber. Your dead man is Arnold Garber—"

14

Asthana knew what the call meant as soon as she saw the look on Wolfe's face. After hanging up to dial Cornwall, Wolfe had to be forcibly dissuaded from going to the office. In the end, Asthana managed to get her partner into a cab that would take her home. Then she headed on foot back to where she had left her own car, glad for the chance to think in private.

As she walked, Asthana recalled the last time she had seen Garber alive, parked in his car near the Battersea Power Station. Garber, who had been a loyal but disillusioned officer of law enforcement, had told her that Putin's regime would never give up control as long as the world needed its energy resources, and that he suspected the agency's current investigation was nothing more than a game being played out between the civilian and military sides of the Russian security services.

Looking out at the power station's four monumental smokestacks, Asthana had asked him what their colleagues thought of his theory. Garber had replied that he hadn't told anyone yet. And he had seemed genuinely surprised, a few seconds later, when Asthana had cut his throat.

Thinking back to that moment now, Asthana knew that she had taken a considerable risk, but to her credit, she had remained calm in the aftermath. Around her, the street had been quiet. After wiping the blade on Garber's shirt, she had left a message for her fiancé, telling him that she was going to be late. Then she had taken the dead man's keys and gone around to the trunk.

After a moment of rummaging, she had come up with a heavy blanket. Returning to the front of the car, she had covered Garber's body so it lay across the seats. When she studied the result, she had been satisfied that the body was not obvious from the street. Then she had locked up the car, crossed to the opposite curb, and stood there in the darkness, thinking very carefully.

Even after the killing, her thoughts had remained clear. She did not think that anyone had seen them leaving the office. For all the world knew, Garber, who was unmarried and lived alone, had gone home as usual after work. If he failed to appear the next day, the agency would suspect that something was wrong. Unless, of course, she managed to shape the story in the meantime.

Once her plan was complete, Asthana had taken out her phone and made two calls. A quarter of an hour later, she had accompanied the car as it was towed by a breakdown truck to Dalston. The mechanic had spoken only after they were safely inside the garage. The vehicle, he had said slowly, would be cleaned and taken to a car breaker in Norwood. He would look after the body himself.

Thinking back to this now, as she neared the office, Asthana was newly incensed at the botched job he had done, but it was too late for recriminations. And in any case, she had more important things to consider.

Arriving at her car, Asthana drove home to Knightsbridge, where she found Devon seated with a laptop at the dining room table. She gave him a kiss. "How are you, darling?"

"Swamped, as usual," Devon said, not looking away from the computer, on which rows of government spending figures were arranged in an indecipherable spreadsheet. "How was the hearing?"

"A disaster." As Asthana spoke, she studied her fiancé in the circle of light from the overhead lamp. She had secretly cast him years ago with a particular role in mind, and even to her critical eye, he was quite handsome, with thick dark hair and a lanky frame that was only slightly too narrow at the shoulders. "Rachel was torn to pieces. I couldn't bear to watch."

She knew that Devon liked Wolfe a great deal, and the sympathy in his eyes now was genuine. "Is there anything I can do?"

"We'll pull through." Asthana checked the pot on the counter and found that the tea was still warm. Pouring herself a cup, she said, "I need to take care of a few things before supper. I'll be down in a moment."

Devon only nodded, frowning at a column of figures on the screen. Asthana gave him another light peck on the cheek, then headed for the stairs, cradling her mug of tea in one hand.

The house was spacious and pleasant, a perfect stage set, with far more room than they could have afforded if her parents had not offered to help. Upstairs, she entered her office and closed the door. Setting down her tea, she checked her email. The only message was from her mother, written in obvious distress, urgently asking whether the tablecloths at the reception would be ivory or champagne.

Asthana closed the email without answering it, then glanced at a picture on the wall. It was the only piece of Indian art in the house, an image of Kalki, the destroyer of darkness, riding a white horse against the sky. He was destined to guide the world into a new golden age, but no one knew what shape he would take, although it was widely believed that he would come from the north. And, like most symbols, the story concealed a deeper meaning.

If asked, she would have been insulted by the implication that any of her choices had been influenced by her background. She had never considered herself particularly Indian, except by accident, and took little interest in the fact that India had always had close ties with Russian military intelligence. Like most things in her life, this decision had been driven by a cold process of analysis, one that had led her to conclude, years ago, that the values her family took for granted would soon be gone.

Garber, she reflected, turning back to her computer, had been right about one thing. The world still ran on oil, and the dislocation between importers and exporters would only grow as petroleum reserves decreased over time. It came down to a simple curve. No matter where you drew the peak, in the face of its remorseless logic, all other considerations fell away. What was required, more than anything else, was a hand strong enough to guide the world through the coming transition. An oil exporter that was also a nuclear power. And this meant only one country.

Putin, she had seen long ago, was not a monster but a pragmatist. He preferred injustice to disorder, which was a choice that could not be avoided. Asthana understood that she had been born at a time when much of her life would be spent in a world where power had shifted east, so when the opportunity arose, she had seen no alternative but to throw in her lot with the forces of history.

As inevitable as the curve was in theory, however, you often ran into trouble in the details. The last few weeks, in particular, had presented a number of challenges, especially now that so much depended on her alone. Which made it all the more important to act decisively.

Opening a new window in her browser, Asthana typed in a name. She took a sip of tea, then clicked on the first result. Scrolling down the page, working slowly and carefully, she began to read.

Half an hour later, she had reviewed most of the information available online. Turning to one of the more recent articles, Asthana studied a picture of a young woman's face. As she looked into the pixels of the girl's eyes, she found that she wasn't sure if she agreed with Wolfe. Maddy Blume, she thought, might be more suited for this kind of work than she seemed. Her face was that of a woman with secrets. Asthana knew the signs all too well.

On an impulse, she unlocked and opened her desk drawer. It was cluttered with pens, pencils, and other odds and ends, but among this deliberate confusion lay a small object with a curved steel handle.

Asthana took out the knife and unfolded it. The hawkbill blade, curved like a raptor's talon, was spotless now, and she had kept it for sentimental reasons, although she used it these days only to open the mail.

She studied the blade for another moment, then closed it. As she put the knife back into the drawer, her eyes fell again on the photo of Maddy. Asthana considered it briefly, then shut the window on her computer screen, although she continued to wonder about the secrets behind the girl's face.

Perhaps, she thought, closing the drawer, it would be necessary to keep an eye on her.

15

"You should have told me," Maddy said to Powell. "Did you know that Tarkovsky had worked with Lermontov?"

Powell gazed out at the lake at the heart of Hyde Park. He had not been looking forward to this conversation, but there was no longer any way of avoiding it. "I knew. But it's more complicated than you think."

"You'd better explain," Maddy replied. "Otherwise, I'm walking away now."

They made their way slowly along the Serpentine. Powell's legs were bothering him, but he was always glad to be outside. It was a bright morning, one of those pleasant London days, of which there had been all too few this year, that made you all the more aware of how summer was passing.

He decided to approach the topic in the way that would seem most reassuring. "You need to understand that there are two competing sides to Russian intelligence. The FSB and its affiliates are what we call the civilian side. At home, they hold the power of life and death, but they're less effective at foreign operations. Lermontov was one of their leading paymasters, channeling money from art deals to agents across the world, and his death was a great blow."

Maddy's voice remained cold. "I imagine that he was very good at what he did."

"He was," Powell said. "And no one has yet emerged to take his place. But there's a second group, the GRU, on the military side. This is a separate world entirely from civilian intelligence. Until recently, they had been growing even more powerful, as the energy companies they controlled spread across the globe. The result is a rivalry that goes back decades. And it culminated late last year."

Maddy kept her eyes on the path, her hands in her pockets. "With the plane attack."

Powell nodded. "Military intelligence thought the civilian side was plotting to seize control of the gas industry. To foil this, they brought down the plane of an opposition leader and tried to pin it on their rivals. It was a very good plan. I should know. But it backfired. The plan was exposed. And as a result, the military side appears to have fallen apart."

As he walked, he was unable to prevent a note of satisfaction from entering his voice. "It's hard to be sure, but the withdrawal seems to have been a messy one. Agents have been left stranded without any way of contacting their handlers at home. Meanwhile, the civilian arm has grown in power, and most of the leading energy companies have come under its influence. So it's no surprise that the remains of the military side are trying to cling to their last source of advantage."

Maddy appeared to understand at once. "You're talking about Tarkovsky."

"Yes," Powell said. "Tarkovsky owns one of the last major oil companies in Russia that isn't in government hands. But his situation is a precarious one. As a banker, he was ready to act when the government privatized state businesses to pay off its debts. He became a billionaire overnight. But he was an upstart, an outsider, and privatization was supposed to benefit the old guard. In order to survive, he had to come to terms with the security services."

Powell headed for a bench by the lake, motioning for Maddy to follow. "Of course, this was true of all energy companies. To avoid being taxed out of existence, they had to set up subsidiaries to distribute the oil and gas. The easiest way of doing this was to partner with organized crime, which already had the infrastructure in place. And this meant dealing with state intelligence, especially in the military, which had strong ties to the mob."

Maddy seemed struck by this. "Tarkovsky's security chief. Orlov. Is he one of them?"

"He's a former military translator, which generally points to an intelligence role. That ring he wears is a sign of this as well. But his contacts, if they exist, are on the military side. These aren't Lermontov's people. And there's no evidence that Tarkovsky was involved with what happened to you in New York."

Powell studied her face as he spoke, hoping that his words would have the proper effect. All the same, he knew that while such distinctions were correct in theory, the lines were not always so clear. Maddy, for her part, seemed to sense this. "So why was he working with Lermontov?"

"It might have been exactly what he told you," Powell said. "We've looked into this very carefully. Tarkovsky spent much of the last few years acquiring Russian art that had been illegally removed from the country. Lermontov had access to work that was sold to raise funds for operations. Tarkovsky may have seen a partnership as the best way to retrieve it—"

Maddy broke in. "No. It isn't that simple. Lermontov killed a friend of mine with his own hands, and he tried to do the same to me. You knew exactly how I'd feel about his connection to Tarkovsky, but you said nothing. Were you afraid I'd refuse the assignment?"

"Of course," Powell said. "But in any case, it wasn't necessary for you to know."

"Well, it's necessary now," Maddy replied. "Before this goes any further, you need to tell me everything."

Looking at her, Powell wondered if she sensed that he was not the same man he had been when they first met. The change had begun with the crash, but there had also been the death of his father, who had passed away four months ago, his mind mercifully gone, after a lifetime of work at Thames House. Studying the files and books that his father had left behind, Powell had come to a decision. If his life had been spared, it was so he could make something real and lasting, even if the rest of the world failed to understand his reasons.

Powell watched a couple in a pedal boat on the lake, the man and woman laughing as they paddled across the water. "Russia will only change if it's forced to do so by its foreign partners. This is why I went to Cheshire. I had no interest in the investment side, but I saw a chance to influence events in a way that might actually matter, and to make sure that the men who did this to me don't return to power again when the wheel comes full circle."

Glancing over, he saw that Maddy had turned away. "So what happens now?"

Powell sensed that she was close to a decision. "It's your choice. I won't blame you for leaving. But I need you." He hesitated. "The documents you've provided are useful. They show that much of the foundation's money is being sent to a range of holding companies that we're still trying to identify. But there's more that you could do for us, at least until this deal is concluded."

She did not reply. After a minute had passed in silence, Powell rose from the bench, thinking of his conversation with Wolfe. Maddy, she had said, had no business being involved, and he knew from long experience that Wolfe was usually right. But this was also the last real chance he would ever have.

"Take your time," Powell finally said to Maddy, who was still looking away. "When you're ready, we'll talk about what comes next."

There was no response. In the end, he only turned aside, moving along the path by the water.

From the bench, Maddy watched him go. Once he was out of sight, she turned back to the other faces along the lake. Her thoughts were clear and cold, but she was no closer to an answer than before.

Powell had used her. The wisest course of action would be simply to end it now. Yet she also remembered the look in Tarkovsky's eyes when he had told her about Lermontov. And she had made a vow to see something through, a promise with consequences that Powell would never understand.

Only one other person in the world knew what she had done. At the museum in Philadelphia, he had seen something in her face, and later, he had come to her, knowing that they both wanted the same thing. In the end, Maddy had done her part. Which was how she had found herself standing outside the house in Fulham, two years ago, when Ilya Severin had killed Lermontov.

Ever since, she had tried to bury this memory as deep as she could. She had told herself that the gallerist's death was the end of it all, that she could move on, but even then, she had known better. Lermontov was only a piece of a larger pattern. If Tarkovsky had been a part of it, she owed it to herself, and to others, to learn more. And if he bore any of the responsibility—

Maddy cut off the thought, afraid, more than anything else, to find out what she might be willing to do. She looked out at the water for another moment, then rose and headed down the path in the opposite direction from Powell.

And she did not realize, as she left the lake, that someone had been watching her the entire time.

16

By late morning, Wolfe's hangover was still there. At the moment, as she sat in the deputy director's office with the door closed, it had been reduced to a dull throb, rising occasionally to the surface as Cornwall tried to get a handle on the situation. "Forensics is sure about the timing?"

"As far as they can be," Wolfe said. "They think he's been there at least six months. If they're right, it means Garber died soon after his disappearance. So all our assumptions need to be thrown away."

Cornwall leafed through the files on her desk. Wolfe had recognized them earlier as a complete set of internal reports, many of which she had written herself, on Garber's presumed defection, all of which could now be consigned to the fire. "And the train ticket to Lausanne?"

"It was bought using Garber's credit card and identification, to make it look like he was leaving the country. The files on his computer are suspect as well. It means we've been chasing a ghost."

Cornwall sighed, removing her glasses. "So let's lay it out. If Garber wasn't the informant, then our mole isn't just guilty of a leak, but of accessory to murder, if not more. It could tear this agency apart."

Wolfe didn't bother denying this. "But it could also work to our advantage. The real informant doesn't know we've identified the body. Only Asthana, Lewis, and a few staff members at the Royal London are aware of it. Garber was unmarried. His next of kin is an aunt in Manchester. If we can, I'd like to hold off on announcing his death for as long as possible, until we can question Rogozin again."

Cornwall seemed to consider this. There was a pair of marks on the bridge of her nose where her glasses had pinched too tightly. "I'll need to inform the board. But I'll try to buy you a day or two. I can't promise anything more."

Putting her glasses back on, Cornwall looked across the desk at Wolfe. "I'm entrusting you with this for a reason. When this is over, you can still go home. I don't want a witch-hunt, but we need to tie this off. Otherwise—"

She left the thought unfinished, but Wolfe knew what she had been about to say.

Leaving the office, Wolfe walked through the cubicle farm on the third floor of agency headquarters. Asthana was seated at her workstation, not far from Garber's old desk, which was still vacant. Before Wolfe could sit down, her partner rose, lifting a finger for silence, and motioned her into an empty conference room. She was carrying a thick stack of folders. "What's the word?"

"We have a day's head start, maybe less." Wolfe quickly described her meeting with Cornwall, then spread out the files Asthana had brought, which turned out to be summaries of personnel records for the entire agency.

Wolfe finished laying out the files, ordering them in separate stacks by division, and took a step back. "Let's start with what we know. We're looking for someone who had access to information about the Karvonen case and could have hacked into Garber's workstation to plant evidence."

Asthana looked over Wolfe's shoulder. "Which points to someone in the intelligence directorate. A hundred names. I'll get the files from corporate services. We can tell them it's part of the restructuring—"

"Which will just make them afraid that they're going to be downsized." Wolfe shook her head, then thought of something else. "And there's one more thing. You need to see Rogozin."

Asthana, who had been stacking the files, glanced up in surprise. "Why me?"

"I can't go myself. I'm being watched too closely. But we need to find out what he knows about Garber. And at this point, you have a better chance than I do." Wolfe began packing up the papers. "We can discuss it later. I'll take care of this. Just get me those records."

After a beat, Asthana left the conference room. Wolfe watched her go, then gathered up the remaining files. As she did, her eyes passed across the names of her colleagues, one of whom, she feared, was a traitor and murderer. Weighing the papers in her hands, she found herself thinking of something she had been told long ago: *Words would only deceive you—*

As she remembered this, she suddenly saw what she had to do next. There was someone she had to see. And before she could come up with a list of reasons to put the thought out of mind, she quickly stuffed the rest of the files into their folders and headed back out to the main floor.

An hour later, Wolfe was in the interview room at Belmarsh, waiting to see Ilya Severin. It was strange to be back. She had not returned since late the previous year, and her last conversation with Ilya had been a phone call lasting less than a minute. Since then, she had made sure he was treated fairly, but she had otherwise kept her distance. Ilya, she had hoped, would understand.

Looking out at the guards, Wolfe wasn't sure what had brought her here again. She had not asked for permission from Cornwall, knowing that it would certainly be denied. Yet she had learned long ago to trust her intuition, which didn't tell her that Ilya would know the informant's name, or even that he would see something that she could not, but only that their conversation might set up a vibration that would lead her, in the end, to the answer.

She was still reflecting on this when she saw a familiar figure in the corridor outside. After consulting inaudibly with one of the guards, he came through the door of the interview room. "Why, hello there," Owen Dancy said. "I wasn't sure if I'd have the pleasure again—"

Wolfe stared up at the solicitor's substantial frame. "What are you doing here?"

"I might ask you the same thing," Dancy said, lowering himself carefully into a chair. "It seems rather strange, given the timing, for you to suddenly decide to see my client now."

"Ilya is your client?" Wolfe heard herself echoing his words. "Since when?"

Dancy smiled. "We came to a private arrangement some time ago. More recently, we've decided to formalize our relationship, now that preparations have started in earnest for his upcoming trial."

Wolfe tried to get her head around this. It didn't make sense. Ilya hated the solicitor's clients and all they represented, and it was unthinkable that he would accept their help. "I want to see him."

"That may be rather difficult," Dancy said. "I just spoke with our friend, and my impression is that he would prefer that you not contact him again. It might give the appearance of a conflict, given the evolving nature of his case—"

Wolfe became aware that her headache had returned. "What are you talking about?"

"I'm hardly at liberty to discuss. However, my client will have more to say at his next court appearance. In the meantime, it seems best for him to refuse any visitors." He gave her another silky smile. "I do hope you understand."

With that, the solicitor rose and headed for the door. Wolfe remained where she was, her head still pounding with that same inner voice, which told her that something was terribly wrong.

17

Later that afternoon, Ilya was seated at his table by the window, reading, when he heard the door of his cell unlock. Looking up, he saw a pair of unsmiling officers in the doorway, both wearing blue nitrile gloves. The older of the two guards spoke. "Time for a spin. Get up."

Ilya rose silently from his chair. He had been expecting this visit for some time. Without being asked, he pulled off his shirt, raised his hands, and turned a complete circle. Then, as instructed, he ran his fingers through his hair to show that it concealed no drugs.

After putting his shirt back on, he took off his trousers. As one of the officers checked the clothes and examined the soles of Ilya's feet, the other tested the bars on the window with a tuning fork. When they told him to get dressed, he could see that they were already bored. "Do you have any contraband belonging to another inmate, or legal papers you do not wish us to read?"

Ilya said that he did not. As the older guard remained behind to begin the full search, the younger escorted Ilya to a waiting room at the far end of the spur, where he was left alone. He was not particularly concerned by what the guards might find, but the overall pattern was troubling.

Security at the prison had recently been heightened, evidently because of Sasha's death.

Ten minutes later, the door of the waiting room was unlocked. Ilya was taken back across the landing, where he found that the search, as usual, had left his cell looking incongruously tidy. Even the book that he had been reading was open to the same page as before.

Ilya waited until the officers had left, locking the cell door behind them. Once he was alone, he went up to the window, where a watch had been looped around one of the bars. Checking the time, he saw that it was nearly five.

He went to the shelf. Among the other odds and ends was a jar of instant coffee. Picking it up, he walked over to the area by the toilet, which was the only part of the cell not visible through the Judas hole in the door. He sat down, unscrewed the lid of the jar, and dug through the coarse crystals with his fingers.

A second later, his fingertips brushed an object inside. Ilya fished out the bundle, which was secured with a rubber band. Undoing the plastic, he removed the larger of two items, the cell phone that he had been given by Vasylenko. Each day, he would turn it on for ten minutes, once at nine and again at five.

He had been expecting a call, so he was not surprised when the phone vibrated a moment later. Ilya answered. "I'm here."

On the other end, Vasylenko spoke quietly in Russian. "You had a visitor."

"Yes. But she went away with nothing. She knows I have nothing to tell her."

"I see," Vasylenko said, his tone of voice revealing nothing of his thoughts. "But I am curious as to why she came at all."

"I don't know. I haven't spoken to her since last year. Whatever she wanted has nothing to do with us." Ilya weighed his words before continuing. "Unless, of course, her suspicions were aroused in some other way."

Vasylenko seemed to sense the unspoken implication. "I do not think so. It certainly had no relation to what happened to our friend. Did something about his passing concern you?"

Ilya had been taught to be careful on the phone, no matter to whom he was speaking. "No. But I have been wondering why security was increased, since he so clearly died of natural causes."

"I do not pretend to know how the guards think," Vasylenko said. "But there are always questions after the death of a *suka*."

The word caught Ilya's attention at once. If Vasylenko was telling the truth, it meant that Sasha had been an informant. "Are you sure?"

"I believe so. Our friend, it seems, was working with the authorities. Thankfully, he knew nothing of importance. But it should come as no surprise that he met such an unfortunate end. Do you understand?"

Ilya felt himself being pulled forward by forces set in motion long before. "I do."

"Good. I do not require love from my men. Nor do I demand perfect loyalty. All I ask is that they understand that our interests are one. On the day I cease to be useful, I will be ready for any betrayal. But that day has not yet come."

The *vor* hung up. Ilya lowered the phone. Then he turned it off and slid it back into its plastic bag, along with the second item, a lockpicking kit that he had obtained what seemed like a lifetime ago.

Ilya stuffed the bundle into the jar of coffee, making sure that it was fully covered by the crystals, and screwed on the lid. Rising, he went over to the shelf by the window and put the jar away. Then he glanced down at the page of the book he had been reading before the guards came.

The Khazars, it noted, were a race of horsemen, bound by the rains, so they naturally worshipped the god of the sky. Turning their eyes to the west and south, however, they had witnessed the growing power of nations whose authority was derived from history and scripture. In the end, the story went, they resolved to seek a more worldly religion that could survive in the land of the Scythians.

According to legend, the Khazar king granted an audience to representatives of three great neighboring faiths. After hearing arguments from all sides, he made his decision. Christ and Muhammad had empires of their own, so instead, he would take a third way, embracing the faith of another tribe of nomads without an earthly army. The warriors of the steppes, he proclaimed, would become Jews.

Even now, it was unclear what form the conversion had taken. Some claimed that the Khazars had practiced a heretical Judaism, while others said that they had carefully studied the commentaries on scripture, tracing their descent back to the brother of Ashkenaz. And most were of the opinion that the change, whatever form it took, had been felt only among the ruling classes.

Yet the result had been the first authentically Jewish kingdom since the time of the Bible. A nation of warriors had opened its borders to merchants and tradesmen, standing as the only barrier between Europe and Islam, dreaming that a lasting empire could take hold where so many others had been consumed.

But in the end, one could never be sure. Even if the new order endured for a time, history, like the steppes themselves, often had plans of its own. And this was true for men as well as nations.

Ilya found himself remembering the day Lermontov had died. Once the gallerist had come to terms with his fate, he had gone to it with equanimity. When the deed was done, Ilya had left the house, only to see a young woman on the street. Earlier, he had told her not to wait, but she had refused.

At the very end, however, it had seemed to him that she sensed the real difference between them, and when they parted ways for the last time, he had keenly felt the gulf that separated their two lives. For all the compromises she had made, she could still go on to find a place in the world, while he was forever estranged from it, as recent events had made all too clear.

In order to finish his work, Ilya thought now, he had to accept his true nature, even if it meant a plunge into iniquity. Yet as he closed the book, another set of words appeared in his mind, and they would continue to haunt him throughout all that followed: *Whosoever is partner with a thief hateth his own soul.*

18

On Sunday, the papers were full of the death of Mark Duggan, a black man in his twenties who had been killed three days earlier by police during an arrest in Tottenham. Several sources claimed that additional shots had been fired, but the details remained unclear. In the meantime, a neighborhood demonstration had resulted in riots and looting, and the city was filled with unease.

Maddy had paid little attention to the news. Instead, she had her eye on a story in the business section, one that might have run on the front page a few days before. Tarkovsky had made his decision. Polyneft would form a venture with Argo, the British oil company, to drill in the Black Sea.

Powell seemed as surprised by the announcement as she was. "I thought we had more time. You're sure you didn't hear any word of this?"

"Of course not," Maddy said into her cell phone. "Is it what you expected?"

"Yes, although we're still sifting through the details." Maddy heard a rustle on the other end as Powell retrieved his notes. "It's a billion-dollar venture. In exchange for capital and infrastructure, Argo will own a third of the company, and the stock swap will make Tarkovsky one of Argo's largest shareholders. There's going to be a signing ceremony in Sochi—"

"I know," Maddy said. "The staff has been talking about it all week. Tarkovsky's new yacht is waiting for him in Romania. He's planning to invite policy makers and executives from both companies. Needless to say, I'm not going."

Overhearing herself, she realized that she was rambling as a means of avoiding the real point. She rose from the dining table in her apartment in Hoxton. "So what do we do now?"

"We'll push forward with the information you've provided. Trying to identify these intermediaries is a nightmare, but it's all the more important, now that they'll be funded with British capital. As far as I'm concerned, however, your obligation to me is fulfilled. Do you think they want you to stay?"

Maddy flashed back on her last conversation with Tarkovsky. "Yes. Even if the Fabergé deal falls through, they have other projects in the pipeline. Tarkovsky seems to think I have useful insights."

"I have no doubt of that." Powell hesitated. "Which reminds me. There's something else. It's probably nothing, but since you know a bit about art, I thought you might have some ideas—"

Something in his voice made her straighten up. She was standing in her sorry excuse for a kitchen, with its square foot of counter space and ancient gas oven that she was afraid to touch. "What is it?"

"It involves Karvonen," Powell said. "After his death, police found a mobile phone buried at the house where he was staying in Helsinki. It had been burned before disposal, but forensics managed to access a list of recent calls, many of which went to a London number. It was for a prepaid phone, long since destroyed, and we have no way of knowing whose it was. The other day, however, this number turned up again. It was written on a card in the wallet of a man named Arkady Kagan."

As Maddy listened, her eyes fell on a picture that she had posted on her refrigerator. It was the only photograph she had of an old friend, taken years ago at a party in the Hamptons. "The man who vandalized the painting at the Met."

"That's right," Powell said. "I got a call about it yesterday from a contact at the Bureau. No one has drawn any public conclusions, at least not yet, but we've assumed for a long time that the number belonged to Karvonen's handler. Which implies that Arkady Kagan—"

"—was working for Russian intelligence." Maddy exhaled, leaning against the kitchen counter. "But why did he attack the painting?"

"I was hoping you could tell me. Even now, the police seem to think that he suffered some kind of breakdown. But can you think of any reason why he'd target this particular work?"

Maddy left the kitchen, heading back to the laptop on her dining room table. "I don't know. It doesn't make any sense."

"Well, think it over. If anything occurs to you, you know where to find me."

Powell hung up. As Maddy set down her phone, a voice in her head, familiar but insistent, told her that this was the time to walk away. Soon, she thought vaguely, it would be too late. But it wasn't that easy. Because even if this new information meant nothing, there was still one more thing she had to do.

Opening her laptop, she looked up directions to an address she knew by heart. Then she got ready to leave.

An hour later, Maddy was standing across the street from an elegant town house in Fulham, which looked much as she remembered. It was evidently unoccupied, the windows in need of a wash, and the front door had been repainted. Since moving to the city, she had avoided coming back, and she still didn't know what had brought her here today. Whatever she had hoped to feel wasn't there. All her feelings had been used up long ago. Except, perhaps, for one.

After Lermontov's death, she had gone back to New York expecting to be arrested at any minute. She had spent two years moving from one job to another, paying down her debts, always waiting to be found out. And when she had been discovered at last, it had been over something completely trivial.

Or so she had thought. Now she wasn't so sure. But that was a problem for later.

What she knew, standing here again, was that she wasn't done yet. There was a question that remained unanswered, and if she walked away now, it never would be. Tarkovsky had known Lermontov. If he had supported his work, even indirectly, he bore part of the blame for the consequences.

Maddy didn't think that Powell would approve of this line of reasoning. She knew it was best to let the dead bury the dead. But she could never forget the promise she had made. And it meant that she had work to do.

She remained there, looking out at the town house, for another ten minutes. At last, she crossed the street and left something on the front steps. Then she turned and headed back to the train.

A red Peugeot was parked nearby, facing away from the house. As Maddy walked up the block, the figure in the car raised a camera and took a series of pictures, thinking they might be useful later.

Asthana lowered the camera. The day before, she had positioned a watcher, a local informant who had done small jobs for her in the past, across the street from Maddy's flat. Today, he had followed his target from there to the train, and when he had telephoned to say that she had gotten off at Parsons Green, Asthana had known at once where she was going.

She wasn't sure when she first began to guess the truth. A routine check of travel records, the sort of thing that anyone at the agency could do without attracting attention, had revealed that Maddy had spent several weeks in London two years ago. And although her whereabouts for much of that time were unknown, she had clearly been in the city on the day that Lermontov had died.

Following up on this slender clue, Asthana had started to look more closely at Maddy's background, and she had finally managed to see what everyone else had missed. Lermontov had killed someone whom Maddy had cared about deeply. Asthana, as much as anyone, knew what a woman like this could do when pushed. The real question was how to use this information.

She climbed out of the car and headed for the house across the way. Going up to the porch, she picked up what Maddy had left behind on the front steps. It was a photograph, weighed down with a small stone, of a young man in a suit, his face slightly flushed, grinning into the camera.

Asthana studied the picture for a few seconds, then slid it into her pocket, where it brushed against something that was already there. Turning, she headed back to her car, moving at a brisk walk. It was almost time for her next appointment, and she didn't want to be late.

19

Crawling through a magnified forest of oak blossoms, a gall wasp searched for a place to lay her eggs, finally inserting the slender needle of her ovipositor into the base of one pale flower. Within seconds, through a miracle of trick photography, the flower burst slowly outward into a mass of convoluted green tissue, a gall, at the heart of which a tiny white grub lay feeding.

Rogozin did not look away from the nature video on his television set as the cell door behind him was unlocked and opened by the guard. On the screen, the gall shriveled and fell to the ground. As it was covered over at once by frost, the narrator's plummy voice continued: *"Plant and insect life is suspended, but unseen changes are nevertheless taking place—"*

A woman was standing just over his shoulder. She spoke calmly. "Hello, Vitaly."

Rogozin turned. It was Asthana. Before saying anything, he looked up at the security camera mounted above the door, which the guard had closed again before departing. The light next to its lens was dark.

"It's off," Asthana said in Russian. "I told them it would make it easier for us to talk."

Instead of responding, Rogozin reached out and lowered the volume on the television, where an adult wasp was emerging from the gall. He gestured toward the edge of the bed. "I was wondering when you'd come."

Asthana sat down. Aside from a few glimpses following the arrest, she had not seen Rogozin in person for some time. "How are you doing?"

"You know precisely how I am doing," Rogozin replied. "Why are you really here?"

Asthana glanced over at the television. On the screen, a different species of wasp was drilling carefully into a gall created by another. When the drill reached the larva at the center of the growth, she knew, the wasp would lay an egg of its own, and in time, the invader would claim the gall for itself, feeding on the body of the grub whose place it had taken.

"They found Garber's body," Asthana finally said. "It was stuffed into a refrigerator in East Acton. The price of working with idiots."

Rogozin continued to watch the drama unfolding on the screen. "And the case?"

"They're still negotiating with the prosecutor's office. You'll end up with a conspiracy charge. It isn't enough to keep you on remand. Wolfe will want you released under a control order. It means house arrest, a tracking bracelet, surrender of your passport. But you'll be able to leave this place." Asthana looked at him evenly. "The real question is whether you'll still be useful."

She reached into her pocket. Her fingers briefly brushed the photograph she had taken from the porch in Fulham, but she passed over it and removed the other item that was there instead.

Asthana held it up. It was the amulet from Rogozin's

home, the one he had shown to Wolfe on the day of his arrest, with the image of a horseman on one side and a gorgon on the other. A few days earlier, she had retrieved it from evidence control. Rogozin eyed it warily. "What of it?"

"I want to know if you remember what you said when you first showed this to me." She set the amulet on the table. "Call the horse and rider whatever you like. Rigden Djapo, Kalki—"

"—or Peter the Great." Rogozin picked up the amulet, smiling faintly. "I remember. No matter what the name is, the meaning is the same."

"Yes. And I believed you. You told me it meant the end of one era and the beginning of another. Something that began as the dream of a few men, only to become greater than we could ever imagine. This change will come soon, no matter what we do. But I wonder if we're still meant to be a part of it."

Rogozin put the amulet down. Her words appeared to have touched a nerve. "I know this has been a difficult time. But that's all the more reason for us to follow through, now that we're so close to completion."

"Are we?" Asthana asked. "I threw in my lot with the military side, years ago, because I believed you were what you claimed to be. The ones who could move between the energy companies and the state. Not the civilian arm, with its plots and counterplots. We were building something. But now it's in ruins. And it's all because of what you did with Karvonen."

His eyes flashed anger. "I did what was necessary to protect what we had made."

"But what came of it? Your army was already depressed, preparing for a kind of war that would never come again.

Now the energy side is gone as well. Whatever influence we had is crumbling. And those networks are impossible to restore. Look at what happened to Arkady—"

"Yet his message came through," Rogozin said fiercely. "The game is not over yet."

His voice softened. For a moment, they were no longer in this cell, but in Cambridge, where they had often talked long into the night. "I know it has been hard. But you need to play your part a while longer. Your presence is even more crucial now. And we still have one ally. Do you understand?"

"I understand very well," Asthana said coldly. "But that was never the issue, was it?"

"No." Reaching out with one hand, Rogozin stroked her cheek with unexpected tenderness. "You were always my favorite child. Karvonen was an instrument, a killer, but you grasped the larger pattern. But none of it will mean anything if you waver. Not when we are so close to the goal."

For a long moment, they sat eye to eye. A second later, Asthana shuddered and drew back from his touch. She turned away, her hand pressed to her lips, as if deep in thought. Rogozin only watched her, waiting.

At last, Asthana turned back. There was a hard gleam in her eyes as she gave a quick nod. "All right. I will do what I must."

Leaning forward, so that she rose slightly from her perch on the bed, she kissed him. If Rogozin was surprised by this, he covered it well, raising his hand again to the side of her face. For an endless second, as their lips met, they seemed to share the memory of all they had been through, separately and together, since their first wary meeting so many years ago.

Suddenly, Rogozin's eyes opened. In the same instant, Asthana pulled back. Reaching out, she took his head in her hands, holding his jaw shut, then pushed him away as soon as she knew that her work was done.

Rogozin rose, staring, from his chair. His right hand, flying to one side, knocked the amulet from the table to the floor. A second later, he fell to his knees, his hands going to his throat. His eyes were still on hers. Asthana could smell the faint bitter scent from the capsule she had placed in her mouth a moment ago, knowing that she only had a few seconds before it dissolved.

She looked down at the dying man. Her voice was soft. "I've made my choice. Russia will be all the stronger with one security service in place. Unfortunately, we picked the wrong side. I'm here to correct that mistake."

Rogozin tried to speak but could not. He sputtered, saliva flying from his mouth in a fine green froth, then collapsed to the floor. A spasm ran down the length of his body, as if someone had given his spine a quick snap. Then the light went out of his eyes, and he grew still.

Silence. On the television set, its sound turned down, a nest of wasps was writhing.

Once she was sure it was over, Asthana knelt and picked up the amulet from the floor. She lifted Rogozin's left hand, which was still warm, and folded his fingers around the medallion. Taking the dead man's right thumbnail, she used it to scratch away a blob of gray wax at the amulet's base. Earlier, she had drilled a hole there and sealed it, as if to conceal something inside.

Asthana took a step back to consider her handiwork, then turned to the door of the cell. As she opened it, her pulse remained steady, and it rose only slightly as she ran into the hallway and screamed at last for help.

20

The following morning, Ilya was escorted from his cell for his day in court. He knew the routine well. After his hands were cuffed in front of him, he was led out to the landing. As he left, he did not glance back. He was not a superstitious man, but he was aware, like every prisoner, that it was bad luck to pause at the threshold when one departed for a journey.

He was brought downstairs by an officer, then led through a series of gates, which the guard had to open and lock behind them as they left the secure wing. As they neared the outside world, the color of the walls changed from blue to green to lavender, the reverse of the order he had seen when he first arrived.

Beyond the receiving spur, it was a cool summer morning. The courtyard was surrounded by a brick wall, thirty feet high, topped with razor wire. At the center, twelve prisoners stood in a row before a white prison van.

As Ilya approached the other inmates, he observed that the group was a mixture of remand and appeal prisoners. It was easy to tell the difference. Many of the men on remand were still wearing their own clothes, and even the ones dressed in standard prison issue had not yet lost a certain light in their eyes.

But among all the men who were standing here, there was no sign of Vasylenko.

Ilya turned his attention to the van. It was a standard security vehicle built from the body of a Eurocargo truck, ten tons or so, with seven opaque windows and doors at the side and rear. Next to it stood the driver and prisoner escort, in black ties and white shirts, chatting with a third guard.

The van followed an identical route each day. After trundling through the prison gate, it would drive fourteen miles to the Old Bailey, where it would drop off some of its passengers for trial proceedings. From there, it would head half a mile to the Royal Courts of Justice, where appeals were heard, thus saving an extra trip, in line with recent austerity measures.

It was the same routine every morning. Today, however, the routine changed.

Waiting in line with the other prisoners, Ilya saw a pair of guards approach from the receiving spur. Like the rest, they were armed with batons but no guns, and after speaking briefly with the driver and the prisoner escort, they mounted the steps into the rear of the van.

This was unusual. Ilya glanced at the inmate standing next to him, a thin, pockmarked prisoner on remand. "Why the extra screws?"

The inmate looked at him with an expression of surprise. "You don't know? Whole city is on alert. Demonstrations over the police shooting in Tottenham. Turned violent. Shops looted, set on fire. Heaving bricks at cops. Worst riot in years, they say. Though if you ask me—"

He broke off, noticing that the guards were watching,

and turned away. Ilya did not reply, but inside, he had already begun to sift through this new information, trying to decide what it meant.

A moment later, the prisoner escort climbed into the van and emerged with a set of leg irons. The inmates, familiar with the drill, allowed themselves to be shackled one by one. Ilya had worn these irons on a number of occasions, and he knew that the shackles, linked by a short length of chain, were each secured by a cylinder lock more reliable than those used for handcuffs.

He was one of the last inmates to be shackled. When the prisoner escort was done, he handed the set of keys to the third guard, who would stay behind. For security reasons, the escort did not carry the keys himself. Instead, the shackles would be unlocked by another officer with a duplicate set at the courthouse.

Once the process was complete, the third guard spoke quietly into his radio, received a transmission in reply, and nodded at the others, who began to load the prisoners into the van one at a time. Ilya was among the last three. He came forward, the chain of his shackles scraping against the ground, and climbed the steps of the prison van. Just before going inside, he glanced back at the receiving spur and saw that Vasylenko was nowhere in sight.

Inside the van, flanking a narrow corridor, were two rows of numbered cubicles. Each cubicle's door had a pair of narrow windows, one set above the other, and a separate lock and security chain. A partition stood between the inmates and the driver's cab. The two additional guards who had entered earlier had taken their seats at the front of the prisoner section.

He was led to the third cubicle from the back, where he sat down in the sweatbox and was locked inside. As the chain across the door was drawn, he looked out the window as two more prisoners were led into the van. Neither man was Vasylenko. The outside door slid shut. A second later, the engine started.

As the van eased its way forward, Ilya wondered what was happening. It was possible, he thought, that Vasylenko's appeal had been postponed at the last minute, or that something else had gone wrong. Without him, they had to begin again. And they might never get another chance—

All these thoughts ran through his mind in an instant. He was seriously weighing the possibility of creating a disturbance to delay their departure when, abruptly, the van halted. Outside his cubicle, the guards seated at the front of the prisoner section exchanged a few words, although he was unable to make them out. The engine died. For a long time, nothing else happened.

At last, through his window, Ilya saw a solitary figure being led across the courtyard. It was Vasylenko. Ilya heard the door of the van open again, and a moment later, he saw Vasylenko come up the central corridor, also cuffed and shackled. There was a pause as the *vor* was locked into his own unseen cubicle. Then the door closed and the van started up again. Looking outside, Ilya saw the tall electric gate at the entrance to the prison roll slowly back, and then they were out on the road.

It was a familiar route. They would head south on the Western Way, then continue on to Woolwich Common, a journey of forty minutes in all. Turning back to the van's interior, Ilya saw that the prisoner seated in the sweatbox across from him was leaning against the window of his own cubicle, his eyes closed, and that neither of the guards was in sight.

As soon he was sure that he was not being watched, Ilya reached up with his cuffed hands, feeling for the small package taped between his shoulders. Reaching down into the collar of his shirt, he pulled the object free. He had secured it there that morning, using a strip of packing tape from the workroom. It was the lockpicking kit that he had smuggled into prison the year before.

Ilya kept an eye on the corridor as he undid the tape and extracted the picks. Leaving the handcuffs for later, since he knew they would take only a second, he began working on the shackle around his right leg.

The process was fairly straightforward, but it was made trickier by the movement of the van as it went over the bumps of the highway. Holding the picks in his mouth, he eased the torsion wrench into the lower part of the keyhole, applying torque to see which way it would turn. Then he inserted a pick, feeling the pins, and raked the lock gently. A few of the easier pins set at once. He turned his attention to the stubborn ones, not hurrying, moving largely by intuition.

A moment later, the van slowed. Ilya halted, his head going up, ready to abandon his work if necessary. From the front of the van, he heard the voices of the guards, their words inaudible, but as he listened, he sensed an underlying tension. A glance out the window told him that they were somewhere in Woolwich, and that the traffic around them had ground to a halt. In the air, there was a faint scorched stench, as if something nearby was burning.

After a pause, the van eased forward and began to turn, heading away from the main road. When they had turned nearly all the way, perpendicular to the stalled flow of traffic, Ilya finally caught a glimpse of the scene outside.

A red bus was parked at an angle across the southbound lanes, blocking the way forward. It was on fire. Flames burned merrily in the windows of the second deck, blackening the surrounding paint and disgorging plumes of smoke. A fire crew was already in place, with a pair of constables directing traffic to an alternate route, motioning mechanically in their yellow vests.

The van finished its ponderous turn, taking the burning bus out of sight. A minute later, they were driving along a narrow road with a single lane running in both directions, heading away from the scene.

Seated in his cubicle, Ilya understood the reason for the detour, and he knew that it had not been an accident. He was also aware that he was running out of time. Lowering his head again, he returned his attention to the leg irons around his right ankle. Just one stubborn pin remained.

At last, the pin set. Ilya turned the lock. And the shackles came open in his hands.

21

"I tried to stop him," Asthana said calmly, with only the hint of a tremor. "I glanced away for a second, and by the time I saw what he was doing, it was too late. His hand was in his mouth. I tore the amulet away, but by then, he had collapsed. I called for help, then went back to try to revive him."

Wolfe turned to Cornwall. "The facts speak for themselves. There's nothing more she could have done."

"I agree," Cornwall said. "But I'm afraid that isn't the real question here."

They were seated together in Cornwall's office. In an hour, Asthana was scheduled to give a preliminary deposition in the inquest into Rogozin's death. For the last twenty minutes, they had been reviewing the events of the day before, which had happened with such unexpected, almost ludicrous finality that Wolfe still had trouble believing that they had taken place at all.

Cornwall, too, seemed to have a hard time accepting this, returning more than once to the same few points. "I still don't understand why you brought the amulet. The coroner will wonder about this as well."

"I've already told you," Asthana said, a note of weariness entering her voice for the first time. "Rogozin had mentioned it earlier to Wolfe, and I knew he'd been sketching it in his cell. I thought if I brought it, it might tempt him to talk. It was clearly important to him."

"Well, now we know why," Cornwall said. "And he said nothing before his death?"

Asthana shook her head. "I told him we'd discovered Garber's body and that we knew he had an informant inside the agency. But he refused to answer any of my questions. The only time he opened up was when I showed him the amulet. He said it was a way of warding off evil. Now I know what he meant."

Taking a deep breath, Asthana began to speak more slowly, choosing her words with evident care. "I'm willing to take full responsibility. I broke procedure by visiting him alone and without recording the interview. It was my mistake. And I'm prepared to accept the consequences."

Cornwall fell silent for a moment. Wolfe could see her working through the situation in her head. Finally, she said, "Well, there's one silver lining. We've removed all doubt about Rogozin's guilt. And we've been lucky in another way. As of now, the press simply doesn't care."

Wolfe knew what she meant. At the moment, no one could think of anything but the riots that had raged throughout the city in response to Mark Duggan's death. The national consciousness had been seared by images of mobs of looters, of police with shields and dogs, of smashed windows and burning shops. More than thirty officers had been injured and two hundred arrests had been made, and it seemed that they were nowhere near the end.

She had sensed the difference as soon as she awoke that morning. Even through her own shock over what had happened to Rogozin, she could tell that the city was on edge. Police had been deployed to Tottenham and other potential trouble zones, with Islington and Stoke Newington on lockdown. Rogozin was yesterday's news. As far as she knew, his death, which a week before might have been the lead story, had been reported only on the inside pages.

Cornwall spoke again, breaking into her thoughts. She was looking at Asthana with mingled coldness and pity. "All the same, I have no choice but to suspend you from the investigation, pending the outcome of the inquest. In any case, I know you have a holiday coming up soon. Where are you going again?"

Asthana smiled weakly. "We're supposed to spend two weeks in Marmaris."

"Well, then. You'll have a chance to get away from all this. And I want you to go home after the deposition. We can discuss the rest tomorrow." Cornwall's tone softened. "Maya, we all wish this had happened at some other time. But we'll get through it in the end."

Asthana only gave a short nod. As the two officers rose to leave, Cornwall spoke up again. "Wolfe, please stay for a moment."

Wolfe had a good idea what the deputy director wanted, but she said nothing. Walking her partner to the door, she gave Asthana's hand a quick squeeze, then whispered, "You know, I've decided to ask Lewis to the wedding. I hope you still have a place at the table—"

Asthana managed to smile at this, although her eyes retained a sheen of sadness. "Of course. I'll let them know."

She left. Wolfe shut the door gently. "Asthana didn't deserve any of this."

"None of us do," Cornwall said. "In her case, it will turn out well enough. The coroner isn't known for moving quickly, but it's clearly a category two suicide. But this isn't what I wanted to talk about. I'm told that you went to see Ilya Severin without permission."

As Wolfe sat down, she saw that there was no point in explaining her reasons. "Yes. But I was turned away by Owen Dancy. I still don't know why Ilya would agree to be represented by Vasylenko's solicitor."

"I wondered about this as well," Cornwall said. "So did the Crown prosecutor. I just got off the phone with the sector director. It appears that Ilya is attending a hearing this morning. The rumor is that he's going to change his plea to guilty and offer to cooperate with the authorities."

Wolfe couldn't believe her ears. "That's ridiculous. He's refused to talk for months. And Dancy has no incentive to help him work with the police. His testimony could only implicate Vasylenko."

"I know. Dancy is playing a longer game. And that's what concerns me. Vasylenko's appeal is being held today as well. It's hard to think of a strategy that could benefit both men."

Wolfe heard the implied question in her words. "But even if Dancy is using Ilya for something else, Ilya wouldn't work with them without a good reason. If you want, I can pay him another visit—"

"No," Cornwall said at once. "That will only complicate things. If the rumors are true, you'll need to clear everything through the Met in the future. Ilya is their witness now. Are we clear?"

"Clear enough," Wolfe said. After being dismissed, she rose and left the office. Outside, the floor was nearly full. Everyone had come in early, waiting, like the rest of the city, for whatever the morning would bring.

When she returned to her cubicle, Asthana was nowhere in sight. Wolfe sat down, trying to put her thoughts into some kind of order. She couldn't understand it. Ilya had refused for so long to say anything about his past, and now, suddenly, he had decided to cooperate with the Met. And although she didn't want to admit it, part of her felt hurt by his decision, as if he had owed her something more.

As she brooded over this, something else occurred to her. Turning to her computer, she called up the day's case listings, confirming that Ilya was scheduled to appear at a mention hearing at the Central Criminal Court.

Meanwhile, at the Royal Courts of Justice, Vasylenko was slated for his own appeal this morning as well.

Something about this second appeal had troubled her for some time. Dancy had waited well over a year to file an appeal that had almost no chance of being granted. Ilya's court appearance, by contrast, had been strangely rushed. And it seemed especially odd to schedule two crucial hearings for the same day—

Wolfe began to feel uneasy. Before she knew what she was doing, she had taken out her phone to dial the main line at Belmarsh. After getting through, she asked for the receiving officer, who answered immediately. "Yes?"

She briefly explained who she was, sensing that the officer was not particularly interested, then asked, "Are today's transports gone?"

"Right on schedule," the officer said. "The van left about twenty minutes ago."

"Just one van?" Her uneasiness, which had begun as a tingle at the nape of her neck, was spreading outward. "There aren't any others?"

"Not these days. One van for two courts. Saves an extra trip. Cutbacks, you know—"

Wolfe broke in. "Listen, can you do me a favor? I need to know if two prisoners were on the transport van that left this morning. Their names are Ilya Severin and Grigory Vasylenko."

"Hold on," the officer said irritably. There was a pause before he spoke again. "Yes, they're on the list."

Wolfe thanked him and hung up. She sat at her desk for another moment, thinking. Both Ilya and Vasylenko had left the prison at the same time that morning, on the same van, on a day when the police were already stretched dangerously thin. She thought back to Cornwall's words from a moment ago. Dancy, she had said, had to be playing another game—

A terrible possibility began to gather in her mind. Before she could give it a name, Wolfe found herself rising from her desk, sending her chair rolling backward. She picked up her coat and keys, then headed for the elevator, already dialing the prison again. Halfway across the floor, she broke into a run.

22

The man behind the wheel of the prison van was an officer named Andrew Ferris, who had worked for the security company for close to eight years. He had risen that morning in Plumstead feeling wary, given the events of the night before. After seeing the images on the news, he had been tempted to call in sick, but when he finally left home, the city had seemed fairly quiet.

All the same, he had been glad for the two additional guards, especially when he saw the burning bus lying across the highway. The sight had sent a pang of apprehension through his ample body, but in the end, it had turned out to be a minor inconvenience, forcing him only to take a detour along Little Heath.

At the moment, he was driving alongside the Royal Artillery Barracks in Woolwich. To his left ran a green fence topped with barbed wire, and beyond that, a row of trees. A brick housing block stood to the other side. Ferris was seated in the cab of the van, a partition separating him from the inmates in the rear, the prisoner escort stationed in the passenger seat beside him.

For most of the drive, inevitably, the two men had talked about the riots. "Police are just standing by," the prisoner escort was saying. "Can't bloody blame them, though, with the budget slashed all to hell. I wouldn't get my head broken over a few boxes of trainers."

Ferris only gave a noncommittal nod. Beyond the intersection, the road narrowed. They went past a wooded training ground, set off from the street by a brick wall, and as they drove by a vacant lot, neither man noticed the three vans, two white, one blue, that pulled into the road to follow.

"Of course, nobody gives a toss for the dead man," the escort continued after a moment. "They're just glad for the excuse to steal. Animals with cell phones. Posting pictures online for all to see—"

He broke off as the blue van, which had been tailing them, accelerated to pass and abruptly cut ahead. A second later, it halted without warning. Ferris slammed on the brakes, narrowly avoiding a crash, as he and the escort were caught by their seat belts, swearing in unison.

To his right, a white panel van pulled up alongside the prison transport, screeching to a standstill. In his rearview mirror, Ferris saw an identical vehicle come up close behind, then saw the blue van reverse to within a few feet of their front bumper, pinning them in place.

Ferris looked to either side, panicked. Vehicles were blocking his way on three sides. On the fourth, a brick boundary wall lay between him and the woods. He was stuck. And it was only now, as he began to grasp the situation, that he really understood the predicament he was in.

The dented rear doors of the blue van flew open and two men holding shotguns slid out, their faces covered by white surgical masks. The one in front spoke loudly enough to be heard through the window: "Hands in the air, please."

While the other figure kept his shotgun trained at the windshield, the first man came around to the driver's side. Ferris, hands raised, risked a glance down at the radio console on the dashboard, then thought of the guards in the back of the transport van. He wanted to turn his head, but he didn't dare.

The man at the driver's door pointed his gun at Ferris's head. Above his mask, his eyes were narrow but startlingly blue. "Roll the window down, turn the engine off, and take out the keys."

Ferris obliged, his hands trembling. Once the keys were out, the gunman asked for their radios and cell phones, taking them one at a time and lobbing them over the wall of the training ground. "How many guards?"

"Two," Ferris managed to say, his mouth dry. "They don't have any guns."

Out of the corner of his eye, he saw three more masked figures come running around to the front of the prison van. One of them dropped out of sight, an industrial cutter in his hands. Ferris heard him get to work underneath the vehicle and realized that he was slashing the brake and power cables.

He heard a metallic clang. Turning, he saw that two of the men who had just appeared were attaching a series of objects to the hood and driver's door with magnets. They were green, round, and about ten inches across, and with a watery rush of fear, Ferris recognized them as limpet mines.

Slinging the shotgun over his shoulder, the man on the driver's side pulled a radio remote from his back pocket and raised the aerial. "You know how this works. We'll blow up the van if you don't do exactly what we say. First, I want the keys for the sweatboxes."

The prisoner escort, who had remained silent throughout all that had happened, found his voice at last. "Go to hell."

Instead of responding, the man glanced over at someone who was standing just out of sight, as if to confirm that all was in place, and nodded. Then he pressed the button of the detonator.

Later, residents in the area would say that they had heard the explosion but assumed it was part of an exercise, since they were used to the sound of ordnance from drills at the barracks nearby. In fact, the remote set off a limpet mine that had been attached to the back door of the van a few seconds earlier, blowing the door off its hinges and rocking the vehicle on its frame.

Inside the rear of the van, the inmates were shouting. Ilya, who had undone his shackles and handcuffs long before, had been counting the seconds since the van halted. From outside, he heard more shouts as the guards inside the van were ordered out. He saw them file past his cubicle, their hands raised. A few seconds passed. And then the chain of his door was drawn back.

A moment later, the door swung open, revealing a figure in a surgical mask. Ilya came out at once and followed the man without a word to another cubicle. The masked figure, who was holding a shotgun and a bunch of keys, unfastened the chain and unlocked this door as well.

Vasylenko was seated inside, his eyes bright. Without being told, Ilya lowered himself to one knee and began examining the shackles around the *vor*'s legs. The man in the mask whispered tensely, "Come on, hurry up—"

Ilya ignored him, getting to work on the cuff around Vasylenko's right ankle. It was easier this time, since he knew the insides of these locks by now, and the shackle snapped open almost at once.

"Never mind the other," the man in the mask said. "Save it for Mare Street."

Vasylenko shot him a look but said nothing as Ilya undid his handcuffs. Then the *vor* rose and went with Ilya toward the rear doors of the van, the loose chain of his leg irons trailing behind him. The man in the mask handed him a mobile phone, then went to open the remaining cubicles.

Ilya and Vasylenko climbed down from the van. Outside, the driver and guards were kneeling in the street, hands bound behind them with plastic cuffs, a man with a shotgun keeping watch. Up ahead, another man in a yellow traffic vest, his face cheerful, was handling crowd control, facing the line of honking cars in the lane behind them, the vans blocking the scene from view.

Hearing movement, Ilya turned to see the remaining prisoners climbing out of the van one by one, their mouths hanging open at the sight. Vasylenko spoke quietly. "This is your lucky day. If you like, you can turn yourselves in at the Woolwich police station. You'll find it ten minutes back the way we came. Or you can run. The police, it seems, have other things on their minds."

The prisoners appeared to get the message. Scattering in all directions, they shuffled away, their shackles ringing against the pavement as they ran. Vasylenko turned to study the officers kneeling on the ground. Finally, he gave a signal to the man standing watch, who yanked Andrew Ferris to his feet. The gunman hauled Ferris around to the blue van and shoved him inside, followed by Vasylenko and the others, a driver already behind the wheel.

Ilya was the last to climb in. He found himself seated

across from Vasylenko, eye to eye with the *vor*, as the doors of the van swung shut. Faintly, in the distance, he heard sirens.

As they pulled into the road, the man holding the detonator slid its range switch to a new setting and pressed the button again. Through the rear window, Ilya saw the prison van and the other vehicles explode into orange blossoms of flame. Then he turned back to Vasylenko as they roared off into the waiting city.

23

When Wolfe arrived in Woolwich, traffic was at a standstill. Through her windshield, she saw flames and smoke. After trying in vain to find a way through, she finally parked illegally at the side of the road, grabbed her warrant card and phone, and ran toward the scene.

Up ahead, a pair of officers stood in the street, trying manfully but without much success to direct traffic to an alternate route. The prison transport van and two other vehicles sat behind them, burning. A few steps away, a sergeant was talking into his radio, which he set aside as Wolfe approached, holding out her warrant card. "I'm Rachel Wolfe. We spoke on the phone a minute ago."

"I know who you are," the sergeant said, drawing himself up slightly. He was clean-shaven and somewhat flushed. "That was the fire brigade. They're on their way. They're stretched pretty thin right now—"

"I know." Wolfe took in the scene. A knot of bystanders had gathered to stare, keeping well back from the blaze. "What about the prisoners?"

"We've picked up a couple, but we don't have enough men at hand to do a real search. A few turned themselves in at the station. We're still looking for the assailants and the two they came to get." The sergeant flipped his notebook open. "Blue panel van, dented rear doors."

"I'll get someone on it," Wolfe said. "On the phone, you mentioned a lead?"

The sergeant nodded. "Just heard it myself. From one of the inmates who turned himself in. He was on remand for robbery, so he had no reason to run. Apparently he overheard one of the attackers. When they were freeing the prisoners, one of them said something about Mare Street."

Wolfe recognized the name. "Mare Street. That's up in Hackney, isn't it?"

"That's right. I've been trying to get a Trojan unit in place, but they're all deployed elsewhere. And it's already sticky on the ground."

Wolfe knew what he meant. Looking at the wrecks of the vans, which were cooking away with no fire crew in sight, she saw what she had to do. "Give me your gear. I'm going there myself."

The sergeant hesitated. "I don't know if that's wise. I can't promise any backup—"

Wolfe broke in. "Listen, you know who I am, right? So you also know why I'm here. One of the men who escaped is someone I've met before. And I'm the only one who can get him back."

Something in her eyes seemed to convince him. After a beat, he motioned for her to follow him to his panda car. Opening the trunk, he unloaded a set of riot gear, including a shield and helmet. As she took the sergeant's baton, she felt faintly ridiculous, but she knew it was best to be prepared. Tossing the equipment into her own car, she headed back to the main highway, pushing it as much as she could, and passed a fire truck coming at last in the other direction.

As Wolfe headed north, she fumbled out her phone and dialed Asthana, who answered a few seconds later. Her partner sounded surprised. "What's going on? I'm just about to go in for the deposition—"

"Cancel it," Wolfe said, relieved to see that the road was fairly clear. "I need you to call Cornwall and anyone you can find at the enforcement directorate. Vasylenko and Ilya have escaped."

There was a long pause. "Rachel, if this is some kind of joke, it isn't funny."

"It's no joke." Driving with one hand on the wheel, Wolfe filled Asthana in as quickly as possible, describing what the sergeant had told her. "The police don't have the resources to handle this. We need to mobilize the agency. Someone has to check security cameras in Woolwich and sweep their cells at Belmarsh. See if we can get a news helicopter to do a pass over Hackney—"

As she drove, continuing to issue instructions as she blew past the posted limit, Wolfe was glad to have something to do, even as part of her brain was piecing together the rest of the story. If Vasylenko and Ilya were working together, with what appeared to be considerable resources, it meant something else was at play. Because no one did anything like this without a reason.

In time, she found herself approaching Hackney. As she neared the neighborhood, she passed another fire crew dousing the hulk of a burning car with foam. Buildings were still smoldering from the night before. Underlying it all was the faint maddening background noise of countless car alarms.

At Amhurst Road, traffic halted. Wolfe stopped, seeing that there was no way past the stalled cars and buses. "I'll have to call you back."

"Okay," Asthana said. "I'll call Cornwall. And I'm coming out there, too."

"Then I'll see you soon." Wolfe hung up. Craning her neck to look past the cars, she saw that this was as far as she could go. She managed to pull over to the side of the road. Her heart was going like mad, but she did her best to collect herself as she slid the baton into her bag, leaving the rest for now, and got out.

She headed on foot up the block. Up ahead, a crowd was milling around in the street, looking at last night's damage. Shops were boarded up and strung with police tape, and a bus shelter on the corner had been smashed to pieces, the ground strewn with broken glass. On the sidewalk before one of the stores, Wolfe noticed what looked like a scatter of body parts, then saw that they were the limbs of mannequins, like the unburied victims of some natural disaster.

Moving past the onlookers, many of whom were taking snapshots of the devastation on their phones, Wolfe continued on to Mare Street, which had been blocked off to vehicle traffic by a line of police vans. In front of this makeshift barricade stood a line of uniformed officers with helmets and plastic shields.

As she scanned the area, looking for the van that the sergeant had described, she observed that the crowd here was noticeably more agitated. A young black man in a hooded sweatshirt, his head large and babylike under its pile of braids, was standing a few steps away. Wolfe caught his eye. "What's going on?"

"You don't know?" He indicated the line of police, his

voice curiously relaxed. "People flinging trash at coppers. They've got three guys from the neighborhood up against the town hall."

She followed his gaze, which was fixed on the long row of helmets. "And what are you doing here?"

"Me?" He laughed. "I'm just trying to get home. But you'll be fine, I'm sure."

Thanking him, Wolfe moved on, more conscious than ever of the tension. Almost everyone had a cell phone out. She studied the crowd, trying to put herself into Ilya and Vasylenko's place, and wondered if the situation here had been part of the plan, or if they had been forced to work around it—

A sound like the rustle of a baking sheet broke into her thoughts. Turning, she saw a pair of men breaking into a store down the street. They were wearing gray hoodies, with scarves wrapped across their faces, and were pulling away the metal barrier that had been lowered across the storefront. A second later, the barrier gave way, peeling back like the cover of a sardine tin, and the men squeezed inside, emerging moments later with armfuls of jeans and sneakers.

Wolfe stared. It was broad daylight. To her astonishment, not only did nobody make a move to stop the looting, but several ran over to join in. The scene was quiet, deliberate, dreamlike.

Turning away, she tried to view the street as Ilya might have seen it. She was about to call Asthana again, hoping that her partner could check a map of the area, when she saw something else. Parked on a side street, three cars from the corner, was a blue panel van. And its rear doors were dented.

She slid the baton out of her bag and approached the

van, coming at it from an angle. There was no sign of movement as she inched up to the driver's window and looked in. It was empty. She headed around back and did the same, edging sideways to the rear window and peering quickly inside. Nothing. As her eyes adjusted to the dimness, however, she saw something on the floor of the van, next to one of the seats. It was a set of shackles.

Wolfe took a step back, mind working furiously. They had left the car here because they couldn't drive on Mare Street, but it would not be safe to stay, which meant they had to move on foot to a second vehicle. Going again to the front of the van, she put her hand on the hood. It was warm.

From behind her came a series of shouts. Heading to the corner, she saw the crowd draw back as the line of riot police began to advance, moving in lockstep to push the onlookers away from the barricades. Most of the bystanders yielded quickly, but a few held their ground.

A second later, at a prearranged signal, the police charged forward in a body. Wolfe took a step back as the crowd scattered, some screaming. After twenty yards, the charge halted, not far from where she was now. She saw that many of the onlookers were breaking off from the main group, and for a moment, she thought the crowd would simply disperse.

Then, as if from nowhere, an object was flung at the police. Wolfe didn't see who had thrown it, but in the instant that it continued to pinwheel forward, she realized that it was a piece of wood, perhaps from a barrier, or a board pried from the front of a shop, or even just part of a chair.

Whatever it was, it struck an officer near the end of the

line squarely in the forehead. He fell to his knees. There was a pause that could have lasted no more than a fraction of a second.

Then the crowd rushed forward. The line of officers wavered, trembling from end to end, and broke as more debris went flying through the air, the mob yelling as it flung itself at the police.

It was a moment that Wolfe would never forget. As the two halves of the scene collided, it felt like the culmination of something that she had sensed, in fragments, for much of the last two years. In a flash, she understood that this was not about Mark Duggan, dead with two bullet holes in his chest. It was about the waste of energy and potential, the broken promises that had piled up for decades, and it made her see how fragile the mask had been all along.

Staring at the chaos, feeling the crowd's energy pass over her in a wave, Wolfe found herself looking across the street at a cluster of men who were not part of the larger commotion. They were moving as a group into the trees of a small park across the way. And one of them was someone she knew.

She took a step forward. Ilya had changed into street clothes, but there was no mistaking who he was, or that the man beside him was Vasylenko. And it was only as she took another step, the noise of the crowd fading to nothing, that she saw that Ilya had seen her as well.

For a moment, the world went quiet. Wolfe felt Ilya's eyes on hers. She heard her own voice rise in a shout, but it was oddly distant, the syllables lost in the empty space surrounding her on all sides.

Then Ilya turned away and the world snapped back into place. The space around her was not empty, she realized, but the middle of a mob that was growing worse by the moment.

As the men continued into the park, Wolfe threw herself into the crush of bodies, pushing past the rioters, feeling herself buffeted in all directions as she searched desperately for an opening. A group of protesters was standing in her way. She lowered her head, carried by pure adrenaline, and plowed forward, managing to break through the crowd at last.

Wolfe made it to the other side of the street, her breath coming in gasps, and crossed into the park. Here in the shade, where it was strangely peaceful, she saw nothing but the trees. Ilya and the others had disappeared.

24

Some time later, a gray minivan parked on a deserted street in Hackney Wick, far from the disturbances elsewhere in the city. As the van stood at the curb, engine idling, the front passenger door opened and a man slid out. With his surgical mask removed, he had a surprisingly intelligent face, with blunt but sensitive features and blue eyes that were narrow but bright.

The man had a canvas bag slung over his shoulder. Keeping one hand on the shotgun inside, he glanced up and down the street, then headed for the steps of a house a few doors down from the van. He took out a key ring, then unlocked the front door, leaving it slightly ajar as he went inside. For a moment, all was quiet. Finally, the porch light winked on.

At the signal, the van's engine shut off and its doors slid open. The first to get out was Andrew Ferris, sweating and pale, with another man's hand firmly grasping his shoulder. A pistol, concealed by a folded coat, was wedged into his ribs. He was followed by the driver, then Ilya and Vasylenko, both in street clothes, who walked up to the house with the others.

One of the men had been left behind in Hackney, after

inciting the riot that had covered their escape. Ilya was impressed by how smoothly it had been arranged. He had seen Vasylenko give the order as they crossed the street, with a man in a red jacket breaking off from the main group as the rest went into the park. Glancing back, Ilya had seen him stoop to pick up a billet of wood.

Then, raising his eyes, Ilya had been startled to see Wolfe standing on the opposite curb, staring at the commotion. He had barely had time to register this fact when the man in the red jacket flung his piece of wood, striking an officer in the face. That had been all the crowd needed. As the street, already tense, exploded into confusion, Ilya and the others had turned to go under the trees.

It was then that he realized that Wolfe had seen him as well. He was normally imperturbable, but in that instant, his blood had gone cold. Her presence, after all he had done to get this far, was enough to destroy everything. And as they passed into the park, he had seen a grain of distrust in Vasylenko's eyes.

Inside, the house in Hackney Wick looked as if it had been deserted for some time, with a child's bicycle leaning against the wall of the entryway. Behind Ilya, the door swung shut. As the others took their hostage into the next room, the one with blue eyes entered the kitchen, along with Ilya and Vasylenko.

Setting his bag with the shotgun on the floor, the man rinsed out a couple of glasses in the sink, drying them off with a threadbare dishrag. Vasylenko sat at the kitchen table, which had a set of plastic chairs. Reaching inside his jacket, he took out a pistol and laid it on the tabletop.

As the man with blue eyes poured them each a drink, the two former prisoners sat in silence. Accepting a glass,

Vasylenko took a sip, then asked carefully in Russian, "Why was Wolfe there?"

Ilya put his own glass aside. "I don't know. She's a clever one. Perhaps she figured it out on her own. In any case, she could not have learned it from me. I didn't know where we were going."

Vasylenko seemed to grant the point. He drained the rest of his drink, then rose from the table, taking the gun with him, and went into the next room. Through the open doorway, Ilya saw him dial a number on his phone.

Next to him, the man with blue eyes was leaning against the kitchen counter, studying Ilya with evident curiosity. After a moment, he poured a drink of his own and said, "My name is Bogdan. We will be traveling together."

Opening his bag, he fished out a large envelope. Ilya took it, then undid the flap and looked inside. The first thing he saw was a passport, Israeli, apparently authentic, with his own picture and a false name. It also contained a wallet with a few credit cards and the usual pocket litter, all of it nicely done. Ilya held up a set of keys. "Are these for anything real?"

Bogdan only grinned at him above the rim of his glass. "You'll find out soon."

The final item was a railway ticket for Brasov in Romania. Ilya studied it, then slid it back inside. "You're from Moldova?"

Bogdan nodded. "Came here to work. Of course, there are no jobs now." He glanced out the window, which disclosed a tired garden. "I'll be glad to go. There is no future in this city—"

He finished his drink. As he raised his glass, Ilya caught

a glimpse of the blue tattoo on his inner forearm. It was the image of a snake.

From behind him came the sound of footsteps. Turning, he saw Vasylenko enter the kitchen again, his phone nowhere in sight. As the old man motioned for the others to follow, there was a thoughtful look on his face.

They went into the next room. Inside, Ferris had been bound rather inexpertly to a chair, his eyes and mouth covered with tape. The other men stood in the corners, smoking. As Vasylenko entered, they straightened up at once, and Ferris raised his head at the sound.

Vasylenko spoke quietly in Russian. "We need to go. Time to clean up."

Without another word, he drew his gun and shot Ferris in the forehead. The spray of blood from the back of his skull sent the driver rocking forward, and he slumped in his chair, his face hanging down toward the floor.

Looking at the body, Ilya forced himself not to react. One of the other men, the one who had freed Ilya in the prison van, laughed.

Vasylenko gestured at the body. "See if there's anything we can use in his pockets."

The man who had laughed came forward. And as he bent down over the body, looking for the best way to search the dead man, Vasylenko raised the gun again and shot him in the back of the head.

Ilya could taste the blood on the air. In the shocked silence that followed, Vasylenko spoke once more, so softly that Ilya had trouble hearing him over the ringing in his ears: "I've been in touch with my source. This fool said something about Mare Street. If we had not managed to leave when we did, the whole plan would have fallen apart." He turned to the others, who were staring at the dead men. "I will not tolerate weakness or stupidity. Are we clear?"

There was no response. Looking around at their faces, the old man seemed satisfied. "Good. Leave these two. We won't be back."

As the others filed out of the room, Ilya remained where he was. Looking down at the bodies, which were lying almost in each other's arms, he saw his own situation clearly. He had chosen to play along, to risk the possibility of violence in exchange for what he might discover, but now it was too late.

What was more, he found that he knew precisely how it would all conclude. The details remained unclear. But it could only end in death.

Vasylenko spoke up behind him. "We are past the point of second thoughts. What are you willing to do?"

"Anything," Ilya said. "But I need to know why we are going to Romania."

Vasylenko told him. It took only a sentence or two. Ilya listened in silence, then turned away from the bodies to look at the *vor*, who was regarding him with what seemed like amusement.

As they left the room, Ilya said nothing, but Vasylenko's words continued to echo in his mind. All along, he had been prepared for the worst, but even he couldn't believe what he was being asked to do now.

"We need you to kill a man," Vasylenko had said. "His name is Vasily Tarkovsky."

25

During the riots in London, a number of observers in the media noticed an increase in sales of baseball bats, both online and at sporting goods stores, which was unusual for a country where baseball had never been particularly popular. One of these bats was leaning against the wall just inside the front door of Maddy's apartment. Buying it hadn't made her feel any better. Instead, it had given her the uncomfortable sensation that she had succumbed to the atmosphere of fear.

She had not gone to work that morning. When she telephoned to call in sick, Elena's response had been frosty. "You should give us more notice in the future. Vasily is leaving for Constanta in two days, and we need to sort out your duties before his departure. We want to make sure that you'll have enough to do—"

Normally, Maddy would have responded with something slightly chilly of her own, but she had more important things to consider. After confirming that she would be in tomorrow, she hung up, glancing at the riots on television, and turned back to the image on her laptop, a picture of *Ovid Among the Scythians.*

As she studied the image on the screen, Maddy wondered what Elena would have said if she knew her real plans for the next two weeks. Tarkovsky's impending departure had left him vulnerable. Until his return, she would be left on her own with the files, which, beneath their surface accretion of detail, contained traces of a darker narrative that she was slowly piecing together.

The first clue had been before her eyes the entire time, hanging in the hallway outside her office door. She had begun to assemble other fragments from the records of Tarkovsky's art transactions and filings for his public holdings, but the picture was still unclear. And she would share it with no one, not even Powell, until she had seen its full shape for herself.

In the meantime, however, she had been presented with another part of the story, the nature of which was still a mystery. Yesterday, the first official photographs of the damaged canvas had been released. The pictures had resulted in another flurry of news coverage, some of which had mentioned her by name, along with other famous acts of artistic vandalism.

Maddy was familiar with these cases, of course. She had read up on the subject years ago, after realizing that she would be numbered among them. Yet the man at the Met seemed different. Arkady Kagan had been born in Russia, served in the army for several years, and emigrated at the age of twenty. In New York, he had worked at a number of undistinguished jobs, mostly in data entry, and according to his friends and coworkers, he had been single, fairly private but not antisocial, and without any obvious signs of mental illness.

And there was another point, not mentioned in any of

the news stories, that put his case in a somewhat different light. This was the fact, according to Powell, that the dead man had been an agent of Russian intelligence.

Closing the article on her computer, Maddy remembered something else that Powell had said. Since last year's attack, the networks within military intelligence had been destroyed, with illegal agents left stranded without any means of contacting their handlers. Which explained why the dead man had been found with a number in his possession for a phone that no longer worked.

And this, in turn, led her to another idea, one that had been gathering slowly over the last day. For much of that time, she had tried to ignore it, but as she considered it now, she was unable to think of anything else.

Maddy rose from the table and began to pace around the room, feeling like a caged animal in its confines. This was a dangerous state of mind to be in. She had been here before, reading meaning into facts and events that had no real significance. But she couldn't let it go.

Arkady Kagan had been abandoned in New York. With his handler's phone disconnected, he would have had no way of sending a message. But there was one other possibility. A dramatic act of vandalism would be widely reported. And if his face and name appeared in the news, sooner or later, it would be seen by the right people. Perhaps he had only intended to be arrested, trusting that the story and the painting's image would be carried overseas.

Which implied that the painting's destruction had been a sort of code. He had chosen this particular work for a reason. And to see what this message was, and whether it had gotten through, she had to look at the incident through the eyes of those who had been meant to see it.

There was, of course, one obvious interpretation. Maddy knew a man who had once been called the Scythian. The more she thought about it, however, the more doubtful she became. Ilya was already in prison and certainly known to military intelligence. Drawing their attention to him would have been beside the point. Moreover, this message, if it existed, had to be one that would be clear to its intended recipient but not to most other observers.

Maddy opened a new window on her laptop, switching to a view of the painting as it had been before its desecration. Here was the poet reclining on the ground, the perfect image of an exile. No one knew why he had been banished. He had offended the emperor in some unknown way, and ever since, his fate had remained one of the most mysterious episodes in classical history.

Whatever it was, Maddy thought, it had been serious enough to send him as far away as his adversaries could imagine. Deprived of his books, he had been exiled to a country where he did not speak the language, at the edge of what was then known of the civilized world, on the shore of the Black Sea—

Maddy paused. On the table, next to her laptop, sat a pile of reference books she had checked out of the library shortly after talking to Powell. One of the volumes was already open. Picking it up, she flipped to the passage that gave the name of the place where the poet had been exiled. She had read it earlier that morning and still remembered its position on the page. At last, she found it.

Ovid, it said, had been exiled to Tomis, now the port city of Constanta in Romania.

Maddy shut the book. Rising from the table, she went into the bathroom, closing the door behind her, and turned on the cold tap. The water on her face was freezing, but it had the desired effect, and the world, which had threatened to blur out of existence entirely, snapped into focus again.

She stared at herself in the mirror, the water glistening on her face, as the pieces came together. Tarkovsky was going to Constanta in two days. From there, he would take his yacht across the Black Sea to a signing ceremony in the Russian resort town of Sochi. This was public knowledge, and had been for weeks, long before the deal itself had been concluded.

What was not public knowledge, at least not yet, was what Powell had told her. Tarkovsky had long been connected to elements of military intelligence. In fact, he was their last remaining source of capital, a relationship that would become all the more lucrative after the Argo deal.

Which meant that a number of rival parties, especially on the civilian side, had good reason to go after Tarkovsky himself.

She tried to consider the problem one point at a time. If Arkady Kagan had learned that an operation was being readied against Tarkovsky in Constanta, he might well have seen only one way to get the message out. He had destroyed a painting that depicted the location in question, in a manner that would make headlines on both sides of the ocean. Only then could he transmit the name of the city above the noise of his own agency's collapse.

Maddy reached out for a towel and dried her face. Then she ran her fingers through her hair, opened the door, and left the bathroom.

As she returned to the living room, she reminded herself that it was necessary to take things slowly. The coincidence of locations was striking, but it might still mean nothing. And it would not be the first time that she read something into a work of art that wasn't there.

All the same, she owed it to Powell to tell him. Her phone was on the kitchen table. Picking it up, she was about to place the call when she noticed something out of the corner of her eye.

Her front door, which led to the hall outside, was open. It had not been open before.

She lowered the phone, then took a step forward. The baseball bat she had bought a day earlier was still leaning against the wall. It was only a few feet away. She took another step.

Behind her, the floor creaked softly. And even as she realized that she was no longer alone, the hood came down over her head.

II

AUGUST 8–14, 2011

The Scythian princes . . . dispatched a herald to the Persian camp with presents for the king: these were, a bird, a mouse, a frog, and five arrows. The Persians asked the bearer to tell them what these gifts might mean, but he made answer that he had no orders except to deliver them, and to return with all speed. If the Persians were wise, he added, they would find out the meaning for themselves.

—Herodotus, *The Histories*

I clearly understand that I am responsible for what I did and do not ask you to soften my fate. Yet let me draw your attention to the fact that I discovered a physical phenomenon unknown to modern science.

—Alexander Barchenko, in a private letter to
Nikolai Ezhov, December 24, 1937

26

Three years earlier, shortly after the series of events that led to her abrupt departure from the art world, Maddy had moved from Brooklyn to a smaller place in Astoria. As she descended from the subway platform on a cold evening near the end of November, she was one of the last passengers remaining on the train. Trudging home through the slush, she glanced back every minute or so, in order to reassure herself that she wasn't being followed.

When she arrived at her front door, which was a rental on the first floor of a tidy brick row house, she paused under the awning, key in hand. As usual, whenever she returned from her latest temp job in the city, she had to spend a moment convincing herself that no one was waiting for her inside.

In the end, she inserted the key firmly into the lock and turned it. Going into the darkened entryway, she shut the door and set down her purse. As she removed her boots, her heart rate began to slow. There was no one here. The danger, as always, was all in her head.

She switched on the light. In the living room, seated in an armchair, was Ilya Severin.

Maddy must have screamed, because before she was aware of any movement, Ilya was out of the chair and holding her firmly by the shoulders. His voice was low but urgent. "I'm not armed. I did not come to hurt you. I only need a few minutes. Then I will go."

She stared at him, heart juddering, her mind still catching up to the fact that this was happening at last. All the while, a more detached part of her brain was already ticking off the relevant points. Her landlord was on vacation. The windows were closed against the chill. If she screamed again, there was no guarantee that anyone outside would hear her in time.

He released her and took a step back. She felt tears come, more instinctive than emotional, and was surprised at the steadiness of her own voice. "If you aren't fucking armed, then prove it."

Ilya seemed to grant the reasonableness of this request. He backed up slowly, his eyes on hers, and undid his overcoat. Beneath it was a rumpled suit, but nothing resembling a weapon.

They regarded each other in silence. It was the first time she had ever really studied his face. He was younger than she remembered, certainly short of forty. His features were nondescript but more angular than before, and his eyes were as black as always. "What do you want from me?"

"Only to talk," Ilya said. "I'm sorry to come see you like this. It was the only way."

Maddy opened her mouth again. She found that she was shaking, her head somehow loose on her shoulders, and she was not entirely prepared for what she said next. "I need a drink."

She took a step forward, still in her coat and scarf. Ilya

fell back, giving her space, as she moved on autopilot into the kitchen. Keeping him in sight, she had to remind herself to breathe as she headed for the refrigerator, her eye briefly caught by the snapshot posted to the door as she opened it.

Maddy bent down, the refrigerator door hiding her from view. Half a bottle of white wine stood on the first shelf. Reaching behind it, she felt for the handle of the boning knife she had placed there weeks ago, one of several she had stashed around the apartment, a form of security born in equal measure from caution and her lingering chemical paranoia.

Glancing at Ilya, she saw that he was looking at the bookshelf by the dining table. She slid the knife quietly into the pocket of her coat. Then she took out the bottle and straightened up.

A used tumbler lay next to the sink. Closing the refrigerator, she pulled out the plastic cork and poured three generous inches of wine. When she turned to face Ilya again, she saw that he had taken out a book to examine it. He put it back, then indicated the table with its two folding chairs. "You can sit if you like."

Maddy managed to pick up the glass, but she remained where she was. "I'll stand."

Ilya only nodded and sat down. He pulled off his gloves, laying them side by side on the table before him. "It's strange, but I don't really know you. Even after our paths have crossed so often—"

Maddy put the wine down without drinking it. Ten feet of faded linoleum stood between her and the Scythian. "Why are you here?"

"I'm looking for Alexey Lermontov," Ilya said. "He has left the country, but it is still too dangerous for him to return to Moscow. Once he goes home, he will be out of reach. I have come to the end of my own resources. And I thought you might have some idea of where he could be found."

Maddy slid her right hand into her pocket, her fingers closing around the knife. "Why would I know this?"

"Because you worked for him. And there are some things a man cannot hide. His habits, his tastes, his affectations. I hoped you might have some insight into this." He glanced again at her books. "I can tell you what I have gathered so far. Perhaps you can say if I am right or wrong."

When she said nothing, Ilya began to speak slowly, occasionally pausing to search for the right word. "You worked at his gallery for several years. It must have been a good position. He was one of the leading dealers in the city, with important clients. And he liked you. He would have kept you on, but you left to start a gallery of your own. It did not go well."

He waited to see whether she had any response, then continued when none seemed forthcoming. "You took a job at an art investment fund, where you were asked to look into a painting purchased by the oligarch Anzor Archvadze. You went to his mansion to see his collection for yourself. It was there that we first met. Of course, I was there to steal the picture."

Maddy found her voice at last. "You were also there to poison Archvadze."

She saw something harden in his dark eyes. "Yes. At the time, I did not question it. I did not learn the purpose of the theft until I was betrayed. The painting was evidence that Lermontov was dealing in stolen art. Archvadze bought it to build his case. Lermontov ordered him silenced and the picture stolen. Later, he killed another man who had also discovered the truth—"

"He was my colleague," Maddy said. "A friend of mine. His name was Ethan."

"I know." Ilya paused. "In the end, Lermontov fled after being exposed. But certain questions remain. It is unclear how Archvadze learned he was working for the security services. Do you have any thoughts on this?"

"No. And Archvadze, unfortunately, isn't around to tell us." Looking down, Maddy found that her free hand had picked up the wine, apparently of its own accord. "And if you find him?"

"I will do what is necessary," Ilya said. "Lermontov may have vanished. But he's still a useful man. His role will be less visible, but his influence will remain. And this is something I cannot allow."

The wine was bad, but it seemed to clear her head. "And why should I help you?"

"You know the answer already. At the museum, I saw it in your eyes. I understand what it means to lose everything. As long as this man is alive, you will never be safe. Sooner or later, he will seek to silence those who threaten or inconvenience him. It's why you're so afraid to put your life back together. And why you keep so many knives in your house."

Ilya rose, picking up his gloves, and set a folded scrap of paper on the dining table. "I won't bother you again. You can contact me here if you wish to talk. But it has to be soon."

Maddy set down the wine, the glass trembling in her hand, and turned away. As she began to see what Ilya's offer really meant, she hated him for coming to her, after she had tried so desperately to face her fears on her own.

But what frightened her the most was the realization, deep down, that she wanted it.

Maddy turned back around, sensing that her decision was already made. "If I agree to this, it won't be for you—"

She broke off. Hearing the sound of the door closing softly, she saw that the chair was empty. Ilya was gone.

27

Maddy sat in the backseat of a parked car, alone, the hood still over her head. It was dark and hot but fairly easy to breathe. The hood had been sewn together from black cloth and smelled mildly of fabric softener. It had been recently washed, perhaps to remove telltale fibers, and this sense of meticulousness, which in another context might have seemed homely, frightened her even more.

Waiting in the car for whatever was coming, she fought away the fear that threatened to overwhelm her, forcing herself to remember what had happened, which was the only way to keep panic from taking hold completely. After the hood came down, she had felt the hard pressure of a gun against her back and heard a man's voice in her ear: "Make a sound, and it ends right now."

He had pushed her roughly toward the door of her flat, which was open from before. Maddy had nearly fallen, but the hand locked around her forearm had kept her on her feet, steering her toward the stairs outside. She felt cool air as they passed through the door of her building and crossed the sidewalk. Up ahead, she heard an idling engine, along with monotonous dance music from a car stereo, the waves of sound pushing thickly through the hood.

She was shoved into the backseat. Her assailant from upstairs slid in beside her and drew the seat belt across her body, the gun pressed against her rib cage. Maddy heard the door close and the music rise as the unseen driver cranked up the volume, and then they were away from the curb.

They had driven for perhaps half an hour. The music on the speakers was a shapeless wall of noise, each track shading imperceptibly into the next, so it was impossible to tell where one song ended and the next began. Maddy tried to remember the turns they made and listen for clues outside, the way one might do in the movies, but she lost her bearings after the first roundabout.

The car stopped at least twice, once at what seemed like a red light, a second time for close to a minute, at the end of which the front passenger door opened to let someone else in. At one point, Maddy heard a siren approaching from the other direction, filling her with momentary hope, but the vehicle, whatever it was, only passed and receded into the distance.

Eventually they came to a highway. After driving along it for some time, they exited onto a side road, the ground uneven beneath the tires of the car, which slowed its progress to a crawl. At last, they came to a stop. The engine was turned off, ending the music. In the ensuing silence, Maddy heard the front doors open and shut, followed by two sets of footsteps.

The man at her side did not move for a long time. At last, his voice came again in her ear: "Stay where you are."

With that, the man opened the rear door and withdrew the gun. Sliding out, he closed the door behind him. Maddy heard his footsteps grow steadily softer as he moved away from the car. And then there was nothing.

Now she sat waiting in the backseat, the lump of sickness in her stomach refusing to dissolve. Her arm ached at the spot where her assailant's hand had clamped down, and she found that she had to go to the bathroom. In the end, she wasn't sure how much time passed, but it might have been only a minute or two before she was startled by the shrill ring of a cell phone.

Maddy jumped at the sound. The phone rang again, sending a vibration through the seat beside her. Reaching up, she pulled off the hood, her hair sticking in strands to her forehead, and found that she was alone. The car turned out to be an old-model compact with grimy tinted windows and vinyl seats creased like the palms of human hands. Through the windshield, she saw that she was parked in a field of dry grass strewn with gray trash and debris.

She looked back at the road along which they had approached, the marks of the tires still visible in the dust, then turned again to the windshield. In the distance, a line of trees stood beneath the white sky. Just before the field ended, there was a decrepit house, its front steps sagging with age.

The phone on the seat was still ringing. Glancing down at last, she thought at first that it was her own phone, although the ringtone was strange. She picked it up and saw an unfamiliar number on the display. Only when she opened the phone to answer it did she realize that it was not hers at all, but a different phone of the same kind, a fact that filled her with even more fear than before.

She raised the phone to her ear. Before she could speak, a distorted voice came over the other end, its words channeled through a voice changer, shifting the pitch downward, so that she wasn't sure if it was male or female: "Look in the pocket of the seat in front of you."

Her eyes fell on the back of the front seat. There was something sticking out from the pocket. Reaching down, she was about to undo her safety belt when the voice abruptly spoke again: "Keep the belt on."

Maddy looked sharply around. The field was still empty. Keeping her eye on the house in the distance, which was the only place where anyone could be watching, she reached into the pocket and felt her fingers close around a manila envelope. As she withdrew it, the voice came over the phone: "Look inside."

She shifted the phone to her other hand. The envelope was unmarked and lightweight. Staring at it, Maddy had a sudden premonition of what might be there. All the fears she had been storing up came rising to the surface, but her hands were steady as she unwound the string on the flap and slid out the contents.

The first thing she saw was a set of pictures printed on uncut photo stock. When she turned them over to get a better look, she felt all her strength drain away. The photos had been taken outside Lermontov's house. One showed her going up the steps, while the second caught her in profile as she left something on the porch, and the last was a shot of her walking away.

Beneath the pictures was a sheet of folded paper. Maddy opened it, already guessing what it was, and saw a photocopy of an itinerary for a flight from New York to London. Circled on the form was her own name, as well as the return date below it, just over two years ago.

"You see, we know," the voice in her ear said, any trace of emotion flattened out by the pitch modulator. "You came to London two years ago to help Ilya Severin kill Alexey Lermontov. Ilya couldn't have done it on his own, but you knew how such a man might be found—"

Maddy closed her eyes, her hands falling open so that the documents fluttered down to the floor. She took a long breath. "You're wasting your time. I have no money. There's nothing I can possibly do for you."

"You're wrong," the voice said. "We need you to perform a service for us. Once this task is concluded, you will never hear from us again. You can resume your life as before—"

Even then, Maddy knew that this was a lie, and that there would be no going back. "What do you want?"

"It's very simple," the voice replied. "We want you to join Tarkovsky on his yacht."

Maddy opened her eyes. The *Rigden*, she knew, would be departing from Constanta in two days, with Tarkovsky and his guests on board, and there was no way she could get an invitation. "Why?"

The voice rasped in her ear again. "That isn't your concern. You will go to Tarkovsky tomorrow. You will convince him to bring you on the voyage. When you leave, you will take this phone instead of your own. Talk to anyone, and we hand you over to the police. We'll be watching you. But if you do precisely as we say, you can walk away from this as if nothing had happened."

Maddy looked at the house in the distance. The sickness in her stomach had spread to every corner of her body. "And if I say no?"

"See for yourself," the voice said. "You can get out of the car now and find out."

The phone fell silent, aside from the faint rustle of the pitch modulator. "And how am I supposed to get on board?"

"Tarkovsky likes you," the voice replied. "I'm sure someone as resourceful as you can come up with a way. Call us when you've done it. Keep this phone on and charged. There's a tube station just up the road."

The hiss of the modulator ceased. Maddy held the phone to her ear for another moment. Then she flung it away so that it struck the back of the driver's seat, bounced off, and fell to the floor of the car.

Keeping her eyes on the house in the windshield, Maddy reached across her lap and undid her safety belt. Nothing happened. Gathering up the pictures, she slid them back into the envelope. She picked up the cell phone. Then she opened the passenger door and stepped out in stocking feet onto the dead grass.

As soon as she was out of the car, she found herself retching, bending almost double, but nothing came out. She squeezed her eyes shut, willing herself to wake up, but when she looked around again, she found herself exactly where she had been a second earlier, her head throbbing with exhaustion and anger as the reality of her situation swept across her once more.

Maddy straightened up and looked back at the car, a Ford Focus, the most common model in the country. The license plates were missing. Going over to the driver's side, she saw that the keys were gone, but a few crumpled pound notes had been left on the seat, enough for a ride home.

If there had been a rock on the ground beside her, she would have smashed all the windows, but instead she turned again to the house by the trees. She took a step forward, then paused.

When she spoke, it was nothing more than a whisper, if indeed she said anything at all. Whatever the words were, they were quickly carried away by the wind and lost at once in the silence.

Opening the door, she gathered up the money. She checked the glove box and found it empty, as were the remaining seat pockets. Going to the backseat, she snatched up the hood as well.

Maddy closed the door, then turned to face the road, which was a hundred yards behind her. She began to walk slowly across the field, not looking back, knowing all the while that she was still being watched.

On the upper floor of the house by the trees, a shadow was outlined against the glass. As Maddy moved away, it withdrew from the window.

Inside the house, a watcher in a leather jacket lowered the binoculars through which he had been observing the car. He turned to the figure beside him. "Are you sure she'll do it?"

Asthana nodded. Her cell phone, a voice changer still attached to the mouthpiece, was clutched in her right hand. "She'll do it. And if she doesn't, we can always get to her in other ways."

28

The overnight train from Paris to Munich, known as the Cassiopeia line, waited on the platform at the Gare de l'Est. Among the passengers boarding its twelve coaches were two men who had arrived at the station some forty minutes earlier. They were dressed in a similar fashion, in casual traveling clothes, and did not attract any particular attention as they entered a sleeping car toward the front of the train.

Walking down the narrow passageway, they reached their compartment. The man in front slid the door open and went in, followed a moment later by his companion, who walked briefly up and down the car, checking their surroundings, before entering and closing the door behind him.

Putting down his bag, Ilya looked around the compartment that he and Bogdan would be sharing. Two berths had been folded down, each set with a pillow and a white duvet. To his right, a door opened into a private bathroom with a tiny toilet and shower. Above the sink, the mirror confronted him with his unfamiliar reflection. His hair had been cut short earlier that day.

Ilya turned back to the main compartment, where his

companion had set down his own bag. Going to the small table in the corner, Bogdan raised the window shade, revealing a view of the station outside, and folded the chair down from the wall. Taking a seat, he drew his bag toward him, opening it, as Ilya sat across from him on the edge of the bed.

Without speaking, the men began to lay out cheese and sausages bought during the walk from the Gare du Nord. From the pocket of his bag, Bogdan extracted a folding knife and used it to slice a piece of sausage for himself. Keeping the knife open, he gave it to Ilya, handle first. After a pause, Ilya took it, knowing that this was not quite the gesture of trust it seemed. Bogdan's real knife, his pike, was somewhere else, probably in his pocket.

They ate in silence, passing the knife back and forth as necessary, as the train left the station. Their journey so far had been uneventful. At St. Pancras, their passports had been stamped without a second glance, and two hours later, they had arrived in Paris. From there, they would travel overnight to Germany, then east to Budapest and Romania. At that point, they would reunite with the rest of the group for the next phase, which would take them, Ilya had gathered, to Moldova.

Bogdan, for his part, had not volunteered any additional information, either out of his own natural wariness or because he, too, was waiting to see where they were going. So far, the other man had struck Ilya as intelligent and careful, and he knew that Bogdan was watching him with the same degree of scrutiny. They had been unable to bring any guns through the metal detectors in London, which meant that they would make the next leg of their journey unarmed.

Once their meal was finished, Bogdan put the leftovers

away, then pulled a bottle and two plastic cups out of his bag. Ilya kept an eye on how much the other man poured into each cup, noting that he gave them both generous amounts. Glancing out the window, he saw that they were heading northeast, the train rolling serenely beneath the steel overpasses. It was shortly before sunset.

Bogdan was looking out at the view as well. Now that the most uncertain stage was behind them, he appeared to relax, although an underlying watchfulness remained. "You spend much time in Paris?"

This was the first time he had asked about Ilya's past, or, indeed, had spoken of anything aside from practical matters since leaving London. "Once or twice," Ilya replied. "You?"

"Not for a long time," Bogdan said. "But I would often pass through in the old days."

Remembering what Bogdan had said earlier about his background, Ilya made an educated guess. "You were a driver?"

Bogdan took a sip of vodka. He was careful, Ilya saw, not to drink to excess. "How did you know?"

"I've known many such men," Ilya said. Sensing that the other man was waiting for him to drink as well, he raised his cup to his lips, keeping his eyes on his companion. "How often?"

"Once a month or so." Bogdan looked out at the darkening sky as the train picked up speed. "After the army. I would drive there from Corjeuti. The only way a man in my village could see any money."

Ilya knew that a network of such drivers made the journey by car on a regular basis between Moldova and France, delivering parcels and picking up cash and groceries from illegals in Paris. "And then London?"

Bogdan smiled for the first time since their departure. "Yes. For a girl. Even after she was gone, London seemed more open, shall we say, to fresh talent. And I had my Romanian passport, so . . ."

He trailed off, since there was no need to spell out the rest. Moldova had been Romanian between the wars, and after it achieved independence, many Moldovans had applied for Romanian nationality. "But now you're going back?"

Bogdan grinned more broadly, although there was a faint tinge of anger there as well. "No money to send home these days. Soon all these places will be the same. Easier to be home when the worst of it comes. And after we are done here, it may not be so bad for us after all."

Ilya watched as Bogdan drank again. "Is that why you want to kill Tarkovsky?"

Bogdan did not reply at once, although the smile lingered strangely on his face. Outside, night was falling. "I do not blame him. He took advantage of the hand he was dealt. Better him than the dogs in the Kremlin."

Ilya sensed an obvious question hanging in the air. "Yet you're ready to let him die."

Bogdan shrugged slightly. "I have no quarrel with the man. But where his money goes is another matter. Hard times are coming, and I intend to be ready. Better to be on the winning side. You see?"

Ilya only finished his drink. It was not hard to read between Bogdan's words. What was happening now was only the latest chapter in a secret history that had unfolded in Russia for years.

Glancing at his travel companion, Ilya wondered how much of this Bogdan had seen firsthand. In the aftermath of the war between Moldova and Transnistria, Russia had sent troops to the latter, unasked, and in order to survive, the local criminals had been forced to reach an accommodation with military intelligence. In response, their rivals in Moldova had thrown in their lot with the civilian side, which had also meant establishing alliances with the network of thieves of which Vasylenko was one of the last remaining representatives.

Looking at his own face, which was reflected darkly in the glass, Ilya considered his predicament. He had been hoping to get close to Vasylenko, learning what he could about the *vor*'s plans before making his final move. So far, however, the others had been careful, and he doubted that he would be left alone with Vasylenko long enough to end things in the way he had intended.

He had wanted to see this through on his own, but now he saw that this was no longer possible. As soon as he had the chance, he would contact Wolfe with what he had uncovered. He had left her one message already. And perhaps, with enough patience, other opportunities would present themselves in the meantime.

The view from the train had grown too dark to see. Lowering the shade, Ilya glanced over at Bogdan. "Do you want to sleep?"

In response, Bogdan switched on the light next to the table. Reaching into his bag, he removed a book of military history that he had bought at the train station and opened it to the first page.

Seeing the shadow of a smile on his companion's face, Ilya understood that he had no intention of sleeping tonight. For a moment, the two men regarded each other in silence. At last, Ilya said, "You can't watch me all the time."

"I know," Bogdan said, not lowering his eyes. "Fortunately, that won't be necessary."

29

"I've spoken again with the museum director," Maddy said. "A board meeting is scheduled for next week, but it's unclear how many votes he has. There's an unwritten rule that once something goes into a museum, it doesn't go out. But I'll keep following up while you're gone."

"Good," Tarkovsky said, keeping his eyes on the view of the garden. It seemed to her that he had something on his mind, although this may have been because she, too, was working up her courage for what she had to say.

They were alone in the sitting room on the second floor of the mansion. All four walls were lined with books, while up ahead, a door, slightly open, led into Tarkovsky's private office. It was the first time Maddy had ever been inside the main house. After getting the call that afternoon, she had put away the files, her hands trembling, and gone up the gravel path through the gardens to the front gable, where a security guard had ushered her inside.

Looking around, she had found herself in a large entrance hall, its exposed beams and thick carpet reminding her, in passing, of another house she had visited many years ago. Before her had stood a massive fireplace with a stepped fireback of cast iron, its shield engraved, inevitably, with the familiar image of a man on horseback, slaying a basilisk with a spear.

It had struck her as an omen, or at least as a sign as to which of two paths to take. And this feeling had only grown stronger as the guard led her upstairs, past a room where someone was endlessly playing the piano, the notes drifting in clusters throughout the great house.

She could faintly hear the piano now, through the closed door of the sitting room, as her employer turned away from the window. "You've done well," Tarkovsky said. "And there are other projects you can work on while I'm away. Assuming that you decide to remain."

Maddy saw the opening she needed. Without hesitation, she took the plunge. "That all depends on you."

Tarkovsky seemed amused by her reply. "And what is it you need from me?"

Maddy paused. From here, she knew, there were two ways she could go. One was safer but less certain, while the other would leave her exposed forever, and in the instant before she spoke, she found herself taking the more cautious approach. "If I'm going to do my job effectively, you need to be honest with me. We need to talk about the real reason you want this egg."

Tarkovsky had listened without visible reaction. "And what reason would this be?"

"I don't think you care about it at all. I think you care more about the horse and rider inside. You mentioned this at the museum, when you said that you saw it as a symbol of Russia's future, but there's more to it than that. And you hired me because you thought I'd see the truth sooner or later."

This was nothing but a stab in the dark, but as he listened, Tarkovsky seemed to grow more watchful. "And what have you seen?"

"The word on the side of your yacht," Maddy said simply. "*Rigden*. It's the name of a line of legendary kings of Shambhala, a mythical hidden kingdom in inner Asia. The final king, Rigden Djapo, is destined to usher the world into a new age. When he's born, white lotuses, like the one painted on the yacht's hull, will fall from the sky. And when he appears, he'll be riding a white horse."

Tarkovsky's features relaxed into a smile. "Very clever of you. But anyone who reads up on the subject for more than a few minutes will uncover the same information. And I don't see how it affects your work."

"Then let me explain." She hesitated, knowing that she was entering dangerous territory. "You're careful to express no interest in politics. You've seen what happens to businessmen with political aspirations. They're killed or they're thrown into prison, like Khodorkovsky. But I know that you care about the future of Russia. Your foundation funds organizations that are pushing for transparency and financial reform. You want to see your country move peacefully into the next stage of its history. And this is what the name of the yacht means."

Tarkovsky was no longer smiling. "And what does that name have to do with this?"

"Shambhala is a political symbol," Maddy said. "A perfect society, ruled by enlightenment and science. It began as a legend in Buddhism, an allegory for spiritual change, but later, people began to wonder if it might actually exist, hidden away in Central Asia, or somewhere to the north, or underground. Its symbol is the color white, especially the white horse and lotus. And if you, of all people, are interested in this story, it means you think these symbols still have meaning."

Tarkovsky turned back toward the window, the panes of which were now lightly dotted with rain. "It has nothing to do with me. Russia has always returned to the same handful of symbols. The Soviet Union once claimed to be Shambhala, the hidden land of plenty, to influence regional politics. Putin himself takes an interest in such myths. There is nothing exceptional here. The idea of a northern paradise goes back to the warriors of the steppes—"

"But symbols have power. You wouldn't have named your yacht after the legend if you didn't think the story was meaningful. It may be a myth, but it stands for something real. A promise that change is coming. I think you want this egg because if you bring it back to Russia, along with the horse and rider inside, the people you want to reach will understand its significance. It's the same reason you've acquired works by Nicholas Roerich. He's a minor painter, but he was also an activist and mystic who took a great interest in the political implications of Shambhala."

Tarkovsky's eyes flicked back to hers. "You're quite good at finding meaning where it might not exist."

"You knew this when you hired me," Maddy replied. "And I've seen enough to make me skeptical of secret forces working to change the world. But I also know how powerful a symbol can be. And if there's a deeper meaning behind this egg, you can't go away for two weeks before we've had a chance to discuss it."

Tarkovsky remained silent. Watching him, Maddy wondered if the approach she had taken was having any effect. Her only hope, as she had seen so clearly last night, was to arouse his curiosity. And the one place where this conversation could continue, given his impending departure, was the yacht itself.

At last, Tarkovsky turned back to her, and this time, he did not look away. "Have you ever heard of a man named Gleb Boky?"

Before she could respond, the door at the far end of the room opened, and Elena entered. Maddy had not heard the assistant approach, and something in her face as she drew closer made Maddy suspect that she had been listening. "I'm sorry to interrupt, but it's time for your call to Argo."

Tarkovsky nodded, falling back into an expression of nonchalance, although his eyes remained fixed on Maddy. "Thank you. I'd say that we're done here. Elena will walk you back in a moment."

"Of course," Maddy said. Rising from her chair, she headed for the door of the sitting area, sensing Elena watching her as she departed.

Maddy left the room, closing the door behind her, and stood for a moment at the head of the staircase, listening to the muffled notes of the piano playing down the hall. For a moment, she thought about throwing herself over the balustrade. She had been so close. Another minute, and she might have been able to bring the conversation around to the yacht.

Looking down the stairs, she saw clearly what she had to do now. Her second option was all she had left. She had been holding it in reserve, knowing that it amounted to a full confession, but even if the consequences were severe, they were nothing compared to the alternative.

Since yesterday, she had gone more than once to call Powell. Each time, standing at the pay phone, she had wavered. Glancing around the street, she had reassured herself that she was alone. Yet she could never shake the sense that she was being watched, and that someone was waiting patiently to see what she would do next. And if she failed to do what they asked—

As she began to gather her courage again, the sound of the piano abruptly ceased. Looking up, Maddy saw a slender girl of twelve emerge from the parlor down the hall. It was Nina, Tarkovsky's daughter. As the girl headed along the landing toward the other end of the house, she glanced back, her dark eyes briefly brushing Maddy's. Then she turned away.

A voice came from over her shoulder. "I don't know what you said, but it worked."

Maddy turned to see Elena standing behind her, a look on her face of mingled disdain and admiration. She had emerged noiselessly from the other room. "What are you talking about?"

Elena smiled tightly. "You're coming with us. Vasily wants you on the yacht. He says that he'd like me to keep an eye on you. So it appears you and I will be sharing a cabin."

At first, Maddy couldn't believe what she was hearing. "He said this to you?"

Ignoring the question, Elena headed for the stairs. "You will pack tonight, and bring your passport. We need to get your visas in order." She glanced down at Maddy's pencil skirt. "And you might want to find something nice to wear. We're leaving tomorrow for Romania."

30

Clifford Hughes was short and muscular, his face mottled with freckles, a scruffy growth of ginger stubble beginning to appear on his face and shorn head. Wolfe observed that he was still wearing his clothes from the day before, although his red jacket was gone, and that a smile was playing across his lips as he studied the three photographs set before him on the table. "Mare Street, innit?"

"That's right." Asthana tapped a figure in one of the shots. "Could this be you?"

Hughes leaned forward. In the photo, a screen capture from a cell phone video taken during the riots, a figure in a red jacket could be seen. "Can't really say. Could be me. Or someone in similar clothes."

At Asthana's side, Wolfe remained silent, her hand resting lightly on a folder on the table. She was tired, but there had been little time to rest since the events of the previous day. In the aftermath of the riots, police stations in the city were packed to capacity, with arrestees sent to outlying areas as the court system worked through its backlog of cases. Even here, in Watford, all the interrogation rooms were occupied, so they had been forced to squeeze into the kitchen, where the door frequently opened and closed as officers came in for cups of tea.

Asthana resumed her questioning. "And what were you doing at Mare Street? Hoping to break an officer's skull?"

Hughes rubbed the top of his head. "I live there, don't I? King Edward's Road."

"And you aren't working these days. Wormwood Scrubs for burglary, wasn't it?"

"If that's what you want to call it," Hughes said easily. "I was alone that morning, watching the telly. Heard the noise and thought I'd go for a look. It seemed like a bit of fun."

Asthana pointed to the second photo. "What about this shot? It looks like you're talking to a group of men near the park. Or is this a different person in the same kind of jacket?"

Wolfe shot Asthana a look. Although she knew that her partner was under a great deal of stress, this was still a leading question. Not surprisingly, Hughes took the hint. "That's right. Lots of jackets like those."

Asthana pointed to the last picture, which showed the man in red throwing something visible only as a blur in the air. "Whoever he was, he threw a piece of wood at an officer at the scene. You're still saying it wasn't you?"

Hughes gave a shrug. "What can I say? It's all a mistake. I've been saying this since I got nicked."

As Hughes leaned back smugly in his chair, Wolfe did her best to tamp down her frustration. Since the prison break, she had been presented with one setback after another. Dancy had gone into hiding, evidently out of fear for his own life, and they had been unable to bring the solicitor in for questioning about his knowledge of his clients' intentions.

She fought away a fresh wave of anger. This was the hardest part of all. She had never pretended to know Ilya well, but she had believed that he would rather die than fall in with Vasylenko. Now, instead, witnesses were claiming that Ilya himself had unlocked the old man's shackles. She was also aware that given her history with Ilya, questions had been raised about her failure to stop him on Mare Street. And the only way to silence these doubts was to bring him back herself.

Wolfe spoke up at last. "Clifford, do you remember the forensic examination you were given after your arrest? It would have been conducted by a scenes of crime officer. He took a sample from the inside of your cheek—"

Hughes's face lit up. "Right, a little man. Pulled a comb through my hair, didn't he? And wiped off my hands."

"Yes. It was a nitrate test. And the results came back a few hours ago." Wolfe opened the folder in front of her, which contained a single printed page. "The tests found traces on your hands of penthrite, a chemical used in high explosives. Similar traces were found on your jacket. And both tested as a match for another set of chemicals found at a scene in Woolwich. Does any of that sound familiar?"

Hughes's eyes were on the printout. His smile was gone. "Can't say that it does."

"Let me explain, then. There was a prison escape that morning. The explosives they used left a residue that perfectly matches the nitrate test I have here. It was all over your jacket, Clifford. And both of your hands."

This was largely a bluff. In the confusion, Hughes's hands had been swabbed only after he had spent the night in his holding cell. Normally, the samples would have been taken immediately, before there was a chance of contamination, and in any case, such chemicals could have come from any number of sources.

Hughes did not seem aware of this fact. He looked with pointed calm at Wolfe, but his hands trembled slightly where they rested against the table. "I don't know about any escape."

"That's hard to believe. As I see it, there are two explanations. Either you were there in Woolwich, with the others, or you encountered them in some other way." Wolfe pointed to a face in the second picture. "I'm most interested in this man. Ilya Severin. Perhaps you spoke to him briefly, and one of the others brushed past you. A moment of contact is all it would take."

Hughes studied the picture. At last, he said, speaking slowly: "Maybe. But—"

"So you were there," Wolfe said. "In that case, you should tell us what you remember about these men."

Hughes hesitated again, as if wondering how much he could safely give up. Finally, he shook his head. "I don't remember anything. And I have nothing to say to the likes of you."

For a moment, Wolfe weighed whether to push things further, then decided that Hughes might be more receptive after another day or two in holding. After they had gone through the closing formalities, a police officer came to take custody of Hughes, who did not say another word. Asthana gathered up the photos, then rose with Wolfe and left the kitchen.

As Wolfe went to find the duty officer, Asthana remained in the hallway of the custody area, checking the email on her phone.

It was lucky, Asthana thought, that Hughes had held his tongue. Listening to him talk, she had wanted to smack him across his blotchy face. He thought he was being clever, but if he were really smart, he wouldn't have said anything at all. Clearly he didn't fully understand the situation, or that the last thing he needed to worry about was the police. And although he knew nothing that could put them at risk, it would still be necessary to keep an eye on him, and perhaps to pass a message along to his parents in Lower Clapton.

Asthana slid the phone back into her purse, then, glancing around, removed a second phone, which had been set to silent mode. There were no new messages, but she wasn't particularly concerned. Before the end of the day, she suspected, she would have the answer she needed.

Rogozin, she saw now, had gone wrong in several ways. He had put too much trust in a single man. Sometimes, for reasons of simplicity or security, you had no other choice, but you also had to take other precautions. And she was about to put a very useful safeguard into place.

Even as this thought passed through her mind, Asthana saw Wolfe turn away from the duty officer and come quickly up the corridor. There was a grim look on her face. "What's wrong?"

"Word just came over the radio," Wolfe said. "They've found Andrew Ferris."

31

Ilya arrived at Brasov at shortly before noon the following day. Leaving the gray railway terminal with a flock of arrivals from Bucharest, he and Bogdan headed for the parking lot, where they came to a halt before a green Vauxhall Corsa. Bogdan gestured toward the vehicle. "Get in."

Remembering the keys that he had been given with the rest of his papers, Ilya unlocked the car. He tossed his bag on the backseat and slid behind the wheel. "Where are we going?"

Bogdan put away his own bag and climbed in on the passenger's side. "Sinaia. Fifty kilometers south. You know it?"

Ilya adjusted his mirrors and glanced at the glove compartment. "See if you can find a map."

Bogdan opened the glove box, rifled through its contents, and emerged with a road atlas, which Ilya accepted. He knew how to get from here to Sinaia, but he had wanted to see whether the glove compartment contained anything else.

They drove without speaking through Brasov, a chilly, spare alpine city lined with apartment blocks from the time of Ceauşescu. As they continued south, the traffic grew light and the sides of the highway became thickly forested, the blue peaks of the Carpathians standing like ghosts in the distance. Looking out at the mountains, Ilya felt as if he were passing out of the world in which he had spent the last ten years of his life, drawing ever closer to his past.

In time, they neared Sinaia, a resort town east of the Bucegi mountain range. Leaving the highway, they turned north, the road narrowing as it wound up through the forest. As they approached a gravel parking area at the shoulder, Bogdan spoke up. "Stop here. We walk the rest of the way."

Ilya turned into the lot, in which a handful of other cars were visible, and shut off the engine. Bogdan told him to leave his bag behind. As Ilya emerged from the car into the cool mountain air, he found that he knew exactly where they were going, but he still wasn't sure why.

The two of them headed on foot up a road paved with cobblestones. Aside from a few hikers in the distance, they were alone in the forest, the slender gray trunks of firs marching up and down the mountain.

They continued in silence for ten minutes. After they had walked half a mile, Bogdan paused, checking to make sure that no one else was in sight, and left the main road, moving deeper into the trees, where an almost invisible footpath led up the wooded hillside.

Behind him, Ilya paused. Bogdan motioned impatiently. "Come on. Not far to go."

After a beat, Ilya followed. As they passed out of sight of the main path, the ground grew steeper. He kept several steps behind Bogdan. It seemed doubtful that they would have brought him this far only to kill him now, but he was well aware that bad things could happen in woods like this.

Finally, through the firs, he caught a glimpse of a building near the crest of the hill. Drawing closer, he found that it was a cottage, two stories high, with flecks of brown paint on its weathered boards. There were no vehicles in sight. A stone wall ran along one side of the house, which seemed to fade into the woods. In the rear yard stood a pile of gravel as white as bone.

Bogdan went up to the cottage and knocked twice. A second later, the door was opened by a man whom Ilya had last seen at the house in Hackney Wick. A shotgun was slung over his shoulder.

Inside, the house was only sparsely furnished. A worn rug lay on the floor, the boards creaking audibly at every step. Looking into the next room, Ilya saw a kitchen table and chairs with the remains of a recent meal.

As Bogdan kicked off his shoes and headed without a word for the couch, the guard closed the front door and began to climb the stairs to the upper story, gesturing for Ilya to come as well. Ilya let him get most of the way up before following, one ear tuned to the floorboards behind him.

On the second floor, which was equally bare, Ilya heard voices coming from a room at the end of the hall. One of them he recognized at once. Following the guard toward the door, he found himself standing at the threshold of a small bedroom facing the clearing below.

The first thing he saw was Vasylenko. The old man was seated at the edge of the bed, in new clothes, with a fresh haircut and shave. He was talking quietly to another member of the team from Hackney, breaking off as the two others came in. The guard from downstairs said nothing, but went at once to the window, the lower sash of which had been raised.

Before the window, a tripod had been set. And on the tripod was a sniper's rifle.

Ilya took in the rifle, then looked around at the others. "Has the time come already?"

Vasylenko smiled. "Not exactly. If it were that easy, we never would have brought you this far." He nodded at the window. "Please, take a look. I'm sure you'll find it interesting."

Ilya went to the windowsill. Looking past the rifle, he saw that the cottage had a fine view of a broad sloped clearing below. Past a field dotted with haystacks, there stood a striking building, a palace with slim spires and towers in the style of a timbered chalet. "Peles Castle."

Vasylenko said nothing. Ilya kept his eye on the window, wondering why they were here. It was a former royal hunting preserve and summer retreat, now a museum, a frequent destination for tourists in this part of the country, a number of whom he could see wandering in the terraced gardens surrounding the palace. He turned away from the view. "So?"

In response, Vasylenko signaled at the guard standing next to the tripod. Bending down, the guard looked through the rifle's telescopic sight, checking the view through the scope, then nodded. As the guard withdrew again, Vasylenko turned his eyes back to Ilya. "See for yourself."

Ilya bent over the scope. He found that its crosshairs were trained on a woman seated on a stone bench in one of the gardens, some five hundred yards away. She was by herself, talking on a cell phone, and although her face was visible only in profile, Ilya recognized her. It was Maddy Blume.

At once, he understood. Ilya turned back to Vasylenko, who was smiling. "Why?"

"Consider it a precaution," Vasylenko said softly. "I have no doubt that you will do exactly what you have promised. But I also know how I would be tempted to act in such a situation. I would play along while I could, waiting for the right moment to take my revenge. This is a safeguard. If you flee, or do anything else to upset the plan, we can kill the girl at any time."

Ilya kept his face still. "What makes you think this girl means anything to me?"

"Only a hunch," Vasylenko replied. "I suspect that you have one weakness. You still think of yourself as a righteous man. And you would not allow this woman, whose life you have already complicated, to die through no fault of her own." The old man paused. "In any case, there's one sure way to find out."

At these words, the guard at the windowsill bent down again over the rifle, his eye at the scope. He adjusted his aim slightly, then waited in silence, his finger resting lightly on the trigger. Through the window, Ilya could just make out the figure of Maddy in the garden below. She had a guidebook in her hands.

Vasylenko looked back at Ilya, his eyes full of dark humor. "The choice is yours. Life or death. Which shall it be?"

32

Maddy had bought the guidebook at the airport that morning, and as she opened it now, she noticed for the first time that its cover bore a picture of the palace in whose garden she was seated. Glancing over her shoulder, she turned to the inside cover, on which she had been secretly taking notes. "Are you ready?"

"Yes," Powell said over the cell phone. "Tell me who you've seen so far."

Maddy shifted the phone to her other hand. She was sitting on a stone bench on one of the terraces, alongside a fountain decked with reclining nudes. Upon their arrival at the palace, she had declined to join the others on the tour. They had been gone for some time, led no doubt by Tarkovsky himself, who took a great deal of interest in the history of this part of Transylvania.

She looked over her notes. "There are something like thirty guests scheduled to travel on the yacht, with roughly the same number of crew. I've seen about half of them. The rest will meet us at Constanta tomorrow. I have a list of names if you want it. Are you ready?"

The voice of Adam Hill came over the line. "I'm ready whenever you are."

Maddy quickly ran down the list. "Tarkovsky and his wife, of course. They're separated, but she's here for the sake of appearances. His daughter, Nina, and her tutor. Elena Usova, Orlov, and the security team."

"Got it," Adam said. She could hear the sound of typing in the background. "Go on."

"There are several board members from Tarkovsky's foundation. Lord Norwood, the former foreign secretary, is supposed to join us in Constanta. I've also seen Sir George Holder, the banker, and Paul Douglas, the former ambassador to Russia, along with their wives. There are at least three executives from Argo and two founding members of Polyneft with their spouses or girlfriends."

Powell came back on the line again. "Good work. But you need to be discreet. You're giving us useful information, but it won't be worth it if Tarkovsky finds out what you're doing."

"I know," Maddy said, reflecting that Powell had no idea what she was doing here at all. "Anyway, I'm not sure how close I can get. I expect that people like me will be kept away from the others."

This statement was addressed to Powell, but it was also intended for someone else. The cell phone she was using was the one she had been given by her abductors, and although she had heard nothing from them since her departure, she suspected that every word she spoke was likely to be overheard.

She had waited until she was at the airport to tell Powell where she was going. Powell had been surprised, but he had also recognized that it represented a rare opportunity. He had cautioned her to remain in the background but to learn whatever she could about the guests, in hopes that it would reveal something about Tarkovsky's intentions in the Black Sea.

Maddy remembered that he had also promised to do something else. "Have you had a chance to look into what I asked about?"

Adam spoke up. "I have. We've been checking out the name Tarkovsky mentioned. I don't know if you've looked at Gleb Boky yet—"

Maddy glanced back at the palace. "Only what I was able to find before I left. He was an officer of the secret police, right?"

"Among other things," Adam said. "Boky was a Ukrainian revolutionary who became a leading organizer for the Bolsheviks. Later, he helped orchestrate the Red Terror, and he was one of the major architects of the gulag system."

Powell spoke up. "My father kept a file on Boky, who went on to run the secret police in Turkestan. The locals were terrified of him, saying that he ate dog's meat and drank human blood, but he was also a gifted cryptographer who developed ciphers for the revolutionists. After the civil war, he became the chief code breaker of the security services, as the head of what was called the Special Section, which focused on cryptography, surveillance, and running the concentration camps."

"I know," Maddy said. "I saw most of this online. But why would Tarkovsky care?"

"Because Boky was obsessed with Shambhala," Adam said. "Along with its other activities, the Special Section was dedicated to investigating the occult. It was located in a secret building, apart from the Lubyanka, and looked at ways of influencing society on a large scale, through the camps, obviously, but also on a psychological level.

Among other things, it researched truth serum, hypnosis, and what we'd consider occult techniques, like mind control."

In Adam's voice, Maddy heard a trace of enthusiasm of a kind that she had last heard many years ago, in the voice of a young man who was now dead. "But why would they waste time on this?"

"From their point of view, it wasn't a waste of time at all," Powell said. "Nearly every intelligence agency has looked into such phenomena. It's a question of competitive advantage."

"And this is where Shambhala comes in," Adam continued. "Boky's lead investigator was a man named Alexander Barchenko, a writer and occultist who was convinced that Shambhala was a real place somewhere in Central Asia. According to him, it was a hidden scientific community of immense power, founded on a mathematically precise system of occult knowledge that could control minds, read thoughts, and predict the future. And he managed to convince both Boky and Felix Dzerzhinsky, the head of the Cheka, to sponsor his research."

Powell broke in. "These were not what you'd call fanciful or sentimental men. I doubt that either believed in Shambhala itself. But they might have thought it worthwhile to investigate traditional forms of mind control, which Barchenko claimed could be found in the East."

"And he did his best to prove it," Adam said. "At first, he tried to organize an expedition to find Shambhala itself, but it was canceled at the last minute. Instead, he and Boky began to look into occult groups closer to home. It's unclear what the results were, but if you look at the history of Russian intelligence, you find references to experiments in mass hypnosis and the use of Tibetan potions to extract confessions. And in the end, their work was transferred to the Institute of Experimental Medicine, the same laboratory that investigated truth drugs and poisons."

Maddy, who had been taking notes on the back page of her guidebook, felt the tips of her fingers grow cold. "What kind of poisons?"

The men on the other end fell silent. "Poisons like the kind we've both seen before," Powell said at last. "These impulses all arise from the same source. There's always been an affinity in Russia between poison and black magic. It doesn't surprise me to see it again here. The real question is why Tarkovsky has taken an interest in this, and why he would mention it to you—"

As Powell spoke, Maddy heard a familiar voice, carried over a distance in the mountain air. Turning, she saw Tarkovsky emerging from the palace, his wife and daughter to either side. Tarkovsky's wife, Ludmilla, whom she had met only briefly, was tall, beautiful, and severe, confirming her suspicion that the oligarch had a definite type with which he liked to surround himself.

She continued to watch Tarkovsky, who was followed shortly thereafter by Elena and the members of his security team. "I can think of one reason. Shambhala is a symbol of social change, or spiritual transformation, which Boky was trying to turn into a science. Tarkovsky is interested in the same thing. As he sees it, the world is about to enter a new era, and he wants to play a role in whatever is coming. It makes sense that he'd be interested in the history of social control in Russia. But I still don't know what he intends to do with it."

Even as she said this, Maddy saw that the oligarch's assistant was waving at her, motioning for her to join the rest of the group. Maddy spoke quietly into her phone. "Listen, I need to go."

"All right," Powell said. "We'll keep working here. Call us again when you can."

"I will." Maddy hung up. Rising from the bench, she wondered what her eavesdroppers had made of this conversation, in which she had left her true thoughts unspoken. Tarkovsky's interest in these matters was only part of a larger picture, one that she had gradually begun to trace, on her own, through the files and records in which it could dimly be glimpsed. It was a story that went back decades, but it gained direction and purpose in the last three years. And if Tarkovsky had found himself drawn to such forces, it came as no surprise that they had also been drawn to him.

Maddy began to head toward the others. As she did, her eye was momentarily caught by a cottage on the hill above the clearing, about five hundred yards away. Then she went to join the rest of the group.

Back in the house in the trees, standing before the window on the second floor, Ilya watched Maddy leave.

At his side, the man at the tripod drew back from the rifle. Vasylenko, who had been observing them in silence for the past minute, spoke at last. "Have you made your decision, Ilyuha?"

Ilya did not turn away from the window. "And what happens when this is over?"

"I let her go," Vasylenko said. "I have nothing to gain

from her death, once our work is complete. And I have no fear that she'll talk."

Looking away from the view, Ilya turned to Vasylenko. "How can you be sure?"

Vasylenko only rose from the edge of the bed. "That isn't your concern. You'll find out soon enough."

33

In the bedroom of the house in Hackney Wick, Wolfe could see several distinct sprays of blood. The bodies themselves had been taken to the mortuary, leaving behind only the thick stench of decomposition, as well as a sour smell, like ammonia, that floated unaccountably above it all.

At her side, the scenes of crime officer produced a set of forensic photographs. "Two bodies. One was Andrew Ferris, the driver who was taken hostage. The other has been identified as Ivan Sturza. You've seen his file?"

Wolfe studied the photos with a connoisseur's eye. "Moldovan national with a Romanian passport. Petty criminal record. Based on video from the riots, he was one of the men at the prison break."

She pointed to the picture on top, which displayed two bodies, one tied to a chair, the other slumped awkwardly across the other. "Ferris, the hostage, was killed first. Sturza was shot as he was bending over the other man's body. And I don't think he was expecting it."

"That's consistent with our analysis," the officer said. "I spoke with the lab in Lambeth. The bullet was smooth, with no rifling, which implies it was fired from a reactivated gun, possibly a converted starter pistol. And they used ammonia to remove trace evidence from the rest of the scene."

"They did the same thing in the van on Mare Street," Wolfe said. "We should check the database for similar crimes. What else?"

"One partial shoeprint in the blood. The men in the house wore smooth gloves. Plenty of latex smears, but no prints. With one exception."

"You mentioned that earlier." Wolfe headed for the door. "Let's take a look."

She left the room, glad to move away from the smell of death, and went back into the hallway, keeping to the approach path. The house itself was small and depressing, abandoned, like so many others, in the recent downturn, which had pushed repossession rates to their highest level in ten years.

At the center of the kitchen stood a warped table with two plastic chairs. The table was covered with gray smears of fingerprint powder, as well as a pair of white cards that marked where two glasses had been found and bagged. Wolfe pointed to the nearest card. "Here?"

The officer nodded. "The only set of prints we found. Clear impressions on one of the glasses. And they belong to Ilya Severin."

Wolfe frowned. "He must have removed one of his gloves. I wonder why—"

Looking down, she saw something else. On the linoleum floor by one of the chairs, in which Ilya had evidently been seated, there was a worn dishrag, apparently taken from the counter by the sink. Picking it up with one gloved hand, Wolfe saw that it had been tied into a loose knot.

She set the rag on the table and carefully undid it. There was nothing inside.

The knot reminded her of something, but before she could put it into words, her partner entered. "I spoke with the sergeant," Asthana said. "They're checking cameras nearby. Ferris was a contractor, but he was still an employee of Her Majesty's prisons, so they're taking the murder to heart."

"Then we'll leave them to it," Wolfe said. After thanking the officer for his time, she and Asthana left the house together, moving past the blue incident tape strung across the entrance. Arriving at their car, Asthana got behind the wheel as Wolfe went over her notes. "I want to try Hughes again. Maybe word of the murders will rattle him further. And then I want to go after Dancy."

"I'll take care of it," Asthana said, heading south on the trunk road. "You see anything useful back there?"

Wolfe thought about mentioning the knotted dishrag, which had continued to stick in her mind, but finally decided against it. "I keep wondering about the resources involved. At least six men on the outside. Vehicles, weapons, a safe house. This takes time and money. But I still can't figure out why."

Asthana did not seem troubled by this. "Vasylenko didn't want to die in prison."

"But that isn't enough to justify the risk. Vasylenko doesn't have the authority he once did in London. The younger generation isn't going to blindly follow a man just because he has the right tattoos."

"Granted," Asthana said. "But a man like Vasylenko can be useful in other ways. He ran extortion and weapons rackets for years. There's institutional knowledge there. It's good to have a man like this around."

"But you don't need to break him out of prison to get the benefit of his experience. It's easy to run operations from Belmarsh. That's what a *vor* does. If they broke him out, it had to have been for a specific task—"

Even as she spoke, she began to glimpse an answer. When you looked at Vasylenko, you saw an old man, but to the right pair of eyes, he was something more. The tattoos on his body weren't arbitrary symbols but the visible signs of the life he had led. His mind, too, was full of signs that had never been written down. And even if you could pass them along to others, they were still only words, at least in the absence of the man whose history gave them meaning.

All these thoughts flashed through her mind in a fraction of a second. Wolfe turned to Asthana. "There's one thing a thief can do that nobody else can. He can talk to other thieves."

Asthana seemed absorbed by the traffic. "I'm not sure I understand what you mean."

"Vasylenko is useful only as a symbol. An icon in the form of a man. He can open doors, guarantee safe passage, draw on the full resources of the brotherhood. But only if he's there in person."

Asthana looked unconvinced. "But you said yourself that the thieves are losing their power in London."

"But not in other countries." Wolfe turned to the last page of her notes. "Ivan Sturza, the dead man, was born in Moldova. That's a country where the old ways still have force. If you want to get something done, you need a *vor* on your side. And if you don't have one already—"

"—you bring him in," Asthana finished. "All right. Vasylenko isn't useful here, but they can take him someplace where he's still valuable. He won't stay in London. But why bring Ilya?"

"I don't know," Wolfe said. "Maybe they have something special in mind."

As she said this, it occurred to her that if Ilya was involved, it could mean only one thing. And she wondered for the first time, with a sinking heart, if Ilya had fired the shots that killed those two men in Hackney.

She was about to say more when her cell phone rang. As she dug the phone out of her purse, her mind continued to follow the thread from before. The next step was to look at the map of Europe, not by country, but by regions of power that had little to do with political boundaries. Somewhere at the heart of that map, she thought, was where Ilya and Vasylenko had gone.

Her cell phone displayed an unknown number. She answered it. "Rachel Wolfe."

The voice on the other end was uncharacteristically nervous. "Wolfe, this is Owen Dancy. I hear you've been trying to reach me. . . ."

34

The following morning, a town car brought Maddy and Elena to the Port of Tomis. Maddy had overslept, having spent much of the night going over the material from her conversation with Powell, only to be awakened by a call from Tarkovsky's assistant. Throwing on her clothes, she had packed and rushed to the lobby, where she discovered that the others had already left.

When they arrived at the port in Constanta, Maddy found herself at a pretty marina. Leaving their car, they headed toward the berth from which they were scheduled to embark. The day was bright and warm, the salt wind blowing her hair to one side as she hurried to follow Elena. Up ahead, she saw a cluster of guests in fashionable casual wear, standing before a sleek white limousine tender.

As they approached the passerelle, a uniformed deckhand with epaulets came up to take their bags, saying that they would be departing in a few minutes. Maddy watched as he stowed their suitcases in the compartment in the stern, then saw that Elena had moved off without a word, going to greet a pair of new arrivals who were standing up the quay.

Maddy took a step back, pretending to look out at the water while really studying the crowd. She couldn't see Tarkovsky, his family, or any of the board members. The executives from Argo and their wives stood apart from the others, and a member of the security team was stationed by the passerelle, his eyes lighting briefly on her face as he observed the scene in silence.

Near the water, standing by himself, was a man who had caught her attention earlier. He was fairly young, perhaps in his late twenties, and a touch on the heavy side. With his hands in the pockets of his jacket and a pair of white headphones in his ears, he seemed less than comfortable here. Maddy had learned a few useful facts about him already, and as she regarded him now, he struck her as a member of a type that she understood very well.

As the others began to board, Maddy climbed onto the tender, where she was shown into a cabin with two rows of facing seats cushioned in nude leather, the skylight open to the sun overhead. She made a show of looking outside until the man with the white earphones had taken a seat at the end of the row. Without glancing over, she sat down beside him, her camera in hand.

A second later, Maddy caught his eye, as if by chance. "Hi there. I'm Maddy."

In response, the man removed his headphones and reached out for a handshake. Aside from a few extra pounds, he was pleasant enough to look at, with a broad open face and a hint of dark stubble. "I'm Rahim. Nice to meet you. So what brings you to this ship of fools?"

"Good question," Maddy said. "The short answer is that I work for Tarkovsky. You?"

"You might say I work for him, too, in a way." Rahim looked out toward the quay as the deckhand cast off the stern lines and climbed into the cockpit. "I was on the yacht design team."

Maddy knew this already, but she made a show of interest. "Oh, so you're an engineer?"

"Not exactly," Rahim said. "I coded the onboard systems. Not the most glamorous part of the process, but still—"

He paused as the tender began to ease out of the marina. As they pulled away, Maddy saw a line of people watching silently from shore. The rest of the passengers were looking out as well, the conversation momentarily halting as they moved past the jetty. Then the tender opened up, its diesel engines rising to a roar, and they headed at full throttle into the open water.

Maddy gazed out at the sea. They were moving roughly parallel to the shoreline, the spray rising to either side as the boat accelerated, cutting like a knife through the waves. To the north lay a line of crowded gray beach, a narrow strip of land between the sea and the lake beyond.

A moment later, Maddy turned to the window across from her and saw the yacht itself anchored in the distance, recognizable by the four petals of the lotus on its prow. Her first reaction, oddly, was one of disappointment. The yacht was large, but it was not as impressive as she had expected, with five decks, a vacant helipad at one end, and a davit and crane at the other. Seeing that it was only a ship like any other, she felt some of her apprehensions fall away. "It's not as big as I thought."

At her side, Rahim laughed. "That isn't the yacht. It's the shadow boat. We converted it from a decommissioned oil vessel. It travels with us, carrying spare fuel and a few extra toys." Glancing over her shoulder, he pointed to the view from the prow. "*That's* the yacht."

Maddy turned, noticing that most of the other guests were already looking in that direction. When the ship in the distance finally came into view, she could only stare in disbelief. “Oh my God.”

She forgot her camera entirely as they drew closer to the yacht, which had been built by Fincantieri in the Muggiano Yard near La Spezia, and from there had traveled up the Mediterranean to the Aegean, through the Strait of the Dardanelles to the Sea of Marmara, and then through the Bosporus Strait to the Black Sea, a voyage of over a thousand miles to where it was waiting now.

The yacht was a monster. With its massive profile of six decks, it looked like a vast wedding cake on the water, its superstructure a blinding white, a helicopter perched on its highest level, visible past the aerials that crowned it like a pair of giant antlers. Yet it was more than just a luxury vessel. Looking up at it, Maddy received an overwhelming impression of power and strength, one that only increased as they drew closer to the ship, the tender dwarfed by its size.

Rahim was grinning. “Four hundred and twelve feet long, with a beam of seventy feet. Not quite in the top ten of the largest yachts ever built. But it’s a gorgeous ship all the same—”

Maddy was still staring up at the hull. “You’ll have to show me around sometime.”

Around her, the cabin grew dark as they passed into the *Rigden*’s shadow. The yacht loomed above them as they approached the raised hydraulic door of the tender bay, six feet above the waterline, where a boarding platform had been lowered. As she watched, the tender slowed and positioned itself so it could be tied up by the waiting deckhands. The engines fell silent. A moment later, the passerelle was extended and the guests prepared to disembark.

Rahim and Maddy, who were seated at the end, were among the last to leave the tender. She rose, feeling the boat rocking slightly beneath her feet, and made her way forward. For a moment, as she was about to mount the passerelle, she hesitated, feeling the immensity of the yacht waiting to swallow her whole, as if it were not a ship but a prison. A second later, she crossed onto the platform, breathing in the salt air, and found herself on the yacht.

Maddy looked around the tender bay, a gleaming space filled with water scooters and kayaks in aluminum cradles. At one end stood the expedition tender, slightly smaller but sturdier than the boat in which they had arrived. Before she could explore any further, she was ushered politely up the stairs to the deck above. Up ahead, she saw that Rahim had joined the rest of the design team, the members of which were looking around, as if in a dream, at the yacht they had helped to will into reality.

Following the others, Maddy emerged onto the boards of the aft deck, blinking in the sudden light. Lined up before her and the other passengers was the crew, smiling and standing at friendly attention. The deckhands wore formal shirts with epaulets, while the stewardesses had shoulder boards with silver crescents. Each had a white lotus embroidered on the left breast.

A woman's voice came from her side. "Miss, would you like to give me your shoes?"

Maddy turned and saw a stewardess, not far from her own age, holding out a pair of slippers. She slid off her pumps and handed them over, taking the slippers in exchange. The shoes, she saw, went into one of two baskets on the deck, in which more than a few red soles were visible.

Putting on the slippers, she moved quickly past the line of crew members, who smiled at her as she went by. Most of the guests were already gathered on the aft deck. Tarkovsky was standing near the railing in a linen suit, a glass of something in his hand, his wife and daughter at his side.

As she saw him, Tarkovsky noticed her as well. He gave her a nod, his eyes on hers. Maddy stared back, feeling, as if for the first time, the full insanity of what she had done, and realized that someone was offering her a glass of champagne. She took it without thinking, managing to resist the urge to drink it all at once. Then she went forward into the sunshine of the yacht.

35

On the roof of the house in Leova, there was a wooden pigeon loft with two pens, one for paired couples, the other for young birds after weaning. An old man stood before the loft with a crested pigeon in his hands, stroking its black neck and tail. Hearing the sound of footsteps, he paused, then put the bird gently back through the trap and eased the door shut.

From over his shoulder came a man's voice. "Peace and health to all honest thieves."

The old man, whose name was Dolgan, turned to face the two figures standing behind him. Only one of them was familiar, although he knew perfectly well who the other man was. "And death to all informers."

As Dolgan came up to kiss Vasylenko on the cheek, Ilya regarded him from a few steps away. He was in his late seventies, dressed in a white shirt and flannel trousers, his teeth stained dark by tea. His posture was slightly stooped, the mark of a man who had spent much of his life in prison, where you kept your head down to avoid knocking it on the bunk above. "And this is the Scythian, I see."

Vasylenko stood aside, allowing Ilya to come forward. "Yes. He has come to pay his respects."

Dolgan studied Ilya's face. "Do you know anything about birds, my son?"

"Only a little." Ilya indicated the loft with a nod of his head. "These are the Armenian breed. They look like strong tumblers."

"Yes, they are," Dolgan said proudly. "We can have *chifir*. Please, come with me."

Moving slowly but without a cane, the old man headed for the stairs that led down from the roof. The weather was cool but pleasant, as it had been since their arrival in Moldova. After escorting them here, Bogdan and the others had returned to the lodging house. On an errand like this, only one man could accompany Vasylenko, and the lot had fallen naturally to Ilya.

Ilya followed the two older men downstairs, closing the door to the roof behind him. They accompanied Dolgan to a table and chairs with a view of the yard outside. The front door had been removed from its hinges, indicating that all honest men were welcome, and that Dolgan owned nothing of his own. As a saint, one of the few criminals allowed to touch money, he wielded tremendous authority, and he was the only man who could get them what they needed now.

When they had each taken a seat, a girl emerged from the kitchen, bringing the ingredients for *chifir* without being asked. She was young and rather plain, her dark hair pulled back from her face, and she did not look at any of the men at the table as she set down the tray and withdrew.

In the fireplace, water was bubbling in a blackened pot. Dolgan gestured toward the saucepan. "Make us some tea."

Ilya rose, knowing that he was being subtly tested. He

extinguished the fire, then added leaves of black tea from a tin. Covering the pot, he wrapped it quickly in a towel to keep in the heat, then returned to the table.

As he sat down, he saw that Vasylenko had lit a cigarette. Taking a short puff, the *vor* passed it to Dolgan, who did the same and returned it. He fixed his sparkling eyes on Ilya. "Your skin is quite pale," Dolgan said. "And unmarked. I find it strange to see a man like this in my house."

Ilya was used to the question implied here. "My skin wasn't always this clean."

"I understand." Dolgan took a pull of smoke and passed the cigarette to Vasylenko. "I know your history. You haven't always been at home in the brotherhood. May I ask what changed your mind?"

"I lost my freedom," Ilya said. "It reminded me how sacred a man's liberty can be."

"A careful response." Dolgan turned his eyes to Vasylenko. "And you are willing to present him to me?"

Vasylenko nodded. "I am. Even if I did not trust his loyalty, I trust his good sense. He knows what needs to be done."

"A quality rare in the younger generation," Dolgan said. "Such men don't always understand the sacrifices that must be made. Although perhaps, before long, even the young will learn this as well—"

Dolgan trailed off, looking out the door at the yard. Ilya wondered what he was thinking. He knew something of the sacrifices that the saint had mentioned, which continued to be felt by the brotherhood, even as those who had struck the original bargain died out one by one.

Years ago, in the gulag, the intelligence officers responsible for maintaining order in the camps had made alliances with the imprisoned criminals and thieves, who had been used to keep other prisoners in line. In the end, however, the arrangement had cut both ways. The thieves had taught the state new forms of violence, but they, too, had been subtly transformed.

Ilya knew that the two old men seated before him now had only been children when these deals were negotiated, but they had inherited these arrangements when they came of age. It was easy to blame them for having lied to their followers, but in his more honest moments, Ilya was aware that he was only in this position because of the choices he himself had made.

As he glanced into the kitchen, however, and saw the girl at the stove, he reminded himself that there were also those who had been drawn into this world through no fault of their own. He had seen another through the rifle scope at Peles Castle. And even if he could no longer protect himself, he could at least make sure that the innocent did not suffer for his mistakes.

The tea was ready. Rising from his chair, Ilya went back to the fireplace and used the towel to raise the lid of the saucepan, seeing that the leaves inside were no longer visible on the water. Taking the saucepan back to the table, he poured the tea through the strainer into the pot, reserving the leaves for later, and finally emptied the *chifir* into a heavy iron mug.

As the two old men watched, Ilya raised the mug to his lips and took three sips, feeling the effects at once. When he was done, he passed it to Dolgan, who did the same before handing the mug to Vasylenko.

They sat this way, drinking in silence, for some time. At last Dolgan, who had taken the last few sips, rose and carried the mug into the kitchen. Going to the sink, he rinsed it out and put it away. As he did, he spoke a few words to the girl at the stove, who went at once into the next room.

When Dolgan returned to the table, he seemed to have come to a decision. "I can see you as far as Yalta. There is a person there who can furnish you with what you require, as long as you travel under my protection. However, before you go, you will need a sign of safe conduct."

As Dolgan spoke, the girl returned to the main room. In her hands, she was carrying a small wooden box. She set it down on the table before Dolgan, who undid the latch and raised the lid.

Vasylenko was the first to speak. Both he and the saint were looking at Ilya. "Well?"

Ilya considered the contents of the box. Inside, there was a set of needles and a coil tattoo machine.

He regarded them for a long moment. Then he turned to the others. "I'm ready."

36

"I had not intended to come forward, but now I have no choice," Owen Dancy said, accepting a drink from a silent waiter. "I've served as Vasylenko's solicitor since his arrest. Last year, he informed me that he and Ilya had reached an accommodation. And he asked me to assist Ilya in preparing his defense."

Wolfe studied the solicitor, who was sweating heavily despite the air-conditioning in the club. "But Ilya was planning to cooperate with the police. That could only have hurt Vasylenko's case."

"Not necessarily." Dancy took a sip of whiskey. "Ilya was prepared to give evidence that Vasylenko had played no part in any criminal enterprise. He was ready to implicate other organized crime figures, most of them deceased or serving long sentences. But not Vasylenko."

Wolfe looked into the solicitor's broad face, searching for any sign of dissimulation. "But you must have known this wasn't true."

Dancy only gave her a weak smile. "I knew that it would help one of my clients."

They were seated before a bow window at a gentlemen's club in Westminster. Women, she had been told, were allowed only in the visitors' room, with its deep leather chairs and reading lamps. A hall at the rear led to the overnight accommodations upstairs. It was there that Dancy had evidently been residing for the past few days, claiming that he felt safer here than anywhere else, as if an assassin might hesitate to violate the membership rules.

Wolfe still had her doubts about why Ilya would have agreed to cooperate with Vasylenko, but she decided to let this pass. "Why did you schedule the hearings for the same day?"

Dancy looked as if he had been expecting the question. "It was necessary to schedule Ilya's hearing as soon as possible, for the sake of Vasylenko's appeal. As it turned out, there was only one date that was suitable. I had planned to attend Ilya's hearing myself and have an associate file an extension for Vasylenko. But I had no idea that an escape was in the offing. No compensation of any kind could possibly make up for the damage to my reputation."

Wolfe saw the solicitor touch his club tie, evidently unconsciously. "So why come to us now?"

"Regardless of what you may think, I have not been standing idle," Dancy said. "And I have concluded that Ilya is far more dangerous than I once believed. I was ready to defend him against the charge of murdering Lermontov, but there are other incidents that are impossible to overlook. The death of Anzor Archvadze, for one, whom Ilya poisoned because of his interference in the illegal art trade. And it appears that he may have killed another man at Belmarsh."

Wolfe stared at the solicitor, whose face was bright with perspiration. "What are you talking about?"

"A prisoner was murdered last week," Dancy said halt-ingly. "He was brought to the infirmary suffering from acute respiratory arrest. The toxicology report indicates that he received a massive dose of nicotine. Such a murder would have required a great deal of ingenuity, of course—"

Wolfe forced herself to keep her voice level. "So what makes you think it was Ilya?"

"He was seen with the dead man shortly before he died. I'm told that traces of nicotine were found in a syringe on the waste ground not far from his cell. It appears that he would have had access to all the necessary materials. And we both know he had the expertise."

Wolfe saw that it was impossible to deny this, but part of her still resisted the implication. "But why would he kill this man?"

"The victim was part of Vasylenko's circle. My understanding is that he had offered to inform on illegal activity within the prison, perhaps including the escape, but was killed before he could talk. It's also possible that Ilya got rid of him to create an opening. You see, I believe that Ilya wanted to get close to Vasylenko, not the other way around. Which means we need to consider the possibility that he, and not Vasylenko, was the one driving the prison break."

Wolfe began to grow angry, although she would have found it hard to explain why. "And what makes you say that?"

Dancy finished his drink, the glass rattling against the table as he set it down. "I knew Vasylenko well. And what I concluded was that his power was long gone. But the more I reflect on Ilya, the more he frightens me. I suspect that what he wants, more than anything else, is revenge. And if so, he may have seen Vasylenko as his best way of getting close to the men who betrayed him."

With visible effort, Dancy rose from his chair. "I've told you everything I can. The authorities at Belmarsh will confirm the rest. If you need anything else, you know where to find me."

He left the room. Wolfe let him go. For a moment, she remained alone at the window, the solicitor's last few words, which were so close to her own fears, echoing in her brain. Looking down at the seat of his chair, she watched as the impression of his heavy frame slowly disappeared.

An hour later, she was at the office, on the phone with Powell, who agreed when she asked for his thoughts. "Vasylenko might still be useful under the right circumstances. Have you read the files I sent?"

Wolfe looked at the stack of folders on her desk, nearly two feet high, that had been delivered the day before. "I'm afraid not."

"You should," Powell said. "My father spent years at Thames House, tracing the relationship between organized crime and the intelligence services. There's one file in particular you should study. It's an orange folder with the image of a double eagle on the cover—"

Seeing the folder in question in one of the stacks, she extracted it with some difficulty. "Yes, I have it."

"Give it a read when you can. It's a collection of what we know about the symbols of the *vory*. Tattoos, codes, ritual questions and responses. These are practical tools, you understand, a means of transmitting secure messages without words. If you send a broken knife to another thief, it means death is on the way. It's called a throw, a kind of symbolic shorthand, and it's precisely the sort of thing that only someone like Vasylenko would know."

Flipping through the folder, Wolfe saw a list of these

significant objects, written in an old man's spidery handwriting. "I'll take a look. You said you had something else to tell me?"

"I did," Powell said. "I'd like you to review some material based on something Tarkovsky told Maddy. She's looking into it now, although I haven't spoken with her since she left with him for Sochi—"

It took Wolfe a second to connect this statement with what she knew about the oligarch's departure, which had been widely covered by the press. "Wait a minute. She's on Tarkovsky's yacht?"

"It's strange, I know," Powell said. "And it wasn't my idea. But she's aware that she needs to be careful. There's more about this in the report. We can talk it over at the wedding, if not before."

At the mention of the wedding, Wolfe glanced at her partner's empty desk. Asthana had taken the rest of the week off, ostensibly to prepare for the ceremony on Saturday, which seemed to belong to another order of reality. All the same, there was no escaping their other concerns, so in the meantime, Asthana had been persuaded to take the lead in the hunt for the informant.

When Wolfe hung up a moment later, she realized that she was exhausted. After listening to Dancy, she no longer knew what she believed, about Ilya or anything else. All the same, she also knew that the solicitor, or his clients, might have good reason to place the blame for the escape on Ilya's shoulders.

She was about to put the file aside when she was struck by another thought. Looking at the list of symbolic objects that thieves used to send a message, she ran her eye quickly down the column. An apple cut in half meant it was time to divide the loot. A piece of bread wrapped in cloth said the police were closing in. And a piece of rope or fabric with a knot in it—

Wolfe read the words, then shut the folder and sat back at her desk. She remembered the scrap of cloth that she had found at the house in Hackney Wick. It had been left under Ilya's chair, tied in a loose knot. Most likely it was nothing. But she couldn't help but wonder.

Because according to the file, it meant: *I'm not responsible for what you've heard.*

37

"This is the finest yacht I've ever seen," Rahim said, looking out at the view from the sun deck. "Tarkovsky wanted something special. Fincantieri had just begun to move into megayachts, so they were eager to show off, but commissions had fallen through after the downturn. Tarkovsky acquired a ship that was under development when the buyer withdrew, but it still took three years to complete."

Maddy thought briefly of what else Tarkovsky had been doing three years ago, when their paths had nearly intersected, and wondered if this yacht was a part of the same story. She and Rahim were seated in a pair of deck chairs at the highest point of the ship, a cantilevered umbrella shielding them from the sun. In the distance lay the coast of Odessa, startlingly clear in the morning light, as the yacht passed slowly through the waters of the Black Sea. "So what did he want?"

Rahim reached for his glass of mineral water, only to find it empty. Before he could say a word, a stewardess had already appeared with a fresh bottle. "Some owners charter their yachts for most of the year, while others conduct much of their lives on board. Tarkovsky is one of the latter. He wanted to keep an eye on his interests in the Black Sea and elsewhere, so he had some unusual specifications. If you don't mind taking a walk, I can show you."

"I'd love that, actually." Maddy rose from her chair, her dress sticking lightly to her back, and followed Rahim to the starboard side. She had studied the yacht's layout very carefully. Below her feet was the owner's deck with Tarkovsky's suite and separate staterooms for his family. Beneath it lay the bridge deck with the wheelhouse, the library, and the oligarch's office, where Tarkovsky had spent much of the voyage meeting with executives from Argo and Polyneft.

Maddy had spent most of her own time on the two following decks, which housed the guest cabins, salons, and formal dining room. After this came the lower deck, including the galley, crew quarters, and tender bay, and finally the bottom deck, with its laundry, storage rooms, and eight diesel engines.

Rahim pointed over the railing toward the hull, which rose in a wall of gleaming white above the waves below. "You can't really tell from here, but this yacht is an ice-class vessel. It has more watertight bulkheads, thicker plate, and stronger scantlings, so it can sail through polar ice if necessary. It's designed for someone who wants to be ready for anything. Alarms, polycarbonate armor plating, and a few things I can't talk about. The latest accessories from Bogotá, shall we say—"

Maddy saw that he was showing off for her benefit. "But that's true of anyone who has the money to afford a ship like this. You make it sound as if Tarkovsky was more interested in something else."

Rahim turned away from the view. "Again, it isn't

something I can talk about. But if I were concerned about what the future had in store, not just for myself but for the rest of the world, this is where I'd want to be."

"That's all very well," Maddy said. "But what happens when you run out of gas?"

Rahim smiled. "Even there, you have options. Let me show you what I mean."

She followed him down to the main atrium, where a spiral staircase wound around the elevator shaft, lined with silver leaf. In the salon, a pair of white flower arrangements in Swarovski vases flanked a large striped canvas, which Maddy had confirmed was a real Gerhard Richter. From the music room came the sound of a piano played with deft but impersonal hands, and as Maddy listened, she wondered how Tarkovsky's daughter felt about her father's intentions.

Rahim went to a touchscreen panel on the wall by the stairs. Maddy, who had seen identical screens in every salon, knew that they marked Rahim's greatest contribution to the yacht's design. Anyone on board, he had explained, could use them to dim the lights or check the weather, but with level-four access, one could control the entire ship from any point on the yacht.

Entering a code of four digits for the highest access level, Rahim called up a fuel report and pointed to the chart on the screen. "See, the main fuel tank has a capacity of a quarter of a million gallons. There's another hundred thousand gallons on the shadow boat. At our current speed, we can go more than eight thousand nautical miles without refueling."

Maddy studied the numbers politely. "And if the crew decides to abandon ship?"

"You downsize to the shadow boat," Rahim said. "Or,

in the most extreme scenario, to the expedition boat in the tender bay. There's enough there to last Tarkovsky and a crew of three for months."

Maddy laughed. "You make it sound like he's preparing for the end of the world."

Rahim restored the touchscreen to its basic level of access. "If you had his money, wouldn't you?"

Maddy only smiled. For a moment, she felt oddly tender toward this awkward young man, who had no real idea of what she had survived. "Until the grid goes down, I say we enjoy ourselves. Maybe I'll see you at dinner?"

"I'd like that," Rahim said. Maddy smiled again and turned away. Feeling him watching her as she left the lounge, she wondered what he would have thought if he had known the truth about what had brought her here, or that she had been looking carefully as he punched in his access code. She had managed to catch the first three digits: a one, a seven, and a zero. And although she had not seen the fourth, she had a good idea of what it might be.

As Maddy moved down the central companionway, she passed a stewardess, who had changed from her formal uniform into a polo shirt and shorts. The stewardess flashed her a smile, which Maddy returned with some uneasiness. Wherever she went, there was always someone on guest watch, keeping notes on what she liked for breakfast or how she took her coffee. For most passengers, such attention would be gratifying, but it also made it hard to go anywhere unobserved.

Heading down the corridor, Maddy reached her own cabin, which was one of eight staterooms on this level. Before unlocking the door, she knocked, but there was no answer.

She went inside, closing the door behind her. There

was no sign of Elena. The room itself was immaculately furnished, with a view of the water not quite as spectacular as those in the other cabins but still sufficiently breathtaking. In her absence, the beds had been made and the laundry taken away.

Maddy went into the bathroom, where her toiletries had been subtly straightened beside the gold fixtures of the sink, next to a basket with ten different kinds of shampoo. Pulling her dress over her head, she ran the water in the tub, and she was about to undress the rest of the way when she heard the sound of her phone.

She ran back into the stateroom and opened the drawer of her bedside table. Inside, her phone was ringing. For a moment, she was tempted to ignore it, but she finally answered the call. "Yes?"

The voice on the other end was as distorted as before, and as soon as it spoke, she knew that there would be no real escape, no matter how far they sailed: "It's time for the second part of your obligation."

Maddy closed her eyes. In the bathroom, the water was still running. "Go ahead."

"The yacht will be paying a port of call in Yalta tomorrow," the voice said. "There's someone there you need to meet."

As she listened, Maddy seemed to feel the hood across her face even now. "How will I know who it is?"

"Don't worry about that," the voice said. "It will be someone you've seen before."

38

At a porch on the outskirts of Yalta, the door opened a crack, revealing a woman in her forties. She was dressed in kitchen whites, with short hair and black eyes, and something in her features seemed familiar, although Ilya couldn't quite place it. She looked them over warily. "Yes?"

Bogdan spoke first, giving her the ritual greeting. "Peace in your house, my sister."

"Welcome with honesty," the woman said without warmth. She glanced over at Ilya. "And this one?"

Instead of speaking, Ilya only unbuttoned the cuff of his shirt and rolled up his sleeve. On the inside of his left forearm, still healing, was a blue tattoo of a coiled snake, its body in an intricate knot.

The woman studied the tattoo, her eyes rising briefly to take in Ilya's face. At last, she opened the door all the way, standing aside to let them enter. Once they were inside, she closed and bolted the door behind them, sliding the pistol in her other hand into the pocket of her apron.

Ilya looked around the house. It was simply furnished and scrupulously neat, with a door in the front room opening into a tiny kitchen. Without asking for permission, Bogdan went in, checking the rooms one by one, while Ilya and the woman remained at the door, standing well apart from each other. After a pause, Ilya spoke quietly. "What is your name?"

The woman responded in a flat tone, her eyes still pointed straight ahead. "Katya."

Taking in her thin features and watchful expression, he decided to play a hunch. "You were in Kachanivska?"

The woman turned to him for the first time, a trace of surprise crossing her face. "A long time ago. How did you know?"

"I can tell," Ilya said. "People like us should know how to recognize each other."

She looked away without replying. Ilya said nothing more, although he knew a great deal about women like this. After serving their time in prison, they got a respectable job in a new town, and although they were careful to seem above reproach, they remained in contact with the thieves. They swore never to marry, to give up all family, and to live and die as brides of the brotherhood.

It was easy to pity such women, but Ilya's own position was not so different. Two days before, he had waited patiently as the tattoo of the snake was inscribed on his arm, the girl watching in silence as Dolgan did the work. Afterward, he had looked down at the bandage, on which a few spots of blood were visible, and could only think that he had been marked again, for all his attempts to break free.

A moment later, Bogdan returned to the living room. From his jacket pocket, he took a slip of paper and gave it to Katya. Unfolding it, she read the words in silence, then motioned for them to follow. Going into the kitchen, she opened a door set to one side of the stove and switched on the overhead bulb. She gestured for them to go down the stairs, but Bogdan shook his head. "You first."

Katya complied without a word, with Bogdan and Ilya following close behind. After descending a few steps, Ilya found himself in the cellar. He saw that it was filled almost to the ceiling with neatly stacked boxes on pallets, some of which had clearly been there for years.

A heavy wooden table stood at the far end of the room. Going up to it, Katya asked the two men to set it aside, which they did. Once the table was out of the way, Katya knelt and turned back the square of carpet, revealing a trapdoor, which she unlocked and opened.

Ilya looked into the niche, which breathed a faint odor of metal and grease. In the dim light, he could make out an assortment of Tokarevs, a Kalashnikov, even a few of the old Stechkins. Ignoring these, Katya pulled out a bundle wrapped in a clean cloth. Inside was a pistol in a shoulder holster, which she handed up to Bogdan, who slid it inside his backpack. Rooting around for another moment, she came up with a black plastic box, which she gave to Bogdan as well.

When she was done, Katya closed and locked the trapdoor again. Bogdan tucked the plastic box under his arm. "That's all?"

"That's all I was asked to give." Katya straightened up. "Put the table back, please."

Walking past them, she headed for the stairs. As she went up the steps to the kitchen, something in the way her profile was caught against the light told Ilya, at last, where he had seen her face before. They were the same features, he realized, as those of the girl at Dolgan's house.

When they emerged from the cellar again, they found Katya in the kitchen. "Is there anything else?"

"Food," Bogdan said. "And a place where we can examine our goods in private."

"All right, but quickly," Katya replied. Leaving the kitchen, they followed her to the rear bedroom, which was empty except for a narrow bed, a dresser, and an icon of the Trinity on the far wall. Katya switched on the light and left without a word, closing the door behind her.

Once they were alone, Bogdan set the plastic box on the bed. Opening the backpack, he removed the pistol. With a grin, he ejected the clip, making sure that the chamber was empty, and handed over the gun.

Ilya studied it. A Glock 19 was not his favorite weapon, but it would do. He checked it carefully, noticing that a rail mount was attached to the barrel, and handed it back to Bogdan.

Setting the pistol on the bed, Bogdan undid the clasps of the plastic box and lifted the lid. Inside, embedded in foam molding, were a silencer and two other objects. Bogdan gestured at the components. "You know these?"

"Yes," Ilya said. "But I haven't used them before. You'll need to show me."

"It's quite simple." Bogdan removed the first object, a small black cylinder the size of his thumb. Picking up the pistol, he slid the device onto the rail mount and locked it in place. He pressed a button on the side, holding it down until a green light blinked on, and held it so that Ilya could see the camera lens. "Lithium battery. Six hours of run time. To transmit video, you slide the range switch here, then hold the button until the light goes to red."

Bogdan pressed the button again, turning the camera

off, and removed the second object, which was the size of a paperback book. “This is the repeater box. You carry it with you until you’re in position. Then you switch it on, place it in your line of sight, and it transmits the image to us.”

Taking the pistol, Ilya studied the camera on the barrel. “And where will you be?”

“Close enough,” Bogdan said. Taking the gun back, he slid off the camera and put it away. “Any questions?”

Ilya watched as he stowed the repeater box. “I still don’t see why this is necessary.”

Bogdan smiled, closing the lid of the box again. “We’ll know that Tarkovsky is dead when we see it on video. Otherwise, we would have no way to verify the kill. Or did you expect us to take your word for it?”

Ilya did not reply. Opening his pack, Bogdan slid the equipment inside and headed for the door. “Come on,” Bogdan said to Ilya, who had remained by the bed. “We don’t want to be late for your meeting.”

39

In the woods, beyond a stone wall, there stood a cottage out of a fairy tale, creaking softly as it revolved beneath the trees. As it turned slowly into view, Maddy saw that a cow's skull had been nailed above the doorway. She began to move on, convincing herself that the dread she felt was only her imagination, and was genuinely startled when the door flew open to disclose the witch inside.

Maddy nearly dropped her shopping bag as the witch spun in her direction, grinning horribly, and extended a crooked finger. Hearing a chorus of squeals, she stood aside as a crowd of children rushed toward the witch, who cackled at them in Russian. Feeling strangely sick, she continued up the forest path, heading to where she would await the expected guest.

The yacht had docked in Yalta the night before. Earlier that morning, Maddy had disembarked with a number of other passengers, going past the sea terminal, which looked out on the gray, crowded beach, and continuing along an embankment lined with cypresses.

She had hoped to wander off on her own, but to her surprise, Elena had proposed that they go shopping. The night before, Tarkovsky's assistant had looked somewhat critically at the dress Maddy was planning to wear to the formal reception scheduled to take place before their arrival in Sochi. Catching up with her on the promenade, Elena had offered to help find something more suitable, and although Maddy had been tempted to decline, she had finally said yes.

They had spent an hour browsing through the boutiques near the marina, at the end of which Maddy emerged with a black number from Stella McCartney. She didn't like to think about what the dress had cost, but she had grabbed it after realizing that she was going to be late. Afterward, Maddy had said she was heading for the cathedral, guessing correctly that her companion would take no interest in this. Elena had gone back to the beach, and Maddy had hailed a taxi, managing to communicate that she wanted to see the children's park three kilometers away.

Her driver had seemed somewhat surprised by this request, and as she looked around now, she found that she couldn't blame him. The park was peaceful enough, but in the shadows under the trees, there was something unnervingly lifelike about the carved, staring figures of trolls and mythic beasts, and she was unable to shake the feeling that she was being watched.

At last, in the distance, she saw the statue she had been told to find. It was a sculpture of a dragon with four heads lying slain on the ground, a hero with a sword posing on its broad back. Standing next to the sculpture was a man with a knapsack, a faded patch visible on its flap. As Maddy drew closer, he seemed to sense her approach, and when she was still a few steps away, he turned around.

When she saw his face, it was as if the witch from the cottage had taken another form, beckoning her forward into the house, or the oven, from which she would never escape. It was Ilya Severin. "Hello, Maddy."

Maddy said nothing. They were just a few feet apart. It had been more than two years since she had last seen his face, and he seemed slightly more gaunt than she recalled, his hair and clothes different in ways that she would notice only later. But his black eyes were the same as before.

Ilya took a step forward. Maddy drew back, her eyes still fixed on his, and in an instant, it all became clear. Ilya could be here for only one reason, and as the full meaning of his presence dawned on her at last, she found herself turning away, moving blindly up the path through the trees.

With startling suddenness, Ilya was at her side. He took her by the arm, gently but insistently, and before she could pull free, she heard him speak in her ear. "Careful. We aren't alone."

Maddy glanced quickly around. Aside from the figure of a grinning cat perched at the edge of the footpath, she saw only a few families, none of whom were looking in her direction. "They're watching us?"

"They've always been watching you," Ilya said. "Don't you know that by now?"

Maddy was unable to speak. She became aware that Ilya was steering her up the path, heading away from the others, and it was only as they moved deeper into the woods that she found her voice again. "Listen. I can't be a part of this. Whatever you came here to do—"

"You don't have a choice anymore." Ilya looked from

side to side as they headed for the zoo, passing a child being led on a tired pony. "I did not intend for you to become involved. I learned only a few days ago that you were on the yacht at all. But now that I am here, I will protect you."

Maddy managed to wrench her arm free. They halted in the middle of the path. "Why should I trust you?"

"You shouldn't," Ilya said. "Not yet. But you need to believe me when I say you're in danger. And I'm the only one who can get you out." He began to walk again. "Tell me what they have told you so far."

Maddy was left with no choice but to follow him through the forest. "Just that I had to get on the yacht and bring someone else on board. If I didn't, they'd reveal everything about Lermontov. Were you the one who told them?"

"I told them nothing," Ilya said, not looking in her direction. "The last thing I wanted was to put you at risk. If they know, it's in some other way. They have been watching you for a long time."

Something in his words told her he was telling the truth. "So why are you here?"

"It's best if you don't know." Ilya kept his eyes straight ahead as they entered the zoo, where a mangy lion was pacing back and forth in its cage. "The safest thing is for you to ask no questions."

They came to a halt before another enclosure, heavy with the smell of sawdust and dung, in which a bear lay with its paws crossed. A few tourists were listlessly regarding the animals nearby. "I don't care about being exposed," Maddy said. "Not anymore. It can't be any worse than this."

"You're wrong," Ilya said. "If I fail to perform this task, you'll be dead. So will I."

He said this casually, as if discussing something that had nothing to do with either of them. Looking over at him now, Maddy remembered the first time they had met, at the house of Anzor Archvadze, who had died a terrible death because he had dared, like Tarkovsky, to involve himself in the operations of this shadow world. "And what if you do it?"

"We will talk about this later." Ilya paused. "I did not want this. I am here because I have no other choice. But I will see that these men pay for what they've done. Both to you and to me."

Maddy heard a flicker of feeling in his voice for the first time. "Is that a promise?"

Looking at the cage, Ilya gave an almost imperceptible nod. "Yes. But that will come later."

They fell silent. Thinking back to their first meeting, Maddy saw again that if she had never entered that house, she could have simply gone on as before, unaware that her world was built on such precarious ground. Yet the trap would always have been there, unseen, even if she had never set eyes on Ilya.

For a moment, she found herself thinking of Tarkovsky. He had trusted her in spite of her past, and now, in return, she would only betray him. Yet part of her was still bound to the Scythian, whose fate had been joined with hers in such unexpected ways. And perhaps, she thought, there might still be a way out.

Maddy spoke without turning from the bars of the cage. "What do you need?"

"Very little," Ilya said. "We will part ways here. You will go back to the promenade and return to the *Rigden*.

I will follow from a distance. And I will arrange to meet you on the yacht."

Maddy laughed. "Well, that's great. But you can't just expect to walk on board."

For the first time, Ilya smiled, although it did not touch his eyes. "That's exactly what I intend to do."

40

Laszlo, the bosun of the megayacht, was tired. Like most of the crew, he was young, fit, and used to hard work, but for most of the morning, he had been keeping watch over the passerelle, greeting the guests as they came and went and making sure that no one tried to sneak on board. For a while, he had flirted with one of the stewardesses, but she had been called away urgently by a passenger, so now he was alone and wondering if he could get someone else to take over.

It was shortly before noon. The megayacht was berthed in the port of Yalta, where it was the largest private vessel in sight. Like any yacht of its size, it inevitably aroused curiosity, and passersby had been coming up all day to admire the ship and shout questions. There had also been a handful of dockwalkers, the kind you saw at ports from Fort Lauderdale to Antibes, approaching to ask if there were any vacancies. The bosun had done a fair amount of dayworking himself, so he didn't begrudge them, but it did become rather tiresome after a while.

Laszlo saw another such figure walking along the quay now. The man was of average height and deeply tanned, dressed in a white polo shirt, khaki shorts, and deck shoes, with a knapsack slung over one shoulder. The bosun knew this type well, so he was not surprised when the man strolled up to the base of the passerelle and waved. "Good morning."

"Morning," Laszlo said. He noticed that the man stopped, properly, before mounting the gangway. No matter who you were, you never boarded someone else's yacht without permission.

The man looked appreciatively at the hull. "What's the length? Four hundred?"

Laszlo had been asked this question at least ten times that day. "Four hundred and twelve."

"Impressive." The man set down his knapsack. "Where are you coming from?"

"Constanta," Laszlo said. "Got in late yesterday. But we're heading out tonight."

"A shame. One doesn't often see such a ship." The man's accent, Laszlo noticed, was hard to place, the kind that came only from a lifetime of wandering. "A long shot, but is there any work available?"

Laszlo smiled. He had pegged the man as a dayworker at first sight. "Nothing today. Just launched last week."

The man grinned back. "I thought so. But no harm in asking. Can I leave a card?"

"Sure," Laszlo said. In his back pocket, he already had half a dozen cards, left by other dockwalkers over the past few hours, which he would throw away as soon as they were out to sea.

The dayworker picked up his bag and mounted the passerelle. Up close, Laszlo saw that his most striking features were his eyes, which were very dark in his tanned face, and something in their friendly but observant expression made him think that the man would have good stories to share.

"The name's Meyer," the dayworker said, pulling a business card from his pocket. As he was writing a number on the back of the card, Laszlo caught a glimpse, for the first time, of the faded patch sewn to the flap of his bag. It was a civil red ensign. Beneath it, there was a second patch, the image of a golden dragon, rampant, with a blue anchor emblazoned on one of its wings.

Laszlo's face lit up. He gestured toward the second patch. "You were at Warsash?"

The dayworker looked up with a smile. "That's right," Meyer said, putting his pen away. "Were you?"

"For my class two deck," Laszlo said. "Right after the merger with Southampton."

"I would have just missed you, then." Meyer gave him the card. "Thought I was getting my chief's ticket. Ended up with my class three instead. Always wanted to work on a ship like this."

Laszlo pocketed the card without looking at it. "Care to take a turn around deck?"

Meyer laughed. "I'd like that very much. You're sure the old man won't mind?"

"We'll stay out of his way," Laszlo said, heading for the steps. "I could use a break. Come on."

The two men went up together. On the yacht's aft deck, a few guests were seated beneath the umbrellas near the wet bar, but most had gone onshore. Tarkovsky, the bosun knew, was in the conference room in the main salon. He was meeting with the executives from Polyneft and Argo, discussing something that was rumored by the crew, who loved gossip, to be a matter of importance for all parties.

Laszlo studied the dayworker. "So where did you end up after Warsash?"

"A few things here and there," Meyer said, turning his eyes toward the marina. "Been mostly in Majorca. Hard to find work these days. My last contract ended in Yalta, so I thought I'd try my luck here—"

He was cut off by an agitated female voice, which came from the deck behind them: "I'm sorry, but something terrible has happened."

Laszlo turned around. It was Maddy, Tarkovsky's art consultant, who had been added to the manifest at the last minute for reasons that remained unclear. Looking at her face, which was drawn with worry, the bosun flashed on all the possible things that could go wrong. "What is it?"

"It's my shoes," Maddy said miserably. "A pair of Louboutins. They're missing from the basket. I put them there when I came back from the beach. Now they're gone, and no one else seems to care."

As Laszlo listened, he saw a stewardess standing a few steps away. The two of them shared a brief glance of commiseration over Maddy's shoulder. "All right. Let's see what we can do."

He glanced over at Meyer, who seemed to sense his predicament. "I'll show myself off," Meyer said at once. "Thanks for the tour. The next time you're here, I can buy you a drink—"

Maddy broke in again. "Look, I don't mean to be rude, but I need to find these shoes. Could we all hurry, please?"

"Yes, of course." Laszlo followed her and the stewardess to the other end of the deck. Glancing back, he saw Meyer going down the steps to the level below. A moment later, he was out of sight.

Laszlo spent the next five minutes searching for the shoes with the stewardess, while Maddy stood by impatiently. Finally, catching a glimpse of red, he saw that the shoes had slipped down by accident behind one of the deck chairs. Taking them into her hands like a pair of lost children, Maddy thanked him effusively, then scurried away to the staircase. Laszlo watched her go, shaking his head, and returned without haste to his station by the passerelle.

Two levels above, on the main deck, Maddy headed for her own cabin, shoes in hand, her heart finally beginning to slow.

Watching the conversation with the bosun from a distance, Maddy had been struck by how relaxed Ilya had seemed. She had never seen him cast away his natural intensity like this before, although she knew that the encounter had been carefully staged. With so many résumés available online, it would not have been hard to learn something about the bosun's background, and a chemical tan and some makeup over his tattoo were all that were required to complete the picture.

She didn't know where Ilya had gone after descending from the deck, but she suspected that he had simply headed left at the foot of the stairs, instead of returning to the passerelle. This would have brought him to the bottom deck, not far from the tender bay. All in all, he had played his part admirably, which made her wonder what else about Ilya might be an illusion.

Going into the cabin, Maddy shut the door and tossed the heels into the closet among Elena's things, where she had found them in the first place. Then she pulled the phone from her purse and dialed.

After a few rings, the distorted voice answered on the other end. "You're late."

"It doesn't matter," Maddy said, her anger rising, as always, at the sound of that mechanical tone. "He's here. What now?"

"That's no concern of yours," the voice said. "If he needs you, he'll tell you himself. Don't ever be late again."

The line went dead. Maddy looked at the phone, then put it down, already filing away her rage to focus on the task before her.

Two thousand miles away, in the bedroom of her house in Knightsbridge, Asthana set her own phone aside with a sense of satisfaction.

There had been a number of possible devices to get Ilya on board, but with Maddy on the yacht, it would have been a shame not to utilize her. It was always best, Asthana had learned long ago, to use every part of the animal.

She heard a gentle knock on her bedroom door, followed by the voice of her mother. "Maya, dear? Are you all right?"

"Just a minute," Asthana said. Rising from the edge of her bed, she switched off the phone and tucked it safely into a drawer of her bureau. Then she went over to the mirror on the wall, gazing greedily at her own reflection. She was dressed in a red bridal sari and scarf, embroidered in gold, with bracelets on her wrists, her hands done in henna, her hair and makeup exquisite.

Asthana regarded herself for a moment longer. Then she turned away from the mirror, smiling, and headed for the bedroom door. After all, it would hardly do, she thought, to be late to her own wedding.

41

Powell arrived shortly before twelve at a posh hotel in Kensington, where a doorman in a silk top hat hurried to open the door. He crossed the marble floor of the lobby, leaning only slightly on his stick, and went up to the clerk behind the front desk, who glanced up at his approach. "Excuse me," Powell said. "I'm a guest at the wedding of Maya Asthana and Devon Malhotra."

The clerk pointed with his pen toward the grand staircase to their left. "Of course. Just follow the steps to the conservatory." He glanced down at Powell's cane. "Or if you need the lift—"

"That's quite all right," Powell replied without hesitation. "I'll take the stairs."

Turning aside, he made his way to the staircase and ascended carefully to the floor above. Beyond a reception area, a pair of doors opened onto a brightly lit space with sloping walls of greenhouse glass. Lotus flowers floated on the pool at the center, with palm trees strung with lights standing to either side, and twenty rows of cream and gold seats had been set before the mandapam.

Powell paused at the entrance, searching for a familiar face among the guests. At last, he caught sight of Lester

Lewis seated alone in a gray suit, checking the email on his phone. Seeing him, Lewis put the phone away and rose for a handshake, although Powell could also sense the pathologist appraising his limp with a clinical eye. "You're looking quite well, Alan."

"As are you," Powell replied, studying the younger man in turn. Lewis was energetic and handsome, of West Indian descent, and a member of a generation of pathologists who liked to treat forensic investigation as a source of interesting problems. Powell wasn't surprised that Wolfe had taken a shine to him, although he still wasn't clear as to the nature of their friendship. "Is Rachel here?"

Lewis pointed toward the front of the room. "She's with the other bridesmaids. See if you can pick her out."

Powell saw a cluster of woman in green saris standing near the palm trees to the left of the mandapam. Most were chattering happily, but Wolfe stood to one side, looking less than comfortable in her unaccustomed outfit. "I'm surprised Maya ended up with only four."

"Are you kidding? Rachel says she lost count at eight. The rest are upstairs with the bride." Lewis lowered himself into his chair again. "You should go over and say hello. She said there was something she wanted to ask you about. I'll save you a seat while you catch up."

Powell thanked him and turned to work his way across the room. As he drew closer to Wolfe, he reflected on how much their relationship had changed since his departure from the agency. They still spoke occasionally on the phone, but he hadn't seen her in person in more than two months, and he knew that she disapproved of some of his recent decisions.

When she caught sight of him, however, the pleasure on her face seemed genuine. He had never seen her hair up before, and as she gave him a hug, Powell thought that the effect was quite fetching. "You look lovely."

Wolfe took a step back, glancing down at her sari. "I still don't know how to walk in this thing."

"I'm sure you'll do fine," Powell said. "How has Maya been handling the pressure?"

Wolfe gave him a sad smile. "It's been hard. This should be a happy day, but it's impossible to forget the rest. I really thought it would be tied off by now." Her expression darkened. "I need to talk to you. Do you mind?"

"Not at all." He followed her to a spot at some distance from the others. "What is it?"

"It's about Maddy." Wolfe kept an eye on the other bridesmaids. "Is she still on the yacht?"

"For now. They're scheduled to arrive in Sochi in two days. As far as I know, she hasn't spoken to Tarkovsky since her departure."

"She might want to keep it that way. I don't think this is a pleasure cruise. You said there were executives from Argo on board?"

"Yes, along with representatives from Polyneft. They're all scheduled to attend the signing ceremony." Powell studied her face. "What makes you think there's something else going on?"

"Because of Shambhala," Wolfe said. "I read the file that Adam sent, and it reminded me of something. I'd heard the name recently, and I finally remembered where. It was in Rogozin's work."

Powell glanced over his shoulder automatically, although it was unlikely that anyone here would be listening. "You mean in intelligence?"

"No. In his published writings. When we were building our case against Rogozin, I read everything he wrote over the past few years. And in several articles, he mentioned a rumor, widespread among journalists in Moscow, that Vladimir Putin had taken an interest in the legend of Shambhala."

In the rising noise of the conservatory, Powell had to lean closer to make out what she was saying. "That doesn't sound like the Putin I know."

"I thought so, too. But Rogozin claims, among other things, that Putin wanted a piece of the polar seabed brought back to him after the *Arktika* expedition five years ago, allegedly because an entrance to Shambhala is supposed to exist at the pole. He also says that Putin authorized funding for a search for Shambhala in the Altai Mountains, although nobody wants to confirm this on the record."

"Naturally. But we have more than enough reason to doubt Rogozin's motives."

"I know. And even if he was telling the truth, I don't think Putin is really looking for Shambhala. He's too practical. It's more likely that a journalist heard a reference to it and didn't understand what it meant. My guess is that it's a code word for something else, in the same way Maddy thinks Tarkovsky sees it as a metaphor for social upheaval. But when I look at Tarkovsky's history, I don't think this is about social change at all. I think it's a code for oil."

As he listened, Powell found that he deeply missed these moments of connection. "If you're right, it isn't the first time Shambhala has stood for something more. Mind if I have a seat?"

They went to the nearest row of chairs, where Powell set his cane aside, glad to be off his feet. "You remember that Gleb Boky, the head of the Special Section, wanted to sponsor an expedition to Shambhala, or so he claimed. But it doesn't seem in character for Boky, much less Dzerzhinsky."

Wolfe was listening intently. "I agree. So there must have been some other reason."

"Yes. But in the end, the expedition was canceled, because a similar expedition was already under way. It was led by Nicholas Roerich, the artist and mystic whose paintings Tarkovsky has been acquiring. He thought he was destined to found a new Shambhala in Tibet, and he received support from Russian intelligence. His brother was employed by the same institute that took over Alexander Barchenko's research into mind control. Roerich himself filed regular intelligence briefs, and a member of one of his later expeditions claimed he had an important mission from Moscow."

Wolfe seemed to see his point. "And it had something to do with Central Asia."

"Exactly. An expedition focused on Shambhala would have been the perfect cover for an intelligence operation. It was a way for the secret services to enter Central Asia without any risk, looking for sources of regional influence, or perhaps for something else. As part of his cover story, Roerich took a land concession for mining in the Altai Mountains, and Shambhala itself, in the old legends, was often said to be underground. Which implies—"

"—that it was a code word for mineral wealth," Wolfe finished. "Boky was a cryptographer. He thought in codes. So you're saying that this expedition was really a covert attempt to look for energy reserves outside Russia."

"And if I'm right, it still means the same thing. If

Putin has an interest in the arctic, it isn't for any mystical reason. It's because most of the giant oil fields in Russia have been discovered. A quarter of the world's undeveloped oil and gas is at the pole, and it's finally accessible because of global warming. Russia has already begun to stake its territorial claims. It's central to its future as a geopolitical power."

"But they can't do it alone," Wolfe said, leaping ahead to the next stage of the argument. "Even if the ice melts, they need foreign technology to extract the oil, which requires deals like the kind Tarkovsky is making with Argo. Forget the Black Sea. The pole is the real prize. He's laying the groundwork for future partnerships to drill for oil reserves where he can't do it himself. Except—"

Wolfe hesitated. "Except that Putin would never allow these resources to be exploited by anyone but the state. He wouldn't give these concessions to a private company. Not without huge political pressure."

"Which is exactly what Tarkovsky is doing," Powell said. "You've seen our report on his finances. His foundation is channeling funds to intermediaries, which disguise where the money really goes. At first, I thought he was supporting military intelligence, but now I think he's funding advocacy groups and opposition politicians. He's building support for something."

"But if that's what Shambhala stands for, then Tarkovsky is playing with fire. Putin would never let those concessions go without a fight. And it means that Maddy has no business being involved—"

Wolfe broke off as one of the other bridesmaids, who had been hovering at a discreet distance, came up and plucked her lightly by the sleeve. "Sorry to interrupt, Rachel, but it's time."

Powell picked up his cane and stood. "We'll talk more later. I'll let you get ready."

Wolfe held his eyes for a second longer, then turned with a smile to the other bridesmaid. As Powell headed back down the aisle, he saw that she was right to object to Maddy's involvement. If Tarkovsky was playing such a dangerous game, it threatened to draw the attention of forces that had a great deal invested in the outcome. And as long as it continued, no one around the oligarch was safe.

For a moment, Powell thought about calling Maddy, but he decided that this could wait until after the ceremony. Arriving at his seat, he gave a friendly nod to Lewis, reaching for his cell phone as the musicians at the front of the room started to play. Powell turned off his phone and slid it into his pocket. Then he settled back to wait for the wedding to begin.

42

Wolfe stood in the receiving area at the rear of the conservatory, a bouquet of white flowers in one hand. She was keeping very still to avoid upsetting her sari. Around her were seven other bridesmaids, all of whom she had met at least once, although she still had trouble telling Kavita from Savita.

Over the shoulder of the bridesmaid in front of her, she watched as Devon received a tilak from the bride's mother, broke a clay vessel carefully underfoot, and began to walk toward the mandapam. He was dressed in an embroidered white sherwani with a red sash, pointed slippers, and a matching sword, all of which seemed somewhat incongruous with his glasses.

Hearing a murmur from the others, Wolfe turned to see the bride approaching at last. In her bridal sari and high golden shoes, Asthana looked delicate, slightly nervous, and heartbreakingly beautiful. In a modern touch, her father was at her side, beaming in his dark suit, and as Wolfe watched them head for the aisle, it seemed possible to forget everything else.

A moment later, the line began to move. Wolfe waited until the bridesmaid in front was almost at the mandapam, then stepped into the conservatory, keenly aware of the two hundred pairs of eyes on her face. Flashes went off as guests took her picture, making her all the more conscious of her sari, which she had been assured would oblige her to move gracefully.

As Wolfe walked gingerly down the aisle, she saw Powell and Lewis seated side by side. She smiled at them as she approached the mandapam, taking her assigned place to the left. From here, she had a good view of the bride and groom, who had lowered themselves into royal chairs on opposite sides of a scarlet curtain. At the other end of the canopy stood the eight groomsmen, in white sherwanis, who had filed in from a separate entrance.

When the last remaining bridesmaid had assumed her place at the end of the line, the cloth between the bride and groom was lowered, allowing them to face each other for the first time. Watching as they gave each other garlands of flowers, Wolfe found that she missed the reassuring structure of belief, having long since abandoned most of the rituals she knew.

As the music ceased, the pandit began with an invocation to Ganesh. The bride and groom stood smiling as their wrists were joined with red cloth, followed by another symbolic bond, a loop of white cotton. In a bed of foil, a sacred fire had been kindled. As Wolfe watched, Asthana and Devon took seven steps around it in bare feet, the clicking of the camera audible over the drum and flute.

When they were finished, the music ended again. Asthana turned to her groom, giving Wolfe a view of her profile. She stood there quietly, looking at Devon, and as the room fell into an attentive silence, she began to speak.

"Devon," Asthana said, her eyes shining, "I'll never be

able to tell you how much you mean to me. You're my best friend, my only love, and you've been there for me through everything. Without you, I never could have gotten through these last few years. And I'm so grateful I get to spend my life with you."

As Wolfe listened, she felt her own eyes grow damp. Several of the other bridesmaids were misting up as well. Wolfe blinked away the tears, wishing that she'd remembered to tuck a spare tissue into her bouquet, and watched happily as Devon squeezed Asthana's hand and began a vow of his own.

"Maya, I've loved you since I first saw you at the reading room in Seeley," Devon said. "My friends said that you were too busy studying to date. What you could possibly see in me, I'll never understand. But I know that you have a poetic side, even though you try to hide it."

Devon nodded to one of his groomsmen, who bounded up to the mandapam. He had something in his hand. Looking past the line of bridesmaids, Wolfe saw that it was a tattered spiral notebook.

Asthana laughed at the sight, clearly surprised. Devon took the notebook, giving his sword to the groomsman in exchange, and turned back to his bride. "I don't know if you remember this. I didn't tell you I was going to do it because I knew that you'd probably say no."

There was a murmur of laughter from the crowd. Devon turned to face the guests. "This is one of my notebooks from college. Not a lot of notes inside, I'm afraid. But Maya wrote something in it when we first began dating. And ever since, it's been one of the most precious things I own."

Devon turned back to Asthana, who had a bemused look on her face, and opened the notebook. Wolfe caught a glimpse of some words on the inside cover as Devon cleared his throat and began to read in a clear, wavering voice: *"Twice or thrice had I lov'd thee, before I knew thy face or name—"*

Wolfe felt the world go away. As the words faded into insignificance, dwindling into mere sounds, she found herself thinking of the last time she had heard this poem, in a prison cell in Paddington Green.

Rogozin, she recalled, had translated John Donne into Russian, sharing his enthusiasm for the poet with all his protégés. Karvonen had only been the latest, but of course he had not been the first.

As Wolfe came back to herself, she found that she was staring at Asthana. Her second realization was that Asthana was looking back. She was still smiling as softly as before, and there was nothing in her expression to indicate that she suspected what Wolfe might be thinking.

For a moment, the two women stood eye to eye. At last, Asthana turned back to Devon, her face still shining with happiness, as he finished the poem and gave the notebook back to his groomsman.

The rest of the wedding was a blur. Wolfe watched as Devon gently put red powder on Asthana's forehead and in the parting of her hair, then hung the sacred thread with its two gold pendants around her slender neck. As they showered each other with petals and rice, Asthana continued to smile brightly.

After a final blessing, the couple turned away from the bridal party to face the crowd, the guests rising to applaud. As they left the mandapam, Wolfe saw Asthana glance back, their eyes meeting for one last time, a smile still playing across the bride's face. Then she looked away.

Wolfe took a step forward. Before she could go any

farther, she felt a hand close on her arm. "Wait," the bridesmaid standing next to her whispered. "Not until they've left the room—"

As bride and groom walked together down the aisle, the music swelling to its height, Wolfe felt frozen in place. Even now, her heart could not entirely believe what her mind was telling her. She saw Asthana lean quickly toward Devon, whispering something in his ear. A second later, they passed through the conservatory doors, and then they were out of sight.

Wolfe waited helplessly with the other bridesmaids as both sides of the family filed out. At last, the girl in front of her moved past the mandapam to head down the red carpet, and Wolfe joined the line, still clinging to her bouquet, her vision filled by the door ten steps ahead.

A second later, she was through at last. The entrance hall was crowded with members of the bridal party. Looking around, Wolfe finally saw Devon standing next to the bride's father. They were alone.

Wolfe ran up to him, no longer worried about upsetting her sari. "Where's Maya?"

Devon seemed confused as well. "She said she was feeling flushed. I think she went to the toilet—"

Without waiting to hear the rest, Wolfe turned, dropping her flowers, and pushed her way past a knot of groomsmen. The restrooms stood at the far end of the receiving area, at right angles to the conservatory entrance. Her sari was still holding her back, but she managed to break into something like a run as she rounded the corner to the ladies' room and pushed her way through the door.

Inside, the bathroom was silent. The row of sinks was deserted. Wolfe checked the stalls. They were empty.

She left the bathroom and headed back out to the reception area, looking around frantically for a red sari. By now, the entire bridal party had emerged from the conservatory, and a number of guests had appeared to give their congratulations, but there was no sign of the bride. Asthana had disappeared.

Wolfe stood there, thinking desperately. Then she turned and ran for the elevator.

43

As soon as Devon began the poem, Asthana knew what was coming. Until that moment, she had been enjoying the ceremony, in a detached sort of way. She always liked being the center of attention, and when she looked around the room, she felt a certain satisfaction at seeing the disparate parts of her life assembled in one place. It was the culmination of all she had ever wanted, although it was at just such times, she knew, that things often came apart.

Hearing the poem's first line, Asthana felt her eyes go immediately to Wolfe, who was looking back at her with dawning recognition. Even now, as she began to understand that there would be no prospect of return, she was amused by the thought of what Wolfe must be feeling. Asthana wanted to savor the sight of so many illusions falling away, but she resisted the urge, knowing that the next few minutes would be the most crucial she had ever known.

She turned away from Wolfe as Devon finished reading, looking up from his notebook with a smile. Asthana smiled back with admirable tenderness, and her expression remained unchanged for the rest of the ceremony, which she fortunately knew by heart. As she went through the motions of the wedding, she considered her situation from all sides, grateful for the chance to think, and remained conscious all the while of Wolfe's eyes on her face.

Asthana had no specific memory of writing the poem in Devon's notebook, but she didn't doubt that she had done so. She had been very young at the time, and she had not yet understood the importance of keeping the two sides of her life firmly separated. A smile, she had learned, could hide a great deal, but only if you were careful not to hint at what else might be unfolding behind it.

Rogozin had taught her this, as he had taught her so much else. Donne, Rogozin said, had lived with a similar division at the heart of his experience. He had been a great lover before he was a preacher, and after his conversion, his passion and wit had turned from the erotic to the sacred, a tension that had never been fully resolved, flowering instead into something rich and strange.

Asthana had listened earnestly to this, as she always had in those days. She had met Rogozin a year earlier, when he had been invited to speak on campus as a prominent writer in exile. Asthana had seen him lecture, and afterward, at a faculty party, she had introduced herself. This meeting had led to another, arranged more discreetly, in which they had talked long into the night, and even then, she had sensed that there was more to him than met the eye.

When Rogozin revealed his true nature, she had taken it as a sign. In retrospect, it was the moment in which she had embraced what she had always been meant to be. Like her recent decision to transfer her allegiance to the civilian side, it had been a choice born of pragmatism, based on a cold appraisal of the historical forces at work, and it was perhaps for this reason that she had written the poem in Devon's notebook. It was a token of a transformation he would never understand, and now that it had come back to destroy her, she had no one to blame but herself.

At last, with a final blessing, the ceremony ended. As Asthana prepared to walk down the aisle with her husband, the applause and music rising to mark the recessional, she saw clearly what she had to do.

When they were almost at the doors leading out to the reception area, Asthana leaned over to whisper in Devon's ear. "Darling, I'm so sorry, but I'm not feeling well. I need to run to the ladies'."

Devon glanced over in surprise, still clutching his foolish sword. "Are you all right?"

"I'll be fine," Asthana said as they passed out of the conservatory, the cheers still echoing behind them. "I just need a moment to myself. Tell my mother that I'll be right out."

Asthana kissed her new husband, her thoughts briefly turning to another kiss she had given only a week ago, and walked away without looking back. She knew she would never see him again.

Rounding the corner, she found herself alone for the moment, the music faintly audible from the next room. Instead of going through the lavatory door, she walked past it to the stairs at the end of the hall. Entering the stairwell, she kicked off her heels, then began to run up the steps in bare feet.

As she hurried to the floor above, she pulled off her veil and unwound the fabric of her sari, which made it hard to move with any kind of speed. Underneath, she was wearing a choli and a long skirt. She dropped the sari in a heap on the landing, then quickened her pace, taking the steps two at a time.

Arriving at the sixth floor, she went through the fire door that led out from the stairwell, finding herself in an empty hall. She headed at once to the elevator bay and stooped down over a potted plant, fishing out the keycard that had been left there in case one of the bridesmaids had to come back. Glancing at her reflection in the mirrored walls, she continued on to the suite they had booked for the day, then swiped the keycard and went into the room.

Inside, the suite was in a state of feminine disarray, with clothes scattered across the bed and draped over the chair by the window. The clock on the nightstand reminded her that she was running out of time.

She began by pulling off her bangles, stripping the bracelets from her wrists and letting them fall to the floor, and quickly toweled off her face and hair. In the closet hung a jacket that belonged to one of the bridesmaids, with long sleeves that would cover up her arms. She pulled it on, then grabbed her purse and slid into a pair of flats. Checking herself in the mirror, she saw with satisfaction that she wouldn't attract a second glance, and that only a sharp observer would notice the henna on the backs of her hands.

Less than a minute had passed since she had entered the hotel room. Leaving everything else behind, she went to the door, opened it—

—and found herself facing Wolfe, standing in the hallway in her bridesmaid's dress.

For an instant, their eyes locked. A moment of understanding passed too quickly for words. Then Asthana lowered her head and plowed forward, knocking Wolfe savagely off her feet.

Caught by surprise, Wolfe fell back, colliding with the mirrored wall. Asthana turned toward the stairs, then felt herself yanked backward as Wolfe managed to grab the collar of her jacket, the seams popping audibly as her partner lunged forward and tackled her from behind.

Asthana wheeled around, slamming Wolfe against the wall as hard as she could. The mirror shattered into spiderwebs, but Wolfe did not let go. Asthana rocked back on her own heels again, turning at the last moment so that the bony part of Wolfe's hip collided with the wall. She heard a sharp exhalation as her partner's grip loosened for a fraction of a second, then managed to break free, nearly stumbling as she sprinted for the door to the stairwell.

Behind her, she heard Wolfe rise, but she didn't look back as she pushed through to the stairs. She descended as quickly as she could, one hand on the railing as she rounded the corner from one landing to the next, and heard Wolfe enter the stairwell above her before the fire door could swing shut.

As they ran, neither woman spoke, knowing that words were a waste of air. Asthana heard Wolfe kick off her shoes, as she should have done long before, but the footsteps overhead grew steadily fainter, and she realized that her partner's sari and hurt leg were slowing her down.

As Wolfe fell behind, Asthana pulled one landing ahead, then two. On the next level, she decided to chance it and took the exit door, finding herself in a corridor on the ground floor of the hotel, a line of housekeeping carts standing to one side. Her heart was going a mile a minute, but she forced herself to slow to a fast walk, hearing the sound of voices close by.

Asthana ran her fingers through her hair, trying to get her breathing under control. Picking a corner at random, she ended up in a service area, looking neither right nor left at the faces around her, although she sensed members of the hotel staff staring. There was no sign of Wolfe.

Up ahead, she saw a pair of doors with panic bars, the two rectangles of glass looking out on the brightness outside. Pushing through without pausing, she found herself in an alley by the hotel.

A second later, she was on Gloucester Road, where pedestrians were strolling along the sidewalk across from the railway station. Slowing her pace, Asthana drew up her head and calmly joined the rest, taking the first side street she saw, and before long, she had disappeared into the city.

44

Tarkovsky looked up as Elena entered his office on the bridge deck, closing the door behind her. As his assistant took a seat on the other side of the room, he turned to Maddy. "I'm sorry. Where were we?"

"We were talking about revising our offer to Virginia," Maddy said. "A new strategy, based on what we discussed before we left. It's an unusual approach, but at this point, it's something I'd be willing to try."

Tarkovsky reached for the teacup on the desk before him, setting it down again when he realized it was empty. "All right. Write it up for my approval. You'll need to make the proposal on your own, before I return from Sochi, so I'll want you to move quickly on this."

"I understand," Maddy said. "I'll have it for your review by tomorrow afternoon."

She watched as Tarkovsky accepted a fresh cup of tea from Elena, who had refilled it from the urn without being asked. This was her first time in the oligarch's private office, which was located just behind the captain's cabin and wheelhouse. It was a refined space lined with bookcases, their shelves set with brass rails. Behind the desk was a window with a view of the setting sun, and, beside it, a separate stairwell leading to the owner's suite on the topmost deck.

Tarkovsky turned to Elena, who had resumed her position from before. "I wanted to confirm our plans for tomorrow. After dinner, I'd like to meet privately with our friends from Argo before rejoining the rest of the party. I'll leave it to you to make sure that the salon is ready."

"Of course," Elena said, writing this down in her leather folder. "And I'll see that the rest of the staff is informed."

"Good." Tarkovsky glanced at Maddy again. "I believe we're done. Elena can walk you out."

"Thank you," Maddy said, rising. As Tarkovsky turned back to his desk, she followed Elena out of the office. Through the window, the sky was growing dark, the swell of the sea faintly visible beyond the glass.

Elena began to walk up the companionway. "I trust your meeting was productive."

Maddy had hoped that the assistant would simply let her go, but it was clear that she wanted to talk. "Yes. It was our first chance to meet privately since Constanta. I've been doing a lot of work on my own, but he wanted to give me some guidance before I head back to London."

"I see." Elena stood aside for a pair of stewardesses. "I'm glad to hear you've been busy. You've seemed rather neglected at times. I wouldn't want you to think you came for no reason—"

Maddy didn't care for the implication here. "You don't have to worry about me."

"I should hope not," Elena said, heading for the stairs. "You've been put in an enviable position. Vasily doesn't allow just anyone to take up his time. It's important that you follow through."

As they went downstairs, Maddy overheard an iciness of tone that she had hoped they had left behind, but she also knew that Elena was under a great deal of pressure. The assistant had been intimately involved in planning tomorrow's formal reception, which she regarded as the high point of the entire voyage, and was clearly determined that the affair go off without any surprises.

At the main deck, they parted ways. Maddy watched as Elena approached the head stew, who was overseeing the other stewardesses in the salon. Then she continued downstairs, emerging on the lower deck, which was devoted to crew quarters and operations. At the moment, there was no one in sight. From the galley to her left, she heard voices, but instead of going closer, she crept quietly along the companionway in the opposite direction.

Whenever Maddy was around the crew, she sensed them watching her attentively, but she had been observing them as well, and she had figured out the time of day when they were most likely to be preoccupied. Dinner each night was an elaborate production with Russian silver service, and afterward, every available crew member reported to the pantry for cleanup. Even with the yacht's ample dishwashers, all the crystal had to be washed by hand.

Heading at a fast walk up the companionway, she reached her destination without encountering anyone else. She had been prepared to bypass the touchscreen by the door, but when she tried it, she found that it was unlocked, presumably for the convenience of the deckhands. Glancing back once over her shoulder, she went in, closing the door softly behind her.

Inside, the tender bay was silent and dark, with only a faint vibration welling up from the engine room located directly below. Maddy kept the lights off, feeling her way slowly past the water scooters and other toys. As her eyes adjusted, she finally made out the silhouette of the expedition tender. Going up to one side, she mounted the cradle and pulled herself onto the foredeck.

A flight of steps led down past the cockpit to the passenger cabin below. Descending carefully, she found herself standing before a closed door, under which a soft line of light could be seen. Maddy gave a gentle knock, then opened the door and went down the steps to the lower level.

As Maddy entered the cabin, she saw several rows of seats standing before the galley. Toward the aft of the tender were two sets of bunks, the head with its toilet and sink, and a table that could be folded down from the wall.

Ilya was seated at the table, on which he had placed an electric lamp. In its circle of light, Maddy saw that he was examining a cylindrical device, evidently a camera, which he set aside as she drew closer. "Are we safe?"

"I don't know what that means anymore." Maddy sat across from him. "If you're asking if the pieces are in place, then yes, we're ready. But I've already thrown away everything I ever cared about."

His dark eyes studied her face. "And are you still willing to play your part?"

"I don't think I have a choice," Maddy said. "There's no other way, is there?"

He only continued to regard her in silence. She had expected him to ask her for more details, or at least to clarify the situation, but instead, she saw nothing but a readiness to do whatever was necessary, a fatalism that left her even more unsettled than before. "Can I ask you something?"

Ilya reached below the table, producing a black plastic case. "Of course."

Maddy watched as he undid the clasps of the box and put the camera inside. "Why do they call you the Scythian?"

It might have been a trick of the light, but she thought she saw a smile pass across his face as he closed the lid again. "Someone I once knew told me I had the eyes of a man of the steppes. He said it only in passing, but the name endured. And perhaps I have something of the Scythian in my heart as well."

Maddy's gaze strayed to the tattoo on his arm. "So what does that mean?"

Ilya slid the box back under the table. "The Scythian is a wanderer. A nomad. Russia has never trusted men like this. They cannot be controlled or contained. Instead of standing their ground, they retreat until their enemies are exhausted. But if they are cornered, none fight more fiercely."

Maddy felt his dark eyes return to hers. "Is that how you see yourself?"

"At times," Ilya said. "But I had reasons of my own for accepting it. The king of the Scythians, according to scripture, was a man called Ashkenaz. Do you recognize the name?"

As she listened, Maddy glimpsed the shadow of something sensitive in his otherwise impassive features, a quality that she had seen before, but only rarely. She realized that it reminded her, strangely, of Tarkovsky. "It's where we get the name of the Ashkenazi Jews."

Ilya smiled again. "Yes. Which is why, when they called

me the Scythian, I let it go. I knew its true meaning, even if others did not. Although, given the choice, I would rather have been a Khazar."

Before Maddy could ask what this meant, Ilya raised a hand, indicating that this topic of discussion was closed. His face became grave again. "But that is all beside the point. We do not have much time, and tomorrow is a very important day. So let's go over it again together—"

45

"I know this is hard, but you need to think carefully," Wolfe said. "Did Maya ever say anything to indicate where she might have gone?"

Devon's voice was flat and unemotional. "No. We hadn't spoken about anything but the wedding for weeks. Not even about that other business." His expression hardened. "You really think she killed Rogozin?"

"I don't know. But it's possible. She was the only one who could have given him the poison, knowingly or not, and—" Wolfe hesitated. "And the more I look at it, the less it seems like an accident."

They were seated in the kitchen of Asthana's house in Knightsbridge, the afternoon light streaming through the small panes. It was the first time that Devon had agreed to see Wolfe since the wedding. Even now, the situation still seemed unreal, although she felt it with every breath she took. She had cracked two ribs when Asthana slammed her into the wall, and it served as a reminder, as if she needed one, that she had no idea at all who her partner really was.

"We've been looking at the records of Rogozin's speaking engagements," Wolfe continued. "He would have been to Cambridge at least twice when you were there. Did Maya ever mention seeing him?"

Devon glanced away. "I don't remember. It was a long time ago. But it wouldn't surprise me. She was reading Russian history. But I never heard his name until after his arrest." When he turned to her again, she was startled by the despair in his eyes. "What is it, exactly, that you want from me?"

"I want the same thing you do," Wolfe said. "I want to find her and bring her home."

Devon struck the table with his fist. "That's not what I meant. You can't ask me to accept that this is the woman I knew. Because it means that everything I believed was a lie."

"I know," Wolfe said, sensing how inadequate these words really were. "I understand how it must feel."

"I don't think you do. Maya was my fiancée. No, I'm sorry. She's my *wife*." Devon laughed bitterly. "You were so clever to see through her mask. But I wish you had done it a few minutes earlier."

Wolfe had no good answer to this. She touched his hand. "You may not believe it, but I loved Maya, too. And I hope there's some other explanation. But I won't know for sure until I can ask her myself. Will you help me?"

Devon pulled his hand away. A second later, he gave a short nod and rose from the table. Wolfe followed him upstairs, where he paused at a door on the landing. At last, with a sudden gesture, he opened it and went inside.

Wolfe had been here many times before, and as she looked around now, she recognized the familiar tokens of her friend, with their curious mix of the intellectual and frivolous. A stack of political journals in Russian sat on the desk, next to a set of bridal magazines. "Do you want to stay?"

"No," Devon said. "I'll be downstairs. I ought to give Maya's mother a call."

He left, closing the door behind him. Once she was alone, Wolfe put down her bag and went to the desk, where she switched on the computer. As she waited for it to boot up, she let her eyes wander across the pictures on the wall. There was a series of photos of Asthana and Devon on holiday at the seashore, a portrait from their engagement shoot, and, set unobtrusively among the rest, the image of a man riding a white horse against the sky.

As Wolfe looked at the figure of Kalki, she felt her anger rise again, remembering the painting in Rogozin's house. The symbol of the horse and rider, he had said, appeared in every culture, pointing in all its guises to the wait, endlessly prolonged, for a savior who would lead the world into the coming era. And as she regarded the picture now, Wolfe wondered if he had given Asthana the same speech.

When she studied the room around her, through her new eyes, its proofs of an ordinary life seemed like an elaborate set, or an illusion. If they were right about the timing, and Asthana had been recruited at university, it meant that she had maintained this front for at least ten years. She had gathered the necessary pieces, rising through the ranks, making friends and allies, furnishing the lie. And it had all been in plain sight the entire time.

Wolfe began rummaging through the desk drawers. At the agency, the situation was a closely held secret. As far as the public record was concerned, Asthana was just another missing person, although certain details had been quietly shared with Interpol. Cornwall was working with the Home Office to map out their strategy, but the betrayal had clearly shattered the deputy director as well.

The first few drawers contained nothing of interest. Wolfe smiled at the sight of a visitor's pass from last year's London Chess Classic, then felt an arrow of regret as she put it down again. When she tried the remaining drawer, she found that it was locked. Frowning, she was about to look around for the key, then noticed that the computer had finished booting up.

She began by checking the email account, only to be told that she needed a password. The browser history had been cleared. Examining the list of recently opened files, she found nothing but drafts of the wedding program, layouts for the table cards, a copy of the catering contract, and a spreadsheet of the seating arrangements, including a line with her own name.

As Wolfe continued to go through the files, she reflected that Asthana had always been among the agency's most methodical officers, and there was no reason to believe that she would be anything else here. Their only hope, she thought, was that her partner had left a trace of her true self behind without knowing it, in private, where all other disguises fell away.

Wolfe closed the last of the files and thought for a moment. Then she went to the web browser again. Clicking on the address bar, she entered a command to check the contents of the disk and memory caches, a directory of online files and objects saved on the hard drive, including web addresses and images.

To her relief, she saw that the files were still there. She began to scroll down the list, eagerly at first, then with mounting discouragement, as she saw that the links seemed to lead to nothing but wedding sites. After she had gone through several pages without success, she was about to resign herself to the fact that this was another dead end when one of the entries caught her eye.

It was a search engine request, dated from just over a week before, for *Maddy Blume.*

Wolfe's mouth fell open. An instant later, she was fumbling in her bag for her phone, remembering what she had told Asthana after the hearing. They had gone to a pub, and after drinking too much, she had let Maddy's name slip. At the time, it had seemed harmless, but now—

Feeling a new wave of dread, Wolfe dialed Powell, who answered at once. "Rachel?"

"I need to talk to Maddy," Wolfe said, eyes still fixed on the link. Scrolling down, she saw that it was only the most recent of several searches, all from the day of the hearing. "Is she still on Tarkovsky's yacht?"

"As far as I know. They're almost at Sochi by now." A note of concern appeared in Powell's voice. "Is something wrong?"

Wolfe checked her watch. It was close to two, and if the yacht was anywhere near its destination, they would be three hours ahead. "Give me her number. I'll explain later. But I have to call her right now."

"All right, hold on." After a short pause, Powell read off the number. "Got it?"

"Yes, thanks." Wolfe jotted it down and hung up. When she dialed Maddy's phone, it rang four times before going to voicemail. She cursed to herself, then left a message, already hurrying for the office door. "Maddy, this is Rachel Wolfe from the Serious Organised Crime Agency. I don't know if you remember me, but I used to work with Alan Powell. You need to call me back as soon as you get this. I believe you're in great danger—"

46

Years before, whenever she was about to step into a strange room, Maddy would imagine a camera before her eyes. When she first arrived in New York, she had often carried an old Nikon around her neck, sometimes not even loaded, but as a sort of license to explore places she couldn't otherwise have entered.

Tonight, however, as she drew closer to the sound of voices and music, this imaginary camera was nowhere to be found. Her hands were empty, leaving her with nothing between her and the salon, but as she hesitated at the entrance, she told herself that she could at least have a drink.

Maddy looked through the door that led to the party. She was wearing the outfit she had bought in Yalta, a black peplum dress with a sweetheart neck, and she had to admit that she looked good. And although it wasn't much, this slender thread of confidence was enough to carry her into the salon at last.

As she entered, Maddy saw that no one else was looking at her, and it occurred to her that this might be the last time she would ever know how this felt. The salon on the main deck was the largest public space on the yacht, its walls cool, white, and inlaid with marble, the lamps casting a soft light across a carpet of olive gray. In the corner stood a baby grand piano, where the pianist hired for the occasion was working his way through something by Prokofiev.

The guests had divided themselves into the usual groups. At the corner near the piano stood the members of Tarkovsky's foundation, chatting with the men from Polyneft. A few steps away, the executives' wives had formed a circle around the captain, a sturdy figure in his forties. For most of the voyage, he had kept to the crew, and Maddy had observed him only from a distance, but tonight, in his dress whites, he was holding court with ease.

She headed toward the center of the salon, where Elena was standing in a long black gown, her back turned, with the faction Maddy thought of as the leftovers. These were the passengers who weren't full guests but not quite crew, either, so they were inevitably all seated at the same table each night. Along with Maddy herself, they consisted of Elena, Nina's tutor, and Rahim, who invited her tipsily to join him and the rest of the design team on the beach deck downstairs.

Maddy declined with a smile and continued toward the bar. The stews were circulating among the guests with trays of drinks and hors d'oeuvres. They had changed before the party into formal uniforms and white service gloves, the women in culottes and vest blouses, the men in dress shirts and slacks. She also saw a few members of the oligarch's security team, who tended to hang at the edges of the room, but there was no sign of Orlov. Or, for that matter, of Tarkovsky.

She accepted a glass of champagne from a stewardess.

Tarkovsky, she knew, had excused himself after dinner to meet privately with the executives from Argo, and they had been gone now for close to forty minutes. These meetings had been taking place on a daily basis, and Maddy often overheard the other guests speculating as to their meaning, with many wondering if there might be something more than the Black Sea deal to announce on their arrival.

Maddy took a sip of champagne and wandered over to the wet bar, where the bartender was mixing martinis for the guests. A display had been set up on the table beside it, with a pair of crystal vases bursting with white lilies. At the center, there was an ice sculpture that had evidently been kept in the yacht's freezer for this very moment. It was the image of a man on horseback.

As Maddy looked at the sculpture, which gleamed softly in the light of the lamps, she remembered, as if for the first time, the events that were being set in motion that night. Putting down her glass, she was reaching out to touch the horse's icy flank when a voice came from over her shoulder: "I wouldn't do that if I were you. My father got mad when I tried it."

When Maddy turned around, she saw that Nina, Tarkovsky's daughter, was standing behind her in a white dress, her hands primly clasped. It was the first time either of them had spoken to the other. Maddy picked up her glass again, not sure what to say. "The image means a lot to him, doesn't it?"

"Obviously. I wish he'd try something new for a change. I don't know why he even pretends to care about art." Nina's brown eyes darted down to take in Maddy's neckline, then looked up again. "Your name is Maddy, isn't it?"

"Yes. I work with your father." Maddy was less than eager to have this conversation, so she turned away slightly, as if to join another group, hoping that the girl would lose interest.

Nina refused to take the hint. "I know who you are. He mentions you sometimes."

Maddy glanced across the room, where Tarkovsky's wife was talking to the men from Polyneft. "Good things, I hope."

Nina only shrugged. She was tall for her age and startlingly pretty, like her mother, with a hooked nose and a small red mouth. For a girl of twelve, she was very poised, the product of several excellent private schools and an ensuing succession of tutors. "Are you coming to live with us, then?"

The question took her by surprise. Maddy noticed that Elena was standing a few steps away, waiting at the bar for a drink, and appeared to be listening to their conversation. "What do you mean?"

"We're going to live on this ship," Nina said lightly. "My father says so. I don't really mind. Of course, no one ever asked me for my opinion. So are you going to be living here or not?"

Maddy watched as Elena accepted her cocktail but continued to hover nearby. "I'd love to spend more time on board, but I'm going home after Sochi. Are you sure your father really wants to live here?"

Nina nodded. "Why wouldn't he? It's safer. There are people who want to kill him, you know. I suppose it's because he's rich, but it doesn't make sense to me. Just because you kill someone doesn't mean you get their money—"

Maddy didn't know how to respond to this. The conversation was long past the point of making her uncomfortable. "I suppose you're right."

Nina glanced down again at Maddy's dress, a smile playing curiously across her delicate features. At last, she said, "I'm sorry you won't be staying with us. You're very pretty."

With that, the girl turned and went away. Maddy watched, not without relief, as Nina rejoined her mother. Raising her champagne, she took a long swallow, suddenly afraid that she might be sick.

At some point, Elena had appeared silently at her side. "She's right, you know. Vasily will stay on the yacht when this is over. It's safer for him. Compared, at least, to the alternative."

Maddy drained her champagne. "What about you? Are you going to live here, too?"

"For now." The assistant seemed about to say something else, then paused, her eyes on the door of the salon. Following her gaze, Maddy saw Tarkovsky step into the room, along with his security chief and the executives from Argo. It was hard to read the looks on their faces, but as they joined the party, it seemed to her that they were keeping something to themselves.

Maddy watched as Orlov went up to one of the guards, speaking to him quietly, then left the salon. "I've heard that Tarkovsky is preparing for the end of the world. Or at least for the coming collapse."

Elena smiled. "That's the least of his worries. He has enough on his mind as it is. It all comes down to power. Khodorkovsky was taken out because he was going into politics. And it could happen again. That's why he's always kept his family at arm's length." The assistant paused. "He's a good man. If I've been hard on those who are close to him, it's because I care about what he's trying to accomplish, and I understand the risks. No one can take power from those who already have it. This is the moral of the Shambhala story."

Maddy looked over at the assistant in surprise. "What do you know about that?"

"You aren't the only one Vasily tells about these things," Elena said. "You know how the story of Gleb Boky ends?"

As Elena spoke, she kept an eye on Tarkovsky, who was giving his wife a kiss on the cheek. Maddy watched the assistant warily. "He died, didn't he?"

"He was arrested," Elena said. "He was accused of being part of a secret society, with branches all over the world, that was trying to predict the future and undermine the state. Perhaps he had become too ambitious for his own good. In the end, they broke him. He confessed that he was going to blow up the Kremlin and assassinate Stalin. He was tried, executed, and cremated the next day. Barchenko was killed five months later. He, too, was charged with plotting against the government and founding a secret society. It was called Shambhala Dunkhor, I believe."

Maddy did not reply. As the music continued to play, she saw Tarkovsky say a few words to his wife, then make his way across the room to the staircase. She watched as he went up the stairs, alone, heading for the bridge deck. Feeling a suffocating dread continue to spread through her body, she tried to take another sip of champagne but discovered that her glass was empty. The moment, she knew, was coming soon. Ilya was on the move.

47

Half an hour earlier, Ilya had emerged from the cabin of the expedition tender. The lights in the bay were dark, and it was with considerable care that he climbed onto the foredeck and lowered himself from the cradle. He was dressed in a deckhand's evening uniform with long pants and epaulets, which Maddy had taken from the laundry room the night before.

Over the last two days, he had come to know the tender bay well, so he made his way through the darkness with ease. He was wearing blue latex gloves and a set of earphones that connected to nothing. In his right hand, he carried a tool bag from the tender's hold, with a screwdriver tucked into his back pocket. Across his face, he had tied a white dust mask.

Going to the door that led to the lower deck, he put his ear to it, listening. He could hear the faint sound of music from two levels above, but otherwise, the ship was silent. Opening the door, he went into the companionway, glancing from side to side. The corridor was empty, but to his left, he heard voices from the galley, where it was the busiest time of night.

To his right stood the main staircase, but he knew better than to approach it, knowing that it would be frequented by the passengers and crew. Instead, he would take the second set of stairs, which stood at the fore of the ship, one hundred feet away. From there, it was three decks and twenty yards to his destination.

Closing the door behind him, Ilya crept along the companionway, passing the crew mess, which was deserted, and the room housing the ship's huge air conditioners. When he reached the steps, he ascended in silence, arriving first at the main deck, where the music was louder. Without pausing, he went on to the next level, ignoring the voices drifting his way from the party.

From above, he heard a set of footsteps. Moving quickly, he went through the nearest exit from the stairs, which led to the guest cabins on the lounge deck. Without turning, he knelt in the hallway, next to an electrical outlet, and smoothly set his tool bag on the floor by his side. Then he fished the screwdriver from his back pocket and pretended to examine the fixture.

Keeping his back turned to the staircase, he listened as someone came down. Whoever it was would see only a deckhand working on the outlet, a pair of headphones in his ears. In the end, the figure on the steps did not stop, continuing down to the main deck. Ilya waited until the footsteps were gone. Then he rose with his bag and resumed his ascent.

He emerged on the bridge deck. Behind him was the wheelhouse, but he did not look back as he went along the companionway, heading toward the owner's office at the end of the hall.

From around the corner ahead of him came a pair of voices. Ilya ducked at once into a nearby doorway, which led to the ship's library. Withdrawing into the shadows, he saw two security guards walk by. He waited until they had passed and the sound of their conversation had faded, then continued to his final destination, which was only a few steps away.

He arrived at the door of the owner's office, which was locked. Earlier, he had cut away the part of the glove covering the first knuckle of his right index finger, which would allow him to use the touchscreen without leaving prints. Glancing back to make sure he was alone, he pressed the screen, which greeted him with a request for a password.

Ilya entered the four digits, then pressed the enter key. Maddy had seen only the first three numbers, but she had been able to guess the fourth. It was the date of the founding of Russia's most beautiful city, visible in the scrollwork of the egg that she had spent so long trying to obtain: *1703*.

A second later, he was rewarded with the option of opening a menu or unlocking the door. He chose the latter and heard the bolt retract. Looking around one last time, he went inside, pulling the door shut behind him.

He crossed the floor of the darkened office, the blinds of which had been drawn. A door next to the desk led to the stairs. Climbing the steps, he found himself at the owner's suite, alone, for now, at the highest point of the ship.

The stateroom was pitch-black, but he kept the lights off. He had studied similar designs by Fincantieri, so he knew the layout well. Closing the door, he could make out the bed and table, the doorway to the dressing room, and, at right angles, the owner's head, with its fixtures of marble and gold.

Ilya went to the table by the window, which looked out on a view of the darkened sea. In the distance, he could see the lights of Sochi. He removed his headphones and mask, leaving on the gloves, and opened the tool kit. Inside were the gun, camera, and silencer, all of which he put aside for now, and the video signal repeater box, which he took out and set on the table.

Turning the repeater on, he checked to make sure that there was a clear line of sight from the box to every point in the room. Looking out again at the view of Sochi, which lay peacefully under the stars, he reflected that in order for the repeater to work, Vasylenko and the others had to be close. Then he drew the curtains and turned away from the window.

He was about to make his remaining preparations when his eye was caught by something at the other end of the suite. Going closer, in the dim light, he saw a large section of pottery, perhaps a ewer, pieced together from several fragments and mounted in a glass case. On it was the image of a warrior on horseback. He was wearing a pointed helmet and a hauberk with long sleeves, and he carried a spear in one hand, while the other was clutching the hair of a captive.

Ilya studied the warrior's face for a long moment, as if trying to commit it to memory, before finally looking away. Taking a chair from next to the dresser, he set it facing the closed door and brought over the rest of his equipment. He screwed the silencer onto the pistol and fixed the camera on the rail mount. Pressing the button to turn it on, he watched as the green light appeared. He slid the range switch to its proper setting and held down the button again. When the light went from green to red, indicating that the signal was being transmitted, he passed the camera once across the room, as instructed, and settled in to wait.

He sat there in the dark, the pistol resting against his knee, his eyes on the closed door of the stateroom. Years of experience had taught him to be patient at such times. It was best, he knew, not to think of the task ahead, and especially not of what would come next. Instead, as his gaze strayed again to the image of the warrior behind the glass, he recalled his last conversation with Maddy. He had mentioned the Khazars, and although they had spoken of many other things at that meeting, he had not told her the significance that their example held for them both.

After their conversion, the Khazars had extended their empire from the Black Sea to the Caspian, building castles of limestone and brick. Yet a more savage nation was growing to the north, making greater incursions into its territory, until, at last, it erased it from the map overnight.

In the end, Russia broke the Khazars. It seized Kiev, then sacked Atil and Sarkel. History had overtaken the tribe of horsemen who, until their conversion, had moved too swiftly to be caught by surprise. With their palaces in ruins, the Khazars melted again into the confusion of tribes from which they had emerged. Travelers said that the few who had not fled to other countries lived in a state of perpetual mourning. The grand experiment had failed.

Looking at the warrior in the display case, Ilya reflected that the lesson was clear. The Khazars had begun as wanderers and had ended by being scattered again, swallowed up once more by the steppes. They had modeled themselves after the children of Israel, but they had not managed to avoid their own fate—

Even as these thoughts passed through his mind, Ilya heard steps on the stairs. He rose from the chair and trained his pistol at the door, holding it at eye level in a combat stance. His heartbeat was as steady as always.

A moment later, there was the sound of the knob turning. The door swung inward. In the darkened opening, Ilya could see the figure of a man, and he closed one eye to protect his night vision just before the lights came on.

It was Tarkovsky, in black tie, his jacket draped over one arm. His face was tired, but when he caught sight of Ilya, he fell back a step. For a fraction of a second, the two men stood eye to eye.

"Forgive me," Ilya said. Then he pulled the trigger and shot Tarkovsky twice.

Tarkovsky did not fall at once. For a moment, he remained standing, his eyes fixed on Ilya's, an emotion unfolding on his face that might have been recognition, a realization that this was the ending that had awaited him all along, his wealth and power no argument against the logic of a machine that would move serenely past him into a future in which he could play no part.

At last, he fell to his knees, toppled sideways to the floor, and grew still. Around him, the yacht continued to function as perfectly as before, a masterpiece of foresight and design surrounded on all sides by night.

Ilya took a step forward. Looking down at the oligarch, he briefly opened his mouth, as if to say a final benediction for the dead. But he only raised his pistol and shot that unmoving body one last time.

48

Earlier that night, a car had pulled up before a dacha on the outskirts of Sochi. The house had not been easy to find. It was surrounded by a brick wall topped with barbed wire, a set of surveillance cameras trained on the area before the entrance. The night was warm and humid, so the guard on duty was in his shirtsleeves, seated on a folding chair outside the gate, a shotgun within easy reach.

At the sound of approaching tires, the guard picked up his shotgun and stood. A moment later, the car came into view, crawling forward along the curve of the driveway, and slowed to a stop, its headlights on. Keeping his shotgun raised, the guard went up to the driver's side, where the window rolled down to reveal the solitary figure behind the wheel.

It was Asthana. "You already know who I am. Are you going to let me inside?"

The guard lowered the shotgun. In his eyes, Asthana saw more curiosity than respect. Then he turned away, slinging the gun over his shoulder, and went to draw the gate back. Asthana rolled up her window again and drove through, watching as the gate closed behind her in the rearview mirror.

She crept along the driveway toward the house, which appeared at the next turn. In her headlights, the dacha was a big summer home with clean Scandinavian lines, the verandah at the front entrance balanced by a wooden deck to the rear. The open layout was bad for security, she thought, but at least the broad windows facing her had been kept dark.

Two cars were parked out front. Asthana pulled up beside them and turned off the engine. Taking a bag from the passenger seat, she slid out and locked up the car. As she went up the narrow path, the gravel crunching underfoot, the door of the house swung open. Inside, there stood a second man, also holding a shotgun, who studied her in silence as she entered.

The man closed the door and motioned for her to follow. Going into the next room, Asthana saw an array of security monitors with views of the grounds in a rack against one wall. Beyond this was a comfortable sitting area with a floor of pale oak. Through the glass of the sliding door that looked out on the deck, she could see the ember of another guard's cigarette.

There were three men in the room itself. The guard who had led her inside was standing behind her. On the sofa, an old man was sipping from a glass of tea, his shoes and socks removed. Another man was seated at a table at the far end of the room, his laptop set next to an array of electronic equipment.

As Asthana entered, the others looked up. Before any of them could speak, she addressed the figure on the sofa in Russian. "Tell your man to stop pointing the shotgun at my back. It isn't polite."

Turning slightly on the couch, Vasylenko observed that she had a view of the entire room in the reflection in the sliding door. He nodded at the man behind her, who withdrew into the hall.

For a moment, as the others regarded her in silence, Asthana had no choice but to see herself through their eyes. Since her unexpected departure from Kensington, her hair had been cut, and only a few traces of henna remained on her hands. Yet she was still a woman, and her skin was still dark, and she knew that she would never truly be welcome within this dying circle.

At last, the *vor* rose from the sofa, his tea still in hand, but did not come any closer. "You're late."

"Actually, I'm right on time," Asthana said, meeting his gaze easily. "You don't have the feed ready yet. So unless I've missed the main event entirely, which I doubt, you're still looking for a signal."

She went over to the table without waiting for a response. The man at the laptop was studying the screen. "The repeater isn't on yet," Bogdan said. "He's still getting into position."

Asthana bent over the computer, which displayed a black rectangle with a time code. "You've been in contact with him?"

"No," Vasylenko said, lowering himself to the sofa again. "But he knows what to do."

Asthana set down her bag, sensing the others watching her warily. They had not met in person before tonight, and until recently they had been on opposite sides. In any case, she did not expect to remain among these men for long, and she wondered what part they really expected to play in the order to come.

Bogdan pointed to the screen. "We just got a signal from the yacht. He's activated the repeater. But the camera isn't on yet—"

Even as he said this, the laptop blinked into life. The image that appeared was being taken in low light, the details rendered in black and gray. There was no sound. Looking closely, Asthana could make out the stateroom, the outlines of a bed and dressing table visible as the camera panned across the cabin. Finally, it steadied against the image of a doorway, and it did not move again.

Vasylenko came for a closer look, standing just behind Asthana as the three of them watched the feed. Asthana remained silent, afraid of breaking the spell that had sustained her all the way from London. It was a transition for which she had always been prepared, and she had embraced it, pausing only long enough to buy a new knife in Solingen.

Somewhat to her surprise, she had found herself thinking less of her abandoned husband than of Rachel Wolfe. Devon had at least been a clean separation, one in which she had never let her mask slip, but her partner had seen through it, if only for an instant. Part of her hated Wolfe for witnessing this moment of exposure, but this was nothing but a sign of weakness. She was moving into a new state of being, as was the rest of the world, and if she failed to accept such a change in her own life, she had no business being here at all.

Even as these thoughts passed through her mind, the image on the screen began to move. The camera bounced for a moment, leaving gray streaks on the video feed, then steadied again on the closed door of the stateroom, as if the man sending the signal had risen. A second later, the door swung open, the image blown out by sudden illumination. For an instant, there was nothing but white. Then the camera adjusted and a figure came into view. It was Tarkovsky.

They watched the rest in silence, the image jumping each time a shot was fired. When it was over, the camera held for another second on the oligarch's body. Then it clicked off and the screen went dark.

As Bogdan sat back from the computer, exhaling, Asthana felt curiously empty. She had imagined this triumph for so long, only to see it reduced to a few noiseless gunshots, and in these first deflated moments, it hardly seemed worth the effort. Later, she knew, it would be seen as her greatest success, one that would allow her to finally assume the role left vacant by Lermontov's death. But she was also aware that it was at times like this that someone like her became expendable.

Vasylenko was looking at her. Without turning her head, Asthana gave him a nod.

The old man took a phone from his pocket and dialed a number. Turning away, he went to the glass door of the dacha, looking out at the view from the deck as he spoke quietly in Russian.

A second later, Vasylenko lowered the phone. When he turned back, his eyes were still fixed on Asthana's face. "It's done. Bogdan, tell the others. I want to go down to the water to watch."

49

Back in the stateroom of the yacht, only a few seconds had passed since the last shot was fired. Ilya lowered his pistol, looking down at Tarkovsky's body, his pulse no higher than before. After a beat, he held down the switch on the camera until the red light had blinked off again. Checking his watch, he pressed the button on the side, starting a countdown for twenty minutes.

Only then did he kneel by the oligarch. As he did, Tarkovsky's eyes opened at once. "Give me a hand."

Ilya helped Tarkovsky up, seeing the oligarch wince. "It hurts," Tarkovsky said. "I wasn't sure if it would hurt—"

"It always does," Ilya said. As Tarkovsky got to his feet, Ilya glanced down at the holes in the oligarch's shirt. They were three inches apart, one almost at the level of his heart, the two others slightly higher.

Tarkovsky followed his gaze. Reaching into one of the holes with his fingers, he dug around and extracted a bullet, which had been flattened into a tiny mushroom. He studied the slug with something like wonder, then handed it to Ilya. "Do you think they believed it?"

Ilya took the slug, closing his hand around its warmth. "We'll find out soon enough."

Tarkovsky laughed, then winced again. Reaching up, he undid his tie and let it fall to the floor, then unbuttoned his shirt, walking somewhat unsteadily through the door to the bathroom.

Ilya let him go. Bending down, he picked up his spent cartridges, then went to the repeater box on the table, which he switched off. He slid the repeater, gun, and camera into his bag, then glanced through the bathroom door. Inside, Tarkovsky had stripped down to his slacks and was examining himself in the mirror. A pair of large brown bruises had appeared on his chest.

The oligarch's dress shirt was lying on the bathroom counter, along with something else. Ilya picked up the vest. It was the type manufactured in Bogotá from multiple layers of pale yellow material, considerably lighter than Kevlar. The vest wouldn't have stopped a Tokarev round, but it was more than effective against the hollowpoints Ilya had been using, two of which were still embedded in the fabric.

Ilya studied the bullets. "You know, I could have killed you with a shot to the head. You were very trusting."

Tarkovsky pulled his dress shirt back on. "Yes. But I didn't trust you. I trusted her."

Leaving the bathroom, Tarkovsky picked up his dinner jacket, which was still lying on the floor, and donned it again. Then he headed to the door of the cabin, glancing back once at Ilya. "Hurry."

The two men went downstairs. In the owner's office, the curtains of which were still drawn, a lamp on the desk had been lit. The two figures waiting there rose as the others entered. One, in black tie, was Orlov. The other was Maddy, who was still wearing her dress from the party.

Drawing closer, Ilya saw something in Maddy's face

that he had never seen there before, a feverish excitement burning deep in her eyes. He wondered if this was something new or a quality that had been hidden there all the while. As he looked at her now, it struck him that he had believed he was here to protect her, but instead, she had saved him. His only consolation was that he was far from the first to underestimate her resolve.

As Ilya joined the others at the desk, he saw Orlov watching him darkly. Tarkovsky appeared to notice this as well. "It's all right, Pavel," Tarkovsky said. "We don't have much time."

Orlov continued to eye Ilya distrustfully, but seemed ready to get down to business. "When is the boat supposed to pick you up?"

"Twenty minutes after the shots were fired," Ilya said. "I have fifteen minutes left. An inflatable raft will approach from behind the shadow boat with its lights off. I won't see them. I will get into the water when the countdown is done. They will pick me up from there."

"And bring you to Vasylenko," Orlov said. "You're sure the others are nearby?"

"Yes. The repeater box I used has a range of twenty kilometers. They are in Sochi." Ilya looked at Tarkovsky, who was listening carefully. "I believe their intelligence contact is also there."

Orlov motioned impatiently with his right hand. "Give me the box. I want to see it."

Ilya took the repeater box from his tool bag and handed it over, observing that Maddy was watching in silence. "Can you track it?"

Orlov studied the repeater. "I think so. We'll have to change the range setting to one they won't be monitoring. Otherwise, they'll see the signal. The camera will need to be on as well, but not recording."

Ilya nodded. "I will switch it on as soon as I get to shore. You can track me that way."

Orlov handed the box back to Ilya, who removed a pair of plastic bags from the tool kit and began to wrap up the repeater and gun. He sensed the security chief watching his every move. "One last question," Orlov said. "How can you be sure that their intelligence contact is there?"

Ilya slid the waterproof bundle into his bag. "I can't. But there will be a debriefing. I doubt they would leave this to Vasylenko alone."

"We'll be following close behind you," Tarkovsky said. "My men will take the tender to shore. Once we've confirmed your location, we will move in. My hope is that we can catch them all together."

Ilya overheard a note of dark satisfaction in the oligarch's voice. "Remember, you have greater resources than I do, but you are in Russia now, and you will be approaching a house containing one or more members of the security services. None of the risks we've taken will mean anything if you fail to follow through."

"You leave that to me," Orlov said. He turned to Maddy. "What is expected of you?"

Maddy spoke for the first time, her eyes moving across the faces around her. "I'll go back to my cabin to wait out what happens next. They want me to keep the phone on, in case they need to contact me."

"Then you should do as you were told," Tarkovsky said. "If they call you, tell us at once. As soon as this yacht comes to port, you'll be in danger, but I'll see that you're protected throughout what follows, regardless of how long it takes. We can talk about the rest of it later."

Tarkovsky turned to Ilya. "I can show you the best way to the aft deck. After that, I'll remain in my quarters for as long as they need to believe I am dead. Orlov, please take Maddy back to her cabin."

Maddy stood. Instead of following Orlov at once, however, she turned to face Ilya. "I don't know if we'll ever meet again."

"I know," Ilya said, holding her gaze. "If you're lucky, this will be the last time."

"In that case, good luck." Maddy paused. "When you see them, tell them hello from me. I want them to know who it was."

Ilya only regarded her in silence. For a moment, he wanted to thank her, but in the end, he said nothing. Instead, he remembered their first meeting, years ago, in a house on the other end of the world. As she looked back, it occurred to him that perhaps she was thinking of the same thing.

At last, Maddy turned and headed for the door of the office, where Orlov was waiting. The security chief entered a code into the touchscreen to unlock it, and the two of them went into the hallway.

Just before the door closed, Ilya saw Maddy look back, not at him, but at Tarkovsky, who was still seated at the desk. And as he watched this last exchange of glances between Maddy and the oligarch, Ilya wondered, not for the first time, what had really taken place between them.

50

One day earlier, Maddy had gone to see Tarkovsky in his office after dinner. That morning, she had encountered him at breakfast in the main salon, talking to a senior geologist from Argo. When he asked how her work was going, she had replied that she needed to speak with him about a few things, and Tarkovsky had invited her to stop by his office later that evening.

When Maddy entered the room that night, she saw Tarkovsky seated at his desk with Orlov. The two men had been conversing in Russian, but the oligarch switched to English as she came in. "Thank you, Pavel," Tarkovsky said, rising. "Please tell Elena that I wish to see her."

Orlov nodded and left the office. Going to the urn in the corner, Tarkovsky refilled a china cup he had brought from the desk. "Tea?"

"No, thank you," Maddy said. She took a seat, watching as Tarkovsky came back to his chair. "There's something we need to talk about."

Tarkovsky looked at her over the rim of his cup. "And what might that be?"

Maddy hesitated, looking within herself for something like courage, but as she spoke the words that marked the point of no return, she found nothing but a strange coldness in her heart. "It's about Alexey Lermontov."

Tarkovsky took a sip of tea, then set the cup down. His face displayed no reaction. "What do you wish to know?"

"I want to talk about your history together," Maddy replied. "You've told me that you worked with Lermontov to repatriate art from overseas, but I think there's more to it than that."

She thought she saw a flicker of interest in the oligarch's expression. "Go on."

Maddy glanced out the window, through which the sun hung like an orange above the sea. "I've been looking at the foundation's history. In the past, you concentrated on issues of social justice and human rights. Then, a few years ago, you abruptly changed course. You began pushing hard for the repatriation of Russian art, and there was no sense that this had ever been an interest of yours before."

"In itself, that doesn't say much," Tarkovsky said, turning the cup around idly on his desk. "Repatriation of artifacts is an important cause for many foundations. My attention would have been drawn to it sooner or later."

"That may be true. But the timing still struck me, because it coincided with your first contacts with Lermontov. I've seen the files. You began doing business with him at the exact moment you started to focus on repatriation. Which makes me wonder. I suspect that you developed a genuine commitment to these issues later, but at the time, I don't think you got close to Lermontov because of your interest in art. I think you became interested in art to get close to Lermontov."

Tarkovsky laughed. "An ingenious theory. But why would I have taken an interest in Lermontov?"

"Because you suspected that he was working for Russian intelligence," Maddy said. "You discovered that the civilian side was selling looted art to raise money for covert operations, which could be a useful weapon for your allies in the military. But you weren't prepared to act on this yourself. You still had to work closely with both sides, as far as appearances were concerned, so you passed the tip along to a man who was ready to use it. His name was Anzor Archvadze."

Tarkovsky's eyes narrowed. "I'm willing to indulge these speculations up to a point, but you're treading on dangerous ground. You should think very carefully before you say anything more."

"I already have. Archvadze's name is in your foundation's records. You met with him on several occasions in the two years before his death. I always knew that Archvadze had learned that civilian intelligence was dealing in stolen art, but I never understood how he found out. Now I do. You told him." Maddy paused. "I also think you told him about a certain work of art, a painting, that was being sent overseas. And I know firsthand what happened next."

"I'm well aware of that," Tarkovsky said. "It must make it difficult for you to remain objective. But even if what you say is true, I still haven't heard any explanation for why I would have done this."

"It isn't hard to imagine. Even at the time, the rivalry between the two arms of Russian intelligence was growing. You saw the chance to take down one of the leading paymasters for the opposing side."

Tarkovsky nodded slowly. "I see. You've thought through this theory with great care. But the trouble with the plan you describe is that it didn't work. Military intelligence, as I expect you know, has been damaged by scandals of its own. And if I wanted to embarrass the civilian side, I would have seen that Lermontov was forced to testify in public. Instead, he disappeared—"

"—and died," Maddy finished. "Yes. But there's one more thing I need to tell you."

Through the windows of the bridge deck, the sky was growing dark. Maddy kept her eyes on the view of the sea as she continued, hearing herself say words that she had never thought to speak aloud, even as she had rehearsed them so many times in her own imagination.

"Several months after Lermontov's disappearance, I was contacted by a man named Ilya Severin," Maddy said. "I'm still not sure why he came to me. We had only been in the same room together for a few minutes, but I think he saw something there, or sensed that we both wanted the same thing. Lermontov betrayed me. He wanted me dead, and he murdered someone I cared about. As long as he was alive, I would never feel truly safe. Ilya said as much—"

Tarkovsky broke in. "You don't need to tell me this."

Turning to the oligarch, Maddy saw that his face had lost much of its color. "But I do. You'll understand why soon."

Maddy took a breath, closing her eyes, and said, "Ilya came to me because I knew Lermontov well. I had insights into his behavior that others did not. Ilya wanted to know if I could help track him down. And I did. It took some luck, but I found him in London. A week later, I flew out there, as part of a longer vacation, and went to a house in Fulham. And I was waiting outside when Ilya killed Lermontov."

She had hoped that this confession would lift the

weight she had carried for so long, but it did not. These were only words, which she had used all her life to get what she wanted, and what really counted was what came next. She hurried through the rest. "I went there to make sure it was really done. And then I walked away. Or so I thought. But now I know that this was never an option."

Maddy opened her eyes. Tarkovsky's expression had remained fixed, but for the first time in their acquaintance, she had the sense that he was having trouble keeping himself under control. "And why come to me?"

"Because I no longer have a choice," Maddy said, feeling for that familiar coldness in her heart's core. "You asked how I knew about your intelligence connections. It's because I'm working for the Cheshire Group. They hired me to pass along information about your foundation's activities in advance of the Black Sea deal. I never meant to stay longer than that. But then the situation changed. And the only way out is for me to tell you everything."

Tarkovsky had listened to this revelation in silence. Some of the blood had returned to his face. "And what is the situation now?"

"I was abducted from my home. I don't know who it was. But I suspect they're involved with the same groups that you implicated years ago, on the civilian side. They knew I was involved in Lermontov's death, and they threatened to expose me if I didn't get on this yacht and bring someone else on board. A man I knew from before." Maddy looked across the desk at Tarkovsky. "It's Ilya Severin. He's on the ship now. And he's here to kill you."

As Tarkovsky listened, his face hardened into something like stone. "When?"

"After the party tomorrow," Maddy said. "The day before we arrive in Sochi."

Tarkovsky did not respond at once. Glancing down at his desk, he picked up his tea, although he did not drink from it yet. When he spoke, his tone was almost casual. "You know, I could call Orlov now. He could easily determine if you are telling the truth. And where Ilya is hiding."

"Yes," Maddy said. "I could give him up to you. But that isn't the smart move."

Tarkovsky finished his tea and set it down with a clink of china. "And the smart move would be?"

"Let it play out," Maddy said, feeling her heart rate rise at last. "If you take Ilya now, none of this will mean anything. But if you follow it to its source, you can get the men who did this. I've spoken to Ilya. He doesn't want this any more than I do. He's here because he thinks it will protect me, but he's wrong. The only way out is to end it. I have a plan. But I can't do it myself. You're the only one with the resources to cut this off at the head."

Looking out the window at the sea, Tarkovsky seemed suddenly tired. "What do you have in mind?"

"First, I need to know I can trust you," Maddy said. "Why do they want you dead?"

To her surprise, Tarkovsky began to laugh. "It's hard to know where to begin. I have not endeared myself to these men by any means. But I suspect you have some ideas of your own."

"I do," Maddy said. "I think it involves the Argo deal. But it's about more than just the Black Sea. You've been meeting with these executives throughout the entire voyage. It's about something else, isn't it?"

After a beat, Tarkovsky nodded. "Yes. Something

larger than you know. The collapse of military intelligence has presented a rare opportunity. We're building something that could change the balance of power in Russia for years. Which is why I refer to it by another name."

Maddy began to dimly understand what he was saying. "You mean Shambhala."

"Yes," Tarkovsky said. "An undiscovered empire. But not the kind you think—"

He was interrupted by a knock on the door. As Elena entered the room, a leather folder in one hand, Tarkovsky glanced over at Maddy, a secret meaning in his eyes. "I'm sorry. Where were we?"

"We were talking about revising our offer to Virginia," Maddy said at once. "A new strategy, based on what we spoke about before we left. It's an unusual approach, but at this point, it's something I'd be willing to try—"

51

That conversation had taken place only the day before, but as Maddy remembered it now, it seemed to belong to another lifetime.

When she came back to herself, she was walking along the companionway with Orlov, fifteen minutes after the images of Tarkovsky's apparent death had gone out over the video feed.

Until then, she had not truly believed that any of this would work. Since their conversation, Tarkovsky had confided only in his security chief. She had not been present at that discussion, but as she glanced over at Orlov now, she sensed that he was as eager as his employer to see this through to the end.

They arrived at her cabin, where Orlov waited as she unlocked and opened her door. "Is there anything else you need?"

"No," Maddy said, going into the stateroom. She kept the door open long enough to look back at the security chief, who had remained in the hallway outside. "Any other instructions?"

"I advise you to remain in your room for the rest of

the night," Orlov said. "Tell us at once if anyone tries to contact you."

"I will." Maddy managed to smile at Orlov. "Thank you for all you've done."

Orlov gave her a faint smile in return. "Thank me when we are both in Sochi."

He turned aside and headed along the companionway. Maddy watched until he had disappeared up the stairs, then closed the door of her cabin and switched on the overhead light.

There was no one else there. Going to the bedside table, Maddy picked up her phone. She stood there for a moment, thinking. Then she went to the door again, opened it, and headed back into the hall.

Maddy glanced around the companionway, seeing that she was alone, and took the stairs to the lounge deck. Around her, the yacht was silent, except for the faraway sound of voices and music from the party on the level below. Moving quietly, still in her black dress, she made her way to the sky deck, which lay at the rear of the ship, the stars shining coldly overhead.

Going to the railing, she paused to look out at the sea. The moon had not yet risen, but in the distance, she could make out the outline of the shadow boat. Feeling the wind on her face, she stood there for a minute in silence, trying to prolong what felt like the last peaceful moment she would ever have.

She looked over the railing at the aft deck. For a second, she thought she saw something by the transom, as if a shadowy figure was moving toward the rear of the yacht, but it might have been just her imagination.

Her phone was still in her hand. She pressed a button

to illuminate the screen, in order to see what time it was, and saw that she had a voicemail from hours before, from a number she didn't recognize.

Maddy put the phone to her ear, looking out at the shadow boat as she listened to the message. A woman's voice began to speak: "Maddy, this is Rachel Wolfe from the Serious Organised Crime Agency. I don't know if you remember me, but I used to work with Alan Powell. You need to call me back as soon as you get this. I believe you're in great danger—"

Even as she heard this, there was a high whine, like the amplified sound of an insect's wings. Something flew across the night sky, leaving a streak of brightness, and then the shadow boat across the water burst into flame.

Maddy recoiled, feeling the push of heat against her face as the explosion lit up the sea. She stared at the burning ship, the hand with the phone falling to her side, and saw something else in the sky above.

Outlined against the stars, illuminated faintly by the fire, a dark winged shape was wheeling around again toward the yacht. A second later, there was another insectile scream, a line of white darting straight in her direction, and a rocket struck the *Rigden* itself.

The explosion threw her off her feet. Maddy fell to her knees, the cell phone slipping from her hand and skittering along the deck as the yacht listed heavily to one side. She saw the phone slide under the railing, caught for an instant in the glow of the flames, and then it was gone.

Maddy crawled blindly forward. Screams rose from the salon below as a third rocket hit the yacht, the deck shuddering beneath her fingers. As the world tilted sideways, she tumbled along with it. Her head struck the railing at the edge of the deck, and then she knew no more.

III

✠

Darius gave it as his opinion that the Scythians intended a surrender of themselves and their country. . . . To the explanation of Darius, Gobryas . . . opposed another which was as follows: "Unless, Persians, ye can turn into birds and fly up into the sky, or become as mice and burrow under the ground, or make yourselves frogs, and take refuge in the fens, ye will never make escape from this land, but die pierced by our arrows." Such were the meanings that the Persians assigned to the gifts.

—Herodotus, *The Histories*

We love the flesh: its taste, its tones,
Its charnel odor, breathed through Death's jaws . . .
Are we to blame if your fragile bones
Should crack beneath our heavy, gentle paws?

—Alexander Blok, "The Scythians"

52

Ilya had heard the sound a few moments earlier. On the aft deck, facing the pool, the two levels of the yacht above had cast a rectangle of shadow. Moving silently onto the deck, Ilya crouched down in this area of darkness, not far from the transom where he would lower himself to the water. He was carrying nothing but a life jacket and the bag with the signal repeater and gun.

Placing the life jacket across his knees, Ilya found the light marker, which was designed to switch on as soon as it hit the water, and tore it off. He was about to remove his shoes and tie them together when he paused, frowning, and turned toward the starboard side. At first, he wasn't sure what had caught his attention. A second later, he felt it again, more in his bones than anything else, nothing more than the faintest of vibrations on the breeze.

Ilya rose to his feet, turning to face the lights of the city a mile across the water. The moon had not yet risen. He continued to look toward the harbor, keeping himself very still, trying to trace that rumor of a vibration to its source. Then he heard it at last with his ears, a low, insistent hum carried across the silence of the sea, and knew at once what was coming.

He dropped the life jacket, keeping only the bag with the gun, and ran forward along the side of the yacht. His first thought was that he had been a fool to believe that they would allow the plan to rise or fall based on his own loyalty. His second thought was that it was already too late.

A ladder on the starboard side led to the deck above. Ilya climbed to the main deck, then ascended one more level to the bridge. Up ahead, he could see the lights of the wheelhouse, with three crew members on lookout outlined against the window. Without hesitation, he opened the door and went inside, aware all the while of the vibration rising on the wind.

As he entered the bridge, the crew members turned in surprise. One of them, he saw, was Laszlo, the bosun he had met on his arrival. Another was an ordinary deckhand, while the third, whose epaulets identified him as the first mate, spoke at once in Russian. "Who are you?"

"You need to sound the alarm," Ilya said. "We're under attack. There isn't time to—"

Even as he spoke, Ilya heard a high whine sear the sky overhead, followed an instant later by the explosion. Turning with the others, he saw the fireball bloom at the shadow boat. As smoke began to rise in the distance, the crew members ran toward the window, their faces lit up by the flames. The deckhand's mouth hung open. "What the hell was that?"

Ilya went to the doorway of the wheelhouse, searching the sky above for any sign of movement. "An unmanned drone. It will have more than one rocket. The next will be for us—"

He broke off as another bright streak flew across the intervening space and a second rocket hit the yacht, shaking it violently. As the alarms on the bridge began to sound, Ilya saw it wheeling toward them again, a slightly darker shadow against the stars, and braced himself as it fired for the third time.

They were thrown to the floor as the final rocket struck the ship, which was already listing. The lights went out. For an instant, the wheelhouse was lit only by the fire burning on the shadow boat, screams rising thinly from the decks below. A second later, the emergency power came on, filling the wheelhouse with yellow light, and as the crew members got to their feet, Ilya heard the hull of the ship creaking dangerously beneath them.

On the bridge, the displays blinked back to life. The first mate managed to pull himself up to check the damage reports. "We're holed below the waterline. There's flooding in the engine room—"

The deckhand stumbled forward, steadying himself against the bulkhead, and groped his way toward the intercom. As the crew tried to raise someone on the lower decks, Ilya thought of Tarkovsky. Heading for the door, he was about to leave the wheelhouse when he heard a gun cock behind him.

Looking back, he saw that Laszlo had taken a pistol from the locker under the console. As the other crew members tried frantically to assess the damage, the bosun kept the gun trained on Ilya. "Put up your hands."

Ilya complied, listening to the alarms going off on the bridge. "We don't have time."

"Shut up." Laszlo looked at him over the sights of the gun. "I saw you in Yalta. Who are you?"

"It doesn't matter," Ilya said. "Listen to me. We need to begin the evacuation."

Laszlo kept the gun raised. Ilya, his pulse booming in

his ears, saw that the bosun was not about to let him go, but he also didn't think that the other man would shoot him. He was about to put this idea to the test when a voice came from over his shoulder: "Officer, stand down."

Ilya turned to see Orlov in the doorway, his face drawn and pale in the yellow lights. "This man is a member of my team," the security chief said. "We were unable to disclose his presence until now. Give me the gun."

After a beat, Laszlo uncocked the pistol. As he handed it to Orlov, the captain came through the door, the head stew and a second deckhand following close behind. Ilya took a step back as they crowded into the wheelhouse, each staring briefly at him in turn as they approached the bridge.

Orlov tucked the gun under his jacket. "I'm here to speak for Tarkovsky. The passengers are safe in the salon. Captain?"

The captain was studying the displays, his broad face lit from beneath by the console. "Tell me everything."

"It was a rocket attack," the first mate said, his voice quavering. "Catastrophic damage on lower and bottom decks. Engines and main generators lost. Without dynamic positioning, we're drifting. Rudder and bow thrusters only."

The captain absorbed this information without any change in expression. "Fire?"

"Flooding seems to have put it out," the first mate said, wiping his brow with the back of his hand. "Fuel tanks are intact. But we have three compartments taking water on the starboard side. Watertight doors closed, but it may be too late. Pumps aren't responding. If a fourth goes—"

"I know." The captain turned to the head stew. "How many were below when it hit?"

The stew's face was haggard. "At least five or six in the galley. A few guests on the beach deck. Is there any word?"

The deckhand at the intercom shook his head. "No response. I'll see what I can find."

"Do it," the captain said. As the deckhand raced out of the wheelhouse, nearly colliding with the bulkhead, Ilya continued to observe from the corner. So far, the crew members had fallen back easily on their training, but he knew that such a situation could change quickly under pressure.

Orlov was studying the damage reports. "Can we evacuate to the shadow boat?"

Laszlo set down the radio. "No. The crew says they have at least two dead. The fire is spreading and may reach the tanks. They're going to set it to go out as far as it can, then abandon ship."

The captain looked out at the fire across the water. "Send the distress call. What about the tenders?"

"Not if we're listing like this." The first mate checked the screen. "Almost twenty degrees. A critical line. Much more and we won't be able to lower the lifeboats on the port side."

"Then we take the others." The captain rested his hands for a moment on the console, his head bowed, then abruptly straightened up. "Prepare for evacuation. If we drop the anchors, it should buy us some time—"

Laszlo broke in. "Captain, we have to talk about the helicopter. They'll need the helipad and upper deck clear for the rescue, and if the list gets any worse, it could slide right over the edge."

The captain closed his eyes for an instant, then opened them again. "Can it take off?"

Laszlo hesitated. "At twenty degrees, it could be hard. I can see if we can secure it. If not, we should just push it off now, before the evacuation starts. I need two men to do it safely."

"I don't have two to spare," the captain said. "We'll just need to take our chances—"

As Laszlo began to protest, Ilya saw that the level of tension on the bridge was rising. He spoke up. "I can go."

The others turned to stare at him. Laszlo sized him up silently for a fraction of a second. At last, he said, "Fine. Dmitri, you, too."

Without another word, Laszlo left the wheelhouse, along with the remaining deckhand. Ilya was about to follow when he felt a hand close around his arm. Turning, he saw Orlov looking at him intently. The security chief spoke in a whisper. "Tell me you didn't know this was coming."

Ilya heard the hint of a threat there, but he did not drop his gaze as they moved out of earshot of the others. "The plan was larger than any of us knew. They put me on board to make sure that Tarkovsky was dead, but they had no intention of letting any of us live. What about the girl?"

"I put her back in her cabin. Tarkovsky is safe as well. But if you've lied to me—"

Instead of finishing, the security chief released Ilya's arm and turned back toward the bridge. Ilya watched him go, then headed for the ladder that led up to the helipad, his bag slung over one shoulder. As he took hold of the rungs, he heard the ship's horn give seven short blasts and one long one, the signal for evacuation, which was repeated as he started to climb.

From below, he heard shouts in several languages as the crew began herding the passengers to their muster stations. As he ascended to the next level, he told himself that he would do what he could to aid the evacuation. Once he was onshore, he would turn his full attention to responding to this final betrayal.

Pulling himself onto the owner's deck, he glanced up as a series of flares soared into the sky, bursting into ribbons of light. Around him, unsecured chairs and tables had slid to starboard, and water was spilling over the edge of the pool. The bosun and deckhand were conferring at the helipad. As Ilya drew closer, moving against the slope of the deck, he saw that the helicopter was straining against its straps. He could tell from their faces that they had decided to cut it loose.

Laszlo motioned Ilya closer. "As long as you're here, you can make yourself useful. We need to open the straps and stanchions. Dmitri will take care of the railing. As for you, whatever your name is—"

Ilya stood aside as the deckhand headed for the helipad's edge. "My name is Ilya."

"Come on, then." As the deckhand lowered the rails, Ilya and Laszlo made their way around the helicopter, releasing all but two of the eight straps, which ran from tiedown provisions on the rotors and body to lashing points on the deck. When they were done, the two remaining straps were stretched taut on their hooks. Laszlo reached into his back pocket and removed a pair of knives. As he handed one to Ilya, he caught the other man's eye. "Tell me the truth. Were you ever at Warsash?"

Ilya took the knife and turned aside, opening its sheepsfoot blade. "Of course not."

Pulling out his radio, Laszlo asked the bridge to switch

on the bow thrusters. As the ship began to turn, they stationed themselves well apart at the two remaining lashing points. Then they glanced over at the deckhand, who signaled that all was clear, and cut both straps at the same time.

At once, the helicopter began to slide slowly across the deck, heading toward the edge of the helipad. Ilya closed his knife and straightened up, watching carefully as the helicopter skated forward on its skids.

It was only then that he realized that the vibration had returned, carried once more across the night air. As soon as he heard it, his heart sinking, he knew. They never would have given up so easily—

Ilya turned in time to see the drone coming straight toward the yacht, low and fast, its insectile hum rising to a scream. He shouted for the others to get out of the way, his own words lost in the hellish whine as the drone descended at full speed and smashed into the highest point of the yacht.

The impact knocked him to the ground. Ilya fell back, rolling along the listing deck, the knife tumbling from his hands, and caught himself on the lowered railing just before sliding over. The bag slipped from his shoulder and fell into the sea. He heard the shriek of metal against metal as the fallen drone plowed forward, crashing into the loosened helicopter and crushing the roof of the owner's cabin as fire rose from the crumpled wreckage of its wings.

As the yacht shuddered, tilting farther to starboard, the mingled ruin of the helicopter and drone collided with Laszlo and the deckhand and took them over the edge, trailing smoke as it slid into the water seventy feet below. The yacht heeled back, groaning, then listed forward again with the sound of breaking glass as mirrors and windows shattered throughout the lower decks.

Ilya was still clinging to the rails. He hauled himself onto the deck, hearing the crackle of flames, and managed to get to his feet. Looking around, he saw that half the deck had crumpled beneath the impact, destroying the owner's suite on the lower level.

He staggered to the edge and looked down. Far below, the drone and helicopter were already sinking. There was no sign of the two other men, but as Ilya watched, water began to seep into the helicopter's wiring, shorting out the switches. As the helicopter sank with the drone, its navigational lights lit up all at once, glowing like a ghost beneath the surface. Then it was swallowed up by the dark.

53

When Maddy awoke, she found that she had been walking for some time without knowing it, her right arm slung across someone else's shoulders. A voice from far away was shouting in Russian. As she was set down with her back to something firm, she opened her eyes to find she was still on the main deck, the world strangely angled, the air tinged with smoke.

She looked over to see who had been carrying her. It was Elena. "Talk to me. Do you know what day it is?"

Maddy's hand went to the crown of her head, where a lump had recently appeared. As she blinked up at the yellow lights, she found that her vision, at least, was clear and unblurred. "Sunday. I think. What's going on?"

"They're evacuating the ship," Elena said, kneeling next to Maddy. The two of them had taken shelter on the starboard side, at some distance from the confusion. "I found you by the railing—"

Listening to this, Maddy suddenly remembered why she had gone out to the deck in the first place. With Elena's help, she managed to rise. The yacht was listing badly, so she had to steady herself against the bulkhead, the pain in her head easing to a dull ache as she got her first good look at her surroundings.

To her right, toward the stern, passengers were moving frantically toward their muster stations, with the stewardesses trying to line them up for a head count. Remembering the smoke, she looked up to see that the deck two levels above was in ruins, flames burning at intervals along the twisted metal. "What happened?"

Elena's voice was without emotion. "The crew is saying it was a drone attack. It fired three rockets, then came around again and crashed into the sun deck. The owner's suite was destroyed."

As the meaning of the assistant's words hit home, Maddy felt sick at heart. "And Tarkovsky?"

"I don't know." Elena glanced over at the stern. "We can't stay here. Can you walk?"

"I think so." Maddy took a step, feeling out the slope of the deck beneath her feet, and found that it was easier with her shoes off. She followed carefully as Elena began to head toward the others. "How bad is it?"

"Bad enough," Elena said. "We're going down. At least four or five of the crew were killed in the galley. People are saying there were guests on the beach deck, too, members of the design team—"

"Rahim," Maddy said, remembering that he had said he was going downstairs shortly after she arrived at the party. She stared at the faces on deck. "Do we know if he made it?"

Elena only shook her head as they joined the rest of the crowd. Maddy saw that all unsecured objects and furniture had slid to one side and were resting against the starboard rail, a pileup of lounge chairs, tables, deck trees.

The passengers, who had also tended to collect at the low end of the yacht, were milling about in uncertain clusters, most still in gowns or black tie, with an air of mounting anxiety on the verge of breaking out into hysteria.

As they headed toward the nearest group, Maddy saw Nina, the oligarch's daughter, moving among the passengers, clutching her shoes in one hand. She slid across the deck to the two women, her mouth clamped in a trembling line. "I don't know where my mother is—"

Elena glanced at Maddy. "I'm sure she's all right. Stay here. I'm going to get us some life jackets."

As the assistant picked her way up the deck to the locker at the far end, where a stewardess was passing out life vests and emergency gear, Maddy led Nina to a spot safely away from the others. "Your mother will be looking for you. It's better if you stay in one place."

Nina glanced down at her stockings, one knee of which had been torn. "My dress is ruined. I don't know how I did that."

"I don't think anyone will care," Maddy said. In fact, she doubted that anyone would notice even if they fell overboard. Watching as runners scrambled to pass out flashlights, she saw that the scene was one of barely controlled panic, as passengers sought out their loved ones or demanded answers from the shorthanded crew, and that it might all spiral out of control at any moment. "Your father built a strong ship. We'll all get out in one piece."

As Maddy spoke, she put a hand on Nina's shoulder without thinking. At first, she thought the girl would pull away, but instead, she pressed closer, putting her arms around Maddy's waist. "I know," Nina said, wiping her nose on the back of her sleeve. "It's all insured, isn't it?"

"I'm sure it is." Maddy almost smiled, but the feeling

died as she reflected what Tarkovsky's true legacy to his daughter would be. Nina was scheduled to inherit much of his wealth when she came of age, but this was nothing compared to her darker birthright, invisibly attached to her father's influence, which meant that she, too, would inevitably be drawn into the game.

A second later, Nina pulled free. Following the girl with her eyes, Maddy saw Tarkovsky's wife approaching from the port side, followed by Elena, who was carrying a set of life jackets as if she had gone to retrieve her employer's dry cleaning. Ludmilla gathered up her daughter, then turned to Maddy, a question in her eyes. When Maddy shook her head, the other woman only looked away.

Taking a life jacket from Elena, Maddy put it on, then did what she could to help the guests around her. A second later, the evacuation signal sounded once more, and the crew began to divide up the passengers. After taking a final head count, the nearest deckhand told them to head for the starboard side, in single file, where the lifeboats had been readied for their departure.

Maddy made her way with the others to a flight of steps that led to the davit below. The panels of the compartment had been slid open, exposing it to the night air, with a narrow walkway leading to an enclosed lifeboat with an orange roof. Because of the list, a gap had opened up between the walkway and the boat, the dark surface of the water visible forty feet down.

Leaning over the gap, the deckhand slid the hatch open and began herding the passengers inside. It was a slow process, and Maddy, waiting her turn on the walkway, was one of the last to board. For an instant, as she stepped across the empty space between the lifeboat and the yacht, she felt the yawning immensity of the sea below. Then she crossed the gap and found herself in a crowded space large enough to accommodate thirty passengers.

Maddy sank into one of the remaining seats, feeling the boat swaying beneath her. Some of the younger men were exchanging forced jokes in Russian, but most had fallen into an exhausted silence. Across from her, Elena was seated next to the oligarch's wife and daughter. Among the others were two members of the design team. Rahim was not among them.

As the remaining passengers climbed on board, Maddy helped the woman next to her with her safety belt, then fastened her own. Through the open hatch, she watched as the deckhand removed the pins and charge cable. After releasing the remaining grips, he got inside and secured the hatch behind him.

Climbing behind the aft console, the deckhand opened the vents, confirmed that all was clear, and instructed the passengers to remain in their seats as he lowered the boat. As the davit swung them over the water, Maddy tried to give Nina a reassuring smile, but the girl did not smile back.

The boat began to descend, moving in fits and starts as the deckhand worked the brake release, the passengers clutching their seats whenever the ropes gave way with another jolt. From where she was seated, Maddy could not see the view outside, and she was surprised a second later by the impact as they fell the last few feet and hit the water with a splash.

As the boat rocked on the swells against the side of the yacht, the deckhand allowed the lifeboat to settle, then released the falls. He started the engine and undid the painter that connected the boat with the deck above. Finally, he sat down, muttered something into the radio, and began moving away from the ship.

Maddy exhaled, the accumulated tension draining out of her body. She leaned forward in her seat, trying to look out the window. For a second, she could see nothing except the black glass of the surrounding waves. Then the view outside stabilized and she saw the lights of the city.

The ride to shore took ten minutes. As they drew closer, Maddy could make out the glow of the passenger terminal, a long steepled building with a red roof that ran along the concrete quay. A rescue crew was already lined up at the marina. Taking the lifeboat in, the deckhand maneuvered it around at a crawl until its hatch was parallel to the nearest berth. As he shifted into neutral, the team came forward to tie up the boat. Then the deckhand cut the engine and opened the side hatch.

Maddy was one of the first to leave. As she was helped onto the quay by a pair of rescue workers, she blinked at the lights of the emergency vehicles. A crowd had gathered to watch the excitement, kept back by policemen and barricades. It struck her for the first time that she was in Russia.

At her side, a volunteer said a few words she didn't understand and held out a rescue blanket. Maddy took it, handing over her life vest in exchange, and draped it over her shoulders like a shawl. Another woman offered her a paper cup of tea, which she almost declined. Then she thought better of it and took two.

A line of survivors had gathered along the water, ignoring the buses that were idling nearby. Maddy went to Elena, who was standing by herself, and handed her a cup of tea, which the assistant accepted without a word. As

Maddy took a sip, she heard the sound of rotors overhead, glancing up as a pair of rescue helicopters flew by and continued toward the yacht.

The passengers stood in silence, looking out at the wreck a mile away. It floated at a strange angle, like a great animal on the verge of sleep, lit by its own emergency lights and by the rescue boats holding station on all sides. In the distance burned the shadow boat, its hull fringed with flame, carrying a wreath of bright water around it as it drifted out to sea.

Hearing a murmur of interest, Maddy saw a second lifeboat approaching. As it disgorged its passengers one by one, she kept an eye on the hatch. She recognized all of the faces, including the executives from Argo, but none of the ones she wanted most desperately to see. Once the last survivor had emerged, Maddy felt her fears, which had faded briefly, return in a sickening rush. If Tarkovsky had been in his suite when the drone crashed, he would have been killed at once.

As she considered the full extent of the betrayal, it hit her for the first time that they had no way of knowing if she had survived. Her phone had been lost in the initial attack. As far as they knew, she was one of the missing.

Which meant that she was free. She could just walk away. And they could do nothing to stop her—

Even as she felt herself seized by this thought, a voice spoke up at her side. "Maddy?"

Maddy turned. Standing a few yards away was a young, attractive woman with short dark hair, dressed in a light jacket and jeans. Around her neck hung a lanyard with a laminated badge. "Yes?"

The woman smiled with what seemed to be genuine relief. "Thank God you made it." She took a step forward, then glanced around the scene. "This area isn't secure. Will you come with me?"

Maddy detached herself from the others, who were still looking out at the water. As she came closer, she saw that the badge around the woman's neck had a curious emblem, the image of a panther leaping across the globe. She had seen this insignia before. "Who are you?"

"I work with Rachel Wolfe." The woman motioned for Maddy to follow, heading for the barricades at the far end of the port. "She asked me to bring you somewhere safe. My name is Maya Asthana."

54

Wolfe's command of Russian had never been strong, shaped as it was by a few semesters of night school, but it served her well enough when necessary. Going up to the security line at the harbor, she approached the youngest man in sight and showed him her badge. "I'm an agent with the Serious Organised Crime Agency in London," Wolfe said in passable Russian. "I need you to let me through."

The officer hesitated. He had the smudge of a goatee on his chin and seemed out of his element as he stood by the barricade, keeping back the line of onlookers. "I'm sorry, but my orders—"

"I have my orders as well," Wolfe shot back. "There were British and American nationals on that ship. If you have a problem with this, take it up with my office. But I need to see your incident commander. Where is he?"

As she spoke, she handed him a card with the number of the office in Vauxhall. The officer studied it uncertainly, then glanced down at her badge. Something in her air of impatience overcame what resistance remained, and he stood aside. "Command center is in the passenger terminal. You can check in there."

"Thank you," Wolfe said, moving past the barricade. She continued toward the terminal building on the harbor until she was safely out of sight, then turned and headed for the quay.

Within minutes of leaving her message for Maddy, she had been on the way to the airport, her every instinct screaming for her to get to Sochi. In the end, she had lucked out and managed to grab the last seat on the next plane to Moscow, racing from there to a connecting flight. All told, she had spent six hours in the air, and while they were not quite the longest of her life, they were close enough that she was very glad to be on the ground again.

Now it was close to midnight, and despite the late hour, the harbor remained crowded with rescue workers, volunteers, and gawkers. A hotel had been opened to house the survivors, but as she neared the water, Wolfe saw that many of them still stood on the quay, their blankets reflecting the light like gold leaf.

Drawing closer to the largest group of passengers, Wolfe saw no sign of Maddy. A second later, she noticed a face that she recognized from the newspapers. It was Ludmilla, Tarkovsky's wife, standing slightly apart from the others, along with her daughter, Nina.

Wolfe quickly weighed her options and saw that she had no choice but to jump in. Going up to the oligarch's wife, who was looking out toward the wreck, she raised her badge and said in Russian, "I'm sorry, but I was wondering if I could speak to you for a moment."

Ludmilla turned slowly to face her. Taking in the badge, she looked up and replied in English. "What do you want?"

Wolfe identified herself and said, "I'm looking for a

guest who was on this ship. Her name is Maddy Blume. Have you seen her?"

Tarkovsky's wife did not respond at once. In her eyes, Wolfe saw a clouded quality that made her think that the other woman was not altogether there. "Do you have news of my husband?"

Wolfe shook her head. "I'm sorry. If you like, I can see what else I can find—"

Ludmilla turned away. "Leave us alone. I don't want to answer your questions."

Wolfe saw that there was no point in pressing further. She was about to leave, hoping to find someone else who had been keeping track of the survivors, when the girl spoke up at her mother's side. "I saw her."

Ludmilla glanced down at her daughter. "Nina, please. You don't need to talk—"

"But I *did* see her." Nina pulled away from her mother's arms. "We were on the same boat. We all left the ship together."

Looking at the girl's mother, Wolfe sensed that she had a limited window of opportunity here. "Do you know where she is now?"

"I saw her leave with another lady." Nina pointed to Wolfe's identification. "She was pretty. And she had a badge like yours."

Wolfe felt as if the ground itself had listed beneath her feet, and a sick dread began to spread through her body. She was about to ask for more information when she felt a spidery hand come down on her right shoulder.

She turned. Standing behind her was a tall police officer in plainclothes, with the kind of cold sparkle in his eyes that she was convinced such men practiced each night in the mirror. "Excuse me," the officer said in excellent English. "My name is Boris Suslov. I am a lieutenant with the Department of Internal Affairs. Would you kindly come with me?"

Over his shoulder, Wolfe saw the officer she had encountered on her way in, along with two others. "What's this about?"

"Please," Suslov said, speaking with the pointed patience of a responsible man with a great deal on his mind. "We merely wish to see if there is any way in which we can assist your inquiries."

Wolfe saw that Ludmilla and her daughter had withdrawn, returning to the main body of survivors. She spent a fraction of a second considering the situation and finally concluded that there was no graceful way out.

Without looking back at the faces by the water, Wolfe followed Suslov as he headed for the terminal, the officers walking a step behind. "We've set up a temporary command center," Suslov said, moving at a brisk pace. "It is customary for all foreign law enforcement to check in there."

"I must have gotten turned around," Wolfe said. "Has anyone on my end signed in?"

Suslov favored her with a thin smile. "I would have expected you to be aware of your own agency's activities. Why exactly are you here?"

Wolfe saw that no additional information was likely to be forthcoming. "There were American and British citizens on that ship. I'm here to make sure they aren't in danger and to get a sense of the situation."

"The situation is clear," Suslov said, approaching the main entrance of the passenger terminal. "This was an act of vicious terrorism, designed to assassinate one of Russia's most respected private businessmen, as well as to cast doubt on this city's security in advance of the games."

As they entered the terminal, Wolfe sensed that Suslov's anger was genuine enough. Sochi was scheduled to host the Winter Olympics in just over two years, and the government had made a massive investment in security and infrastructure. "What has the law enforcement response been so far?"

Suslov continued past the marble pillars into the terminal lobby. From somewhere up ahead, Wolfe heard ringing phones, although the command center itself remained out of sight. "Officers have been called in from throughout the region. We are pursuing all leads with every available resource."

As two of the officers remained behind, they climbed a flight of stairs to the landing, the sounds of the command center falling away. Going to a closed door, Suslov waited as the last officer came forward to unlock it, then turned on the lights and stood aside. "Here we are."

Wolfe went in and saw at once that the office was empty except for a desk, a television mounted to the ceiling, and a map of Sochi tacked to the far wall. She turned back. "What's this?"

Suslov was still in the hallway. "We'll have someone to see you in a moment."

With that, he closed the door in her face. Through the frosted glass, Wolfe saw him speak briefly with the officer, who remained where he was, before heading down the corridor again. She understood, too late, that she had been shunted unceremoniously to one side. Going to the door, she was about to demand to be let out when she realized that she needed somewhere to go first.

After a moment's thought, she went to the television set and turned it on. All of the local channels were devoted to ongoing coverage of the disaster. She cranked the volume up high enough to discourage anyone who might be listening, then pulled out her cell phone.

Powell answered before the second ring. "Tell me you've already found her."

Wolfe looked at the footage of the burning shadow boat on the news. "No. I'm being given the runaround. The terrorism narrative is already locking into place, and anything I share with the police here will end up with state security. Any word from the embassies yet?"

"I'm working on it," Powell said. "Our best chance is the embassy in Tbilisi. They're closer than St. Petersburg, but they won't be able to get a team there for at least three or four hours."

"That won't work. I'll need to do this on my own." Wolfe paused. "Alan, she's here."

Powell didn't need to be told what she meant, or what the implications might be. "And you think she has Maddy."

"Yes. So I need you to get me some information." Wolfe went over to the map of the city on the wall, searching for the port where she was now. "I've been thinking about that drone attack. In theory, you can fly it from anywhere, but they'd want to stay off the satellite networks. Which means—"

"—it must have been controlled from nearby," Powell said, jumping to the next point at once. "What are you thinking?"

"It would have to be line of sight, which means on the water. And somewhere with privacy and space. A drone big enough for three rockets would need room for take-off, maybe even a pneumatic launcher. This wasn't a backyard operation." Wolfe's eyes flew across the map. "South of the port is all commercial. It would be somewhere to the north. A dacha with all the necessary security in place. There can't be that many that fit the bill."

"Give me ten minutes," Powell said. "I'll send whatever I find to your phone."

"Thanks." Wolfe hung up. Checking the drawers of the desk, she found a recent street atlas, which she took. Then she switched off the television, opened the office door, and stepped out into the hallway.

The officer standing by the door looked at her in surprise. "Where are you going?"

"I have everything I need, thanks," Wolfe said in Russian, already moving toward the landing. A second later, she was heading downstairs to the night beyond, and she did not turn around as the officer called her name.

55

Half an hour earlier, as they headed for the parking lot south of the harbor, Asthana had removed her jacket and handed it to Maddy. "Here, take this. And give me that blanket. We don't want to attract attention."

Maddy unwound the sheet from her shoulders and took the jacket in exchange. "What are we worried about?"

Asthana balled up the blanket and shoved it into the nearest wastebin without breaking stride. "We don't want to run into the *politsiya*. I don't have any jurisdiction in this city, and I'm not exactly here in an official capacity."

As they continued toward the secluded space where she had parked, Asthana noted that while security was tight at the port, it slackened considerably away from the water. This was lucky, because a great deal of what she had just said was true. She was acting on her own initiative here, and she didn't yet know how it would play at the dacha. "How are you feeling?"

"I hit my head on the yacht, but I'm fine," Maddy said. "What are you doing here if you aren't here officially?"

"Consulting on another case," Asthana replied. "A lot

of back-and-forth in advance of the London games. Wolfe caught me at the office this afternoon, just after she called you. I'm the only other officer here."

They arrived at the car. Asthana unlocked it with her key fob and was about to slide behind the wheel when she saw Maddy hesitating at the passenger's side. "Is something wrong?"

Maddy looked at her across the roof of the car. "Where exactly are we going?"

"A safe house," Asthana said. "We need to sit tight until we can get you to the consulate, and it's a long drive to St. Petersburg. In the meantime, we need to keep away from the police. Otherwise, you'll end up in a back room at the Department of Internal Affairs, and that isn't where you want to be."

Asthana waited for her words to hit home. After a beat, Maddy opened the door and got in. Climbing inside, Asthana started the engine and backed out, keeping her headlights off. A moment later, they were heading for the service drive that ran parallel to the water, which she hoped would allow them to circle back to the main road without attracting attention.

Soon they were heading north toward the dacha. As Asthana drove, she felt in control of the situation at last. She had been weighing her options ever since it became clear that many of the passengers would survive. At first, she had feared that this would leave her with some undesirable loose ends, but she had finally seen that it could also be a source of leverage.

She glanced over at the woman in the front seat, who had fallen into an exhausted silence. Asthana had left the dacha an hour earlier, saying only that she wanted to keep an eye on the harbor. With luck, she could convince the others that Maddy was more useful alive than dead, at least for now. And if the situation changed, it would be easy enough to get rid of her.

First, however, it was necessary to determine what she knew. Reaching out with one hand, Asthana switched the radio to a news station, but she kept the volume turned down. "The reports are saying it was a drone attack, but they can't seem to agree on the details. Did you see it?"

Maddy closed her eyes. "Yes. It knocked me out. I didn't see the crash. By the time I woke up, we were already evacuating." She opened her eyes again. "Has there been any word on Tarkovsky?"

"I was about to ask you the same thing," Asthana said. "You didn't see him?"

"Not since I left the party. I don't know what happened next. He wasn't on the first or second lifeboats." Maddy turned back to the view from the window. "Have they said who was behind the attack?"

"Only rumors. Sochi is on the front lines of two different conflict zones. Abkhazia is twenty miles south, and you've got the usual rebels in the Caucasus. A hell of a place to host the Olympics. The lines are so tangled that there's no telling who did what. At least not until we can conduct a proper investigation."

Something in this last statement seemed to catch Maddy's attention. "Why was Wolfe worried about me?"

Asthana had been expecting the question. "I'm not sure. But she told me a few things. That you were working for Alan Powell, for one—"

Out of the corner of her eye, she saw Maddy start. "How did she know that?"

"Powell must have told her. She didn't say much, but I could tell she wasn't happy. I think she was afraid it would come out sooner or later, and it would raise questions, especially after the attack. Everyone on that yacht will be scrutinized. It's better if we deal with it from London." She paused. "It's hard. I know. But once this is over, you can resume your life as before."

Maddy only glanced away again, looking out the window at the night beyond.

As they continued north, Maddy rested her head against the glass, as if tired, and did not speak again for a long time. Inside, however, her mind was racing, and she was afraid that the beating of her heart would give her away.

We need you to perform a service for us. Once this task is concluded, you will never hear from us again. You can resume your life as before—

Maddy turned to look at the woman behind the wheel, whose face passed through alternating bands of light and dark. It occurred to her that Wolfe had left her original message hours before the attack, which meant that if the officer had been afraid for her safety, it could only have been about something else. "Do you have a phone? I should let Wolfe know I'm okay."

"We can do that back at the house," Asthana said, keeping her eyes on the road. "It's just a few minutes from here."

Maddy only nodded. As she turned back to the window, she casually put her hands into the pockets of the jacket that Asthana had given her. Both pockets were empty. A second later, as Asthana glanced away to make a left turn, Maddy reached out and unlocked the door on her side of the car as quietly as she could, resting her fingers on the handle.

She looked through the windshield at the featureless

street. They had been on the road for fifteen minutes. To her right, she could make out a line of trees, while to her left, past the dark blocks of apartment buildings and hotels, stood the water. They were heading north, away from the city center, toward the resort areas that ran along the edge of the sea.

At last, leaving the road, the car began to slow. Looking ahead, Maddy saw a long driveway with a steel fence. A man was standing next to the gate with what looked like a shotgun in his hands.

As they came to a stop, Maddy tightened her grip on the door handle, seeing that a few yards of open ground stood between her and the trees. If she was going to run, it had to be now. Through the windshield, she watched as the guard turned to open the gate. She reached for her safety belt. And then she paused.

If she ran, Maddy thought, she would not get far. Not with an armed guard nearby. And if they had been willing to let her die on the yacht, they would not hesitate to kill her now if she forced their hand.

But if they had brought her here, it meant that they had reason enough to keep her alive, if only to find out what she knew. And if that were true, she had one advantage. She knew that Ilya had not killed Tarkovsky. And there was a chance both men might still be alive.

With this thought echoing in her mind, Maddy let go of the door handle, which had grown slick beneath her fingers. No more running, she thought. Not if this was how it was meant to end.

As the guard opened the gate, Asthana eased the car forward until they were moving along the gravel driveway. In their headlights, Maddy could see the dark outline of a dacha.

She was surprised by the sound of her own voice. "So there's no hood this time?"

Behind the wheel, Asthana stiffened. For a second, Maddy caught a glimpse of the other woman's true face, the one lurking behind the mask that she had so carefully worn. Then, strangely, she smiled.

"No," Asthana said at last, turning back to the house up ahead. "Not tonight."

56

Shortly after midnight, the shadow boat exploded. The incident commander in Sochi had concluded that there was no way to fight the fire safely, given the risk from the hundred thousand gallons of diesel fuel. As a result, after the surviving members of the crew had been evacuated, rescue launches had maintained a respectful distance as the ship smoldered quietly and drifted out to sea.

Finally, the fire crept forward far enough to reach the tanks, rewarding the news cameras with a satisfying burst of flame. As the fireboats went in, the burning ship was visible for miles, a sooty candle kindled in the darkness around the city. The resulting footage was shown repeatedly on all stations, along with images of the sinking yacht, which continued to list in the direction of greatest damage.

At the port itself, crews from state television had been allowed to film the rescue from designated points near the water. One of these crews happened to be nearby when a third lifeboat approached the harbor shortly after the explosion. Instead of the enclosed boats that had been observed earlier, the latest arrival was an inflatable raft with a trolling motor, evidently pressed into service after the angle of the yacht had rendered the remaining boats unusable.

In the lights of the cameras, eight men and women could be seen as the raft tied up at the quay. Most were in life jackets, with several dressed in survival suits of orange neoprene, which had black face seals that left only the eyes and nose visible. The cameras caught them climbing out of the raft one by one, with most of the attention directed to a photogenic female who turned out to be the ship's purser. In her life vest and culottes, she cut an attractive figure, and at the approach of the reporters, she agreed to be interviewed for Channel One.

Only the most alert of the newscast's viewers would have noticed the man in the life jacket caught briefly in the background of the camera frame, moving away from the water. Declining the offer of a blanket, he pulled off his life vest and left it on the dock, continuing along the quay until he was at a safe remove from the cameras. At the moment, most of the rescue crews and volunteers were clustered at the southern end of the port, so he headed in the other direction.

Orlov rounded the corner and entered a region of shadow, sheltered from the rest of the scene, where a line of smaller boats stood at a separate marina. Only then did the security chief turn to face the two figures, both of whom had also emerged from the raft, who had detached themselves from the others to follow a few steps behind, dressed from head to toe in immersion suits.

Once they were alone, one of the men pulled off his hood. It was Ilya. He breathed in deeply, grateful for the air on his face after the suit's stifling confines. Before he could take the rest of it off, however, he heard a voice from behind him: "Stay where you are, please."

Ilya turned and saw that Orlov had drawn the pistol he had taken from the bosun on the bridge. He was not aiming it yet, not exactly, but there could be no question about his intentions. "What are you doing?"

"I can't let you go," Orlov said, still holding the gun by his side. "You know this as well as I do."

Ilya had no trouble reading the meaning in the security chief's eyes. "I've told you all I can. I did not know the attack was coming. If these men are still in the city, I will find them. You need to give me that chance."

For one tense moment, they stood eye to eye. Then the third man, the one who had not yet removed his hood, spoke up for the first time. "That's enough. Help me get this off."

Orlov looked over at Tarkovsky, who had pulled the hood away. At last, he slid the gun into his waistband and went to assist the oligarch. Ilya watched them for a second, then quickly removed the rest of his suit, keeping an eye on the others. Tarkovsky, for his part, continued to look out at his yacht, the shadow boat burning beyond it, with no trace of emotion on his face.

It was not difficult to guess what he might be thinking. Shortly after their final meeting, Tarkovsky had gone to the library on the bridge deck. If he had been in his suite when the drone struck the yacht, or if the ship had not been more solidly built than its attackers had expected, he would have been killed. And as Ilya considered what he must be feeling now, he saw a way to use it.

He also understood how blind he had been. This assault would have required years of preparation, which explained why Vasylenko had been allowed to remain in prison for so long. After the war in South Ossetia, he knew, Georgian arms had appeared on the black market in great quantities, including parts of drones shot down over Abkhazia. The remaining components would not have been difficult to acquire. All that was needed was a man with the ability to deploy them, which was why Bogdan, with his military training, had been included in a project that had otherwise drawn most of its resources from the civilian side.

Once his immersion suit was lying on the ground, Tarkovsky turned toward the line of survivors at the far end of the quay, his wife and daughter among them. "I want to see Ludmilla."

"Not yet," Orlov said. "You need to wait until we know more about the situation."

Tarkovsky sighed. Beneath the suit, he was still wearing his tuxedo shirt from the party, now rumpled and damp with perspiration. "And what exactly do we think the situation is?"

These words were directed at Ilya, who was standing to one side. He seized the opening. "It would not be safe for them to leave yet. If they're in a secure location, they would wait until morning."

Tarkovsky began rolling back his shirtsleeves. "But you don't know where."

"No," Ilya said. "But I have an idea. It would be secluded, a place where four armed men would not attract attention. In the old days, they could fall back on Vasylenko's connections, but not now. Sochi has cleaned house in advance of the games. The networks are no longer there. Am I right?"

Orlov had been listening closely. "Perhaps. Minalyan, who ran most of the old gangs, was killed two years ago in Moscow. They would not have been able to rebuild so quickly. So where would they go?"

"Inside the system. State security must have a presence here. And if I were them, I'd want to keep an eye on Vasylenko."

"A safe house, then." Tarkovsky looked out at the wreck on the water. "But where?"

Ilya turned to Orlov. "You must have contacts. Someone who would know where the safe houses would be—"

Orlov shook his head. "No. That information is closely held. And the two sides don't share their toys."

Ilya wanted to push back, but he fell silent instead. For the first time in years, he felt tired, the energy he had stored up for so long draining inexorably away. He also knew that what the security chief said was true. Any contacts that Orlov retained would be on the military side, a world apart from civilian intelligence. To find Vasylenko, he needed information from within the same agencies that had carried out the attack, which meant that all was lost. Unless—

Out of the depths of his exhaustion, Ilya felt an idea flicker into flame, and before it could fade, he turned to Tarkovsky, remembering something that Maddy had said in their long conversation the night before. "You have one connection there. The man who told you about Lermontov."

Even in the shadows, Ilya could see Tarkovsky's face grow dark. "What do you know about this?"

"I know enough," Ilya said, aware that he was playing his last card. "I know you had a contact who said civilian intelligence was funding its operations with stolen art. Only a man at the highest ranks of state security would have known this. He must have been sympathetic to your cause. If he isn't dead or in prison, he can tell us where these men would have gone."

Tarkovsky's eyes remained fixed on his. After a long moment, he said, "I have nothing more to offer you. My men have their hands full here. If you go after Vasylenko, you go alone."

"I understand," Ilya said. "I ask for nothing else. All I need is a car and a gun."

For a moment, the three men stood in silence. Ilya sensed in his bones that Vasylenko and the others were still in the city, but he also knew that they would not remain there for long.

When Tarkovsky spoke again, facing the water, his voice was as quiet as death. In his eyes, Ilya could see two pinpoints of light from the distant fire. "All right. I'll make the call."

57

As promised, there was no hood this time. When Maddy entered the sitting room at the dacha, she looked at the men around her and saw them looking back. Vasylenko she recognized from his pictures. She had never seen the guard at the door or the man at the laptop. All the same, she knew that if any of them were allowing her to see their faces now, there was no way they meant for her to leave here alive.

Behind her, Asthana said something in Russian to the guard who had let them in, who withdrew. Taking a chair from the corner, she brought it over to the center of the room. "Sit down."

Maddy complied, not taking her eyes from Vasylenko, who was seated on the sofa by the fireplace. In person, he was smaller than she had expected, but he did not seem fragile or tired. Instead, he had visibly drawn into himself, like a fist, as if the passage of time had left him all the more determined to stay alive. And she understood at once that all she had done for the last three years had only been to avoid finding herself in the same room as this man.

The man with the laptop was packing up an assortment of electronic gear. He spoke angrily to Asthana. "What is the girl doing here?"

"Insurance," Asthana said, sliding a second chair across the floor until it was facing Maddy. "If Ilya made it off that yacht, he'll be coming for us. With the girl here, he may have second thoughts. We can keep her alive until we're safely away. Then we can let her go."

As Maddy listened, she wondered why they were speaking in English instead of Russian, then realized that this conversation was meant for her ears. They had no real intention of letting her walk away. And if she wanted to make them see otherwise, her window for doing so was closing already.

Throughout this last exchange, Vasylenko had said nothing. Finally, he gave a nod to the man in the corner, who tucked his laptop under his arm and stood. He did not look at either woman as he left the room.

Asthana drew the curtains of the sliding glass door. Watching her, Maddy could sense the tension in the air. Although Vasylenko had remained silent, she thought she knew something about men like this, and that he would not be pleased to be taking orders from Asthana.

Once the curtains had been drawn, Asthana went to the chair she had set across from Maddy and took a seat, almost close enough for the two of them to touch. She got down to business at once. "Is Ilya alive?"

When Maddy said nothing, Asthana smiled reasonably, as if she were conducting a job interview. "Let me explain how this works. The more information we have, the better we can plan our response, which works to your benefit as well. I know a lot about you. You've always put your own interests first. And if you refuse to talk, we can find out in other ways."

Glancing over at Vasylenko, who was still seated in silence, Maddy pretended to consider this point. She responded slowly, as if the words were being drawn out against her will. "I don't know if Ilya is alive. All I did was get him on board. Did he kill Tarkovsky?"

"That isn't really your concern," Asthana said. "You knew all along what our intentions had to be, and you performed more than capably. If it matters, I can tell you that the situation was resolved as intended."

"I know," Maddy said, speaking more quickly. "I was there when the rockets hit. And I would have been killed if I had been on the lower deck, or if the yacht hadn't been built so well. But it's all the same. You've still won. Even if not everyone gets to share in the spoils."

Maddy looked over at Vasylenko, addressing him directly for the first time. "I'm curious about you. I know why you agreed to fight for this cause, but I wonder if your men really know who they're working for. I've been told that collaboration used to mean death, at least among true thieves—"

Without a word, Asthana came forward from her chair and drove a fist into Maddy's stomach. Maddy doubled over, gasping, the weave of the carpet going in and out of focus as Asthana spoke in a low voice. "That was a warning. Don't think you know who we are just because you read it in books."

"I know enough," Maddy managed, feeling new dispatches of pain with every word, her hair hanging in her face. "I know Tarkovsky was standing in your way. The state controls almost all the oil in Russia, but you wanted the rest. And you couldn't just kill him like you've done with others."

With an effort, she straightened up in her chair, looking up at Asthana, who was still standing. "If you wanted him dead, you could have used a sniper. Or poison. I don't need a book to tell me that. But you had to make it look like it was someone else. You told me so yourself."

Asthana sat down again slowly. "And what, exactly, do you think I told you?"

Maddy flung the hair back from her forehead. "You said it was being treated as a terror attack. The rumors were in the air already, so you could pin it on anyone. Abkhazia, maybe, if you want to go to war against Georgia again. Islamists, if that's more convenient. When they pull that drone out of the water, I'm sure they can trace it wherever you want. Everyone wins. But that doesn't mean the thieves get to share in the glory. Not once they've done their part."

She turned back to Vasylenko, dreading another blow, but also knowing that this was the only chance she would have to say these words. "Ilya knew this. They need you for now. But there isn't room for you in the new order. Not when so many others are waiting in the wings. And it won't be long. They already know you'll take orders from a woman."

Silence fell. For a long moment, Maddy could hear nothing but the sound of her own labored breathing.

At last, Vasylenko rose from the sofa. Without looking at Maddy, he took out his revolver and opened it, allowing the bullets to fall into his hand with the air of a man sliding out a cigarette. He pocketed all but one cartridge, which he reinserted into its chamber, then closed the cylinder.

Asthana stood, her eyes on the *vor*, and asked something in Russian. Vasylenko gave a short response, only a few syllables, but they were enough to send Asthana backing into the corner.

Maddy sat there, heart thudding, as the old man studied her from a few paces away. Finally, he glanced aside, looking at nothing in particular, and asked, "Do you know how Russian roulette began?"

It was not the kind of question that seemed to require an answer. Vasylenko began to walk in a slow circle around the carpet, the gun held loosely in one hand. "It was invented by army officers, out of boredom. They were part of a closed world, with no possibility of change. It made them wonder if it was best for a man to kill himself. Many did. But some of them found another way."

Vasylenko raised the revolver, still pointing it at the ground, and spun the cylinder. As it came to a stop, he said, "For a thief, there is no need for games like this. One's life is a game. I learned in the camps that there is only one rule. A dead thief is good for nothing. Which is what Ilya never understood."

With one easy motion, he pointed the gun at Maddy's head. She heard herself exhale, her breathing growing quick and shallow as she forced her eyes shut. The pounding of her heart seemed very far away. She found herself fascinated, almost impersonally, by the thought that this was how it would end, as if this was the moment that had always been awaiting her, after all she had done to survive.

Vasylenko's tone of voice remained conversational. "I do not take orders from women or Chekists. So I want you to think carefully before you answer my next question. Did Ilya get off that ship alive?"

Maddy did not reply. As she waited for the click of an empty chamber, or for a shot that she would never hear, she told herself that it didn't matter what she said, any more than it mattered if there were six bullets or only one. This had never been a game of chance.

When she spoke, it was with the deliberation of one who knew these words might be her last. "I don't know if Ilya made it. But he would have been on the aft deck. If he was there when the rockets hit, he would have survived. And if he's alive, it means he's coming for you."

In the silence that followed, Maddy felt the resolve that she had saved for these last few words begin to slip away. She listened for the click, or for nothing, waiting without hope for either to come—

—when instead, from somewhere outside the house, an alarm began to sound.

Her eyes flew open as Vasylenko withdrew the gun. Looking at the faces around her, she saw that the alarm was not her imagination, and at once, her arms and legs began to tremble.

From behind her came the sound of footsteps. When she turned, she saw the man with the laptop run into the room. Looking at the scene, he took in the situation at once, then spoke a few urgent words in Russian.

Vasylenko holstered his revolver. Without so much as a glance at Maddy, he said something to Asthana, who came forward, her own gun drawn, and hauled Maddy out of the chair. "Get up."

Maddy got to her feet, her legs somehow managing to keep her upright, and met the other woman's eyes. In Asthana's face, she thought she saw something like fear. "Looks like Ilya is here after all."

"It isn't Ilya," Asthana said, pushing Maddy into the hallway. "It's Wolfe."

58

Wolfe had checked two other locations before arriving at the dacha, using the addresses that Powell had sent to her phone and the map she had lifted at the terminal. The first two had been dead ends, vacation homes that she had seen at a glance weren't suitable for an operation like this, and even as she pulled over to the side of the road, a hundred yards from her latest destination, she couldn't shake the feeling that she was here on a fool's errand.

It didn't help matters that she was working on her own. She opened her driver's side door, making sure that the interior lights were off, and slid out of the car. Her equipment had been riding on the seat beside her. It wasn't much, just her identification, penlight, and handcuffs, which were all she had been able to bring on the plane. She checked that her phone was on silent mode, then closed the door, leaving it unlocked, and approached the final address on foot.

The street was very quiet, like the rest of the city, the eyes of which were squarely fixed on the port. As Wolfe crept along the road, she noted that at least the situation was promising, with trees to her right and the sea somewhere off to her left, beyond the houses lined up at the shoreline. Based on aerial photographs, the dacha she was approaching was set apart from the rest, with several acres of land, some of it wooded, but also with a fenced clearing.

Wolfe continued onward until she was across the street from the driveway of the dacha. Glancing to both sides, she headed in, keeping to the trees that extended to the edge of the drive. After a minute, she came within view of a brick wall topped with wire. A security camera was pointed at the area immediately before the gate, and a few feet away, a man was seated with a shotgun in his lap.

She halted at a safe distance, her eyes on the guard, whose head was a darkened cutout. As she watched, he rolled his head from side to side, stretching his neck, and for a second, his profile was caught by the yellow light. Then he turned away again, leaving his face as indistinct as before, but in the instant that his features had been visible, Wolfe had recognized him. It was one of the men she had seen on Mare Street on the day of the prison break.

Wolfe took a step back, not making a sound, and withdrew again into the trees. Once she was out of sight, she paused, halfway between the house and the road, and began to think.

She had known that the prisoners had been broken out for a reason, and she had suspected that they were heading east, using Vasylenko's connections to obtain safe passage. Whatever they were planning had been significant enough to risk the danger and expense of their escape. And as she considered the situation now, she saw that such men might be very useful for the project that had unfolded here in Sochi, especially for someone like Asthana.

For a minute, Wolfe remained where she was, torn between going back to her car and getting a better sense of the scene. At last, moving as quickly as she dared, she retraced her steps through the trees until she was back on the main road, where there was still no sign of life. She went down the street from the driveway, counting off her paces as she walked past the other homes, and finally saw a gap between two of the neighboring houses.

Picking her way carefully toward the shoreline, she ended up on a concrete embankment, about twenty feet wide, that sloped gently down toward the sea. Most of the houses had boat shelters on their lower levels, with metal tracks allowing the boats to be winched down to the water. Wolfe moved through the darkness along the concrete, stepping over the clumps of reeds that had sprouted at the waterline, and when she had taken the same number of steps as before, she found herself at a pier that could belong only to the dacha she had just left.

There was no fence here. Two large motorboats covered in tarps were moored at the pier, which was the sectional kind that could be screwed in separate pieces into the seabed. To her right stood a boathouse, with a footpath moving up a grassy slope toward the dacha itself. From here, she could not see the main house, but at the crest of the hill, there was a faint yellow glow.

Lowering herself to the ground, Wolfe felt her way forward on her hands and knees. A line of trees stood to either side, screening the dacha from its neighbors. As the ground began to level off, she flattened herself completely into the grass, advancing one inch at a time until the house came into view at last.

Wolfe studied the layout. The rear of the dacha was twenty yards from where she was lying, with a wooden pergola and trellis. Past the deck, a sliding door led into the house itself. Beyond the glass, the curtains were drawn, but the lights were on inside, and as she watched, she saw a shadow of movement.

On the roof, two security cameras were trained on the area directly to the rear of the house. A man was leaning against the pergola on the left side of the deck, smoking. She could see a pair of binoculars hanging from his neck, tucked neatly beneath the strap of his shotgun.

Wolfe lay there, watching, for another minute, although the situation had been clear at first glance. She had no choice but to call it in, sitting on the house in the meantime until backup arrived.

Keeping an eye on the dacha, Wolfe edged out of the guard's line of sight. When she was a few feet away from the trees to her left, she began to withdraw, and she had just started to inch backward when her other eye was caught by an object fastened to a nearby tree.

It was an infrared motion sensor. Wolfe recognized it at once and froze, but her left foot was still moving, and before she could pull it back, it was too late. The colored lights of the sensor blinked on, and from up ahead, a shrill alarm sounded. Wolfe closed her eyes. *"Shit—"*

She heard footsteps and a shout in Russian, followed at once by a shotgun being racked, which put to flight any thoughts she might have had about trying to make a retreat. Opening her eyes, she saw the guard standing ten yards away, his shotgun pointed straight at her head, and faintly heard him order her to get to her feet, keeping her hands in sight.

Wolfe complied, rising to a standing position with her arms up, the fact of her stupidity pounding in her brain in time with the shriek of the alarm. Keeping the shotgun on her, the guard pulled out a radio with his free hand and pressed the button to talk, saying something in a low voice.

A response came over the radio, unintelligible to her ears, but the guard seemed to have no trouble understanding it. He slid the radio into his pocket again and took a step forward, his shotgun aimed at waist level, and there was no telling what he might have done next if a hole had not suddenly appeared in his forehead, sending him toppling over to the ground.

Wolfe spun in the direction of the gunshot to see a darkened figure emerging from the trees to her left, his pistol raised as he neared the circle of brightness cast by the house. It was Ilya.

For a fraction of a second, their eyes met. Then Ilya indicated the body. "Hurry."

Wolfe didn't need to be told twice. As Ilya kept his pistol trained toward the dacha, staying out of camera range, Wolfe ran forward and pulled the shotgun from the dead guard's hands. Yanking up his shirt, she found a pistol in a breakfront holster, which she pulled out and tucked into her own belt a split second before her head snapped up at the sound of approaching steps.

She fell back as a shotgun blast tore through the area where she had been standing an instant before. As she rolled, she caught a glimpse of Ilya taking cover in the trees as the guard who had emerged from around the house fired again, and she did not stop moving until she had covered the open ground between her and the deck, ending up in a low crouch on its sheltered side.

A second later, the alarm ceased. In the ensuing silence, Wolfe heard nothing but her own ticking pulse, her cracked ribs aching with every breath. Her hands were shaking, but only slightly, and they stabilized considerably as she checked the shotgun and found that it held six shells.

From the other end of the deck, she heard whispers. At least two guards were taking cover at the far side of the house. She couldn't piece together their words from here, but it was easy enough to imagine what they were saying. Either they would split up, or they would radio for someone else to approach from the opposite direction, cutting off both lines of retreat.

With her back to the deck, the shotgun raised, Wolfe tried to remember what she had seen of the layout. If Ilya stuck to the trees, he would be unable to get a good shot at anyone at the other side of the house or on the deck, which was protected on that end by the pergola.

Wolfe looked over her shoulder at the deck behind her. A yard away, she saw a spot where the latticework had come loose, creating a narrow opening. Under the boards, there was two feet of headspace, and before she was fully aware that she had made the decision, she rolled onto her belly and squeezed herself into the darkened gap with something that was not quite a prayer.

Pulling her legs in after her, she found herself lying on a patch of rough ground covered in loose boards, the slats of the deck six inches above her head. A few flattened beer cans were rusting nearby. She turned herself around, the dirt gritting softly beneath her knees, and settled in to wait, her shotgun pointed at the place on this side of the house where she expected the next attack to come.

Almost at once, before she was ready, a pair of legs appeared in her area of vision, visible from the knees down. Wolfe fired through the latticework, the gunshot deafening, her face stung by blowback as the guard fell, howling, his shins blown away. The spent shell skittered off somewhere into the darkness as she racked the shotgun and fired a second time, cutting off the man's screams, and she was about to crawl out when she heard footsteps on the deck overhead.

Before she could move, the second guard fired down through the boards, missing her by inches. She felt a searing pain in her leg as a few stray pellets bit into her left calf, but she still managed to roll onto her back and fire up blindly, blowing a hole through the deck where she thought the guard might be standing. A hail of splinters flew in her hair and face as she racked the shotgun again. She heard the second guard's body fall. Then nothing.

Blood trickled warmly down her leg as she spat wood chips, wiping her eyes with the back of her arm, then rolled onto her stomach again and crawled to the spot where the first man had fallen. As she climbed out, she saw Ilya coming her way, gun raised. "Can you walk?"

Wolfe rose to a crouch, testing her leg. It hurt like hell but she could move. "Yes."

They took shelter behind the deck as Ilya searched the dead man. "At least two more inside," Ilya said, his head down, so close that she could see the tendons standing out on his neck. "We need to go in now. The noise will attract attention. And I don't know who else will be coming."

He pulled an ammo pouch from the dead man's belt and tossed it to her. Wolfe fished out the shells and loaded them into her shotgun, her ears still ringing. "What exactly are you planning?"

"I'm here to finish this," Ilya said, taking the dead guard's pistol. "Once and for all. This is all I ever intended."

"I know." In the faint light, Wolfe saw a gleam in his eyes she had never seen there before, as if the air of calm he wore like a shield remained only precariously in place. "But it won't be that easy. They have a hostage."

For the first time, Ilya turned to look at her directly. "Is it Maddy Blume?"

Wolfe felt a jolt of surprise, but she pushed it away as something that could be addressed later. "Yes. Which means we can't just go in."

Ilya was silent for what felt like a long moment, but which really could have been only a second or two. When he spoke again, it was with the voice of a man who had examined all courses of action and settled on the best of a bad lot. "All right. But we need to work together."

59

A minute later, the radio crackled in the dacha. When the alarm went off, the men and women inside had withdrawn into an inner room, without windows, its only furnishings a table, two chairs, and a bed, on which Maddy was now seated. Bogdan, who was holding her at gunpoint, looked sharply at the radio on the table as a voice came over the speaker: "If you're listening, pick up now."

These words were the first they had heard since the two men guarding the front of the house had gone around to check on the initial gunshot. Reaching out slowly, his pistol still trained on Maddy, Bogdan picked up the radio and pressed the button to talk. "Who is this?"

"My name is Rachel Wolfe," the woman on the other end said. "Your men outside are dead. I want to talk to Asthana."

Bogdan glanced over at Asthana and Vasylenko, who were seated in the corner. After a beat, Asthana extended her hand for the radio. Holding down the button, she paused for a moment, her eyes on Maddy as she finally spoke. "We have someone you know here. If you try to move in, you know what will happen."

"I do," Wolfe replied. "I imagine you've thought this

through very carefully. You've always been careful, as long as I've known you."

Asthana sensed that Wolfe was testing her, trying to see if a reference to their past together would arouse any reaction. She pressed the button again. "I could say the same of you."

"Which leaves us with a problem," Wolfe said. "If you have any ideas, I'm all ears."

Asthana took a moment, as if thinking, although she had decided long ago what her course of action would be. "I'll go to the sitting room. You can see it from the rear yard. I'll open the blinds and turn on all the lights. You can watch to make sure I'm unarmed. Then I'll go on the deck, carrying the radio, nothing else, and walk down to the pier in plain sight."

After a pause of a few seconds, the radio crackled again. "See you in five minutes."

Asthana set the radio down. Maddy had been watching the entire time. "So what does that really mean?"

Ignoring the question, Asthana spoke in Russian to the others. "I can take care of this. There will be no deal."

Bogdan was clearly agitated. "I don't like it. We should kill the girl and go."

He spoke in Russian, with no sign on his face of what he might be saying. Asthana did not look at Maddy, who had continued to watch them in silence. Part of her knew that Bogdan was right, and that it would be best to end things now. Yet she also knew Wolfe. And she was aware that the other woman would never rest if the night somehow concluded with both of them still alive.

She looked over at Vasylenko, who was reloading the bullets into his revolver one by one. Asthana knew that he understood, from personal experience, how costly such an unresolved issue could be. "I can assess the situation. If she's on her own, this won't take long."

Vasylenko loaded the last remaining bullet, then snapped the cylinder closed. "Very well," the *vor* said. "Meet with her if you must. I trust that you will do what is necessary—"

Five minutes later, outside the house, Wolfe waited alone in the dark, lying on the ground leading up from the water.

In her hands were the binoculars she had taken from the guard Ilya had shot. Through the lenses, she studied the dacha as someone drew back the curtains in the sitting room. As Asthana came into view, she observed that her partner had cut her hair, but her face was still that of a woman she had loved, and for a second, she felt another stab of anger and regret.

Wolfe watched as Asthana stood in the center of the sitting room and turned around slowly, raising her jacket to show that she was carrying nothing but the radio. Going to the sliding door, she opened it and went out on the deck. Then she closed the door behind her and headed down the steps, barely looking at the bodies, the radio in one hand as she descended the narrow path.

Lowering the binoculars, Wolfe rose and began to move back toward the water, keeping Asthana in her line of sight. She halted on the pier, next to one of the covered boats, and watched as her partner drew closer, coming carefully down the slope of the embankment. It seemed to take a very long time.

At last, Asthana paused a few steps away. For a moment, the two women stood there in silence, looking across at each other on the pier, the water sparkling to either side in the moonlight.

Asthana was the first to speak. "If you're ready to do business, show me your hands."

Wolfe responded by unslinging the binoculars from her neck and setting them down. Raising her arms, she turned around to prove that she was carrying nothing else. "I didn't expect it to end like this. Did you?"

"No," Asthana said. "I can't say that any of this has gone according to plan."

In the other woman's voice, Wolfe heard a false note, as if she were confessing to a regret that she did not really feel. "Tell me. What would have happened if I hadn't found out?"

It might have been her imagination, but she thought she saw Asthana smile. "Nothing. I would have been a good wife. You would have been close to my children if you had stayed. How is Devon?"

Wolfe wondered if she really cared or if this was another tactic to distract her. "He's not doing well. He thinks it was some kind of mistake."

"And he's right. I never wanted to hurt him." Asthana paused. "None of this was personal, Rachel. I hope you understand that—"

Wolfe felt her anger rise again and pushed it away, knowing that any emotion would only play into Asthana's hands. "What was it, then?"

"It was about being on the right side," Asthana said, as if this were the most reasonable sentiment in the world. "About surviving what we both know is coming. If you saw things as I did, you might have done the same."

"Don't be so sure," Wolfe said, hating the tremor in her own voice. "It's no good being on the right side if you can't share in the victory. Tarkovsky may be dead, but there's no way out of this. At least not for you."

"Is that what you really believe?" Asthana took a step forward, bringing her face into the moonlight. "Let me tell you what I think. If you made it this far, it had to be on your own. You figured I was heading for Sochi and tracked me here based on what you could guess about the attack. Am I right?"

"Close enough," Wolfe said. "You were careless. I knew from your computer records that you were interested in Maddy."

"And I have you to thank for that." Asthana smiled. "You always were a smart one, Rachel. Too smart, I think, to share information with the police. And if you had a team flown in, we would have heard the chatter. Which means you're by yourself. It's impressive that you took out the guards. But if you're really alone, there isn't much else you can do here."

"That may be true," Wolfe said. "How many men do you have in the house?"

"The two you've left standing," Asthana replied. "Along with the girl. You can work out the numbers yourself."

Wolfe, who had already known the answer to this question, wondered if Asthana's honesty on this point came from calculation or overconfidence. "No. But it still leaves the problem of how we're going to do this."

Asthana's smile grew even more glittering than before. "It doesn't matter. It's done."

Raising the radio in her right hand, Asthana released the button on the side, which she had been holding down throughout their conversation. "You see, they're already gone. They went out the front door as soon as they heard there was no one else. And as for the rest, we can settle it ourselves."

As she spoke, she put both hands behind her back. Wolfe heard the sound of adhesive coming loose as Asthana pulled free what was taped to the bottom of the radio, the blade a bright gleam in the moonlight.

Wolfe saw the knife coming and fell backward, not fast enough, the slash grazing a point just below her breastbone as she landed hard against the boat at the pier. She felt a white line of pain from the cut and remembered the two wounds they had found on Garber, one on the side, one in the throat—

Asthana flicked the blood from the blade and took another step forward. "I'm sorry, Rachel, but I can't just let you walk away. It's your own fault. You were always too trusting—"

"I know," Wolfe said. She went down on one knee as Asthana came forward again, her shirt sticky with blood as she reached beneath the edge of the tarp and pulled out the pistol stashed inside, bringing it up and around to squeeze off two shots even as the blade sought her neck.

Asthana halted, staring down at the pair of holes in her chest, and dropped the knife. She looked back at Wolfe, eyes wide, and seemed on the verge of saying something very important as she fell dead to the pier.

Wolfe rose, knees trembling, and kicked away the knife, which went sliding over the edge into the water. Looking at her partner's body, she opened her mouth to speak, but the words died on her lips. Then she remembered where she was and ran up the embankment toward the dacha.

A minute earlier, soon after word came over the radio that Wolfe was alone, the front door of the house had opened from the inside.

Bogdan emerged first, gun raised, and checked the area around the porch, which was clear. The car was parked to one side of the driveway, twenty feet away. He took a step forward, then another, finding that all was quiet, and finally signaled for the others to follow.

Maddy was the next to appear, walking slowly because of the revolver that Vasylenko was pressing into the small of her back, his other hand clamped on her arm. Her face was calm and still. She knew very well what was coming. From the moment it became clear that Wolfe was here on her own, she had known that neither of them was going to survive.

And yet her first thought, as she stepped out on the porch, was how beautiful the trees were in the moonlight. The night was peaceful, with no sound except for the murmur of insects, and for a moment, she found herself thinking of the evenings in her childhood when she would fall asleep in the car and her father would carry her inside, even if sometimes she had only been pretending.

As Maddy headed for the car that was waiting for her now, she became aware, all at once, of a decision she had made long before. She would not get into that car, no matter what they said. After the fever of her life so far, if it had to end like this, it might as well be here.

Maddy was still coming to terms with this realization when Bogdan halted before her, as if struck by a sudden thought, and fell to the ground. Her mind caught up to the sound of the bullet only later, and at first, the two events did not seem connected. When she looked down at Bogdan, however, she saw that the back of his head was gone, his feet making small hyphens in the gravel.

Vasylenko clutched her arm more tightly and raised the revolver so it was pointed at the side of her skull.

They turned in a tight circle, as if they were partners in a dance, and looked out at the trees as Ilya stepped into the light, his gun drawn and aimed at the *vor*'s head.

Maddy felt the pressure of the pistol at her temple as Vasylenko spoke in a whisper. "Another step and she dies."

Ilya halted, but he did not lower the gun. On the ground, Bogdan made a choking sound that was almost a chuckle, then grew still.

Maddy saw Ilya's eyes flick toward hers. In the instant of shared comprehension that followed, she found herself thinking of a moment at a museum, long ago, when she had asked him to spare another man's life.

Looking into his eyes, Maddy asked a silent question. Ilya seemed to understand, and he gave her an almost imperceptible nod.

Maddy began to speak. There was no need to raise her voice, since these words were meant only for the man at her side. "It won't work. You were wrong about Ilya. He never cared about me. If he went along with the plan, it wasn't for my sake. Tarkovsky is still alive."

A convulsion of disbelief seemed to pass through the old man's body. For an instant, Vasylenko's revolver fell back a fraction of an inch. "Even if that were true, it only tells me that he would never let you die. You see yourself as an honorable man, Ilyuha. But let me remind you of what you really are. You—"

Maddy did not see Ilya fire. She only heard Vasylenko fall silent before he could finish his sentence, his head snapping back as the bullet passed between his eyes, Ilya watching with no change of expression as the man he had once seen as another father collapsed in the dust.

Ilya put his foot gently on Vasylenko's hand, which

was still clutching the gun. When he looked up, Maddy saw that his eyes were glistening, although the rest of his face was as impassive as before. "Are you all right?"

Maddy managed to nod, overcome by a sense of unreality that might have been due to physiological shock. "And Tarkovsky?"

"He's alive," Ilya said. When he blinked, the shine that had appeared so briefly in his eyes was gone.

Hearing the sound of steps, they both looked to see Wolfe approaching from the side of the house, gun drawn, her eyes on the bodies on the ground. There was fresh blood on her shirt. Taking in the scene, she said nothing, but only lowered her pistol as she turned to face Ilya.

For a moment, Maddy saw something pass between the two of them, an unspoken exchange in which she had no part.

A second later, Ilya turned away, the gun still in his hand. Wolfe stood looking after him in silence as he walked toward the gate at the end of the drive, which led out to the road beyond.

Just before he was out of sight, he removed the clip from his pistol and let it fall to the ground. Clearing the chamber, he tossed the gun off somewhere into the woods. Then he vanished into the darkness.

60

Wolfe had been in this neighborhood before. As she walked down the narrow street in the Shoreditch Triangle, she noticed a familiar building to her left. Although the upper floors had been repaired of all traces of fire, she recognized it as the apartment house where Karvonen had lived. She thought about mentioning the coincidence, then decided against it, given the nature of the errand she was here to run.

The morning was typical December. Arriving at the gallery, Wolfe paused for a moment to check her reflection in the window, then went inside. The gallery itself was in disarray, with canvases leaning against the walls where temporary labels had been taped. Through a door at the rear, she could see a storage room in which a television was playing the news.

As Wolfe began to leaf through the catalog proofs on the counter, Maddy came smiling through the doorway. Wolfe sensed that the other woman had seen her coming, but had retreated into the back room to make a more appropriate entrance. "Sorry about the mess. We're still getting ready, you know—"

For a moment, the two women hesitated awkwardly on the verge of a hug, then settled for a handshake instead. "I've been meaning to stop by," Wolfe said. "It's been busy on my end."

"I'm not surprised." Maddy indicated a pair of folding chairs. "Please, have a seat."

Wolfe sat down as Maddy went over to an electric kettle in the corner. She liked what she saw. In a white blouse and jeans, Maddy looked comfortable in her own skin, if not exactly relaxed. "How's the gallery coming?"

"Lots of fires to put out," Maddy said, pouring two cups of tea. "Elena seems to enjoy it. Of course, she doesn't know half of what can go wrong. But she's been a good partner. We have a lot in common. She wants to make a name for herself, and she knows most of the Russian buyers."

"It must be hard to break into that world, especially if you're not from around here."

"It could be worse." Maddy lowered herself into a chair. "When I left my gallery job, after the story broke about Arkady Kagan, I took a flash drive with my employer's contacts. I figured it might be useful one day."

Wolfe accepted a cup, which she set on the nearest box to steep. "What does Tarkovsky think of that?"

Maddy toyed with the label of the tea bag. "He doesn't know. Tarkovsky isn't really involved. He helped me get the lease, but if I succeed or fail, it'll be on my own terms. That's all I've ever wanted."

Wolfe reflected that this was probably true. She didn't really know Maddy at all, although they had spent a fair amount of time together, both during their departure from Sochi, taken under diplomatic cover, and in the ensuing political fallout, which was just beginning to die down. A ship could be salvaged, a painting could be restored, but systems did not easily heal.

"I suppose Tarkovsky is busy enough as it is, with a new boat to build," Wolfe said, lifting out the tea bag and setting it neatly on the saucer. "And I heard the announcement last week. Oil rights in the Kara and Barents Sea, in partnership with Argo and Exxon. Those concessions will be worth a lot more as the ice melts. It sounds like he got what he wanted."

Wolfe watched Maddy to see if she would take the bait. After a second, she did.

"That isn't entirely true," Maddy said slowly. "I think he wants more. I've spent a lot of time wondering about this, and he doesn't tell me anything, of course. But the answer was right in front of me."

"You mentioned this on the phone," Wolfe said. "I'm still not sure what you meant."

"It's Shambhala." Maddy paused, as if gathering her thoughts, then said, "I never understood why it meant so much to him. Tarkovsky isn't a romantic. He only cares about his own interests, which happen to involve a more open society in Russia. I didn't realize that Shambhala wasn't just a symbol, but a specific plan of action. And the clues were in the story itself."

Maddy looked around her unfinished gallery. "Shambhala is an ideal society. It embodies the kind of social change that Tarkovsky wanted for Russia. But it only works because it's hidden away. In the real world, there are always complications. Shambhala has it easy. It can prepare itself in secret, untouched by politics, and will show itself when it's ready. That's why the stories always put it in some faraway place, in the Altai Mountains, in Tibet—"

Wolfe suddenly knew what Maddy was going to say next. "Or the North Pole."

Maddy nodded. "That's the thing about the pole, right? It's pristine. The last empty spot on the map. Tarkovsky can build something there without interference. He even designed his yacht with this in mind. The government is willing to tolerate this because it doesn't have the technology to get the oil on its own. But in the meantime, something else is growing."

"An example," Wolfe said, seeing her point. "A stable partnership between a Russian company and foreign partners. Any closer to home, and it would be assimilated. But up there, in the ice—"

"—Tarkovsky can make something that can't be touched," Maddy concluded. "He knows the government will leave him alone as long as it needs him. The ice will buy him some time, at least a few years, to lay the groundwork for a change that needs to happen either way. When the state finally sees what he has done, it will be too late. Other investors will demand the same transparency and accountability. It's the only way Russia will ever move forward. Or so he hopes."

As Wolfe listened, she caught a glimpse, not for the first time, of the qualities Powell had seen in Maddy. "Will it work?"

Maddy paused again. "I don't know. Most attempts at reform have been crushed. But the need for change is there. It's deep underground, but sometimes it breaks out. The hard part is knowing what shape it will take."

"I know," Wolfe said, thinking back to the violence she had seen on the streets of this city. London itself had grown quiet again, but similar convulsions had continued in more distant lands, and as she considered the impulses that brought them to the surface, she thought of Asthana, who had been willing to do whatever it took to hasten the change she was convinced was coming. If she was ever tempted to forget this, the scar on her chest was reminder enough.

There was an extended silence, not altogether comfortable, as Maddy went to refill their cups at the electric kettle.

While Maddy added more hot water, her back turned to Wolfe, she reflected that she had not told the entire truth. Part of her work for Tarkovsky would forever remain a secret, but as far as the public was concerned, she had done well. Virginia had agreed on a deal, allowing the egg to spend half the year in Richmond and half in Moscow, a compromise suited to its divided nature.

Afterward, Tarkovsky had expressed gratitude for what she had done, and he had offered to back her gallery openly. Maddy had declined at once. Change, she knew from experience, could not be imposed from the outside but had to come from within. She suspected that Tarkovsky knew this as well, which was why she believed his investments at the pole were only part of the story.

This, she knew, was why the color white had always been associated with Shambhala, where white flowers were supposed to rain from the sky whenever a new king was born. White was the color of ice, but also of purity and rebirth. Shambhala was a symbol of transformation, a process that took place invisibly, one soul at a time, before you were aware it was coming. But it could take hold only when a country, or a person, had the freedom for change to endure.

As Maddy returned to where Wolfe was seated, she

decided to learn how much freedom she really had. "How's Powell doing?"

"He's right where he wants to be," Wolfe said, taking back her cup. "Keeping an eye on events, trying to see past the veil. The official position in Moscow is that it was a terror attack, but rumors of an intelligence angle are everywhere. Powell thinks that heads are rolling, and the fallout will last for decades."

Maddy, who had guessed as much, knew that this would buy Tarkovsky breathing room as he continued to build his vision in the north, as well as closer to home. "What about the gangs?"

"Powell is under the impression that the state has broken off all ties with the *vory*," Wolfe said. "They were on their way out anyway. When Moldova, of all places, is cracking down, you know you've outlived your usefulness. The attack just happened to hurry it along."

Maddy thought of the respected young solicitor, Owen Dancy, who had been found at his club with a plastic bag over his head, a peculiar suicide that had been widely reported in the press. "And Ilya?"

Wolfe set her cup down untouched. "Personally, I don't think we'll hear from him again. He waited until we had enough evidence to connect the plan to the system that set it in motion, then took out the last of the old thieves. Without Vasylenko and his kind, the brotherhood is dying. Even if it emerges again, it will be very weak. That's all he wanted, ever since he went after Lermontov. But he's the only one who understands his reasons. That's why he always worked on his own."

Before Maddy could respond, she saw Wolfe glance out the window. "Looks like my friend is here."

Following her gaze, Maddy saw a man standing on the

pavement outside. She had met Lester Lewis briefly before, shortly after her return to London. Seeing them, Lewis raised a hand in greeting but lingered on the street, perhaps sensing that the two of them wanted to be alone.

Wolfe rose from her chair. "I'm staying here, you know. The agency is being pulled apart, but I should still have a job when the dust settles."

Maddy stood as well. "I'm glad to hear it. I was hoping you'd stay in the city."

"Well, we'll see how it goes." Reaching into her pocket, Wolfe fished out a business card. "Before I forget, I should mention that I'm looking for someone to consult on cases, on a freelance basis, involving art crime. Fraud, art trafficking, that sort of thing. It's still a big headache at the agency, and we don't always have the expertise we need, so we're always open to outside help. If you can think of anyone who fits the bill, you should let me know."

Wolfe handed her the card, then turned to leave the gallery. Maddy remained where she was, watching as Wolfe went to join Lewis, who took her by the arm as they strolled together up the street.

Maddy glanced down at the business card, studying it with a faint smile, then looked at the television in the next room, which was turned to news coverage of recent protests over parliamentary elections in Moscow. Tens of thousands of demonstrators were chanting in the snow, filling most of a city square with flags and signs. She had seen these images before, but as she watched the footage now, one small detail caught her eye. The protesters were wearing white ribbons.

Epilogue

Tens of thousands of Russians took to the streets in Moscow on Saturday shouting "Putin is a thief" and "Russia without Putin," forcing the Kremlin to confront a level of public discontent that has not been seen here since Vladimir V. Putin first became president twelve years ago. . . . A photographer circulated photographs of a riot police officer holding a white flower, a symbol of the protest, behind his back.

—"Rally Defying Putin's Party Draws Tens of Thousands," *New York Times*, December 10, 2011

At the house in Leova, the front door had been put back on its hinges. It had always been one of the nicer homes at the edge of the city, with tables and chairs set up in the garden, but now the lawn was showing signs of neglect, and the curtains on the top two stories were drawn.

Ilya studied the house from a distance. He had parked up the dirt road and walked a quarter of a mile. In the field across the way, children were chasing one another with guns made of folded paper, among the small flowers that had sprouted with the coming of spring.

Climbing the steps, he tried the door, which was locked. There was no sign of movement in the windows. He was raising a hand to knock when he noticed the sound of music. Moving quietly around the house, keeping to a strip of shadow, he found himself facing the rear yard.

On the porch, a girl was seated in a lawn chair, facing away from him. She was smoking a cigarette, her hair tied back with a kerchief, and had evidently been working in the garden. On the table behind her lay a pair of canvas gloves and a trowel, along with a cassette deck that was playing a song from America.

Ilya came up softly and pressed a button on the tape deck, silencing the music halfway through the fourth verse. The girl glanced back, then straightened up so quickly that her chair tipped over and fell sideways to the ground.

"It's all right," Ilya said, opening his hands to show they were empty. "I'm not here to hurt you. I only came to talk."

The girl took a step backward. He saw that she recognized him. "Dolgan isn't here."

Ilya remained where he was. "I know. I've been in town for a week. No one seems to know why he was arrested, but I'm sure they'll come up with a charge. Apparently there are limits to protection these days, even in Moldova."

Moving slowly, so as not to startle her, he reached down and righted the fallen chair, then took a seat at the table. "You can sit down, if you like. But I won't be long. Are you here alone?"

The girl swallowed. "Yes. There used to be many visitors. But they're staying away. And I have nothing else."

Ilya observed that she was keeping her fear under control, but that it could break out again at any moment. "You're taking care of the birds?"

She shook her head. "I let them go. A few wouldn't leave. I feed them when I can."

"It can be hard to give up the old ways," Ilya said. "Even when your cage is opened. Or when it has fallen apart on its own."

He paused, weighing what the best approach would be. "It isn't just happening here," Ilya continued at last. "I've seen it with my own eyes. The thieves are dying out. They've been overtaken by stronger forces. But some things can't be undone. Their works live on, even if their empire does not."

The girl glanced down. Following her eyes, Ilya saw that she was looking at his arm, which still bore the tattoo he had received here nine months earlier. He had left it there as a reminder.

"When I was your age, I lost my own parents," Ilya said, his eyes still on the snake. "I was told they had died in an accident. Really, though, they were taken from me so I would become what the brotherhood wanted. But that doesn't make me less guilty. If I changed, it was to turn into something I had been all along. I learned this when I tried to change again. Do you understand?"

The girl only stared at him. Ilya glanced away, looking out at the garden, and thought of his own recent travels. Almost unconsciously, he had retraced his steps, working back across the places he had visited over the last year. And it was only in Romania, near the palace in Sinaia, that he had seen the truth at last.

After their fall, the Khazars had vanished, dispersed among the steppes they had once ruled. Yet even now, signs of their presence could still be seen, if you looked carefully enough.

Shortly before the empire's decline, several tribes had broken from the king and gone west. Allying themselves with the Magyars, they had fought bravely in a series of bloody wars and ultimately found refuge in the Carpathians. Their images were still unearthed there from time to time, mounted on horseback with hauberks and spears, like the one he had seen in the owner's suite of the yacht.

Looking at these warriors, it was hard to believe that such a nation could change its underlying nature, even for a moment. Yet the signs were there, in the tombs of the Khazars themselves, who had once buried their dead with their horses, like Scythians, but later had inscribed their gravestones, even those of the poorest among them, with the menorah and the staff of Aaron.

This was the lesson of the Khazars. The legends stated that the conversion was a political decision, decreed by the king and the ruling class, but in fact, it had begun among the people. Jews from Constantinople had sought refuge on the steppes, bearing their laws and history, and almost invisibly, a gradual transformation had occurred, on all levels of society, one imperceptible step at a time.

Tarkovsky had understood this. Ilya suspected that this was why the oligarch had taken such an interest in Transylvania, where the last traces of the empire could be found. The Khazars were the secret model for the transformation he hoped to enact in Russia, building it from the ground up, not imposing it from above. Change could arise only from within. But it could also be helped along.

These thoughts, which had been growing slowly within him for a long time, passed through his mind now in the space of a few seconds. He turned back to the girl, who had remained standing, and rose from his chair.

"I know a house in Yalta," Ilya said quietly, reaching into his jacket pocket. "When I was there, I met a woman. Years ago, she was sent to prison, and when she went to work for the thieves, she gave up her only child. But perhaps it isn't too late for them to make a life together."

From his pocket, he withdrew an envelope, about a quarter of an inch thick, that was held shut with a rubber band. A name and address had been written on the front. The girl watched as he set it down on the table, then looked up at him again. She did not move to take it.

Ilya gave her a nod, as if she had spoken, and turned away. As he did, he pressed the button on the tape player, which resumed where the song had left off: *"And she fears that one will ask her for eternity—"*

Descending the steps of the porch, he went around again to the front of the house, not looking back until he was standing at the edge of the lawn. The children across the way had disappeared, leaving only a few guns of folded paper on the ground. For the moment, he was alone.

He looked down at the white flowers that had sprouted in the dirt, some of which had been trampled underfoot. For all their strength, he thought, the Khazars had not survived, but had been destroyed by a trick of history.

Ilya headed up the road, his hands in his pockets, moving away from the house. There were no guarantees. A revolution was more likely to die than endure. Yet one still had to believe that change was possible, for men as well as nations, even if it came like a thief in the night.

ACKNOWLEDGMENTS

Many thanks to David Halpern, my agent; to everyone at the Robbins Office, especially Kathy Robbins, Louise Quayle, Arielle Asher, and Micah Hauser; to Danielle Perez, Kara Welsh, Talia Platz, Jessica Butler, and the rest of the team at New American Library; to Jon Cassir and Matthew Snyder at CAA; and to Mark Chait, Eileen G. Chetti, Alla Karagodin Holmes, Trevor Quachri, Stanley Schmidt, and Stephanie Wu. Thanks as well to my friends and family, to all the Wongs, and to Wailin and Beatrix.

Read on for an excerpt from
Alec Nevala-Lee's

THE ICON THIEF

Available now from Signet

Prologue

In Russia, the outlaw is the only true revolutionary. . . . The outlaws of the forests, towns, and villages . . . together with the outlaws confined in the innumerable prisons of the empire . . . constitute a single, indivisible, tight-knit world. . . . In this world, and in it alone, there has always been revolutionary conspiracy. Anyone in Russia who seriously wants to conspire, anyone who wants a people's revolution, must go into this world.

—Mikhail Bakunin

Andrey was nearly at the border when he ran into the thieves. By then, he had been on the road for three days. As a rule, he was a careful driver, but at some point in the past hour, his mind had wandered, and as he was coming over a low rise, he almost collided with two cars that were parked in the road ahead.

He braked sharply. The cars were set bumper to bumper, blocking the way. One was empty; the other had been steamed up by the heat of the men inside, who were no more than shadows on the glass. A yellow field stretched to either side of the asphalt, flecked with mounds of debris.

Andrey waited for what he knew was coming, barely aware of the music still pouring from his cassette deck. As he watched, the door of one car opened, disclosing a figure in a fur cap and greatcoat. It was a boy of twelve or so. His rifle, with its wooden buttstock, seemed at least twice as old as he was.

As the boy approached, Andrey reached into a bag on the floor of the van, removing a fifth of vodka and a carton of Bond Street Specials. He rolled down his window, allowing a knife's edge of cold to squeeze through the gap. As he handed over the tribute, something in the boy's eyes, which were liquescent and widely spaced, made him think of his own son.

The boy accepted the offering without a word. He was about to turn away, rifle slung across one shoulder, when he seemed to notice the music. With the neck of the bottle, he gestured at the cassette deck. "What band?"

Andrey did his best to smile, painfully aware of the time he was losing. "*Dip Pepl.*"

The boy nodded gravely. Andrey watched as he carried the vodka and cigarettes over to the other car, speaking inaudibly with the man inside. Then the boy turned and headed back to the van again.

Andrey slid a hand into his pocket, already dreading what the thieves might do if they asked to search the vehicle. Withdrawing a wad of bills, he peeled off a pair of twenties and held them out the window. When the boy returned, however, he waved the cash away and pointed to the stereo, which was singing of a fire on the shore of Lake Geneva: *We all came out to Montreux—*

"Cassette tape," the boy said with a grin. "*Dip Pepl.* You give it to me, okay?"

Andrey's face grew warm, but in the end, he knew that

he had no choice. Smiling as gamely as he could, he ejected the cassette, silencing the music, and handed it to the boy, who pocketed the tape and went back to his own car. A second later, the thieves pulled over to the road's scalloped edge, clearing a space just wide enough for Andrey's van to slip through.

Easing the van forward, Andrey drove through the gap, keeping an eye on the thieves as he passed. Once they were out of sight, he exhaled and took his hands from the wheel, flexing them against the cold. Reaching up, he lowered the sun visor, glancing at the picture of the woman and child that had been taped to the inside. After a moment, he raised the visor again and turned his eyes back to the road.

The following morning, unwashed and weary, he arrived at a town on the river Tisza. Studying the ranks of buses preparing to cross over to Hungary, he saw a familiar face. The driver seemed pleased to see him, and was especially glad to load a cardboard box from Andrey's van into the back of his bus.

Andrey followed the bus across the border. At the customs checkpoint, he said that he was a businessman looking for deals in Hungary, which was true enough. Sometimes the officers wanted to chat, but today, after a cursory search, they waved him through without a second glance.

Driving slowly through the countryside, he caught sight of the bus parked at a roadside restaurant. The driver was leaning against the wheel well, smoking a cigar, which he ground out at the van's approach. The package in the rear was untouched. Handing the driver a carton of cigarettes, Andrey loaded the box into the van again. Back on the road, his mood brightened, and it grew positively sunny when, in the distance, he saw the city of Budapest.

He drove to a hotel on Rákóczi Road. In his room, he locked the door and set the box on the bed. The lid was secured with tape, which he sliced open. On top, there lay a loaded pistol, which he set aside, and ten rectangular objects wrapped in newspaper. Nine were icons taken from churches and monasteries throughout Russia, depicting the saints of a tradition in which he no longer believed.

The last painting was different. Andrey unwrapped it gently. It was no larger than the icons, perhaps twelve by eighteen inches, but it was painted on canvas, not wood. It depicted a nude woman lying in a field, her head gone, as if the artist had left it deliberately unfinished. Her legs were spread wide, displaying a hairless gash. In one hand, upraised, she held a lamp of tapered glass.

Andrey studied the painting for a long moment, stirred by feelings that he could not fully explain, then wrapped it up again. Casting about for a hiding place, he finally slid it under the bed, in the narrow gap behind the frame, which was just wide enough to accommodate the slender package. He put the gun back in the box, along with the icons, and went, at last, into the bathroom.

The shower stall was no larger than a phone booth, and the water took three minutes to grow warm, but by the time he climbed beneath the spray, it was steaming. Closing his eyes, he allowed his thoughts to wander. After the exchange, he would replace his lost cassette and buy ten kilos of the best coffee, five to sell, the rest to bring home. Even his son could have a taste.

He was still thinking about coffee when he emerged from the shower, naked except for the towel cinched around his waist, and saw the man who was waiting for him in the next room.

Andrey froze in the doorway, drops of water falling onto the rug. The man, a stranger in a corduroy suit, was seated before the louvered window. He was very thin. Although his age was hard to determine, he seemed to be in his early thirties. Behind his glasses, which gave him a bureaucratic air, his eyes were black, like those of a nomad from a cold and arid land.

"My name is Ilya Severin," the stranger said, not rising from his chair. His legs were crossed, the tip of one polished shoe pointing in Andrey's direction. "Vasylenko wants to know why you're here so early."

Andrey felt beads of condensation rolling down his back. "How did you find me?"

"We have eyes on the road." Ilya hummed a few bars of music. *Smoke on the water, fire in the sky—*

Andrey thought of the gun in the cardboard box, which lay on a table across the room. "I was going to make the delivery. But—"

"But someone else wanted to see the icons." It was not a question, but a statement.

"Only to look. Not to buy. I was told that I could bring them to you as arranged." As he spoke, Andrey was intensely aware of his heart, which felt exposed in his bare chest. "He's from New York. I was never told his name."

Ilya's expression remained fixed. If this information was new to him, he did not show it. "All right," Ilya said, his voice affectless, as if he were reading off a column of figures. "Show it to me."

Unable to believe his luck, Andrey crossed the room, the grit of the carpet adhering to the damp soles of his feet. As he approached the box, he forced himself to concentrate. He had never shot a man in his life, but had no doubt that he could do it. He only had to think of how much he had to lose.

He reached the table. Deliberately blocking it from view, he undid the flaps. The gun was at the top of the carton. Andrey reached inside, picking up an icon with one hand and the pistol with the other.

With his back to Ilya, Andrey said, "If you see Vasylenko, tell him that I am sorry." He turned around, the icon hiding the pistol from sight. "I meant no disrespect to the brotherhood—"

There was a muffled pop, as if a truck had backfired in the street. Andrey felt something heavy strike his chest. At first, he thought that the stranger had punched him, which made no sense, because Ilya was still seated. Then he saw the gun in the other man's hand. Looking down, he observed that a hole the size of a small coin had been drilled into the icon that he was holding.

Andrey fell to the floor, the towel around his waist coming loose. He tried to raise his pistol. When he found that he could no longer move, it seemed deeply unfair. He made an effort to picture his son, feeling dimly that it was only right, but could think of nothing but the painting under the bed, the headless woman lying in the grass. It was the last thing that he remembered.

As soon as Andrey was dead, Ilya, whose other name was the Scythian, rose from the chair by the window. Kneeling, he pried the icon out of the courier's hands, looking with displeasure at the damage to the wood. He put the icon back into the box, then left his gun next to the body.

Ilya sealed the carton and tucked it under his arm. He glanced around the room, asking himself if he had forgotten anything, and concluded that he had not. Leaving through the door, he was gone at once. Under the bed, the headless woman lay, unseen, at the level of the dead man's eyes.

1

The voice in her earpiece, with its soothing drone of encouragement, reminded Maddy of nothing so much as the sound of her own conscience. "Talk to me," Reynard said. "What do you see?"

"It's packed," Maddy Blume said, seating herself in the last row of the salesroom. Across the open floor, which was half the length of a soccer field, a temporary wall had been erected, with fifty rows of chairs set before the auctioneer's rostrum. The seat that she had been assigned was less prestigious than those in front, but it offered the best view of the crowd. "Our friends from Gagosian are here. And that girl who works for Steve Cohen."

"How about the skybox?" John Reynard asked through the earpiece. "Who's there?"

Maddy looked up at the balcony. "The curtain is drawn aside. Someone's there, but I can't see who."

She turned back to the crowd on the seventh floor of Sotheby's, where the chairs were rapidly filling. At the rear of the room, specialists from Christie's, the other great auction house in New York, were standing to observe the proceedings, while in a far corner, roped off from the rest of the audience, news crews trained their lenses on the ranks of attendees.

Across from her sat a trim Israeli, a cord running from one ear to the cell phone in his hands. She knew that he was buying on behalf of an investor in Tel Aviv, but at the moment, he seemed more interested in her legs. Maddy, who had blossomed only in her late twenties and, at thirty, sometimes feared that her face had been marked by recent disappointments, took a certain pleasure in this. She was a tall young woman with striking, almost sibylline features, and she always dressed carefully for these events, knowing that she was here to represent the fund.

As Maddy scanned the crowd, her eye was caught by a man in a navy blazer who was seated near the back of the room. His hair was short, emphasizing the blocky lines of his face, and his build was that of a boxer. "There's one guy who seems out of place. Cheap suit, bad shoes. He's on the phone. Maybe it's nothing, but it sounds like he's talking in Russian—"

"I'll make a note of it," Reynard said. As she watched the auctioneer mount the rostrum, Maddy knew that there was no need to spell out the rest. Russian money had been a primary driver of the art market for years, so any attendee with a Slavic appearance was automatically a person of interest.

"Good evening, ladies and gentlemen," the auctioneer said, dapper as always, placing a cup of water next to his hourglass gavel. "Welcome to the final auction of the summer season. Before we begin—"

As the auctioneer ran smoothly through the conditions of sale, Maddy wound up her call with Reynard. "They're about to get started. I'll call you back as soon as our lot is announced."

"Fine," Reynard said. "I'll have Ethan standing by in case there are any surprises."

He hung up. Maddy removed the earpiece and turned to a fresh page in her notepad, checking to make sure that her phone was charged. Only then did she look at the canvas hanging at the front of the room. It was a painting of a headless woman lying in a field of grass, a glowing lamp in one raised hand.

A slide of the first lot of the evening, a nocturnal street scene by Magritte, appeared on a pair of screens. "Lot number one," the auctioneer said. "And I can start here with the absentee bidders. Two hundred and eighty thousand, two hundred and ninety, three hundred thousand. Do I have three hundred and ten?"

One of the clerks seated behind the counter raised his hand. He was one of only a few men stationed by the phones, with the rest consisting of the young women known as auction babes. Maddy, who had spent an uneasy year working these phones herself, knew the type well.

"The bid is with Julian at three hundred and ten," the auctioneer said, calling the clerk by name. "Do I have three hundred and twenty?"

A woman in the front row gave a slight nod. Bidding continued for another minute, with the woman, a buyer for a major corporate collection, prevailing for five hundred thousand. Maddy took notes on the bidding structure, using the shorthand that she and Reynard had developed. For the next forty minutes, as one lot followed the next, she wrote down paddle numbers and kept an eye on the faces around her, which, with their varying degrees of excitement or indifference, gave her an intuitive sense of each work's true value.

When her own lot drew near, she knew that countless eyes were watching her as well. Without particular haste, Maddy donned her earpiece and called Reynard. The fund manager answered at once. "Are we up?"

"In a minute," Maddy said, doing her best to sound calm. As she spoke, the previous slide vanished and another took its place, reproducing, on a greater scale, the image of the headless nude hanging at the front of the room.

"Lot fifty," the auctioneer said, pausing to take a swallow of water. "*Study for Étant Donnés*, or *Given*, by Marcel Duchamp, showing at my left. And I have outside interest here. Nine hundred thousand, one million, one million one hundred thousand, one million two hundred thousand. With the order at one million two hundred. Do I have one million three hundred?"

An auction babe raised her hand, rising from her chair in her eagerness. "Bidding!"

"Bid is at one million three hundred thousand. I have one million four hundred." The auctioneer said this without pausing, indicating that they had not yet reached the absentee bidder's limit. "Against you, Vicky."

The clerk whispered the new bid into the phone, listened to the response, then nodded. Her bidder would go higher.

"One million five hundred thousand," the auctioneer said. "I have one million six."

The process repeated itself several times. As had been previously arranged, Maddy, with Reynard on the phone, did nothing. She kept an eye on the Israeli seated across from her. His client was rumored to be a likely bidder, but he had yet to signal, which implied that either his price point had been exceeded or he was waiting for the right moment to jump in.

Maddy held back as the price climbed toward three million dollars, nearly twice the record for a Duchamp. Presale estimates had the study selling for between two and three million, but privately, the fund had calculated that the price might go much higher, given the mystery surrounding the work's reappearance. Finally, at three million one hundred thousand, the phone bidder exceeded the absentee bid. The auctioneer scanned the floor. "Do I have three million two hundred?"

Maddy looked over at the Israeli, whose paddle remained in his lap. "Tel Aviv isn't budging. I think he's been outbid."

"Duly noted," Reynard said. "This doesn't change our assumptions. Go for it."

Maddy raised her paddle, feeling a slight but pleasurable rush. The auctioneer smiled. "Bid is on my left at three million two hundred thousand. Do I have three million three hundred?"

The phone clerk checked with her bidder, then nodded. Turning back to Maddy, the auctioneer invited her to raise her bid. Although Maddy was more than ready, she forced herself to count off three seconds before nodding back. It was best to maintain a constant pace. By taking her time now, she would buy herself a few seconds to think as the bidding became more intense.

For a full minute, Maddy alternated nods with the clerk at the telephone. After every bid, she whispered the current price to Reynard, who did not reply. There was no need for him to issue instructions, at least not yet. According to their pricing model, she was free to go as high as five million dollars.

The bids reached four million and continued to rise. At four million two hundred thousand, Maddy sensed hesitation in her opponent. The clerk spoke into the phone, then waited. Finally, after a pause in which the crowd maintained an absolute silence, the clerk nodded.

"With Vicky at four million three hundred," the auctioneer said. "Against the lady at four million three hundred thousand dollars." He turned to Maddy, waiting politely for her response.

Maddy dutifully counted off three seconds, but knew that they were almost done. She was about to nod one last time, raising the bid to the final price, when the Russian at the rear of the room, who had been seated in silence since the auction began, raised his paddle into the air.

There was a murmur of excitement. The auctioneer was momentarily thrown off his rhythm, but quickly recomposed himself. "On my right at four million four hundred," the auctioneer said, moving slightly away from the rostrum. He glanced between Maddy and the phone clerk, extending his hands like a symphony conductor. "Do I have four million five?"

Maddy, flustered in spite of herself, whispered: "The Russian just made a bid."

"It doesn't matter," Reynard said, although he sounded surprised as well. "Take it to five million. We'll regroup from there."

"Okay," Maddy said, nodding at the auctioneer. Four million five hundred thousand.

Without hesitation, the Russian waved his paddle. Four million six hundred thousand.

The auctioneer, along with the rest of the room, was waiting for her response. Maddy counted to three. Before she could nod, however, the phone clerk raised her hand. Four million seven hundred thousand.

The Russian bid again. Four million eight hundred thousand. By now, the attendees were craning their necks to get a better look at the bidder, who was waving his paddle as if trying to swat a fly, his phone nowhere in sight.

"This guy won't stop at five million," Maddy whispered, watching as the phone bidder took it up to four million nine hundred thousand, only to have the Russian bid again. "What do you say?"

When Reynard failed to respond at once, Maddy knew that he was updating the pricing model with the latest information. At last, the fund manager said, "Okay. We can go up to seven million."

As soon as she heard this, Maddy caught the auctioneer's eye. The auctioneer gave her a smile, as if she had paid him a personal compliment. "Five million one hundred thousand," the auctioneer said, drawing out the syllables. "With the lady at five million one hundred. Do I have five million two hundred?"

The Russian, implacable, bid again. As Maddy studied his face, it seemed to her that he was bored, as if he felt that they were drawing out a process that had only one possible conclusion. Before she knew it, the price had blown past six million five hundred, more than twice the presale estimate. For the first time, she began to consider the possibility that she might lose.

She watched as the Russian bid seven million. As the auction babe conferred with her client, the room fell silent. Maddy sat still, heart thumping, waiting for Reynard to update the model.

Finally, after a long pause, Reynard sighed into the earpiece. "Too high. Let it go."

Maddy found herself blushing with shame, keenly

aware of the news crews clustered in the far corner. She wondered if coverage of the auction would mention her by name. "All right."

"Don't let it get to you," Reynard said. "He doesn't understand the winner's curse."

But the lot wasn't over yet. As the auctioneer continued to play for time, repeating the current bid, drawing out the words for as long as possible, the clerk finally nodded. Seven million one hundred thousand.

Without a pause, the Russian raised his paddle in the air. Seven million two hundred.

Maddy, reduced to the status of a spectator, watched as the Russian and the clerk took the price even higher. As the bidding passed ten million and headed for eleven, the Russian raised his paddle and held it there, a lighthouse bid, signaling that he was willing to buy the painting at any price. It was a strange gesture, since the rival it was designed to intimidate wasn't even in the room, but it seemed to work. With the bid at eleven million, the clerk spoke into the phone, listened, and spoke again. The silence deepened, the room watching and waiting.

Finally, after a hush that seemed endless, although it could have lasted no more than a few seconds, the clerk shook her head.

"Eleven million dollars with the gentleman on my right," the auctioneer said, relishing the moment. "At eleven million, are we all through? Fair warning at eleven million. Last chance, fair warning—"

The auctioneer rapped his gavel against its block. "Yours, sir, at eleven million. And your paddle number is?"

Before the Russian could read off his number, his voice was drowned out by a burst of applause. Maddy watched, drained, as the Russian was surrounded by members of the Sotheby's staff, who formed a protective circle as the news crews charged forward for a picture.

There was a camera in her purse, a piece of paper taped across the bulb to soften the flash. Switching it on, she took a picture of the Russian, who was handing his paddle to a representative of the auction house. It caught him with his face turned toward hers, arm extended, revealing a length of sleeve. When the flash went off, he glanced briefly in her direction. Their eyes locked. Then he looked away.

As the murmur of the crowd rose to a roar, Reynard shouted into her earpiece. "We need to fix our pricing model. And we need this guy's name." The fund manager's voice, normally so controlled, was cracking with emotion: "Find out who the buyer is. If he's as big as he looks, he's going to move the entire market, and we need to be ready for it. You understand?"

Maddy nodded, knees weak. She slid the camera back into her purse, then raised her eyes to the balcony. Behind the glass of the skybox, outlined against the light, a darkened figure was looking down at the salesroom. Before she could make out his face, he turned aside, drawing the curtain, and was gone.